❋ A Season of Betrayals ❋

A Season of Betrayals

A Short Story and Two Novellas

(The Sound of Falling Leaves, Sita Betrayed
and *The Housing Society)*

by

QURRATULAIN HYDER

Edited and Introduced by
C. M. NAIM

kali for women

A Season of Betrayals : A Short Story and Two Novellas
was first published in 1999

by

Kali for Women
B 1/8 Hauz Khas
New Delhi 110 016

ISBN 81-86706-01-1

Typeset at Comprint, 69 Arjun Nagar, New Delhi 110 029
Printed at Raj Press, R-3 Inderpuri, New Delhi 110 012

Contents

Acknowledgements

I would like to thank the author, Miss Qurratulain Hyder, for allowing me to attempt the translations. She was always generous with her advice, and also equally gracious when I took the liberty not always to heed it. Her kindness to me is immense. Of course, I cannot even begin to thank her for the hours of pleasure and reflection that all her writings have given me over the years.

Suzanne Schwartz Gilbert not only provided her translation of "The Housing Society" but readily gave me permission to revise it as I saw fit. I must thank her for this exceptional act of trust. She, on her part, wishes to thank her former teacher at Oakland University, Prof. Munibur Rahman, who supervised the original work.

Frances Pritchett found time in her busy life to go over the translations of "The Housing Society" and "Sita Betrayed". The final versions owe much to her. Tauneel Mian suggested many improvements in my translation of "The Sound of Falling Leaves". I'm grateful to both.

C.M. Naim

Introduction

The days and months that preceded and followed August 1947—when the Indian subcontinent became free of colonial bonds—were filled with most horrific acts of physical violence. The killings, rapes, plunder and arson that occurred on a massive scale at the time, moved the great Urdu poet Faiz Ahmad Faiz to call that 'Freedom's Dawn' "a pock-marked and night-bitten morning", and his words became the mantra for a whole generation of Urdu writers on both sides of the new international borders. It was also a time of other, equally rampant violations that were not any the less scarring for not being patently physical. These were violations of trust; they wounded and maimed the psyches of their victims, leaving the bodies intact. And their time—that season of betrayals—lasted longer than just several months.

These betrayals were of many kinds. In the arena of public life, for example, there was the abandonment by the Muslim League leaders, particularly of U.P. and Bihar, of the very people whom they had vociferously claimed to represent, as they rushed off to gain positions of power for themselves, in Pakistan. Then there was the abandonment of avowed ideals—not to say the Mahatma's wishes—by the stalwarts of the Indian National Congress when they accepted—some would say, with ungainly haste—the division of the country in order to pursue their own vision of a highly centralised polity. Instead of leading to a devolution of power to the common man—the individual *citizen*—the emergent polity in Pakistan soon turned into a nightmare military dictatorship. While in India, where the abolition of princely states and zamindari briefly created the effect of a radical change, there eventually developed a feeling of increasing disillusionment as the 'consensual' politics of the Indian National Congress quickly showed its true face as shameless manipulations of caste and religion.

At the level of personal lives, too, there were many betrayals. One may rightly say, of course, that the physical violence let loose during those 'communal riots' was nothing but an extreme violation of the trust that had existed, or should have existed, between human beings. But even otherwise, there were innumerable incidents that occurred between neighbours, between friends, even between members of the same family, that were betrayals of established ties and expectations. As masses of people moved from one country to the other, a person suddenly found his neighbour had left, even though there had been no fear of violence, or a friend was shocked to discover that his boon companion had emigrated overnight to some distant place. And who can say that those who went away did not at some time or other feel a twinge of guilt for what they had done to the trust that others had placed in them?

From the specific perspective of the Muslims of Bihar, U.P., Rajasthan, Central India and Hyderabad, such sudden, large-scale and continuing emigration had never occurred before. Its consequences in terms of a permanent severing of familial ties—along with what the latter entailed as rights and responsibilities—were unprecedented. Perhaps the worst sufferers in that regard were the women of middle-class Muslim families. House-bound and ill-educated, they had mostly been raised to wait for their male elders to find them husbands, for whom they could then continue to perform their traditionally designated tasks. But now male elders and prospective grooms went away to Pakistan, while the two nations steadily used legislative controls to make their return impossible. It must be difficult today to imagine how it was in the Fifties for countless Muslim girls and their parents, particularly in the so-called *sharif* families of North India that had fallen on bad days after the abolition of zamindari and enforcement of the Evacuee Property Act. (Ismat Chughtai's memorable short story, *Chauthi ka Jora*, "The Wedding Dress"—partly incorporated in her script for the film *Garm Hawa*—perhaps best communicates that particular nightmare.)

At the time, most major Urdu writers—they were almost all men—wrote about the horrors and brutalities that some human beings could deliberately inflict upon others in the name of religion. Sa'adat Hasan Manto, Krishna Chandra, Khwaja Ahmad Abbas, Qudratullah Shihab and numerous other male writers produced a powerful 'literature of the riots'. But, to the extent these and other male writers remained focused on just the physical violence, their fiction—particularly of the less talented, though not any less sincere, among them—often read like a list of horrors. (Usually these horrors were ascribed to the two communities or nations in a carefully calibrated equal measure.) Only later, did some of them—Rajinder Singh Bedi, for one—turn their attention to the other, less overtly bloody tragedies: what had happened and continued to happen to individuals and families at those human sites where there had been no 'riot' and yet there were any number of victims. Women writers, on the other hand, focused their attention from the beginning on the non-physical and less tangible tragedies of divided families, abandoned parents and siblings, and shattered loves and trusts. Perhaps because these were their own experiences. Prominent among the latter was Qurratulain Hyder, who may also have been unique among all writers, women and men, for having experienced and written about such tectonic upheavals on all the emergent borders—in India, and in both West and East Pakistan. Interestingly, she first responded in the form of novels, as if the magnitude of the events demanded a larger canvas, and only later turned to shorter genres. In some sense, however, she never stopped examining the consequences of those events, as is evident even in her most recent works.

The present collection—two novellas and a short story— contain three of Hyder's best-known shorter fictions about that particular time of trials and betrayals. The first no- vella, "Sita Betrayed" ("*Sita Haran*"), is dated 1960 and was published in *Naya Daur* (Karachi); the second novella, "The Housing Society" ("*Housing Society*"), is dated 1963; it, too, first appeared in *Naya Daur*; the short story, "The Sound of Falling Leaves" ("*Patjhar Ki Avaz*") dates from around the same time and was the title story of the collection that came out in 1967 and won the Sahitya Akademi award in 1968. The three, besides being some of my own favourites, also form, to my mind, a fair representation of Hyder's thematic concerns and stylistic predilections, as will be- come clear below.

The chief protagonists of the three works are women: Sita Mirchandani, a Hindu refugee in India from Sindh; Salma ('Choti Bitiya') and Surayya, Muslim girls from very dif- ferent social classes in U.P., who are forced to move to Pakistan; and Tanvir Fatima, another Muslim born in U.P. but narrating her story in Lahore and not quite sure why she is there. In fact, this uncertainty, this not quite know- ing what happened to them and why, is a feature common to these and several other female characters in Hyder's fiction. Not that they are befuddled, unintelligent, or in- ert; rather, they seem unmoored, though not unnerved, by the cataclysmic events around them. It is important to note that despite the crumbling away of the social and economic certainties of their childhoods and adolescent days, these women do not fail to shore up new lives for themselves. They are not benumbed into total inaction. However, there does remain a deep emptiness at the cen- tre of their lives which they repeatedly—and vainly—seek to fill through new human contacts. One reason is that the cataclysms have not dislodged men from their essen-

tial position of authority and control. In fact, the changed
times seem to provide the men with ever-new channels for
exercising dominance.

Arguably, some contemporary readers might see these
women as ineffective, or worse. Others might scorn them
for repeatedly placing their love and trust in the hands of
men who eventually only betray them. These would be
unfair judgments. I feel if she were accused of not allowing her female protagonists any 'agency', Hyder might well
reply, "Guilty as charged. But that's the whole point."
Hyder's female characters live within a patriarchal society
which, of course, still exists, and her censure of that insti-
tution of control and exploitation is unequivocal. If her
protagonists do not assertively challenge patriarchy, they
are not its eager accomplices either. When they make any
compromise with it—as, Surayya does for example, near
the end of "The Housing Society"—it is for the sake of
that most basic of all human needs: survival. On the other
hand, there may be seen a 'heroic' quality in their apparent naivete: they would rather suffer than give up the very
human habit of trust—which, it must be conceded, is basic to all our relationships and institutions. Sita
Mirchandani in "Sita Betrayed", despite betrayals by a series of men, must remain alive to her own essentially felt
need: it is as if, for her, ceasing to search for a shared and
lasting experience of love would mean self-annihilation.
This particular stance, this curious way of giving meaning
to one's existence, is also hinted at in "The Housing Society" when Surayya quotes a line of verse: *"But for this endless illusion, man would die"*.[1]

The female protagonists of these fictions also feel a
deep, ineluctable separation from their surroundings,
despite all the surface congeniality that their lives seem to
offer. They live in a state of exile that is more internal
than obvious. Sita Mirchandani, a Hindu, feels lost in a
predominantly Hindu India; as do her Muslim counter-
parts, Salma and Tanvir Fatima, in the overwhelmingly

Muslim Pakistan. Sita may have internalised the history of Sindh—in fact, she remembers many histories—but the wound of separation from Sindh itself is so deep that no tie to any other place heals it. So she wanders, from Delhi to New York, back to Delhi, then to Colombo, on to Paris, and again to Delhi. Her story ends with her back in Paris, but again facing the prospect of having to return to Delhi or go somewhere else. Tanvir Fatima, more sedentary and more modest in looks and talents than either Salma or Sita, shares her story with us while sitting in a drab flat in a nondescript alley in Lahore, but to the extent the particularities of the burgeoning capital of Pakistan's largest province have any meaning for her, she could just as well be in Toronto, Bradford or New Jersey.

The title of the novella, "The Housing Society", refers to what was once considered the apex of wealth and power in Karachi: a residence of your own in the prestigious Pakistan Employees' Cooperative Housing Society (P.E.C.H.S.)—commonly known simply as the 'Society'. For a couple of decades, the 'Society' remained the summit towards which the more ambitious clawed and scrambled through various intermediary stages. Now, of course, it has been surpassed by other, fancier, addresses.

The narrative of "The Housing Society" consists of three strands: the lives of three families which intersect for one brief moment in U.P. some years before the Partition and which, unbeknown to the protagonists, again intersect in Karachi a few years after 1947. (The denouement takes place at a lavish housewarming party in the 'Society'.) The element of coincidence is as prominent in this novella as it is in "Sita Betrayed". It is, in fact, a favourite device with Hyder, and serves well to maintain the self-contained world of a novella. In addition, it sharpens the didactic impact of the bewildering changes brought about by the radical post-Partition transformations. Simply put, the fortunes of the family—Salma and Salman's—that earlier had power and wealth, now go into decline, while the two families—

Surayya's and Jamshed's—that once seemed fated for genteel poverty are launched on an upward trajectory that seems boundless. This predictable narrative, however, is saved by the fact that all the protagonists are drawn with an even hand. And when their experiences of childhood are recalled in the context of their new lives in Karachi, it becomes clear that they are just like everyone else, neither exclusively good nor exclusively bad. The trajectories that their lives took in the wake of the political and social upheavals of 1947 could not have been predicted even a few years earlier.

The narrative flow of the two novellas is familiarly chronological, but staccato and rapid. The scenes shift quickly, and though their firm linearity doesn't allow for a truly montage-like impression, the final effect on the reader is much like that of watching a fairly fast-moving film. It means, for example, that there are no moments of reflection and introspection, nor are there any authorial asides. What we do get are auditory flotsam and jetsam—snatches of forgotten songs, bits of poetry, even old doggerel—functioning very much like the musical sound-track of a movie. They help to recreate the 'reality' of the events as located in historical times—what in cinematic terms would be called the *mise en scène.* They also underscore the emotional contents. Hyder's aural memory is formidable, and she prefers to rely on it—as also on a memory of smells—to evoke for us particular places and times.

This poetic or musical 'scoring' of the prose narrative may seem odd to some. A reader not familiar with Urdu culture, for example, may look askance at the set-piece near the end of "The Housing Society" when two reporters drunkenly recite bits of a "Progressive" poem. But most *Urduwallas* do quote poetry all the time, and what the two reporters do is no different from what so often takes place in any gathering of Urdu speakers after "the night has spread its dark tresses" and nostalgia reigns supreme. The shards of the poem make the scene 'real' by placing it in a history. They also sharpen the realisation we only gradually come to, that the two drunks, crying over Salman's fate, are in fact lamenting the passing of their own innocent and idealistic days of not too long ago.

The use of such textual fragments is more prominent and deliberate in "Sita Betrayed", where in different sections liberal use is made of quotations from (or references to) three famous texts: Vishakhadatta's play, *Mudra Rakshasa;* Malik Muhammad Ja'isi's sufi love-tale, *Padmavat;* and Tulsidas' devotional epic, *Ramacharitamanasa.* The fifth century A.D. Sanskrit play is set in the fourth century B.C. when the mighty Mauryas began their reign. The play, however, does not celebrate that event. It focuses on the fate of Rakshasa, the exiled chief minister of the deposed Nandas, who was too loyal and trusting, and who was therefore easily destroyed by that great 'realist' Kautilya, political guru to Chandragupta I. The question of personal loyalty within the context of political shifts, the experience of exile, the folly of undisciplined trust—these are some of the themes that the play shares with the novella. Perhaps it is not insignificant that fragments from the play are heard in a scene in Delhi, that eternal Indian site of contestations over political power and loyalty.

Ja'isi's famous sufi *premakhyan* or love poem, *Padmavat,* written in the fifteenth century, is considered a masterpiece in Avadhi and predates Tulsidas' *Ramacharitamanasa.* It is one of several such works by Muslim poets who belonged to the Shattari sufi order. One distinguishing feature of that order was its several masters' extensive interaction with Hindu yogis, even to the extent of adopting many yogic practices in their own instructional methods. In a similar vein, the Shattari poets made use of indigenous tales and legends for their mystical allegories. In "Sita Betrayed", the quotations from *Padmavat* occur in the section set in Sri Lanka, the legendary Singhaladwipa of the poem. On the surface, they indicate the 'rootedness' of Jamil 'and Irfan even after they have moved away from

Avadh and its syncretic milieu. More deeply, they high-
light certain ironies. In the poem, King Ratan Sen, who is
already married, sets off for Singhaladwipa to find Padmini
with whom he has fallen in love on mere hearsay—on a
parrot's word, to be exact. The poem pays scant attention
to the grief of the first wife, but glorifies for its sufistic
aims the love between Ratan Sen and Padmini. In the novella, Sita, Jamil's first wife, goes to Colombo, hoping that
Irfan, who claims to love her, will help her gain custody of
her son from Jamil and also her legal freedom from the
marital tie. She achieves neither; on the other hand, the
two men manage to bond together as they exchange verses
from the *Padmavat*. Neither the medieval poem nor its
modern users show any concern for—or even an understanding of—Sita's anguish.

The use of Tulsidas' poem may seem more obvious, but
it, too, is limited in purpose. The Sita of Hyder's novella
cannot possibly be confused with that absolute embodi-
ment of innocence and virtue, the Sita of Tulsidas. Sita of
the Ramayana, born in Mithila, comes as a bride to
Ayodhya, follows her husband Rama into exile, where she
is abducted by Ravana, who carries her off to Lanka. After
being rescued and after the end of Rama's period of exile, she returns to Ayodhya, only to be exiled by her own
husband on account of mere rumours. And though she
returns to Ayodhya one more time, her sufferings end only
when she is swallowed by Earth, her true mother. Sita
Mirchandani thinks of herself as a daughter of the land of
the Indus, and to the extent she has internalised the histories of several places, she may even be perceived as a
daughter of the earth. But there the parallel ends. The
two vastly different Sitas have only one thing in common:
the 'agency' in the lives of the two women seems to lie
exclusively in the hands of men.

Like "Sita Betrayed", "The Housing Society" also has
collage-like segments in its narrative: the petition of
Surayya's mother; the old songs that Jamshed and Surayya

remember; the fragments of poetry with which the two journalists console themselves. But there the songs and verses merely serve nostalgic impulses; they do not play the same structural role that the fragments of the classics in "Sita Betrayed" do. What is interesting and consistent, of course, is that while Hyder gives no physical descriptions of her protagonists to help us visualise them, she gives us plenty that we can use to hear them in our mind.

❖

Qurratulain Hyder was born in 1927 to two highly creative, original and earnest individuals.[2] Her father, Sajjad Hyder, a product of the M.A.O. College, Aligarh, was an enlightened man who expounded his liberal views on the education and welfare of women in essays and stories, and also through various organisations. Besides being a pioneer short-story writer in Urdu, he also translated short stories and novellas from Turkish, which he had learned from Haji Isma'il Khan, a friend of Sir Sayyid Ahmad Khan. Haji Isma'il Khan started a magazine called *Ma'arif* from Aligarh in 1896 on the lines of *Sarwat-o-Funoon*, a forward-looking Turkish magazine. Sajjad Hyder, still an undergraduate, worked as its Assistant Editor and transcreated considerable Turkish short fiction into Urdu for it. From 1904 to 1907, he worked as dragoman for the British consul at Baghdad and came in close contact with the Young Turks. Later he visited Turkey several times. An avowed Turcophile—he adopted a Turkish word Yildirim, thunderbolt, as his pen-name—Sajjad Hyder saw in the rise of the Kemalist movement a glorious future for all Muslim societies.

Qurratulain Hyder's mother, Nazar Sajjad, was an equally liberal and socially concerned person. She, too, wrote fiction, both novels and short stories. These were particularly popular with the emergent female readership in Urdu. She was also very active in promoting educational and social reforms among Muslim women. Hyder has memorably celebrated the lives of these two immensely creative individuals in her two-volume *Kar-i Jahan Daraz Hai,* which is itself a unique book in Urdu, being a semi-fictional account of her family that goes back to the time when her ancestors first arrived in India from Central Asia, and progresses right up to her own days, till 1978.

Hyder was educated mostly in Lucknow, first at the famous Isabella Thoburn College, then at the University of Lucknow, where she obtained a Master's degree in English literature. She also studied painting and music, and has always been avidly interested in various other arts.

Hyder's father passed away in 1943. She and her mother were in Dehra Dun in 1947 when India became free and communal riots broke out at many places, including Dehra Dun. Mother and daughter were able to escape to Lucknow, and in December 1947 they left for Karachi where Hyder's only brother had preceded them. In Pakistan, Hyder worked for the Department of Advertising, Films and Publications, working on documentaries, particularly in what was then called East Pakistan. Subsequently she moved to England, where she worked at the BBC. In 1961, she returned to India and lived in Bombay, first as the managing editor of *Imprint,* then as Assistant Editor at the *Illustrated Weekly of India.* Since 1984, she has lived in Delhi and has held various posts, including visiting professorships at the Aligarh Muslim University and Jamia Millia Islamia. Her writings have brought her several major awards, including the Sahitya Akademi award in 1968, the Soviet Land award in 1969, the Ghalib Modi award in 1985, the Iqbal Samman in 1987, and India's most prestigious Jnanpith award in 1991. The Government of India honoured her with a Padmashri in 1984, and the Sahitya Akademi chose her as one of its permanent Fellows in 1994.

Hyder's literary career began at a very early age when she started contributing to some of the celebrated magazines of the time that specially catered to women and children. Soon her short stories began to appear in the best literary magazines of Urdu, and the first collection came out in 1947. Her first novel, *Mere Bhi Sanam-Khane* ("My Idol-houses Too"), followed soon after. Set at the time of the Partition, it movingly displayed the tearing apart of the lives of ordinary individuals as they got caught in the vortex of events that they understood only dimly, if at all, and the destruction of that syncretic *Ganga-Jamni* (Indo-Muslim) culture that was once the primary defining element for much of elite society in the towns and cities of the Gangetic plain. The novel's title (borrowed from a couplet by Iqbal: *"You have your idol-houses; I, too, have mine /My idols are perishable, and your idols are too"*) aptly described the young author's view of those calamitous days: a disillusionment of immense magnitude, a tragic falling from grace of many gods. Notably, she did not write like an outsider writing about other 'victims' and thus feeling a need to point a finger at someone 'guilty'. Instead, her voice was that of a victim who chooses not to accuse anyone, for who is there to accuse but another victim?

Since then she has published three volumes of short stories, six novels, several novellas, the two-volume family saga mentioned earlier, and several translations, including Henry James' *Portrait of a Lady*, Truman Capote's *Breakfast at Tiffany's* and T. S. Eliot's *Murder in the Cathedral*. She has also published English translations of her own works, including a couple of novels, *Fireflies in the Night* and the more recent *River of Fire*, as well as a collection of short stories, *The Sound of Falling Leaves*. Another memorable publication is *The Nautch Girl*, her English translation of nineteenth century Urdu version of what was perhaps the first piece of 'modern' fiction written in Persian (ca. 1790), and possibly also the first Indian novel.

During her literary career, Hyder has had her share of controversy, too. In the early Fifties when the so-called Progressives had the dominant voice in Urdu literary circles, Hyder was accused of being bourgeois and reactionary, given to morbid nostalgia and employing a literary style that, to the Progressives, seemed slight or brittle if not outright flippant. Ismat Chughtai even wrote a parody of her fiction, entitled "Pom Pom Darling". Hyder's real crime, in fact, was that she preferred to write exclusively about what she knew best. She wrote mostly about upper-crust people and did not denounce them in the manner expected by the votaries of Socialist Realism. But her detractors were utterly wrong to think that she wished for a return of the good old days. They demanded of her a kind of crude class-consciousness, but themselves showed no understanding of the immense pain—private as well as public—that she felt as life around her changed. Hyder was never oblivious of the economic ties that existed between people as well as between classes of people, she was simply more concerned with the human bonds of trust, loyalty and empathy—values that are often not quite defensible through cold logic. Later in Pakistan, some literary critics, pointing to her apparent affection for that *Ganga-Jamni* culture of the past, faulted her writings for being 'anti-Pakistan'. Understandably, her readers in Pakistan, as in India, showed better judgment than the critics.

In almost all her writings Hyder has been concerned with Time, that faceless presence which transforms all appearances and which we ignore only at our own peril. Though this inevitability of change is our only permanent reality,[3] Hyder persistently urges us to recognise both its faces, one of gain and the other of loss. A linearly progressing time brings about changes. Should we then take sides? Should we say that change is progress? Or should we say it is decline? Either, according to Hyder, would be simplistic and perilous, for such issues are not settled by a reference to the material world alone. What counts, for her, is the human spirit and relationships it generates and nurtures. That is where the linearity of time seems to curve into a spiral, urging us to recognise a past that never quite disappears. This, of course, may have depressing side, too: the more things change, the more they remain the same. What, then, is our choice as individuals? Here it may be worthwhile to recall the characteristically modest, even self-mocking, remarks that Hyder made in 1991 in her acceptance speech at the Jnanpith Award function: "My concern for civilisation values about which I continue writing may sound naive, woolly-headed and simplistic. But then, perhaps, I am like that little bird which foolishly puts ups its claws, hoping that it will stop the sky from falling."

I may be stretching the point but it seems to me that what Hyder tacitly offers us is nothing but that wise Candidean response: even in the best of all possible worlds, it is best not to neglect to tend our garden. Certainly, through the several thousand pages of her writings, she has shown herself to be an eloquent witness to that truth.

❖

NOTES

[1] This existential attitude is most effectively expressed in an extraordinary couplet by the sixteenth century Persian poet, 'Urfi' who died in India:

> *Don't be proud if you were not deceived by the mirage;*
> *Instead, fault yourself for not being thirsty enough.*

Iqbal, the most influential Urdu poet of this century, admiringly quotes this couplet in his lectures on the reconstruction of religious thought in Islam.

[2] Her maternal uncle Mir Afzal Ali named her after the remarkable Persian poet, Qurratulain Tahira. A Baha'i martyr—she was executed in 1852—Tahira was nevertheless admired as a heroic figure by many Muslim intellectuals at the time, including Iqbal. Mir Afzal Ali's mother, Akbari Begum, was the author of the famous novel *Gudri Ka Lal* (1907).

[3] Iqbal: *sabat ek taghayyur ko hai zamane mein.* "Only change has permanence in Time."

❀ The Sound of Falling Leaves ❀

The Sound of Falling Leaves

This morning I was standing at my backdoor arguing with the vegetable vendor over the price of cauliflower. Upstairs, in the kitchen, rice and lentils were boiling on the stove. The servant had left for the market. In the bathroom, standing in front of the dull mirror over the chipped sink, Viqar Sahib was admiring his face, humming a tune, and shaving. As I argued with the vendor my mind was busily planning the evening meal. Just then a car stopped near us. A woman leaned out the car window, then opened the door and stepped out. I was counting my change and didn't pay her much attention, but when she came closer I raised my head and looked at her.

"Oh! . . . It's you!" she almost shrieked.

I froze. Her face looked as if she had seen a ghost. The horror I saw in her eyes at that moment still haunts me. I can't forget it. I could go mad thinking about it.

This woman—I still can't recall her name, and in the morning, out of sheer embarrassment, I couldn't even ask her—she and I used to students together at St. Mary's in Delhi. That was some twenty years ago. I must have been only seventeen then. But I was a healthy girl and looked big for my years, and people were already talking of my beauty.

There used to be a custom in Delhi: women with eligible sons or male cousins would make the rounds of all the schools, looking over the girls. If they liked one they would send a proposal to her parents. Somehow I came to know that the mother and aunts of this girl had noticed me in the assembly on Founder's Day, and were keen to make me their daughter-in-law. They lived on Nurjahan Road, and the 'boy' had recently started at the Reserve Bank of India making two hundred a month. A proposal was sent to my parents, who lived quite far from Delhi in

Meerut. But my mother had loftier plans for me—also, at my age, it was too early for marriage. The proposal was immediately turned down.

Later we were briefly together in college, but then she got married and left. Now, after so many years, we met again this morning in an alley behind Lahore's Mall Road.

"Come upstairs and have a cup of tea," I said to her, "We'll have a good chat."

She replied that she was looking for an in-law's house— that's how she happened to wander into my lane—and promised to come later. Then, right there in the middle of the alley, she told me about each and every one of our college friends. Salima married a Brigadier; she now had four children. Farkhunda's husband was in the Foreign Service; her eldest daughter was in a school in London. Rehana was now the Principal of a college. Sa'diya had been to the States where she picked up a whole bunch of degrees; now she had some topnotch job in Karachi. This girl even knew about our old Hindu friends. Prabha's husband was a Commodore in the Indian Navy; they were living in Bombay. Sarla was now a Station Director with the All India Radio, currently posted somewhere in South India. Latika had made a name for herself as a painter in New Delhi. She chattered on, but I couldn't forget that first look of horror in her eyes.

Then she said, "Whenever some of us get together in Karachi we always think of you."

"Really!" I laughed, but it sounded hollow.

I know what words they must have used to remember me by, those witches. Friends, indeed! To tell you the truth, women are their own worst enemy. She didn't even bother to ask me what I was doing in that wretched alley, at the back door of a decrepit house—she already knew. Women have an intelligence service of their own—it can put even Interpol to shame. Not that I have ever tried to hide anything. I'm insignificant, not worth much talking about. Nobody gives a damn for me. Neither do I.

I'm Tanvir Fatima. My father, who lived in Meerut, was a zamindar, though not big. Our family observed strict purdah; I was kept in seclusion even from my cousins. But as my parents' only daughter I was their darling, they pampered me beyond measure. I did well at the local school and won a few awards, so my parents sent me all the way to Delhi, to St. Mary's, to matriculate. From there I went to Aligarh. That was the best time in my life, those four years at Aligarh Muslim Girls' College. What a dream of a place! I'm not sentimental, but the memory of it still lingers. The large, enclosed yard of the college; the brick-lined paths; the lush grass; the patter of raindrops on the trees; the annual fair in the city where all the girls from the college would run around covered from head to toe in black burqas; the narrow verandahs of the hostel; the tiny rooms which had such an air of domesticity about them—it almost breaks my heart when I think of that place.

I returned to Delhi, to do my M.Sc. There at the college I met all those girls—Rehana, Sa'diya, Prabha, the rest. I've never much liked girls. In fact, I don't like most people. You only waste time with most of them. I felt quite superior in those days. Physical charms can do that to anyone; they turn your head in no time. And I was a rare beauty— as they say, one in a thousand: fair, translucent skin; reddish blond hair; tall and slender. When, on occasion, I'd put on a brocade sari, I looked like a Maharani.

The War was going on, or perhaps it had just ended. I don't exactly remember. In any case, life in Delhi was in full swing in those days. All the college girls—daughters of rich businessmen and big-shot civil service people— Hindu, Sikh, Muslim—were being whisked around in the their fathers' limousines, from one social event to another. A play at Indraprastha College. A concert at Miranda House. A party at Chelmsford Club. Lady Irwin College . . . Lady Hardinge College . . . St. Stephen's College . . . Roshanara Club. . . Imperial Hotel. . . The Gymkhana Club. They were like settings from the Arabian Nights. And ev-

erywhere one ran into crowds of young men—unmarried
military officers and civil service internees. Such fun!

One day, together with Prabha and Sarla, I went to a
garden party at Daljit Kaur's; she was the daughter of a
millionaire Sikh—a building-contractor—and lived in a
mansion on King Edward Road. There I met Major
Khushwaqt Singh.

He was a Chauhan Rajput from somewhere near Jhansi:
very tall and sturdy and extremely dark of complexion. He
had long moustaches, swept upward and twirled to a sharp
point. When he laughed his brilliant white teeth dazzled
you. He adored Ghalib's poetry, and quoted a verse in every other sentence. Though his laugh was boisterous, he
would bend his head most graciously when talking to people.
He immediately invited all of us to a movie the next day.
Sarla and Prabha were killjoys, even rather old-fashioned
in some ways. They never went out with boys. Since
Khushwaqt was a friend of Daljit's brother, I didn't know
what to say. Then Sarla whispered in my ear, "Don't ever go
to a movie with him. He is no good." So I remained silent.

In those days, Delhi was buzzing with the tales of two
'loose' girls: how they were running around with men and
making fools of their genteel parents. I had heard about
them and felt somewhat nervous. They seemed so strange,
almost mysterious, even though they looked just like the
rest of us: pretty, nicely dressed, even modish. In our hostel, we'd often talk about them. "People have given them
a bad name for no reason," Sa'diya would say after a great
deal of thought.

"Of course. They can't be that bad!"

"The fact of the matter is," Sarla would add, "Our society is not prepared yet to accept modern, educated girls."

"Well, some girls tend to lose their sense of balance,"
Rehana would comment.

We just couldn't believe that any girl, who looked just
like us, could do such horrible things.

The following day, at dusk, I was walking to the labora-

tory when, near Nicholson Memorial, a long, maroon car
crept up close to me and stopped. Khushwaqt leaned out
the window, and his white teeth lit up the twilight. "Well
ma'am, so you've forgotten our appointment?"

"What! What?" I was totally confused.

"Ma'am, you must come with me. Evening's no time
for you to lock yourself in the lab. In any case, what good
will all your studying do?"

I cast a quick glance all around—without really intend-
ing to do so—and got into the car, pushing myself deep
into one corner.

We went to Connaught Circus and saw an English film.

Same thing the next day.

After that, for one whole week, I went to many places
with him. He was staying at Maidens Hotel. By the end of
the week I had become the mistress of Major Khushwaqt
Singh.

I'm not the literary type. I haven't read Chinese, Japanese, Russian, English or even Urdu Poetry. In my opinion, reading literature is a sheer waste of time. I've studied science since I was fifteen. I don't know what Meta-
physics is, or what is meant by 'mystical attraction'. I had
no time then for poetry or philosophy, nor do I have any
now. Likewise, I'm not given to using big, ambiguous,
mysterious words.

Within a fortnight most of the college knew about us.
But I paid no attention; I've always carried a curious confidence in myself. In any case, I wasn't much of a socialiser.
Now Sarla and company looked at me as if I were a Mar-
tian or had horns growing out of my head. After I'd leave
the Dining Hall the girls would talk about me for hours.
Their 'intelligence service' kept them fully informed about
Khushwaqt and myself: where we had been the previous
evening, which shops we frequented and what gifts he
bought me, in which New Delhi ballroom we had danced
last night (Khushwaqt was a fabulous dancer; he taught
me, too, to dance well).

Khushwaqt used to beat me up quite a bit; he also loved me more intensely than any man could have ever loved any woman.

Several months passed. Soon it was time for my M.Sc. (Previous) exams, and I became totally engrossed in my studies. After the exams ended, Khushwaqt said to me, "Darling, my love, let's go to some quiet hill-station . . . Solan, Dalhousie, perhaps Lansdowne?" I went to Meerut for a few days; later, telling my father (my mother had passed away when I was in my Third Year) that I had to start studying for the Finals right away, I came back to Delhi. We couldn't go to any hill-station in North India where we could have run into people we knew. So we decided to go far south, to Ooty, and spent a month there. Then Khushwaqt's leave ended and we returned to Delhi and stayed in a bungalow in Timarpur.

A week before my classes were to start, Khushwaqt and I had a big fight. He beat me like never before; he hit me till my face was bloodied and my arms and legs were left with dark bruises. The reason for the fight was his wretched fiancée, an Indian Christian, who had suddenly turned up in Delhi and was going around saying obscene things about me. The crafty bitch had been in the Army during the War and had met Khushwaqt on the Burma front. Somehow she had made him promise her marriage. However, now that he had met me, he was determined to end their engagement.

That night, in that desolate bungalow in Timarpur, he pleaded with me on his knees. With tears in his eyes, he said, "Marry me, or I'll die." But I replied, "No, never, not even if the world comes to an end." I was a Sayyid's daughter, my family was old and noble, how could I marry a jet-black Hindu and ruin my family's name! I was dreaming of that fair-skinned, handsome scion of some elite Muslim family who was sooner or later going to come with a large procession to marry me. We'd see each other for the first time in a mirror under a veil of flowers. I'd be dressed like a princess and go to his parents' house. There his high-spir-ited sisters would stop us at the door, insisting that he pay them some money as the custom required. Then the tradi-tional singers and dancers would perform. . . .

I knew how these Hindu-Muslim marriages always ended! Quite a few Muslim girls in Delhi had married Hindus—moved by love or just to be progressive—but within a year it was all over. It always ended in a pitched battle. And the children suffered the most; they belonged nowhere. Anyway, when I wouldn't accept, Khushwaqt lost his temper and hit me again and again. Two days later, he went off with that black bitch Katherine Dharamdas to Agra, where they got married in a civil service.

At the beginning of the new term, when I arrived at the hostel, my head and face were all bandaged. I had written to my father that I had been working in the lab when the apparatus exploded, that as a result I got a slight burn on my face but there was nothing to worry about. The girls, of course, knew the whole story; they didn't even pretend ignorance and ask what had happened. I could've been kicked out of the hostel after such a scandal, but Khushwaqt happened to be on very good terms with the Warden. Everyone kept their peace. Also, no one really had any proof. After all, it's only too easy to give any col-lege girl a bad name.

I still remember the scene that morning, like it hap-pened only yesterday. It was around ten or eleven. The girls were arriving in tongas from the railway station. There was a crowd of them on the lawn, near the old banyan tree, busily sorting out baggage and loudly exchanging news and greetings. When I got down from my tonga and they saw my pale, bandaged face, they fell silent as if they had seen a ghost. I asked one of the servants to carry my suitcases and marched off to my room. Later, when I joined them at lunch, those bitches were the soul of politeness and amiably chatted with me about this and that. Of course, without saying so, they made it clear that they knew all about my 'accident' and were avoiding the topic only to save me from embarrassment. That evening, at the dinner table, their leader announced her verdict: psychologically speaking, in her opinion, I was a 'nympho'. (I had stayed behind in my room, studying at my desk by the window, but the news immediately reached me through one of my own 'spies'.) There were, of course, many other comments: "One rotten apple can spoil a barrel." "No wonder people say girls shouldn't go to college." "That's why parents don't like giving us freedom." And so on.

I agreed with every one of those comments. I myself used to wonder: why do fairly reasonable, well-educated girls suddenly turn bad? One theory said, only the girls with low IQs turn bad, intelligent ones don't ruin themselves knowingly. But I have seen highly intelligent, supersmart girls running around with men. A second theory proposed a host of reasons: excessive desire for fun, love of luxury, search for romance and adventure, sheer boredom, rebellion after a restricted childhood. . . . They must all be true. What other explanation can there be?

I had just finished the first-term exam when Khushwaqt reappeared. He phoned me at the laboratory and asked me to meet him at Nirula's that evening. I went. He had left Katherine at her parents' and had come to Delhi on some pretext. This time we flew off to Bombay for one week.

Now we started meeting every second or third month, and a year went by. Then one day, he sent a dear friend of his to bring me to him at the airport; he was on his way to Lahore from Lucknow and was stopping in transit for a few hours. Faruq turned out to be the son of an extremely wealthy Muslim businessman. He was by no means young . . . must have been almost forty. Married, with children; tall like a camel; dark-complexioned. He had the looks of a wild man, with manners to match. And his English was simply terrible.

This time when Khushwaqt left Delhi he never came back; by then I had become Faruq's mistress.

With Faruq, I entered Delhi's high society quite properly, as his fiancée. Muslims are allowed four wives. So there was nothing wrong—religiously speaking that is—if, in addition to his middle-aged, conservative and illiterate first wife, Faruq wanted to marry a modern, educated girl who could be by his side in mixed company. In any case, anything goes among the rich. It's only us, the middle class, who insist on dos and don'ts. During the long, mid-term break, Faruq took me all over India. I'd simply write to Father, "I'm going with other students on a university-sponsored tour." Or, "I've been invited to an important conference." Faruq also loaded me with gifts of jewellery. I was doubtless anxious to keep up my academic record, but I didn't do well in the final exams. After the last test I went home to Meerut.

That was the time communal trouble started in Delhi; soon it had spread everywhere. Faruq wrote to me in Meerut that I should leave immediately for Pakistan, where he planned to join me later. I was already thinking of doing just that. Father was crazy with worry: he didn't want me to stay in India where the honour of decent Muslim girls was going to be in constant danger. Pakistan for him was different: it was an Islamic country. Because of our property Father couldn't leave Meerut. My two brothers were still in their teens and, after Mother's death, Father had sent them to my aunt in Hyderabad. Then the results were announced: I had passed, but just barely. It broke my heart. And so when there was a lull in the riots I took the first available flight to Lahore. Faruq came with me. He planned to open a branch of his business in Lahore; it was to be in my name, and I was to marry him there. He had no intention of leaving Delhi permanently, for his father was a fanatic 'nationalist'. Instead Faruq intended to visit Lahore every other month or so. Lahore was just a big mess at that time. If you knew the right people you could get the finest of homes abandoned by the Hindus allotted to yourself, but Faruq didn't know a soul here.

The most he could manage was a small house in Santnagar, which he got in my name. There he set me up, and in order to provide me company, had the family of a distant relative move in with me. They had come to Lahore from India as refugees and had no other shelter.

The change in my life was sudden and drastic; it left me stunned. I just couldn't understand what had happened. One moment there had been my gay and abundant life in undivided India, the next I found myself in a dark and dingy house in the Lahore of '48. Allah be praised! What terrible days these eyes have seen!

I was in such a state of shock that I didn't even try to find a job. Not that I was short of money at the time: before going back to Delhi Faruq had deposited ten thousand rupees in a bank in my name. (Only ten thousand. When he himself was a millionaire! But at the time I was too numb to think. Even now few things make sense to me.)

Days turned into weeks, weeks into months. I'd sit on my bed all day long, chewing betel and listening to Faruq's 'aunt'—or whoever that old woman was—telling stories of their past wealth and their frightful *hijrat* to Pakistan. Once in a while I'd help her young daughter, who was in high school, with her math assignments. Her son looked after Faruq's business, which was only nominal.

Faruq would visit us five or six times in a year. Life in Lahore was gradually returning to normal. His visits would add some color to my days. His 'aunt' would prepare Delhi dishes specially for him. I'd visit a hairdresser on the Mall and get my hair set. Evenings we'd go to Gymkhana Club. There, at a corner table and with a glass of beer in front of him, Faruq would tell me the news of Delhi. He'd either talk relentlessly, or suddenly fall silent and gaze at all the unfamiliar faces in the room. Not once did he mention marriage. I didn't say anything either. I was no longer interested in the subject. Nothing made any difference anyway. After Faruq's return to Delhi I'd write him every two weeks to assure him about ourselves and his business. I'd also ask him to bring saris on his next trip from certain shops in Connaught Circus and Chandni Chowk—one still can't get decent saris in Pakistan.

One day a letter arrived from my uncle in Meerut: my father had passed away. "Who has lived for ever, not even the Prophet!" I'm not terribly sentimental, but Father would have given his life for me. I was devastated. Faruq wrote me several letters full of loving, consoling words. They helped. "Say your prayers regularly," he'd write. "These are bad days. A dark time has come upon the earth. The day of judgment is imminent. You can't even be sure of your next breath." Like all business men, Faruq was terribly religious and superstitious. He used to visit the shrine at Ajmer every year. He had faith in all sorts of astrologers, palmists, soothsayers, psychics, necromancers, what have you. For one whole month I said my five daily prayers without fail. But every time I prostrated myself before God I felt a mad desire to burst out laughing.

There was then a great demand in the country for women teachers who could teach physical sciences. The principal of a local college who knew about me, offered me a job and wouldn't take no for an answer. I finally gave in, though I don't like to teach. After some time, a girls' college in another, rather distant city enticed me away. I worked there for several years. Often my students would ask me, "You're so sweet, Miss Fatima, why don't you marry your millionaire fiancé ?"

I had no answer for them.

This was a new country, these were new people, a new society. Here no one knew my past. Any number of decent men could have readily married me. (But what could I do, I don't find good-natured, normal-looking gentlemen very attractive.) Anyway, who cared in Lahore what had happened in Delhi? Some of the most notorious girls of those days now go around looking so very virtuous! I personally know at least two.

By now Faruq's visits had become quite infrequent. We'd meet like a couple married for decades that had exhausted all topics of conversation: now was the time for peace and rest and stillness. Faruq's daughter got married in Delhi; his son left for Oxford; his wife suffered from asthma; his business spread to several countries; he built a new bungalow in Nainital. Faruq would tell me his family and business news, and I'd silently prepare betel leaves for him.

One summer vacation when I returned to Lahore I ran into Sayyid Viqar Husain Khan, an old friend of Faruq's. He, too, was one of a kind. Tall and heavy, dark as midnight, about forty-five: he looked like a giant in a children's book. I had first met him in Delhi, where he used to run a dancing school.

Scion of a good family of Rampur, Viqar Sahib had run away from home as a boy. Working in circuses, carnivals and touring theatres, he travelled all over the world and married all kinds of women. When I met him in Delhi his wife at the time, whom he had seduced into running away with him, was the daughter of a Marwari moneylender in Calcutta. I had seen her some twelve or fifteen years ago: short and olive-skinned, she had a tragic air about her. But the word was that she was a most devoted wife; even when she ran away, tired of being maltreated by him, she always came back after a few days. Viqar Sahib had rented a flat on the third floor of a building in Connaught Circus, that's where he ran his school for ballroom dancing. He, his wife and two Anglo-Indian girls made up the teaching staff. During the War he made a lot of money with his Sunday morning "Jam Sessions". (I once went to one of them with Khushwaqt.) The rumour-mill had it that Viqar Sahib's wife was so devoted to him that he'd order her to gain the confidence of particular girls and then bring them home to meet him. And sh'd do it, too. Once I remember she came to our hostel and followed some girls around, insisting that they come and have tea at her place.

After the Partition, "having lost", as the saying goes,

"everything", Viqar Sahib arrived in Lahore and got himself a flat allotted in an alley behind Mall Road. Here he started his school again. In the beginning there weren't many takers: who could think of ballroom dancing when hearts were full of grief? Before the Partition that flat had housed a music school run by Arya Samaji Hindus: it had a nice hall with a wooden floor, two side rooms, a bathroom and a kitchen, a wooden balcony in the front and rickety stairs that led up to it. From the balcony dangled a sign: "Hindu Mata Sangeet Mahavidyalaya". That sign was taken down and replaced by another; it said, "Viqar's School of Ballroom and Tap Dancing". Pictures of Gene Kelly, Fred Astaire, Frank Sinatra, Doris Day and others were cut out of American film magazines and pasted on the peeling walls of the hall. Viqar Sahib had brought along a small collection of records from Delhi; now, with money borrowed from Faruq, he bought a gramophone and some old furniture. Thus the school got going. God bless college dandies and fashion-hungry wives of the nouveau riche—in just a couple of years Viqar Sahib's business had picked up nicely.

Viqar Sahib was a close friend of Faruq's, so he considered me his 'sister-in-law' and I looked upon him as my 'brother-in-law'. He would often come by to see how I was doing as would his wife, who sat with me for hours and talked about her domestic woes. The poor woman showed me all the affection of a sister-in-law. The two were childless, and made a sad, colourless, uninteresting couple. As they say, it takes all kinds . . . .

One day I got into a bad argument with the principal of my college. She had recently returned from the States and nothing at home could please her. I was hot-tempered myself and no easier to please. I shot off a resignation letter to the College Committee and returned to Santnagar, Lahore. By then I was tired of teaching. I could have easily got a fellowship and gone overseas to do a Ph.D., but kept delaying it till 'tomorrow'. Tomorrow I shall go to the

USEFI where they hand out fellowships. Tomorrow the British Council. Tomorrow the Ministry of Education. But that tomorrow never came. Days turned into weeks. I said to myself: does it matter? What have I to do over there anyway? I was waiting for something, but I didn't know what.

Then one day Viqar Sahib came to me highly agitated. "Your Bhabhi," he said, "had another of her crazy fits. She got new papers made and left for India . . . for good."

"What happened?" I asked rather casually, and put some water to boil for tea.

"I divorced her, that's what happened," he replied. "She'd become very argumentative. She'd fight with me all the time." Then he settled himself on a cot opposite me and, in a most husbandly manner, reeled off his complaints against his wife, how she was to be blamed for everything and how blameless and right he was.

I listened to his tale half-heartedly, for I couldn't care less. Everything in life seemed so trivial, so colourless, so utterly without meaning or purpose.

After some weeks, he came to me again. "The servants are driving me crazy," he grumbled. "What sort of a 'sister' are you? Can't you stop by just once in a while and put your 'brother's house in order? Tell the servants what to do? Must I run the school and the house too?" He complained as if I was naturally obliged to look after his domestic needs.

A few days later, I packed up my things and moved in with Viqar Sahib; I also assisted him in the dance lessons. After a month—last Sunday, in fact—Viqar Sahib sent for a maulvi and, with two of his ridiculous friends as witnesses, married me.

Now I stay busy in the house all day long. My looks are a forgotten tale. Though I hate parties and noisy affairs, my home constantly rocks with dance music. But now, this is the only home I have.

I have offers of jobs from several colleges; they want me

to teach Chemistry. But how can I find time for it? The house demands so much. As for servants, you hire them today and they're gone tomorrow. I've never asked for much. At most I desired a modest house, a car to make it easy to go some place, and a few things in the house to receive guests properly. Enough to keep one's dignity before one's peers, that's all.

We now make about fifteen hundred or two thousand every month—more than enough for the two of us. If you can be content with your fate you can automatically save yourself from grief.

Marriage provides a roof over a girl's head. But the girls today are so different. I don't understand them. They get so out of hand. The more I think about it the more lost I feel.

I've never even flirted with anyone. Khushwaqt, Faruq, and this dark giant of a husband; except for these three I don't even know a fourth man. I don't think I was a bad girl. I don't know what I was then . . . or what I am now. Sa'diya, Prabha, the girl whose eyes filled up with horror when she recognised me—they probably know me much better. What use is it now to think of Khushwaqt? So much time has passed. By now he must be a Brigadier or even a Major General— fighting the Chinese in Assam, perhaps, or sitting in some Officers' Mess in Rajputana, smiling under his up-swept moustaches. Or perhaps he died long ago in Kashmir. Who knows!

On dark nights I lie in my bed, my eyes wide open. Science has revealed to me so many secrets of this world. I have read countless books on Chemistry. For hours and hours I have thought. But I get scared. On dark nights I get very scared.

Khushwaqt Singh! Khushwaqt Singh! What can you possibly have to do with me now?

(1959)
(Translated by C. M. Naim)

✻ Sita Betrayed ✻

Sita Betrayed

(1)

It was an ordinary afternoon—not unlike so many others—when Sita Mirchandani, Ph.D. (Columbia), heard the news that Jamil had remarried. The clock on the wall continued to tick away the seconds. Birds in the November sky kept circling as before. And in the Asian Theatre Institute, children remained engrossed in their puppetry lessons. Sita had gone to see Lalita. Then at three she had come to Hima's house to go with Shahzad to the rehearsal of *Mudrarakshasa*. Still later she had been invited by the members of the Modern Theatre to a dinner at the house of Mrs. Dolly Sen. Her life was very busy—and very empty!

At two-thirty Sita had taken a bus from Mathura Road for Alipur Lane. Arriving there, she had walked down the long, red gravelled road of the "Yellow House", calling out cheery hellos to the girls sitting on the terrace, and had entered the gallery of the garden cottage attached to the "Blue House". Shahzad's room was next to the entrance; when Sita peeked through the door he was sprawled on his bed, comfortably snoring. She had started to walk down to Hima's room when the phone in the gallery began to ring. Then, as she picked up the receiver, the clock rang out the hour. It was Bilqis shouting at the other end: "Hima? Has Sita arrived there?"

"Hello. Bilqis? This is Sita. What's the matter?"

"Oh! You are there already! . . . No—nothing special. It was just—er—it was just so funny. You know what Pradip said to Kamran?"

"Bilqis!" Sita said firmly, "Why did you call just now?"

"For no reason—just for the heck of it." Bilqis' voice was calmer than usual. "I just thought I should catch up with the news. Did you remember to give Hamida's message to Lalita?" Then for the next twenty minutes Bilqis had gossiped about the city's amateur theatre network.

The clock sounded the half-hour.

"Bili dear," Sita had said with some exasperation, "did you call here just to tell me this nonsense?"

"Well—er. . . ."

"Have you received a letter from New York?"

"Ye-es." All the eagerness had gone out of Bilqis' voice.

"What's the matter, Bilqis?"

"Jamil Bhai—Jamil Bhai has got married."

'Tick-tock, tick-tock,' the clock sounded. Shahzad turned in his bed and the springs groaned. Outside, near the rose bushes, Hima's baby son began to cry. In the dining room, Bishan Singh slammed shut the buffet door.

"Who's the girl?" Sita's voice came from the bottom of some deep well.

"Some European. . . ."

Miles away in Chanakyapuri, life in Bilqis' home was going on as usual. Children were shouting. Tea things were being rattled. Chhoti Khala was scolding the gardener. Bilqis' young niece was sprawled on the drawing room rug listening to the tape-recorder: *All my life long I remained a prey / to her coquetry* . . . 'Close that door' . . . 'Hey, stop talking, will you' . . . 'Wonderful, wonderful' . . . *to her coquetry*. . . 'Please, read that line again' . . . *All my life long.* . . . Some poet had recited that ghazal at Bilqis' house last week and Sita was quite fond of it. But with all those noises in the back, she was unable to hear Bilqis clearly.

"Speak up, will you?" Sita had almost shouted. "There's too much going on at your end."

"It's some European girl." Bilqis had tried to speak above the din. "I don't know the details. Jamil Bhai has only written that she works in his office at the United Nations. It could be anyone. (Hey, Muzaffar, what are you doing here? Go play outside, will you.)" Then she had added, "Must be some wretched waitress—or some typist."

"He can marry Elizabeth Taylor, for all I care." Sita had responded calmly. She had sat down in the chair next to the telephone table. The gallery was full of dark shadows, and unusually cold.

"Well, the trouble with that, Sita dear, is that Elizabeth Taylor's already married. And I hear that Princess Margaret might also get married soon. Those were the two girls that he liked in all the world—the third was Nargis, but she too found a husband not so long ago."

Bilqis Anwar Ali, being one of the country's finest stage actresses, had resumed her normal voice. She had received that year's Best Actress award from Delhi Natya Sangh, and in the next production of the Modern Theatre she was set to do a tremendous tragic role. How then could she let her voice betray what she was really thinking?

"Bilqis . . . ."

"Yes, Sita dear?"

"So, okay. I must go now and talk to Hima. See you this evening. 'Bye."

" 'Bye, Sita."

(2)

Bilqis put the receiver down and walked through the lounge to her own room. In the middle room Chhoti Khala, wrapped in a deep purple shawl, was busy talking to some relative from Tulsipur. On the back lawn children were playing cricket, while the late autumn sun filtered into the lounge through the window-panes. Reaching her room, Bilqis picked up the letter which lay half-open on the box of Kleenex on her dressing table. She started reading it over again. Her beloved cousin had written—in one brief paragraph, after a lot of other chitchat:

"Last Sunday I married a girl from Spain. She works in my section and is very decent. Not an intellectual. But she went to Smith College, which is a very aristocratic place. So rest assured, your sister-in-law is not some 'shop-girl'.

Because all you 'native' girls firmly believe that your good-
for-nothing brothers come to the West, then take home
'shop-girls' or, as you put it, 'laundresses'. God, you folks
are such snobs! Anyway, I'll send you a picture later.
Carmen is not overly beautiful, but in a sari she will look
very Indian. Dark eyes and all that, as the poet said. Pass
this news on to Mother. Rahul is well. He has already become quite fond of Carmen. He's also getting to be rather
chubby. Carmen and I went to see him at his school yesterday.

"You should come here next fall. These magnificent
forests are then ablaze with colour. I hear that you might
get a scholarship to come here to study acting. When do
you come? Carmen and I will go to Boston for Christmas."

Jamil had written not one word about Sita. Sita, who
was the mother of his son Rahul.

Back in 1951, Bilqis had received a similar letter from
Jamil, again from New York. (That day, too, she had been
hurrying to go to a rehearsal. All the same people, the
same world, the same whirligig of activities.) After the usual
gossip, Jamil had written:

"There isn't much else to tell you. Sorry, I forgot. Last
week I got married to a Sindhi girl. She is studying Socio-
logy at Columbia. She is from the Amil caste, which is considered very high among the Sindhis. So Mother should
be happy that at least I didn't tie myself to some low-caste
American. Now you, my child, must be dying to know what
she looks like. Well, she is extremely fair—all pink and
cream—and rather beautiful. As you know, I am always
stingy when it comes to praising women's looks—even a
little praise can turn their heads. But Sita is in fact quite
attractive. She is a bit taller than you. And though she
doesn't speak Urdu very fluently, if she were to dress in
old-fashioned clothes she would look like any Syed's daughter from village Tulsipur, district Faizabad. So rest assured.

"We have already decided we'll call our son Rahul. Yes,
Rahul. I guess I'll have to explain—you are so dumb. Rahul

was the name of the son of Gautama, the Buddha. You must be shocked by the idea of my wife already discussing these matters. The trouble, little girl, is that you're still an A-class old fogey. Despite all your fancy education and your progressive pretensions, you continue to be very feudal. Sita is a New Woman. She is not a rustic like the rest of you. In any case, our son will be called Rahul, and if it's a daughter, her name will be Gulrukh."

A shiver went down Bilqis' spine and she put the letter back on the dressing table. It was so dreadful. The two letters were almost identical. The same man had written them. She forced herself to open the wardrobe and started selecting a sari for the evening. Now she had to get ready for the rehearsal of *Mudrarakshasa*. Within half an hour they will all be together, all the old friends—Lalita, Rakesh, Kamran, Hamida, Shahzad—all the familiar faces. Life would go on just as before.

(3)

Something fell in Hima's dressing room across the gallery. By then Hima had wrapped a towel around her wet hair and stepped into the garden. Another door of her room opened out toward the Jamuna and had thick, yellow rose vines hanging over it.

Sita put the phone down, and for a moment leaned against the gallery door, staring outside. Then she lifted the curtain and stepped into Hima's room. There was no one there. Sita saw that on Hima's dresser there was an arrangement of several picture postcards and a portrait of Hima's Maratha husband, who was away in London doing some advanced training course. The cane bassinet for the baby lay near the bedstead and on the sofa was draped an electric blue sari from Cuttack that Hima had bought only that morning on Queensway. The baby's milk bottle stood on top of a copy of Chughtai's *Indian Paintings* on the corner table. The dull rays of an autumnal sun were scattered

across the red tile floor. And ragged, yellow leaves blown
about by the wind outside, knocked against the glass panes
of the windows and doors. Otherwise there was desolate
silence.

After a few moments there was a clattering sound in the
room next door. Hima's younger brother, Shahzad, leapt
off his bed with a thump—then the sound of the shower
being turned on came from his bathroom. Sita looked
outside. Hima's mother was sitting outside her bedroom
on a cane stool, reading the Gita. What an old-fashioned,
religious woman she was! The mother of such highly educated, modern young people and yet so old-fashioned. Her
own mother was equally religious. As was her mother-in-
law. As was Bilqis' mother. These tiny, weak women, doll-
like, wrapped in shawls and *dupattas* . . . these women who
constantly prayed for their children's happiness, who
looked for good and bad omens, who fasted and
prayed. . . . 'Mothers can be so ridiculous,' Sita thought.
She was a mother herself. And so was Hima, who, since
yesterday, seemed to have forgotten all her German Philosophy and was frantically consulting different doctors
about her baby's flu.

Sita walked through the gallery and down the steps into
the garden. At the other end of the lawn, on the terrace of
the "Yellow House", Uma-ji was sitting with her son trying
to teach him Hindi. The formal path had rows of huge
roses blooming on both sides. Sita stepped off the path
and came out on to the terrace. On hearing her steps,
Uma-ji raised her head and smiled. Then she bent over
the book again and said to her son, "Now read: *Bundele
harbolon ke muh hamne suni kahani thi, khoob ladi mardani
veh tho Jhansi wali Rani thi.*" *

But the boy began to argue, "No, I won't, Mummy. You
must first give me a rupee."

---

* We heard it from the mouths of the gallant Bundelas, how she fought
like a man, this Rani of Jhansi.

"Come on; don't be so naughty." Uma-ji tried to be stern. "Read!"

"What does *mardani* mean?" the boy asked.

"Brave, courageous." answered Uma-ji, and began to laugh.

The boy began to read, rocking his body back and forth to the rhythm of the poem. Sita stopped for a few moments to watch this peaceful scene, then she entered Hima's old room—where Hima had lived before her marriage. Her books still lay in disarray on the shelves. The walls were decorated with Manipuri caps and wooden figurines of Jagannath-ji. There was also a cabinet full of gods and goddesses. Its middle shelf had a tiny bed made for Devi. Every Tuesday, Devi had her dress changed. There were so many gods and goddesses in this house that sometimes Sita got rather nervous. But Hima looked at them as merely a part of the room's furnishings. Hima was not religious—neither was she irreligious. She was just a normal sort of girl. It was only Sita's crazy mind that kept constantly asking questions about religion, about politics, about death and life and everything else in this world. As for Hima, she had now started taking her baby every Tuesday to the Kalikaji temple in the company of her mother and aunts.

Sita left that room, passed through the drawing room, and came out into the front verandah. It faced the private road that joined Alipur Road. She could see Hima's cousin Pramila returning from her office. Pramila waved to her then disappeared in the mango grove. Sita turned around and wandered through the rooms once again. She had always loved this house. Coming to this house and spending time with its residents always gave her a wonderful sense of comfort and security. How peaceful their lives were! They had no mental, emotional or psychological problems. For nearly seventy years this family had lived like this, spread over five or six houses. Their ancestors had been court-chroniclers and *munshis* for the Mughals, and the Mughal kings had given them the title of Rai Raja. Hima's grandfather had been a Persian poet; her great-grandfather had written an important Persian dictionary, and his father had compiled a biographical dictionary of Persian poets. Hima's mother would sometimes use Urdu phrases and idioms that would go over Sita's head. Then she would say, "Hey girl, your in-laws are from Lucknow. You had better learn the language now." Then she would frown and add, "Well, those in Lucknow, what do they know of Urdu—they are from the East after all. . . ."

It amazed Sita no end to see how cultured, refined, properly set in their ways and totally apolitical these people were. Such a great upheaval had taken place—but they had calmly stayed put in their homes. As for Sita, she went through a number of refugee camps in India before she reached Delhi in '48. Here she met Hima at the house of Bilqis's elder sister, Farkhunda Baji, who was an M.P. From dawn to dusk, there would be a crowd at that house—Hindu refugees from Pakistan and frightened Muslims from Delhi—and Farkhunda Baji would share their grief and pain and try to help them all. At that time Hima, who had just finished the I.A.S. training course, was working in the Ministry of Rehabilitation. That day Bilqis had beckoned a scared-looking girl sitting in one corner of Farkhunda Baji's drawing room to come near, and then said to Hima (who had just arrived driving a long, maroon Nash), "Hima, remember how Uma-ji was asking yesterday about someone who could do Sindhi-style embroidery on saris? This is Sita—her mother does extremely beautiful embroidery."

"Oh, how wonderful!" Hima had said. "Can you get me a cotton sari embroidered? How much will it cost?"

"Ten rupees. . . ." Sita had replied, and the words had felt like poison on her tongue. She could feel her whole body tremble—she was just an indigent refugee, an object of pity for others.

Then one day she accompanied Bilqis to Hima's house. The various members of Hima's extended family had their houses next to each other, and each house was known by its separate colour. Hima lived with her parents and brothers and sisters in the "Blue House". Her senior uncle lived in the "Yellow House", the middle uncle in the "Red House", and the junior uncle in the "Green House". They were all fabulously lively and jovial people, who loved their friends and were devoted to each other. Their daughters studied in schools and colleges. So did the sons: Shahzad, Mahtab, Iqbal, Gulzar, Nihal, and many more. None of them, however, was the least bit snobbish. Despite that, Sita remained a bit withdrawn in the beginning. She was young then, and also extremely sensitive. Whenever Farkhunda Baji or Hima behaved like older sisters towards her, Sita felt she would burst into tears.

Why was she cursed to remember every tiny act of kindness? One summer night she had gone with them to Connaught Circus to see a late show of Nargis' latest film. A flower-seller was sitting in the arcade with strings of juhi flowers. No sooner had Sita turned to look at him than Ni'mat Chacha went and bought her a garland. Later, when they went there another time, Ni'mat Chacha did the same on his own—"I know you like white flowers, Sita." Now Ni'mat Chacha was somewhere in Uttar Pradesh running a farm. He had a family of his own. Shahzad had grown too; in fact he had been selected for the I.A.S. a few years ago. Recently he had been transferred to the capital. Hima was married and staying in her father's room in the Garden House while her husband was away in London. Now she was so busy taking care of her child that she had no time for Sita, while Shahzad was equally caught up in his "Theatre Movement". Hima's girl cousins had all finished their studies and found careers. A few of them had also been married off. The boys had grown up too. Iqbal and Mahtab were officers in the Army, and were posted in Kashmir.

A lot of changes had occurred in this family during the last nine years. This house, which had always seemed a haven of refuge, now looked somewhat different. Perhaps because she herself had greatly changed. But these rooms, the carpets and antique furniture, the paintings, the tiles on the floor, the flowers in the garden—they were all still the same. For her this house was still like a safe and quiet ship anchored in a harbour; every once in a while she came here to harmonise herself to its peace. Down there, beyond the long, serpentine, silent road, gently flowed the Jamuna. 'Is so much peace really possible?' Sita walked through all the rooms, then returned to the one which was once Hima's.

"Sita! What are you doing in there? Come outside, crazy girl. It's so damp in there." That was Hima's mother, who was walking towards the room of gods and goddesses, her wooden slippers clacking on the hard floor. Sita followed her to the room but stopped at the door.

"Come on. At least greet them, you silly girl. How will that hurt you? After all, God is in everything. There's no reason for you to be scared. Listen, two of my nieces also married Muslims. That seems to be the fashion these days. But no one threw them out. Their father gave such a big party.. . . . Take my own Hima—she married someone not our caste and went off to live in Maharashtra. So what did we do? Nothing. Such are the times." And she opened the cabinet and lit a tiny lamp before all the figurines and pictures.

Sita stepped into the room and stood before the cabinet. Tiny clay figures of gods and goddesses were arranged like toys. Behind them were photographs of many sadhus and yogis, each with its garland of marigold flowers.

Sita had not known Hima's mother for very long, that's why she was always a bit nervous around her. Back in 1948, when Sita was in Delhi, Hima's mother had been in Lucknow with her brother. Three years ago, when Sita had returned from the States for a few months, she had met her for the first time. The old lady was sitting, as usual, on her cane stool on the lawn, reading the Gita. Hima had introduced them: "Amma, this is Sita."

"*Adab Arz*," Sita had said, raising one hand to her forehead.

Amma had pushed up her glasses and, blinking her big,

pink-streaked eyes, looked at her intently. Then, with a
faint smile, she had said, "Your name is Sita, but you say
'*Adab Arz*' instead of '*Jai Ram-ji*'!"

Outside as they got into Hima's car, Sita had said with a
snort, "Hima, your mother has strange ideas. Why should
I say '*Jai Ram-ji*?' I'm not a silly Hindu."

Amma was now busy changing the flower garland hung
across the photograph of a young sanyasin whose eyes
seemed to draw the viewer into themselves. In the photograph she was sitting on a deer skin, a string of tulsi beads
around her neck and her hair loose on her shoulders. She
was staring into the camera. There was a vichitra-vina
placed in front of her. In the next photograph, the same
sanyasin was seated on a settee alongside a young sanyasi
whose eyes were more magnetising than hers. The sanyasi
was extremely handsome.

"Amma—where does he live?" Sita softly asked, pointing at the picture.

"Him? He has abandoned his earthly body."

Oh—what a pity! How handsome he was!

"And she?" Sita indicated the sanyasin.

"Radha-ji? She too left her earthly body two years ago."

"Were they. . . ?"

"Yes. In the world's eyes they were husband and wife.
Radha-ji had been married to him when she was quite
young. But they never lived like husband and wife."

Nonsense!

Amma was now changing the costume of the devi.

"Amma, you must have met some very powerful sanyasis
in your life, haven't you?" Sita asked after a pause.

"Every sanyasi that I was honoured to meet possessed
amazing spiritual powers," Amma replied, closing her eyes
soulfully.

"Oh!"

"Today the devi has to go to Hima's aunty's place."
Amma said, adjusting the coronet on the goddess's head.

"That's nice."

Sita walked out of the room.

Meaningless—how utterly meaningless life was!

A few of Hima's cousins were standing around on the lawn. Hima, in her pink housecoat, was pacing up and down, trying to get her baby to sleep. Shahzad, too, had emerged. He had a friend with him who was so handsome that Sita couldn't look away from his face. He was very young—couldn't have been more than twenty-six. And his eyes—they were simply bewitching.

"Hello, Sita. This is Kailash." Shahzad introduced them.

"Hello."

"Are you coming to our rehearsal, Mrs. Jamil?" The young man asked her in a voice that was terribly relaxed and intimate. All these theatre people were so strange.

"Dr. Mirchandani," Sita corrected him gently.

"Oh! I do beg your pardon. . . ." Then he whispered to Shahzad, "Did I drop a brick?"

"Of course not," Shahzad replied, "makes no difference." Then he turned to Sita, "Are you coming with us, or should I come back later to get you?"

Sita was gazing at Kailash's eyes. This made Kailash quite flustered; he hastily turned away and began to talk with Pramila.

"Sita. . . !" Shahzad asked a second time.

"Yes? . . . No," she said with a start, "No, you go ahead. I'll come with Hima."

Hima was still worried about her baby. His fever had not come down, leaving him too restless to sleep. She didn't hear what Sita said.

"Hima . . . !"

What's the use of it? It's all so useless, so meaningless.

"I'm sorry, Sita. What were you saying?" Hima finally looked up. "No, I can't go. How can I? Just look at Anand."

"O.K., Sita." Shahzad said. "You should come to the Coffee House at six. Kailash will pick you up from there." The two young men walked away across the lawn to the car.

Over there, on the terrace of the "Yellow House", all

the girls in the family were busily knitting, munching pine-nuts and comfortably chatting about 'normal' things.

Hima called the ayah to come and clean the baby's milk-bottles.

"Hima—I'm going home," Sita said, getting up from the lawn chair.

"Home?"

"Yes . . . Karol Bagh. From there I'll go on to the theatre. Good night!"

"Good night, Sita."

She picked up her bag and walked down the gravel road towards the bus stop.

(4)

Kamran was standing behind a pillar, fiddling with something. Then he bent over a coil of wires lying on the floor and turned on a switch. A dim white light spread over the stage. The actor playing the 'Stage Director' addressed the empty auditorium:

This will do. I have been instructed by the audience to stage a new play today, a play by the poet Visakhadatta, the son of Maharaja Bhaskara and the grandson of Governor Vateshvaradatta. The play is a heroic drama, entitled The Minister's Seal. In fact, I am extremely happy to stage a play for an audience like this that is so appreciative of good literature. For even a fool can reap a rich harvest, if his seed falls on good soil; the abundance of his crop does not depend on the sower's skill. So I had better get home and call my wife. . . . Here we are. Well, well, what's going on here? It looks as if we're having a celebration. All the servants are unusually busy at their jobs. One is carrying buckets full of water, another is mixing incense, a third is fashioning garlands of all kinds of flowers, and still another is humming while she pounds with her pestle. All right then, I'll call my wife and ask what is happening.*

---

*This and all subsequent italicised quotations from the play are from *Two Plays of Ancient India*, translated and introduced by J. A. B. van Buitenen (New York: Columbia University Press, 1968).

Crrrash! A big plywood board fell to one side and Sardar Pradip Singh lumbered forward in his overalls, holding a hammer.

"Pradip! Must you do this now?" shouted Bilqis from somewhere in the auditorium. "You're making a wreck of me. Where is Shahzad?"

Pradip shouted at some stagehand, "Hey you, drag these boards over to that side."

"Talented treasure of household economy!" that was Rakesh, still speaking his lines. *"Loyal promoter of Love, Wealth, and Faith! / Leave for the moment, domestic tactician, your / Science and Arts, and come here at once!"*

Now the 'Actress' came forward: *"Here I am, my lord. Be good enough to grace me with your orders."*

Bilqis shouted, "Rakesh, can you go ahead a few lines and start from 'Cruel Grasper'?"

"Look," Rakesh declaimed. *"Look, a Cruel Grasper wants to violate the Moon's Immaculate Realm . . ."*

'It's seven and Sita hasn't come as yet,' thought Bilqis as she looked at her watch.

Now 'Chandandas', the confidant of the defeated Minister Rakshasa, was speaking: *"Clouds are thundering overhead. But, alas, my love is far away. What is happening? Life-preserving herbs are far away on snow-capped mountains, while a coiled cobra nestles just above my head."*

And then it was 'Chandragupta' speaking about the "fortune of kings":

She flees from the severe, but does not stay
With those whose meekness is inspired by fear.
She hates the foolish but no more does love
the very learned. Trembling for the bold,
She mocks the overcautious. Alas!
Luck, like a courtesan in great demand,
Demands the utmost to be served and pleased!

"Sita-ji has arrived." Kamran announced to Lalita, sticking his head out the window in 'Chanakya's house'. Sita crossed the hall and sat down on the steps of the side verandah where it was dark. Kamran pressed another switch and a doleful yellow light spread over the stage.

Now 'Chandragupta' was saying:

The autumn sky flows like a river, slowly,
And pure, with here and there a late white cloud
Emerging like a sandbank. All around
The skies are noisy with the gabbling cries
Of cranes, and when night falls clusters of stars
Dot the heavenly pond with lotuses.

"Sita!" Bilqis called, coming out on the verandah.

"Hi, Bili."

Bilqis sat down near her. "It's cold out here. Let's go inside."

"No. It's all right."

"What took you so long? We made coffee and waited for you. You also got some calls."

"From whom?"

"I don't know." Then Bilqis added, "Listen, Sita, you didn't let me finish when I called you. You hung up on me."

"Why, what more could you possibly tell me?"

"That's true, but. . ." Bilqis shifted nervously. "You see, Sita dear, last night Manjhli Khala called from Karachi. Qaisar is getting married next week, and Manjhli Khala insists that you should attend. Bari Khala cannot leave Tulsipur because Asghar Bhaiya is ill. So you will have to represent her." She cleared her throat. It was chilly on the verandah but she could feel herself perspire.

"Karachi?" Sita's heart skipped a beat. "Karachi?" she repeated.

"Yes, yes . . . where else." Bilqis was again in full control of herself; she turned on her acting voice. "Let's go. It should be fun. We'll meet all the Pakistani relatives. You know, I haven't seen them in nine years. We shall also visit Baji in Lahore, then come back in a week or ten days. What do you say?" But she couldn't look Sita in the eye, and nervously flipped the pages of the script. "You should come along, really. Then next month I'll be gone to that theatre seminar in Bombay."

"I know, I know. You're very busy . . . very important. The entire theatre movement in India depends on you, doesn't it."

"Don't talk rubbish . . . . Hey, why are you crying? You silly girl . . . . Really!" Then she tried to be funny. "Come with us to Karachi. Just think, I've never been to a 'foreign country'. I must see at least one."

Sita remained silent.

"Come, instead of going to Mrs. Sen's we'll go straight home. Then after dinner, we'll play Scrabble . . . making only Latin words this time. . . . Why were you so late? Did you go home first?"

"Yes. I . . . I wanted to sit quietly with Mummy for a while."

"You didn't tell her, did you?"

"Yes . . . I did."

"What did she say?"

"Nothing. She merely said, 'It's the fruit of our Karma.'"

In the hall the voice of 'Chandragupta' again grew loud. He was repeating his lines: " . . . *a late white cloud emerging like a sandbank. . . . and when night falls clusters of stars . . .*"

"I too got a letter from Manjhli Khala," said Sita in a low voice. "Also from Barey Bhaiya. Just now I also told Mummy that Manjhli Khala had invited me for Qaisar's wedding. She said, 'You must go. Your true home is with your in-laws. It's your *jeth* who lives in Karachi, and a *jeth* is the same as a father-in-law. If they ask you you must go.' And more in the same vein."

Bilqis kept her eyes fixed on the flowers growing below the verandah. The fog was growing thicker. She got up and with the firm gait of a responsible director strode back into the hall, to listen to the deep and resonant voice of 'Chandragupta'. He was saying:

. . .and when night falls clusters of stars
Dot the heavenly pond with lotuses.
Fall shows the swollen waters of the rivers
Their humbler place, and makes the paddy fields
Bow under the proud burden of their ears.
It cures the peacocks of their frenzied lust
As of a poison, and to all the world
It thus imparts its old propriety.
The autumn, like a messenger of love,
At last has taken Ganga down from heaven
Where she had quarreled with her Lord,
A God of many mistresses, and leads
Her, glibly telling many tales of love,
Grown calm but thin from suffering,
To her new husband, all the rivers' lord!

Now the Bard proclaimed:

The Autumn cleans the heavens as with ashes
That mirror white the whiteness of the kasas,
Washing the dark hide of the nightly sky,
Spotted by clouds, with moon's wide net of rays;
It wears the moon like a white skull about,
And smiles with the white flecks of swarming swans:
May Autumn, wondrously resembling Siva,
No less divinely, wipe away your cares!

And then it was 'Chanakya' declaiming:

To all the sandy shores of the four oceans,
Whose waters are churned by monstrous fish,
Where thick palm forests cast their heavy shadows,
Your command has spread, accepted by a hundred kings
Like they would a garland made of dewy flowers.

"Bilqis." It was Kailash calling. He stepped out the door
at the far end of the hall and came towards the stairs.

"Yes?" Bilqis asked, turning to look at him.

"What would you like me to write for the Introduction?" Kailash kneeled down on the floor. "Give me an outline— I'll take care of the rest."

"Just write that this is the fourth classical offering of the Modern Theatre."

"How original and profound!"

"Well, then add . . . ." Bilqis scratched her head.

"Summaries of all the acts? But what should I write at the beginning?"

"I can't see here in the dark," Bilqis muttered, opening her file. "Just write: this play was written in the fourth century, in the Gupta Period, and that Prince Visakadatta was its author. It was first staged in Pataliputra during the reign of Emperor Chandragupta II, who ruled from 375 AD to 412 AD. Better check in the book though."

Sita stood up. "I'm going out for a bit."

Bilqis didn't hear her; she was engrossed in her play again. Like Hima, she, too, had little time for Sita. "Then you must write," she continued with Kailash, "that it is a very serious political play. And in the next paragraph, compare the Sanskrit drama with the pure art theatre. . . . Has Renu got the layout ready?"

"She can't do that until she gets the galleys back from the press," replied Kailash.

Inside Chanakya was saying:

The fires that burnt their corpses blaze today
And cast upon the sky, where patient vultures
Circle about on wide unhurried wings,
A cloud of smoke. . . .

Sita made a full round of the building and returned to the verandah. Bilqis and Kailash had gone inside. 'How time flies!' she thought, and sat down on the stairs.

Now they were rehearsing the fifth act and Bhagurayana, the false friend of Prince Malayaketu, was advising the prince, *"Your Highness, in this world of politics it all depends on the immediate objective whether a diplomat is a friend, an enemy or neither—not on sentiment, as with ordinary beings. . . Look, your Highness, politics, which makes friends of enemies and enemies of friends, brings on a man's reincarnation even while he is alive, a reincarnation with all old memories wiped out."*

A 'Servant' entered the stage, *"Victory, your Highness! One of the camp police, Dirghacaksus, wants to inform you that he has arrested a man with a letter, who tried to leave the camp without a permit."*

And now 'Prince Malayaketu' was thundering:

Let the columns of dust
That rise from the hoofs
Of my thundering horses
And are cut from their base
By the flowing rut
Of my elephant forces
Rain down on my foes
Till their women's rouged cheeks
Are withered and shaded,
And the bumblebee blackness
Of their beautiful curls
Is coarsened and faded!

A group of young people, earnestly talking, walked down the verandah towards the Green Room. There was the noise of a car being started in the portico. The moon crept out from behind the jacaranda tree.

'After a little while these people will go on to Mrs. Dolly Sen's. There they'll sprawl on the carpet in her smoke-filled drawing room and noisily carry on their "professional" talk.'

Sita heard Kailash say to Pradip, "Before we go over to Mrs. Sen's, let's go and wet our whistles."

She, liked to wet her whistle too. These boys didn't know that; otherwise they'd invite her immediately. In their

group, no girl drinks. Now it's eleven. Then it will be midnight. Time disappears only when you're drinking. . . .
And Kailash is so handsome.

Inside they were coming to the end of the play, and
'Samrddharthaka' was speaking:

Friendly our friends may be
when we dine and wine them at parties,
When they desert us and leave,
enemies could not be worse!

'How appropriate!' Sita smiled. 'Who deserted? Who is
left? What suffering? Damn . . . damn . . . damn!'

And now at the beginning of the sixth act, 'Rakshasa'
was slowly speaking:

Oh the ugliness of a ruined garden!
The white pavilion, carefully laid out,
Has like a clan of noble deeds collapsed.
. . . .
The trees bear no more fruit than policies
That were frustrated by a bitter fate.
And like the mind of a misguided sage
The ground is covered with some futile straws.
And, breathing sighs of pity for the friends
That came to grief, the hooded cobras seem
To bandage with the shreds of cast-off skin
The open wounds which whetted axes cut
In these tired branches that which the long plaint
Of nestling pigeons moan in agony.
And croaking that their heart has dried, the trees,
In desperate ailment of worm-eaten canker,
Their skin, unsoothed by shadow, withering,
Hope in their plight for mercy from the fire.

Somebody started switching off the stage lights. Kamran
called her from the hall, "Sita-ji!"

Sita was startled.

"Phone for you . . . a Mr. Chowdhry."

She got up and went to the room behind the stage. Bilqis and Kailash were bent over the table, busily composing the Program Notes.

"You are getting many calls today," Lalita said, briefly raising her head from the script.

Sita picked up the receiver. "Hello?"

"Hello. Sita?"

"Yes?"

"This is Qamrul, Sita. I arrived from Calcutta just this morning—with our play for the Festival. Tried to contact you several times. Finally they told me you'd be at Bilqis's rehearsal. How's she doing?"

"How are you, Qamar?"

"Fine, fine. You tell me. When did you come from New York?"

"It's been a long time. You have been in India for quite some time, too, haven't you?"

"That's right. And I'll be going to Moscow in March with the play. But let's talk of the old days. Was New York heartbroken when I left? And how is old Jamil? . . . Did you see him afterward? . . . What's your programme now? . . . Listen, Sita, I very much want to see you. Why don't you come over to the Constitution House right now? We'll then go to the Ashoka together. Projesh Babu has invited us to his party. . . No, you won't be gate-crashing at all. . . What, you don't know Projesh? You've certainly wasted your time. . . No, I won't accept 'No' for an answer. You must come. . . Good. Come right away. . . ."

Sita kept bantering cheerfully with Qamrul, as Bilqis stopped writing and stared at her in disbelief.

(5)

Just half an hour after talking to Sita, Abul Fasahat Qamrul Islam Chowdhry was on his way to the Ashoka Hotel. Madhuri

Rangarao had come in her car a few minutes earlier and said, "Hurry, they're waiting for you at the party." By now he had forgotten that he had invited Sita to the Constitution House.

Qamrul Islam Chowdhry was from Murshidabad and possessed a mellifluous voice. Also long, thick eyelashes, a softly dark complexion, and somewhat romantic features. He was the kind of man adoring college girls could die for. After completing his M.A. from Calcutta, he went into producing "progressive" plays. Then he acted in some films, wrote poetry in English and Bengali, and toured China, Russia and Eastern Europe with delegations of artistes. Finally he went to the United States where his English poetry was 'discovered'. When his first book of poems was recently published in London it caused quite a stir in literary circles. Both the *New Statesman* and the *Times Literary Supplement* had carried articles about him. After such international acclaim, he had become even more desirable in women's eyes.

Qamrul Islam Chowdhry was also a braggart and an utterly irresponsible person. He was usually unemployed and constantly borrowed money from friends which he never repaid. Fortunately for him, he happened to be the kind of man who never had to bother to fall in love with any woman—women themselves eagerly fell in love with him. Except for Bilqis, who couldn't care less for him, and always called him a pompous ass. She found his posturing intolerable, and considered him utterly unprofessional.

But Madhuri Rangarao had fallen for Qamrul head over heels. A perfect specimen of South Indian beauty, she was more attractive—and obedient—than Sita. In any case, Qamrul Islam Chowdhry was not sure how Sita might treat him now, and he firmly believed in the old adage about a bird in the hand being worth two in the bush.

(6)

The bride had left some time ago. Manjhli Khala was

wandering around the house, hiding in corners to shed her tears. Barey Bhaiya was trying hard not to cry anymore. Now that the guests were leaving, the sofas and chairs under the huge tent lay in disarray. Children were playing upon the plush carpets and pillows where, earlier, the wedding ceremonies had been performed. The city's 'high society' was taking leave of the hosts and departing in a string of cars. Inside the house, Bilqis was sitting in the midst of a crowd of relatives, cracking jokes and laughing. Her cousin Nadir, smartly dressed in a black sherwani and white churidar, had tired of offering cigarettes to the guests and was sprawled on a sofa. His sister-in-law was standing in one corner of the tent, encircled by Nadir's friends, with whom she was hotly debating the "Kashmir issue".

"I'm doomed. Just look at her," Nadir muttered to himself anxiously; then he went off to order some more coffee for the guests.

Sita was still standing in the corner, still arguing vehemently, when a strikingly good-looking man, holding a cup of coffee, walked by. As their eyes met, he gave her a sad smile, as if he understood—or was at least trying to understand—the intense grief reflected in her own eyes. His hair reminded Sita slightly of Jamil's, and she felt a momentary stab of pain. A little earlier she had seen that man talking rather eloquently with Bilqis. Bilqis had appeared to be acting equally polite.

Just then one of the numerous cousins came to her with coffee. Sita asked her, "Who is that gentleman?"

"Why that's Irfan Bhai!" the girl replied and walked away.

Then Nadir came near her, carrying a plate of dry fruit and nuts. After some hesitation, Sita asked him the same question, "Who is that gentleman?"

"What! You haven't met him yet? I'll fetch him right away." Nadir strode off. "Irfan Bhai, come here please. How is it that you haven't yet met our Bhabhi?" Then he returned with that man in tow. "Sir, meet our Jamil Bhai's wife Dr. Sita Jamil."

Out of habit she gracefully raised her hand in greeting, "Adab Arz."

"Adab," the man replied. "Please come and sit with us. You must be tired from standing. You know, I've been listening to your 'speech' for half an hour."

The three of them walked over to a sofa far away from the others and sat down.

"I was only trying to explain my views on the issue, but no one seems willing even to consider the other perspective. All of you immediately become emotional." Sita continued passionately, "Try some logic for a change! It seems to me even the educated people here are so naïve."

"Every case is emotional," Irfan said with a smile, "the rest, merely argument."

She gave him a surprised look. Just then Nasir—another cousin by marriage—joined them. "Bhabhi-jan, would you like some coffee?"

"What do you think of Karachi?" Irfan asked. (He thought, 'What a stupid question to ask!')

Now Nadir, Nasir and Irfan began to chat with her casually. Irfan asked, "What sort of Doctor are you? The kind who prescribes medicines—or the other kind?"

"She sells medicine for aching hearts." Nasir—being a younger cousin of her husband—had the right to flirt with her.

Everyone here had been so generous and so friendly ever since she had arrived. The traditional *mirasins* of Tulsipur, who had migrated to Pakistan along with their patrons and lived in Lalukhet in the city, had sung a song on her behalf last night: "*My mother-in-law told me to give the beggar a pinch of flour/ I was so innocent I gave him my sister-in-law.*" Nadir, in particular, was constantly coming up with different ideas to entertain his Bhabhi. They were trying so hard to make her happy. All because Jamil had taken a second wife without divorcing her.

Manjhli Khala had said to her many times, "We stand ashamed before you."

Barey Bhaiya had said, "Too bad that fellow isn't here. I'd have given him such a hiding. He knows what my anger is like."

Manjhli Khala showed Rahul's photograph to all the guests. "Just look at him. A piece of the moon. Just like his father. . . ."

"Our Bhabhi-jan is a very learned person." Nadir proudly informed Irfan.

Irfan raised his eyes and looked at Sita. She became flustered. Just then Barey Bhaiya walked over to them; Sita immediately covered her head with her sari. The three young men got up to show respect.

"*Dulhan,*" Barey Bhaiya addressed her as the bride of the house, "Bilqis says that she'd like to go back next Sunday. What do you think?"

Next Sunday . . . so soon? She felt scared. She'd go away so soon and perhaps never get to see this man again?

"We wanted you to stay a bit longer. After all this, too, is your home," Barey Bhaiya continued. "But Bilqis says she must get to Bombay as soon as possible."

"But, Barey Bhaiya, we were planning to take them to Lahore by car," said Nadir. "Come, Bhabhi-jan, let's go inside and talk to Bilqis."

She said goodnight to Irfan and accompanied Nadir inside.

Later that night, when she was helping the other girls lay out the dowry, Manjhli Khala had suddenly asked her, "*Dulhan,* did you seen Irfan?"

"Ye-ye . . . yes."

"His mother has written to Delhi and asked for Bilqis' hand in marriage for him." Manjhli Khala continued, "That's why we wanted Bilqis to come here for sure—so she could look him over. But she's so crazy I don't know if Irfan would please her."

"Oh!" Sita, like a devoted daughter-in-law, showed interest and concern in family affairs. "He seemed nice enough to me."

"He is nice. But if only Bilqis would see that."

"What does he do?"

"He holds a very high post. Gets nearly two thousand a month. What more could a girl want?" Manjhli Khala said, making neat piles of the wedding gifts. "And he comes from a good family too. From Hardoi. You know Hardoi, don't you?"

"No . . . Yes."

"That crazy Bilqis says she'd never migrate to Pakistan. What are we to do now? Irfan is a Pakistani."

Sita remained silent.

Manjhli Khala said, "You should go with Nadir tomorrow to see your old family house."

The day before they left for Karachi, she had taken Bilqis to her house in Karol Bagh for the first time. She had never done that before. In fact, she had never even revealed her correct address to any of her friends. But when she was packing for the trip to Karachi, her mother had said: "Sita, you must invite Bilqis for a meal. This is terrible that I've never met your *nand*." Sita had been working in a government office for a few months; it was from there that she phoned Bilqis and invited her for dinner that evening. Bilqis immediately called Hima and told her about the invitation. Then she added, "I'll come and get you." Later, at noon, when Bilqis ran into Sita in a restaurant in Connaught Place, she said, "I'll go to Old Delhi to pick up Hima and should be at your place by eight."

"To pick up Hima?!"

"Yes . . . is something the matter?"

"Why did you invite her?"

"But Hima is such an old friend of yours," Bilqis remonstrated. "What's wrong in inviting her? I actually thought you must have called her already."

"Bilqis—Hima lives in a fancy house. How can I invite her to my place? I don't even have enough space to sit. You are my relative, with you it doesn't matter."

"Sita!" Bilqis was flabbergasted. "And you go around all

the time talking of class consciousness. . . ."

"That's right," Sita said with some heat. "But I also happen to have some pride."

"Good Heavens! . . . Now what will I say to Hima?"

"What can you. . . ?"

And so that evening Bilqis, with Hima in tow, arrived at the address in Karol Bagh which Sita had given her. Sita's younger sisters were looking out for them from the window. Sita's mother opened the door. It was a small, dark and narrow house that had been abandoned by some lower-middle-class Muslim family during the Partition riots. Mummy led the guests into the main room and invited them to sit on the carpet. There was a cot laid out against one wall, and a row of steel trunks arrayed against another. A large, glossy print of Lord Krishna hung above a massive almirah. After a while, Mummy probed behind the almirah and pulled out another framed print. It said in Arabic, "There is no God but God, and Muhammad is His Prophet."

"It was left behind in this room," Mummy said to Bilqis. "I took it down and put it away—just in case one of us might do something improper by mistake. I've asked Sita several times to take it over to your house, but she keeps forgetting. Now you must remember to take it with you."

"Yes, Mummy," Bilqis had answered.

Mummy brought trays of food to where they were sitting on the carpet. Hima and Bilqis leaned back against the wall and merrily talked to Mummy and to Sita's younger sisters, Lila and Mohini. Sita sat opposite them, against the other wall, and watched them in silence. On the wall opposite her there was still another print; it showed Hanuman flying through the air holding a mountain on his palm. 'I also tried to fly to the skies holding the mountain of life on my palm. . . ,' Sita thought.

"Bibi," Mummy said to Bilqis, pouring water into glasses, "In Karachi, in the Amil Colony, we had a two-storied house with eighteen rooms."

Sita looked at her with annoyance: 'What comfort does she find in telling that story to everyone?'

"And, you know, in that house Doctor Sahib—that is Sita's Daddy—had marble floors put in six rooms. . . ."

"Come on, Mummy, be done with all that," Sita interrupted her with some disdain.

"No, Bilqis, it's true. You must go to see the house. It has blue glass in all its windows. And its name, 'Daulat Rai Mahal', is written high on its front—you can see it from quite a distance. When you leave Jamshed Road and turn onto Motilal Nehru Road. . . ."

"All right, Mummy, all right. We'll go to see it," Sita again interrupted. "Here Hima, take some more of this. . . ."

Just then Daddy came into the room. "So. . . ! Is she telling her tales of 'Daulat Mahal' again?" he asked with a laugh. "She won't give up the habit easily!" Then he sat down near them on the carpet and said to the guests, "Bibi, today you've come to our humble place for the first time— though we have known each other for several years. Please think of it as our 'Mahal', and come back soon."

"Nadir will take you to see your old family house after breakfast tomorrow," Manjhli Khala reminded her.

"No. . .there's no need. . .I don't really want to see it," Sita replied.

Manjhli Khala fell silent.

A week passed, as they stayed on in 'Chandpur House'. That was the name of the double-storied Scandinavian-style home of Sita's brother-in-law which he had built in the 'Housing Society' area.

"Why do you folks persist in parading yourself as petty ex-ta'aluqedars of Avadh? What difference does it make now if—before 1947—you owned some petty estate named Chandpur in the district of Faizabad?" Bilqis began to quarrel with her Pakistani relatives in her usual fashion. "Why must you 'refugees' cling to those old names in Pakistan?"

"Didn't we have a 'Chandpur House' in Lucknow—on Jopling Road?" Manjhli Khala replied, with no passion in her voice. It reminded Sita of the way her Mummy had talked. She felt bored, and began to look out the window.

His car came up the driveway and stopped. He got out, climbed the steps of the verandah and entered the dining room. Bilqis disdainfully continued to spread butter on her toast.

During that week he came to 'Chandpur House' every day, morning and evening. He would sit for hours talking to all and sundry, always looking for some opportunity to sit near Sita without letting it become too obvious that he was seeking her company. Manjhli Khala thought he was coming because of Bilqis, and was very happy. If someone shows such devotion, she thought, the girl will have to say yes. She immediately sent off a letter to Tulsipur, to Bilqis' mother—who was her older sister, saying that by the grace of God the marriage was just about settled.

The younger crowd mostly spent their time in the verandah in front of Nadir's room. One afternoon they were all sitting there having tea when Irfan turned to Sita and said: "Why are you in such a hurry to go back? After all, we Pakistanis aren't all that bad. Please stay a few more days."

"I don't dislike any race in the world. It's you non-socialists who talk of religious fanaticism and. . . ."

"But really, Bhabhi-jan," Nadir interjected, "please stay another month. I'll get your visa extended in no time at all."

"How can I stay? Your Intelligence people wouldn't leave me alone if I did."

"Now come on, Sita!" Bilqis said with a laugh. "You aren't important enough to give sleepless nights to the Intelligence people." Then she added, "But if you keep going on like this for a few more years, Interpol might send their men after you."

Sita looked at them cheerlessly. Ridiculous—how ridiculous the world was!

"What was your maiden name?" Irfan asked. He was flipping the pages of a magazine.

"Mirchandani."

"When we were children in Hardoi," Irfan said, "a Sindhi civil engineer was appointed there. His name was also Mirchandani. One day he came to visit us. Our servant came inside and announced: '*Machchardani* Sahib has come.' Then for several day he referred to him as '*Mirchdani* Sahib'. I still remember that incident." Then he added, "You see, at that time we had seen or met very few Sindhis. A couple of Sindhis had shops in Lucknow's Hazratganj, that's all."

"That's right," Nadir spoke up. "Bilqis, do you remember that Sindhi owner of the fruit-mart? How you asked him about Indira Walters' marital and mental state and he promptly replied, 'Yes, madam, she is mad and married both'? How we laughed!"

"That is funny," Irfan said with a chuckle, then began to turn the pages of the magazine.

'Absurd—totally absurd,' Sita thought.

Suddenly she turned to Irfan and asked, "Do you know how they give someone the 'third degree'?"

"Why? What made you think of that?"

"Nothing in particular. Must every thought be logical?"

Irfan looked at her intently for a moment, then tried to change the subject: "Have you heard that joke?"

"Which one?"

"The one about the weekly meetings of left-wing writers in New York. Most of the people at those meetings used to be from the FBI. One day a writer got up and addressed the group by saying, 'Comrades, and gentlemen of the FBI.'"

"Ho, ho, ho. . . ." Nadir found it extremely funny.

Then they all laughed, but it was hollow laughter.

Every evening she would wonder: what can we do?

"Let's go to a movie, Bhabhi-jan," Nadir would suggest.

"Not again!"

She would get into arguments with Irfan: "No one here has any political understanding. You don't have good books. . .not even good movies. There is only one half-way decent newspaper. What do you think would be the mental state of someone brought up on the cartoons of the *Morning Star*?"

"Bhabhi-jan, please!" Nadir would plead. "You'll really get us into trouble. Why must you say such nasty things in every gathering?"

But Sita took no notice of Nadir's pleas, and continued to wrangle just the same.

Irfan's leave was over; he had to return to his job in Lahore. It was decided that they would all go together in two cars. That evening Sita was sitting alone in the verandah, flipping the pages of the latest issue of *Life*, when Irfan arrived. For the first time there was no one else present.

"We are all set to leave the day after tomorrow, Doctor Sahib," he said, and sat down in a chair, not too close.

"Please don't call me Doctor Sahib."

"What should I call you then? Mrs. Jamil? Begum Sahiba? Shrimati-ji?"

"You know I have a simple enough name: Sita."

She was the wife of Bilqis's first cousin, and if he were to marry Bilqis he would become her *nandoi*. He had a right to joke with her, that's why he was always teasing her. Or perhaps . . .

"When is your 'Ramchandra-ji' coming back to his 'Ayodhya'?" Irfan asked. He had not been told that Jamil had taken a second wife. It was after all a family matter and Irfan was still an outsider.

"His term has been extended for another two years." Sita replied. "Have you ever been to New York?"

"Yes."

"When?"

"When you weren't there."

"I have been there since 1949."

"I, too, went there in 1949. But we must have moved in quite different circles. When are you going back?"

"I haven't decided yet." She nervously looked toward the door, praying that Bilqis or someone would appear and put an end to this topic.

Then it so happened that the night of the morning they were to leave for Lahore Bilqis came down with flu. Naturally the departure was postponed. With Bilqis confined to bed, Sita had to go out with Nadir and Irfan by herself. She was popular among Nadir's friends. They had not seen a real live Hindu girl for many years, and they greeted her with open arms. When Nadir invited some of his 'intellectual' friends to Chandpur House to meet Sita, Manjhli Khala peeked through the window and remarked: "Is this Nadir's tea party or Shiv-ji's wedding procession? What a wild bunch of people!"

"They have been invited to meet Bhabhi-jan," a girl informed her.

"Sure. Your Bhabhi-jan is pretty strange herself." Manjhli Khala responded.

Irfan had begun to call her 'Sita' and act familiarly with her. Qaisar, for whose wedding they had all come, had returned from her in-laws' place and was to leave with her husband for Peshawar in a couple of days. There was going to be a big formal dinner at Chandpur House for her in-laws. Bilqis was now well and Nadir wanted to take them to see a movie before the dinner. That afternoon, when Sita got dressed in a hurry and was about to leave, Bilqis called to her from her room.

"Yes, Bili?" Sita stopped at the door.

"You're leaving already?"

"Yes. You come to the Palace Hotel at five-thirty, I'll be at the bar."

"At the bar?"

"Yes. I've asked Dick to meet me there. He was with me at Columbia. Now he's come here for the World Bank. Yesterday I ran into him on Elphinstone Street. Why do you ask?"

"Sita darling"—Bilqis got off the bed and put on her dressing gown—"You have become too emancipated. This is Pakistan, not America or England."

"Oh! I didn't think. In that case you should come to Irfan's house by quarter-to-six. I'll ask Dick to drop me there. Irfan's house is not far from the Palace. I know because we dropped him there yesterday."

"Irfan's house?" Bilqis sounded more worried. "Darling, he's a bachelor. Lives by himself. You can't go to his house.

"My God!" Sita gave up. "I'm sorry; I don't want to shock you any further."

"Listen, the guests for the dinner will start arriving soon, and you'll have to get properly dressed when you come back. Better tell Nadir to forget the pictures."

"Yes dear," Sita said in her most obedient voice.

After seeing her American friend in the bar of the Palace Hotel, Sita walked over to the reception desk and called Irfan. She was expected back at Chandpur House, but felt she had to spend that evening alone with him.

A few minutes later Irfan arrived, together with his friend Usman. The three of them sat down in the lounge. Sita looked stunning in a dark red Canjivaram sari. Irfan looked her over leisurely before settling on a sofa near her, then recited a couplet with a smile:

Mela hai chand-ganj mein suraj-gahan ka aj
*Tum kis liye na ghairat-e shams-o-qamar gaye**

Sita cracked up. "You 'Urdu-wallas' are really something! Nadir is right. Around you folks I don't have a chance."

"And no ordinary 'Urdu-wallas' either," Usman added. "They hail from Lucknow and quote only Rind and Arzu."

After a while Usman took his leave; he had to go some-

---

* "They're celebrating the sun's eclipse in Chandgunj (Moon Town) today. Why aren't you there, you who eclipse both the sun and the moon?"

where. Sita and Irfan were left alone. By now it was rather dark outside, and people were beginning to wander over to the restaurant, Le Gourmet.

"Would you like some coffee?" Irfan asked. He didn't know that after sunset Sita usually needed something stronger than black coffee. He was watching her intently. "You are really very beautiful."

"Thank you."

Then he looked at her hair.

"Don't you put sindur in the parting of your hair?"

"I do, but you see . . . I . . . I misplaced the sindur box soon after I got here. In fact, Manjhli Khala has also reminded me about it several times. She doesn't like to see my hair without the line of sindur. 'It's not a good omen,' she says. I do want to reassure her. Can I get sindur in Karachi?"

"I don't know," Irfan replied. "Ask someone to get it for you."

"Can you get me some—please." Then she stopped, and her face turned crimson.

How dreadful! Why did she ask this man to find her some sindur? Something that she would use in Jamil's name! Oh, my God! What must he be thinking? Sita decided she will tell Irfan the whole truth.

"I'm afraid you don't know . . ." she began. "There is no one to put sindur for. Jamil has left me." Then she turned away with a frown, blinking her eyes to hold back the tears.

"No, I do know; I knew it even before anyone had told me," Irfan said to her gently. "That day when I first met you at the wedding, I could see in your eyes how terribly sad you were." He suddenly got up from the sofa. "Come, let's go to Chandpur House. You shouldn't be late for Qaisar's dinner. After all, you're a daughter-in-law of the family."

"And you shouldn't be late either." Sita replied in a soft voice. "You're going to be a son-in-law of the family."

"Certainly not. You know very well Bilqis doesn't care for me."

"And you? You don't care for her either?"

"Definitely not. But you don't have to believe me." Then he added, "Come on, let's go."

That night Irfan left soon after the dinner ended. But when he reached home, sleep eluded him. The loneliness was unbearable. In desperation he called Usman.

"I'm going to Azam's stag party," Usman told him. "Why not join us at the Gymkhana Club?"

"I can't go to any more parties tonight."

"Just come over," Usman insisted. "We'll sit in a corner by ourselves and talk about your Sita. As the poets says, 'Come, let's talk of the beloved's charms.'"

"All right—I'll see you there."

The club was close by; it took him just a few minutes to walk over there. Usman had not yet arrived. Irfan found himself a chair in a secluded corner of the verandah.

'Sita . . . Sita. . . .'

"Sita Jamil seems to be quite a flirt. . ."

Irfan was startled. On the other side of the palm plants a party was in full swing. Perhaps the stag party to which Usman had invited him. Irfan continued to listen to the conversation with closed eyes.

"Looks like a real man-eater."

"But claims to be very Progressive."

"Well, the Left always believes in high moral standards."

"You know, the Russians are said to be quite Victorian in these matters."

"Nonsense. With them, anything can be shared."

"I guess you don't know any better."

"And perhaps you've been brainwashed by that gentle lady."

"Come on! . . . That poor thing—who can she brainwash? It's you. Your heart has been sealed by God himself. For your kind, ignorance is bliss."

"I don't see why you must judge someone's private life by her political beliefs."

"I do feel sorry for you. You met just one of them—and

a very confused one at that—but you're pronouncing judgment on all leftist women. What a shame that, of all people,
Sita Jamil comes here! It seems we can import only B-class
movies from India, or phonies such as Sita . . ."

"Never mind. The grass always looks greener on the
other side of the fence."

"I think she talks too much. The other night at Rahman's
dinner she held her own against everyone for a whole hour."

"I hear she's a good dancer too. Kathakali. . . ."

"For heaven's sake! Women don't dance Kathakali."

"All right, all right. I'm not a dancer that I should know."

"She's really a nice girl. Her only fault is she drinks a bit
too much."

"But that's what I like most about her."

"Of course. You're the last king of Avadh!"

"I hear she's left her husband."

"Is that right? Then we have a chance."

Irfan got up and silently walked away.

The next morning he ran into Sita at the gate of
Chandpur House.

"You left too early last night," Sita said. "There was a lot
of singing afterwards."

"I see."

"Then late at night I called your flat, but your servant
told me you had gone to the Gymkhana Club."

"I see."

"What's the matter with you?" Sita sounded a bit scared.

"Sita."

"Yes?"

"People are saying all sorts of things about you. I don't
like that. Do people in Delhi also gossip about you?"

"I don't know. They must. . . ."

"And you don't care?"

"No!" she said firmly. By now they had reached the front
steps. "Please come inside. We were waiting for you," she
added coldly.

Inside, there was much crying and wailing going on. The Karachi ladies were taking turns embracing the ladies from Delhi and shedding copious tears. Even Bilqis was wandering around sniffling. The men, too, had their handkerchiefs out to dab at their eyes. Irfan saw the scene from the gallery door and could barely suppress his laughter.

All the Indian relatives were returning by plane—except for Bilqis and Sita. They were to go to Lahore with Nadir and Irfan. Some Karachi cousins were also travelling with them. The entire party came out and filled two cars. Sita sat with Bilqis in Nadir's car. The others got into Irfan's Chevy. "May Imam Zamin protect you all!" shouted the people who remained. Then the two cars went down the winding Forty Second Street, onto Drig Road, and set off for Thatta.

(7)

"The great city of Thatta!" Nadir announced briskly as he parked the car in front of the mosque built by Shahjahan.

In the full heat of the day they walked around the mosque, then stepped into the narrow street called the "Lane of the Baniyas". Just then a strong gust of wind blew through those decrepit, mud-and-reed houses, and for a moment Sita felt they were inhabited by all the wretched and homeless souls in the world. She silently fell behind the others. After a while Irfan joined her.

"Do you know why they named this place Thatta?" Sita asked, removing her sunglasses to wipe off the dust.

"No."

"Because in Mughal times this city was so prosperous that *thattha* [crowds] of people from all over Asia used to fill its streets."

When they returned to the cars, Bilqis whispered to Sita, "Listen, I want to talk to Nasim Baji and the others, but I can't do that in Irfan's presence. In his car both he and I would feel needlessly constrained. So why don't you go in

Irfan's car; I'll sit with Nadir and ask the others to join
me." And so it came about that when they left Thatta, Sita
had to sit by herself in Irfan's car. Now they were crossing
the big desert.

Sita turned to Irfan, "The other day you asked me what
I thought of your Karachi—now I ask you: what do you
think of my Sindh?"

He shot her a quick glance but remained silent.

"What bothers me now is that on my return Daddy is
sure to pester me with questions. 'Did you see that place?
Did you go through that village?' And Mummy asked me
to check and see how our old home in Karachi was. I never
got around to doing even that."

"What did your father do in Karachi?"

"He was a doctor—he had his own clinic in Ram Bagh."

"Ram Bagh?"

"Yes, there's a Ram Bagh in Karachi. Why? Have you
never been there?"

"Oh yes. . . . But now it's called Aram Bagh."

A line of camels was crossing the horizon. Suddenly a
goat tried to run across the road and Irfan had to brake
hard. Sita nearly fell on top of him. "I'm sorry," she said,
hurriedly sliding away.

"No, no. It was my fault." Irfan was equally flustered.
"Now—now I suppose your father has his clinic in Delhi?"

"No. He's been ill for some years. He can't manage his
practice any more. My brother is an engineer in the Bhilai
Steel Works; he supports the family."

"Oh."

"Look over there. You see that tree? When we'd go to
Hyderabad we'd always stop under it to rest. Once I hurt
my leg badly. . . ."

He remained silent and concentrated on driving.

"Don't you see that this is my land? My fields—my villages—my saints' tombs?" Sita asked with some anguish.

"I didn't know you were so sentimental," replied Irfan.

"When you come to Delhi and cross the Jamuna Bridge

then I'll see if you're sentimental or not, too".

"I don't let myself get caught in memories."

"Well, I'm glad you told me."

"In any case, why would I come to Delhi?"

"Because that's where your future in-laws live."

"There you go again. Talking nonsense about in-laws. Like all women." Irfan snorted, and stepped on the accelerator.

He had kept his car ahead of Nadir's, making sure that he and Sita were visible all the time to the people in the car behind. 'How careful he is,' Sita thought. For a while she remained silent. A truck went by, raising dust. Now they were passing an ancient graveyard.

"The whole of Sindh is full of graves," Irfan remarked.

"Do you know how old this land is?" She was apparently determined to add to his knowledge.

'What a talkative girl,' Irfan thought. 'Why doesn't she stay quiet for a while? Perhaps she is trying to cover up her nervousness.'

"No, I don't," he replied loudly. "I was always weak in history."

"Mummy used to tell us that according to the Puranas the children of Prince Sibi flowrished in Baluchistan while Bharat, the brother of Ayodhya's Rama Chandra, sat on the throne of the Sindhu Desh. She used to say: 'Kaliyuga began soon after the *Mahabharata*, that's why the later Puranas don't tell us much about Sindh.'"

"Is that right? Tell me some more."

"You don't have to make fun of me."

"Oh no! I'm not at all. Please do continue. I'm truly interested."

"The Greeks called this place Indo-Scythia, because the people of the Lower Sindh were Scythians, not Aryans."

"Really? You see, I wouldn't know the difference. I'm really very ignorant. But lo continue. I like listening to your voice."

"Oh God!"

Now they were quite close to Hyderabad.

"The Scythians were from West Asia. When they came here they spread as far as Rajasthan and Gujarat, and were later called the Rajputs."

"Amazing!"

"In ancient times, there was a large temple of Brahma in Mirpur Khas—and Multan had a huge Sun Temple. In Sehwan, the Aryans had built temples to honour Shiva."

"Have you ever been in a temple?" Irfan asked.

"Of course. I visited many temples when I was a child. There were so many temples in Tandu Adam—that's why it was called the Kashi of Sindh. And in Hemakot, there was a temple for Mahadeva. I went there once with my aunt. And that temple on Clifton in Karachi, I used to go there with Mummy every Shivratri. My grandmother worshipped Kali. In our community, Kali is also called Thar Mai—Mother of the Thar Desert." Sita fell silent for a few moments, then continued. "Mummy is a great devotee of Rama. When she lived in Karachi, she always wanted to make a pilgrimage to Ayodhya. Later, when I married Jamil, I told her that Jamil's ancestral village, Tulsipur, is only a few miles from Ayodhya. Isn't that strange?"

"Not particularly," Irfan responded with a shrug. "You tend to make even the most ordinary event extremely dramatic."

"I do? . . . You think I'm a complete idiot, don't you? As a matter of fact, we have a saying in Sindhi: A woman's brains are in her heels, and after sunset not even there. Perhaps you agree with that? But you know something? I intend to go to Sadh Bela."

"You must. After all, you're on a sentimental journey."

"Oh, shut up."

"My, my! You must treat me with respect."

"Like hell!"

"Tell me, why do you Hindus make such a fuss if someone cuts a branch of a pipal tree? In Hardoi, every time the *ta'zia* touched a pipal tree, it used to cause a riot."

"Because Lord Mahadeva lives in pipal trees."

"I see. . . ." He burst out laughing. Then he said, "The pipal trees had a lot of significance in our lives too. Mother believed that witches lived in pipal trees. And that the martyred saints were buried under them. There was a pipal tree in front of our house in Hardoi. Mother would never allow us to play under it at dusk. She was afraid some spirit would possess us. Every Thursday she had a lamp lit under that tree." His voice sounded heavy.

"Look, who's being sentimental now?" Sita asked.

"Oh, shut up!"

Now they could see the tall 'wind-catchers' that are put up on all the houses in Hyderabad.

"I bet you'll start sniffling soon." Irfan pulled out his handkerchief and offered it to Sita. "Here, take this. Just in case." Sita had to laugh.

Turning onto the road to the Circuit House, Irfan said, "Sita, you should complete that story you were telling me: what happened in Sindhu Desh. The Scythians came here. Then what?"

She sat up properly, as if she were in the university library. "Then Buddhism grew strong here. But there were also Saraswat Brahmins and Rajputs and Jats. When the Muslims attacked Aror, its citizens fled to the Punjab. My mother is an Arora from Lahore. Even after they converted to Islam, the people of Sindh held their old beliefs in respect. They built shrines for saints, but each saint had one Hindu name and one Muslim."

"Really? Is that true?"

"Yes. Raja Bhartari came to be know as Lal Shahbaz. Pir Pattu, as Pir Sultan. Zinda Pir as Khwaja Khizar. Udero Lal became Shaikh Tahir, and Lalu Jasraj is Manghu Pir."

"Manghu Pir!" Irfan exclaimed. "The Manghu Pir of the crocodiles, near Karachi?"

"The very same."

"I don't believe you!"

"You should meet Daddy sometime," Sita said smugly.

"He knows a lot about the history of Sindh. Even now he frequently reads the *Chach Nama*."

"Tell me some more."

"Well, just as the Hindus have a god or goddess for everything, so the Muslims of Sindh have Pirs. They have Pirs for songs, Pirs for clay pots, Pirs for cradles—the entire Sindh region is a land of Pirs. Did you know that all the snake charmers were Muslims, but were also Shaivite Yogis and also followed Gorakhnath? The month of Ramadan was also sacred for the Hindus; and the Hindus used to make offerings before the *ta'zia*s of Muharram. Was that how it used to be where you lived, too?"

"Yes. . . ."

"I must say religion did work as an opiate for our people for many centuries—and then it worked as dynamite."

"Now don't start that again—please! I'm starving. As soon as we reach the Circuit House you must get us some food."

"You're such a reactionary! It's useless to tell you anything."

Later that night, after supper, Nadir lit a cigarette for Sita, then he, Bilqis and others left the room to sit in the drawing room. Sita remained seated at the dining table, pulling off the petals of a flower she had picked from the centerpiece. Across the table, Irfan leaned back in his chair and watched her puff at the cigarette.

"I didn't know that you also smoked."

"What do you mean 'also'?"

"Er . . . nothing. You look unusually sad tonight." He quickly changed the subject. "Did you see the garden? Doesn't it look pretty?"

"Yes."

"It's a full moon tonight—that's why."

"Yes."

There was laughter from the drawing-room.

Irfan could think of nothing to end her gloom. Psychologists say that if you want to make someone relaxed and less worried you should talk about his or her childhood.

"Tell me about your childhood." Irfan asked like an expert.

"You sound as if you're Freud himself."

He laughed, but it sounded hollow.

"And next you'll tell me about your own childhood. Excuse me, but that's such a hackneyed technique."

"My God! You don't give a man a chance, do you?. You should've been a lawyer."

Once Jamil had also told her about his childhood. He had said with much feeling: "Our house is a bit away from the river Ghaghra. My mother is a very fine cook. My younger sister's name is Qaisar. She's such a pain. Now she lives in Pakistan with Barey Bhaiya. Once I tricked her into going to the attic, then I locked the door behind her. That got me quite a spanking. I have two aunts. Farkhunda Baji is the daughter of the younger aunt. She's so patriotic, my Farkhunda Baji—and caring, like an angel. You never went to see her in Delhi. I wish you, too, would become like her. She has a younger sister, Bilqis. When we were in Tulsipur, Bilqis and I used to sneak into Barey Bhaiya's guava orchard and steal fruit. Then Qaisar would tell on us. . . ."

"Rubbish . . . just rubbish." And suddenly Sita realised that her bitter tone had hurt Irfan's feelings. She had responded to his concern with rudeness. She had no intention of making him angry. In fact, she had never had any intention of making Jamil angry either. But then what had happened?

"I . . . I was born here . . . in Hyderabad." She said, feeling somewhat guilty, and raised her eyes to look at him—to see if he was listening. "We were four brothers and sisters. . . ." Her voice choked.

"The fact is," Irfan said, "the fact is that I had never come to Sindh before the Partition. That's why I'm asking you so many questions. I really have no idea what sort of places Lahore and Karachi and Hyderabad Sindh were before India was divided. Or what sort of people lived here."

"One 'people' is here, in front of you."

Irfan had to laugh. "You're amazing." Then, becoming serious again, he said, "You see, Sita, you think I'm very unsentimental. But this question of a lost home bothers me, too. In West Berlin, in Hong Kong—I have seen homeless people everywhere. In American cities I met people who had fled from Eastern Europe. In Jordan I saw the terrible plight of the Palestinian refugees. . . . The reason I seem to get into arguments with you, or try to turn everything you say into a joke, is that we live in a time when four hundred million people have suddenly gone through a metamorphosis. Their thoughts, their feelings, their reactions to events—all have changed. You and I—we have nothing in common any more. I don't know what you people think, or what you read or do. When Bilqis talks about her life in the theatre in Delhi, she seems to be talking about another hemisphere. . . ." He paused briefly. "Now we've started talking politics again. Which I hate."

"You were asking me about my childhood."

"Yes . . . yes."

"We were four brothers and sisters," Sita began, like an obedient child repeating lessons. "At first we lived here, in Hyderabad. Our house was in Hirabad; my grandfather had built it. Then Daddy started his clinic in Karachi and also built us a new house there. I was sent to grammar school, then to St. Joseph's College. We had a big family. So many relatives. Uncles and aunts and cousins. Some of them lived in Amil Colony, some in Larkana, others in Hyderabad. I have only one brother, but two sisters. The three were quite young at the time of Partition." Her voice gradually became sadder. "When Partition took place, we took a ship to a port in Kathiawar. In the three months after August, hundreds of thousands of refugees fled from here by whatever means they could . . . . ,

"A special train for the refugees was running from Mirpur Khas to Marwar Junction, where transit camps were set up. Those who went from here were mostly urban people—professionals. They couldn't be settled on farm lands. Finally they were sent to the refugee camps in Bombay Presidency, Madhya Pradesh and Rajasthan. My own relatives ended up everywhere—Ahmedabad, Jodhpur, so many places. A large number of Sindhis were sent to Bhopal."

"Where did your family go?"

"We first went to Gandhi Dham, then to Ulhas Nagar. These were new settlements for the Sindhis. Daddy's ailment started in Gandhi Dham. Like other refugees he, too, received financial aid for two years. But it stopped at the beginning of 1950. There were some special camps for the elderly and the ill. So Daddy was sent there for a short time. Then we all came to Delhi. Of course, by then the Sindhi refugees had scattered all over the country in search of jobs and opportunities." She drew a long breath.

The people in the drawing room had started a game of rummy. Irfan lit a cigarette for himself, but didn't offer one to Sita.

"Now we are a people with no land of our own," Sita continued. "The Punjabis at least got the eastern part of Punjab."

"Doesn't your father do anything now?"

"No. Didn't I tell you? He's always ill. We are Amils, and Amils were mostly professors, doctors, lawyers and people like that. It's a caste, like the Kayastha caste you have in U.P. When the Kulhoras and the Talpurs were the rulers in Sindh, the Amils worked for them as administrators. That's how their name came about."

"Are you Brahmins?"

"Of course not. Amils are Khattris. Now, after the emigration, all that has changed. Amils and Brahmins have set up shops on sidewalks. The old customs, the pirs and faqirs, all the shrines and temples—they were left behind here. But the real religion in this land was Sufism, and that Sufism never let us become religious fanatics."

For a few moments there was silence. Sita picked up a fork and began to draw lines with it on the tablecloth.

"Can you read Sindhi?" Irfan asked.

"Why certainly! You think I'm a such a memsahib that I wouldn't know my own language? I'm sure you must have picked up some Sindhi by now."

"No-o-o," Irfan answered slowly. Then he asked, "What did you write your dissertation on?"

"On that same topic—'The Social Revolution in India after 1947'. There must have been much work done on this subject in your country too. I'd like to get the names of some books. My main focus was 'The Refugees from Punjab.'"

"Sita," Irfan suddenly said, "It's well past midnight. You'd better go to bed."

"All right." She obediently got up, wished him good night, and left the room.

The fillowing morning she was standing in the verandah of the Circuit House when the gardener brought a bouquet of flowers. Irfan was also standing nearby.

"Some flowers for the mistress, master," the gardener said.

"Then give them to the mistress. . . ."

Sita flounced away inside.

When they were getting into the cars, Irfan said to her, "Listen, yesterday your chattering nearly drove me crazy. I want some rest today. You should go in Nadir's car."

When they were passing through Khairpur, Sita suddenly said, "I want to see Pir Allah Bakhsh Jamali."

Her companions looked at her astounded.

Sita pulled her notebook out of the purse and read out the Pir Sahib's address. "He was a close friend of Daddy's. Daddy had asked me to see him even if I didn't see anyone else."

They had to drive around for quick a while searching

for the Pir Sahib's mansion. Finally Bilqis said, "Let's go on to the State Guest House; we'll ask someone there." On their way they saw the mansion in the distance.

By the time they finished tea, it was getting dark. "I should have remembered the sun sets early in winter," said Nadir. "Irfan Bhai, you should take Bhabhi-jan to see the Pir Sahib. There's no need for all of us to go there."

"Now I have to deal with you again," Irfan grumbled, opening the door of the car for her. "I thought I was rid of you."

When they got to the Pir Sahib's mansion, Irfan said, "You go in. I'll come back for you in an hour."

"Why, why won't you come in too?"

"I . . . I feel a bit nervous meeting Sindhi landlords." Irfan looked somewhat abashed.

"Is that so!"

"Well, you tell me. He must be some real old-time feudal type. I won't understand his language, nor he mine. And it would be terrible to have you, an outsider, interpret for us."

Sita was looking out the car window at the garden. "When I was a child I used to come here with Daddy. Daddy was the Pir Sahib's family physician. And my grandfather, Har Bakhsh Mirchandani, was the most prominent lawyer in Hyderabad. You must have heard of him."

Irfan hadn't. He lit a cigarette and remained silent.

"Grandfather was the Pir Sahib's legal adviser. Like other big landlords, the Pir Sahib was also always involved in legal battles."

Irfan pressed the car horn, but no one appeared. Sita continued, "You know. . . ."

"No, I don't," Irfan interrupted with a smile.

"You know how the Hindus prospered during British rule and how the Muslims almost totally pawned themselves to Hindu money-lenders? Well, the Sindhi Muslims were different. They never developed a middle class. The big landlords took shelter in their feudal mansions and locked their doors to the outside world. Perhaps they're still doing the same."

"That's the story of all the Hindus and Muslims," Irfan countered. "Perhaps that's why Pakistan was formed."

Sita paid no attention. "As a child I was fascinated by the marvellous clothes and ornaments of the Pir Sahib's wives. You can't imagine how backward, yet how wealthy these people really are."

Just then a tall Sindhi servant came out of the house. He had thick moustaches and was wearing a wide, flaring, black shalwar. He approached them with folded hands and led them to the drawing room. Sita immediately went into the ladies' section of the house. Irfan settled himself on a sofa. The room was filled with priceless furniture, while the floor was covered with precious carpets. The windows had curtains made of the heaviest silk, tied back with golden cords. After a few minutes, Pir Allah Bakhsh Jamali entered. He had a thick gray beard, and large, heavy-lidded eyes. He bent down to take both of Irfan's hands in his own in greeting, then silently sat down on the sofa next to him. A few minutes later tea was brought in an ornate silver service. The Pir Sahib poured and made a few innocuous remarks. Slowly they began to talk politics. Sir Firuz Khan Noon was the Prime Minister and things were not looking up for the country.

Then the Pir Sahib rose and went inside. When he returned with Sita, he had tears in his eyes which he wiped away with a large silk handkerchief, as he patted her hair with affection. When Sita talked in Sindhi to the Pir Sahib, Irfan keenly realised what a stranger he was in that place.

The moustachioed servant put a big suitcase in the car.

Irfan started the engine and as they swung out of the gates, remarked in jest, "You seem to have hit them for quite a few presents."

"I haven't looked. He has given things for Daddy and Mummy and for everyone else. The things must be quite expensive. These people are extremely sentimental, and also extremely generous."

"Hunnh!" Irfan snorted. You put so much value on sentiments . . . yet you also claim to be so very logical. What a
fraud you are!"

The next day their cars passed through the city of Khairpur.
On both sides of the street were dilapidated old buildings
made of crumbling bricks. And under their leaning arches
stood dignified old Sindhi Muslims, conversing. They had
flowing beards, and as they talked they frequently bowed
and held their palms together as if in supplication. Low
musical voices, delicate gestures—it was a strange and
bewitching way of life that Irfan had not seen before,
though he had lived in these parts for nine years.

"I'm truly amazed," Irfan said to Sita, shifting gears, as
they drove past the court buildings. "Isn't it strange that
I'm a resident of this country but you're an alien?"

"Over the years I've grown accustomed to it," Sita replied. "The last time I came from New York to India with
Jamil, Manjhli Khala came from Karachi to Faizabad to
see her favorite nephew. It was she who showed me all
the sights of Lucknow and explained to me the old rituals
and customs at Tulsipur and Chandpur. But when we arrived in Lucknow from Faizabad, it was I who took her to
the police station to have her arrival and departure entered in the records."

The cities of Sindh were filled with desolation and dust.
Their Civil Lines had streets on which sand blew in from
the desert, and pock-marked old office buildings stood, a
dismal reminder of the Raj. Over the entire sub-continent,
from Peshawar to Madras and from Bengal to Sindh, the
English had created an architecture, a mood, an identical
pattern of problems for the districts, and now they were
gone. They had left behind identical courthouses, parks,
Dak Bungalows, railway stations, high-ceilinged waiting
rooms and their heavy, ugly furniture. The Circuit House
of Sakkhar where they had just arrived could easily have
been in Bulandshahr or Bodh Gaya. The cook, who had

come rushing to greet them and who, after saluting the
sahib, had asked "What time would you like your *chota
hazri?*", could have been called either Rasul Bakhsh or
Gurbachan. The gardener was either Chiragh Din or Ram
Khalawan. Yet the world had changed. Men had changed.
But had they, really? No one was willing to honestly answer that question.

"I must go to Sadh Bela," Sita said for the second time.
"We used to go to the annual fair there, and always had so
much fun."

In the late afternoon, they took a motor-launch to the
island of Sadh Bela, which stood in the middle of the river
like an ocean liner. On arrival they climbed up the stairs.
There was a large pavilion whose walls had verses by Kabir
engraved on them. On the small hillocks there were many
buildings—big and small temples, a hostel for boys, a club
house—but they all looked desolate, haunted. The other
members of the party were soon tired and sat down on a
bench near the steps, but Sita and Irfan kept wandering
around. When Nadir saw Sita climbing the steps of a dark,
brooding temple some distance away, he muttered, "Poor
Bhabhi-jan! I feel so sorry for her."

The temple walls had strange, even hideous and frightening stone figures fixed to them. And under the figures
there were graffiti: "Devi Ma, I'm going to India. Be kind
to me. 12 November 1947." "Bhagwan, I'm running away
to India. Please forgive me. 25 September 1947." "Great
Mother, I'm leaving you behind. Now I'll never be able to
make offerings to you. Please always be kind to my children. 19 December 1947."

Sita and Irfan continued to look for more such heart-
breaking sentiments until the sun had sunk in the waves
of the Indus. On the next hill there was a banyan tree and
yet another desolate temple. Inside, in the heavy gloom, a
life-size statue of Radha lay overturned on the floor. Irfan
felt very agitated. "Let's get out of here," he said.

Later, when the two were seated on the marble steps of

the club house, Sita suddenly asked him, "Doesn't it look
like a ghost town?" Then she continued, " My grandmother
would sometime say to me, 'Last night I had a very nice
dream about you. Some saint's gentle spirit must have
flown over our house.' Or, 'Last night I had a very bad
dream. Some cobbler's evil spirit must have passed by our
backyard.' She believed that certain evil spirits take the
form of children with four fingers on each hand. Or that
evil spirits fly through the air, glowing like lamps. . . . Look,
look," she raised her hand to point, "do you see something glowing over there . . . like a lamp?" Then she added,
"Sadh Bela is the graveyard of my people."

She got up, then sat on another step. "How dark it is!
And in this darkness all my ideals, all my longings and
regrets glow faintly—like will-o'-the-wisps. Just now, when
I closed my eyes for a moment, I felt as if Bhairon's dog
had attacked me and I couldn't escape because I was surrounded by witches riding hyenas." She grabbed Irfan's
hand, her own cold with fear.

"We had a terrible custom," she continued after a few
moments. "When someone died unmarried, the corpse was
wrapped in a red cloth, then carried to the burning place
to the beating of a drum—as if the death was also a wedding for that person.

"You see this river Sindh—my people believed that west
of it, where the moon sets, lay the land of death. And any
Sindhi who while alive gave a cow in charity to a Brahmin,
could cross the river, when he died, holding on to that
cow's tail. Then, in the month of Bhadon, on the night of
the full moon, he would return in a boat which his relatives were expected to set loose on the river two days earlier.

"In the month of Chaitra, there used to be a huge fair.
You see, this river was in fact our biggest god because it
flowed through a desert. The ancient Egyptians considered the Nile to be a god for the same reason. And in this
very city of Sakkhar there was a temple of Darya Devata,

whom the Muslims called Darya Pir or Khwaja Khizar. The
Hindus of Southern Punjab used to call him Darya Sahib.
Just think, how fascinating their beliefs were."

That night she lingered till late on the terrace of the
Sakkhar Barrage, telling him the story of the river Sindh.
Suddenly she fell silent. Irfan looked at her. Leaning over
the parapet wall of the massive, awe-inspiring dam, she
seemed utterly alone, entirely helpless, and totally a
stranger. The waves of the Mehran were restless and noisy.
The lights of the barrage stretched for miles. The surrounding desert was an expanse of centuries. And in the
midst of all this stood one poor, lonely girl!

Below them the waves glistened in the moonlight. On
the two banks shone the lights of the twin cities of Rohri
and Sakkhar. On the seemingly endless bridge there was
an equally endless procession of vehicles and people. This
Sindh of November 1957 was very different. So different
indeed that it could offer no sense of belonging to Sita
Mirchandani of Karol Bagh, Delhi.

As they were leaving Sindh to enter Punjab, Nadir said,
"Well, Bhabhi-jan, we really got to see a whole lot of your
Sindh. And Irfan Bhai even had the honor of meeting your
Pir Allah Bakhsh Jamali."

"Sindh is not mine—nor does it belong to Pir Allah
Bakhsh Jamali. It belongs only to those wretched *haris*
whom you have never felt any need to think about," Sita
replied with some heat.

"Long live the Revolution!" Nadir shouted with glee.
Irfan felt very happy: finally Sita was returning to her normal, combative mood, eager for political debates.

Beyond Bahawalpur, the forests of Panjnad and the
confluence of five rivers looked bewitching in the light of
the full moon. As they drove on, the moonlight grew
brighter. Irfan pointed the car down the straight road cutting through the wilderness, and said to Sita, "Night in
the wilderness! You'll have to forgive me if I suddenly begin to recite the jingles of Akhtar Shirani. In our Urdu

textbooks, we used to read: 'The mornings in Benares; the evenings in Avadh; the nights in Malva.' We could, of course, understand the reasons for Benares and Avadh, but a night in the wilderness didn't make any sense. What could be there, we'd wonder, except dirt and dust? But now I know what that proverb meant." Then he asked, "You must have seen the dawn in Benares as well as Avadh's merry evenings?"

"Yes, I have."

In the moonlight pouring into the car Sita's gold bracelet suddenly flashed—she had been playing with it for some time.

"That's a lovely bracelet—is it Italian?" asked Irfan.

"Yes."

"Did you get it in Naples?"

"No, in Canada."

"Canada! There are hundreds of countries in the world—what made you go to Canada of all places?"

"My uncle has a business there. After Partition he wrote to Daddy, 'Your financial condition will no longer allow you to educate Sita properly. Send her to me.'"

"That must have made you very happy?"

"Of course it did. There I was, a 21-year old, extremely sensitive girl, who had passed through several refugee camps only to end up in a tiny house in Karol Bagh; who had to take a wretched bus every morning to go miles away to Ramjas College; who was suddenly told she was she was being sent abroad. It was like a fairy tale. . . . My uncle had no children. He and Aunty had been living in Canada for nearly twenty-five years. His business was all over the place—they spent several months in New York every year. So they sent me an air ticket and got me admitted to Columbia."

"And there you fell into the company of the Reds."

Sita laughed. "I had fallen into the company of the Reds even while I was in Delhi. I had a cousin, Shyam Narayan Arora, who had fled to Delhi from Lahore. He wrote short stories in Urdu—you might have read some of them. He was a dyed-in-the-wool leftist. There used to be a weekly literary meeting at his house, where people would read stories and poems about the Partition riots."

"Then. . . ?"

"Then what?"

"What happened in New York?"

She remained silent.

He didn't have the courage to ask her the question he so badly wanted to ask.

"Perhaps . . . perhaps you wish to know about Jamil?" Sita began after a few moments of silence—like an obedient pupil answering her teacher. "I met Jamil in a leftist gathering. McCarthy's witch-hunts had not yet started and there were plenty of left-wing groups in Greenwich Village which had mostly Jews and Negroes in them—and only the rare Indian. Jamil had just arrived in New York from India to work at the United Nations."

"And then. . . ?"

"Then what? Bang, bang!"

"How eloquent!"

"Why not? After all, I married a master of eloquence." Then she continued, "You know, after I met Jamil, I started taking a strong interest in Urdu. Jamil loved Urdu literature, and now that I wanted to be with him I had to share his interests and think and do things the way he liked. Often he would start talking to me in Avadhi. When I would make fun of him, he would retort, 'Madame, my relatives and I speak the language in which the great Tulsidas wrote his Ramayana. . . .'

"Before we got married, I used to go to Jamil's apartment directly from the campus, and there a Sikh friend of his would teach me Urdu. But that Sardarji also fancied himself a story writer and every day I had to listen to his latest masterpiece. He would walk back and forth in the room as he read to me, and say, 'One day soon I shall surpass both Krishan Chandar and Bedi.'

"I had no trouble learning Urdu. After all, it has the same script as Sindhi. I remember, two years after our marriage Jamil wrote to his sisters, 'My wife can beat you all in her command of Urdu.'"

Suddenly she asked, "Should I tell you how low I can get?"

"What do you mean?"

"When I first met Jamil, a mutual friend told me that he was a cousin of Farkhunda Baji. I then met him with an open mind, otherwise I might have snubbed him in the beginning."

"Ahha! So you snub people in the beginning?"

"Just listen, will you? I met Jamil but didn't disclose to him that I also knew Farkhunda Baji and Bilqis. Because he had told me right away that he was engaged to some relative of his who was a cousin of Bilqis' and a distant 'niece' of his own. These crazy 'cousin-marriages' among you Muslims never cease to amaze me. Anyway, if I had told him about Farkhunda Baji, he would have immediately cabled Delhi—'Getting married to Sita Mirchandani.' And you can imagine what Farkhunda Baji and Bilqis would then have thought of me. The worst kind of ingrate, to say the least. The two had taken such good care of me in Delhi, but now there I was in New York seducing their cousin's fiancé."

"Don't use such vulgar words about yourself."

"But they are the right words. All girls make a play for men one way or another. Their *modus operandi* may differ, and silly folks like you may call it Love, but that doesn't mean anything. The one goal—the one burning desire— of every girl is to catch some fool and make him marry her. The rest is nonsense."

"What fine ideas!"

"Why, thank you, sir."

A lock of hair had fallen over her forehead; Sita pushed it back and closed her eyes. "The night I first met Jamil I went back to my hostel and said to Grace—my roommate:

'Until now I've been an encyclopedia, but now I know I'm a woman. . . .'

"Before our marriage I would often get mad at Jamil, but as quickly make friends again. Once Jamil remarked: 'One moment you growl like a tiger, the next you purr like a cat.' I immediately said: '*Lahaul va-la quvat* . . .'— that was one of the first things I had learned to say from him. He then said: 'You're the stuff that old-maids are made of.' Jamil was a king of words."

Several miles went by in silence. Then Irfan asked, "What about the marriage, how did that happen?"

"One afternoon we were coming back on the subway from someplace. That's when Jamil proposed."

"On the subway?"

"Right in the middle of the rush hour."

"That was hardly romantic."

"Exactly. Jamil hated humbug. At one station we had to get off and take separate trains. The crowd had pushed me far away from him. As I was struggling to get on my train, he shouted: 'Sita . . . Sita . . . will you marry me?' Then he looked at his watch and added: 'Give me an answer . . . there isn't much time.' And I turned towards him as the doors were beginning to close and shouted back: 'Yes.'"

"Then what happened?"

"Then? . . . I didn't tell my aunt and uncle but the next week, at the house of an Indian friend, we got married. A lot of pictures were taken—some of them even appeared in the evening papers. My friends were delighted and had a lot of parties for me. Still I didn't tell my uncle. I was scared, though I was then twenty-four. Uncle learned of it from the papers. He nearly died of the shock. He loved me very much—he thought of me as his daughter. But when Jamil went to his office, he refused to see him. Aunty turned out to be more sensible, even though she is rather old-fashioned. I think women usually have more common-sense than men. Also, the years in America had mellowed

her. She arranged to meet Jamil in a drugstore, and liked
him a lot. That was one thing about Jamil: he could win
over a woman in no time. Then Aunty wrote to Mummy:
'Sita has married . . . the boy is not from our caste . . . his
name is Jaimal.' Later, she would often laugh and say:
'Jamil . . . Jaimal . . . there's only a difference of a few
vowels.'

"After some time Aunty shared her secret with Mummy;
she too readily accepted the theory about the vowels. She
told Daddy: 'The boy is Hindu, but extremely progressive
. . . doesn't believe in any religion . . . in any case, no
Hindu boy cares much for religion these days.' And Daddy
accepted it. He had heard such 'progressive' talk from his
own children.

"But a few months later Jamil and I jointly wrote to
Daddy and told him everything. Daddy wrote back to me:
'I'm doubtless angry with you, but it's all right if you are
happy.' And to Jamil he wrote what every bride's father
writes to his son-in-law: 'Sita is my beloved child . . . she's
been brought up with much love . . . please never hurt her
feelings.'"

She laughed.

"Poor Daddy. He's such a literary person. In his letter
to Jamil he quoted from Tulsidas: 'Just as Himalaya gave
Girija to Mahesh and Samudra gave Lakshmi to Hari; just
as Janaka gave Sita to Rama—so we, my son, are giving you
our Sita.' Jamil was overwhelmed—after all, he was from
Tulsi's land. . . We Amils are fairly open-minded, but
Mummy's family is staunchly Arya Samaji. She has never
told them that her daughter had married a Muslim. They
still think that the husband is a Hindu from U.P. named
Jaimal.

"When our Rahul was born, my parents were delighted—
more so by the fact that Jamil had not objected to my giving the boy a Hindu name. Two years later, Jamil got leave
and we returned to Delhi. Farkhunda Baji . . . Bilqis . . .
everyone greeted me with so much love that I felt embar-

rassed. Mummy had explained to her Arora relatives that
the husband was from Lucknow, that's why he spoke such
excellent Urdu and swore by '*Khuda*'. But these refugees
were already angry at the U.P. people in general, and never
forgave Mummy for letting me marry a non-Sindhi. Jamil
and I stayed in Delhi for just a few days; then we went to
Tulsipur and Chandpur. I visited Faizabad and Lucknow.
We holidayed in Kashmir. Then returned to the States.

"That same year a boy came to New York from Calcutta
to study acting. He had a long name: Abul Fasahat Qamarul
Islam Chowdhry."

"Qamarul Islam Chowdhry?" Irfan was taken aback.
"Who writes poetry in English? Whom they call 'India's T.
S. Eliot'?"

"Yes, the same. Of course, at that time he wasn't at all
famous and was only a struggling actor. But he had worked
in several 'progressive' Bengali films, and had also written
some good poems in English. Soon enough he became a
regular in our group. . . ."

"Then what happened?" Irfan prodded.

"You aren't planning to write it all down, are you?"

"Don't be silly."

"In those days. . . . But never mind, there is no sense in
talking about those days."

"No . . . no. You must tell me." Irfan persisted. "Don't
hide anything from me."

"Why? Are you my analyst with a plan to cure me?" Sita
mocked him. "I warn you, don't even think of it."

"For heaven's sake!"

"All right, all right," Sita hurriedly said in a conciliatory
tone, "What was bound to happen happened." Then she
continued, "Who really knows what happened! At the university, I struggled with my academic work. At home I took
care of Rahul and cooked meals. We still had the same
circle of friends. Our other activities were much the same
too. And yet, I don't know why, Jamil gradually turned into
a reactionary. I could have tolerated that, but he also

started drinking much too much. He would return home from the bars very late at night and I'd sit at the table with his dinner waiting for him. And Qamar would be there keeping me company."

"And, no doubt, also offering you his sympathies. That's quite a racket." Now it was Irfan's turn to mock.

"Isn't that your own racket right now?" Sita shot back. "No, it wasn't a matter of sympathy, Irfan. I truly don't know what happened. We float along with events and don't quite know what's going on. I'll tell you how Qamar and I came to be close. One day Qamar stopped me on the campus and said: 'Come to my apartment this evening—a friend of mine who teaches elocution is coming over. I'm sure you'll enjoy meeting her.' By then Jamil and I were keeping quite different hours. He would often eat at the U.N., then go off to bars with his friends. . . .

"Jamil never flirted with other women—that I am sure of even today. He was always faithful to me. And yet, who knows what happened. . . . Usually it's another woman who breaks up a home."

"Or another man." Irfan quietly remarked.

"That's true." Sita nodded in agreement. "In any case, we trusted each other completely; there was never any question of suspicion. . ." Her voice was choked.

"Here," Irfan offered her a cigarette.

"Thanks." She lit the cigarette. "The reason I smoke is not because I think smoking symbolises women's liberation. I just picked up this bad habit when I was in college in the States. You don't mind, do you?"

"No. Of course, not." Irfan's foot pressed down on the accelerator. 'Who am I to object to her smoking? Why did she ask me that question?'

"What were we talking about . . . ?"

"We?"

"Oh, excuse me. Living with Jamil for so many years I picked up his habit of using 'we' instead of 'I.' Isn't that the way they talk in your Avadh? I was very careful then in

such matters. I diligently imitated Jamil's accent in Urdu,
and greeted people with '*Adab Arz*' instead of '*Namaste*'.
No girl could have changed herself as much as I did to
adapt to Jamil's ways. I even began to drink a lot so that I
could keep him company in the evenings. But whenever I
tried to accompany him to a bar he got angry. 'Can't you
leave me alone for even a minute,' he would shout at me.

"While we were in Tulsipur, Muharram came. They observe Muharram in a big way in Jamil's family. I, too, would
put on a black sari and devoutly attend the *majalis* with my
mother- and sisters-in-law, despite the fact that I think all
religions are silly. How could I be concerned about the
Shi'ahs and the Sunnis when I have no interest in Islam
itself? But because Jamil belonged to a Shi'ah family I
thought all Shi'ahs were wonderful."

"Some wise man has said, 'Women are such fools.'"

"It may be true . . ." She fell silent.

"What are you thinking of now?" Irfan asked.

"Nothing. I just remembered that Muharram in Tulsipur.
The time I spent there was like a dream. I also saw strange
things. In quite a few of those *majlis* there would be refugee women from Sindh and Punjab. Farkhunda Baji told
me that that was happening at many places in U.P. See,
how cultural patterns change? There were empty houses
in Tulsipur, left vacant by those Syeds who had emigrated
to Pakistan, but no refugee would occupy them. They
thought it would be disrespectful towards the Syeds. . . .
Here in Sindh and the Punjab they had always respected
them as the descendants of the Prophet."

"God almighty, Sita!" Irfan exclaimed. "You're bursting
with information. There's no end to what you know."

"Won't you even let me talk?"

"I was merely thinking about Jamil—poor fellow must have
felt he had married not just a girl but an entire library."

"Very funny," Sita mocked him.

"Please continue."

"Well, that evening I went to Qamar's apartment. All

the bohemian crowd was there. I tell you, Irfan, when I saw that girl, Jennifer Crane, I was quite taken aback. And then, we were all flabbergasted when Qamar introduced her to us as his fiancée. But we were intellectuals, after all, and intellectuals consider it a duty to act differently from the rest of the world.You see, Jennifer Crane was monstrously fat, while Qamar is a slim, rather handsome man."

"Yes, I remember seeing him once in a film shown at the Indian High Commission."

"Jennifer had a very pretty face, but the rest of her was huge. That only made her look grotesque—a mermaid's face on an iceberg's body. Qamar had met her at some theatre workshop in Boston. She followed him to New York. She was considered quite a good teacher of acting. She was also a poet and published poems in *New World Writing* and the *Hudson Review*. We were all very impressed by that. Then we had a big celebration and a lot of toasts. Jennifer, being a bohemian herself, could make fun of her obesity. She would analyse her psychological problems in front of everyone. She even pressed Qamar to flirt with other girls in her presence so that she could analyse her feelings of jealousy and pain, and write better poems.

"Qamar didn't marry her, but she moved in with him. We took no notice of it. That sort of thing bothers only old-fashioned moralists."

"Yes, yes. We all know that. Come to the point."

"At the end of the year Qamar went back to Calcutta. A short time later Jennifer followed him, and the two actually got married. Afterwards, however. . . you aren't getting bored, are you?"

"I don't answer silly questions," Irfan retorted. "You just continue with your story."

"But it's a long story."

Just then Nadir brought his car alongside and honked the horn. They had arrived in Multan.

As their cars entered the city, Nadir suddenly sang out loud:

Aur Diwan Sharar Multani
munch safed aur munh pe jawani.
*Aur Diwan. . . .**

"How delightful! I never heard anything more inappropriate," shouted Irfan, leaning out of his car window. "Please continue."

"I don't remember any more," Nadir replied, laughing to cover his embarrassment.

As they were getting out of the cars at the local Circuit House, Nadir said, "It's really amazing how some things from our childhood never leave our memories. Irfan Bhai, you should explain this. After all, you're an expert in psychology."

"Is that true?" Sita asked, frowning in mock annoyance. "No wonder he kept asking me, all the way, about my childhood."

"You see," Nadir said, "as a boy I had read a funny poem in *Nairang-e-Khayal*, which was about 'Karma', the English movie that Devika Rani had made. It was just delightful—like Akbar's poem '*Dilli Darbar*'. But now I remember only one verse from it." He turned to Bilqis, "Do you remember more?"

"Jamil Bhaiya knew the entire poem," Bilqis said, "he knew thousands of verses by heart." Then she looked at Sita and fell silent.

"*Aur Diwan Sharar Multani*," Nadir tried to save the situation, "*aur Diwan Sharar Multani*." He repeated the line until they all sat down on the chairs laid out on the verandah.

"Would you like to hear some more nonsense, Bhabhijan?" he asked Sita, with fake heartiness.

"Sure, sure. Let's hear some more," Sita replied. Her voice was full of maternal affection—after all, the poor boy was her *devar*.

---

*"Then there was Diwan Sharar Multani with a white mustache and youthful face."

Nadir and Bilqis quickly started a hilarious duet. How anxious they were to make her happy!

Flinging himself on a chair close to Sita, Irfan said, "How about some history of Multan now?"

"Oh shut up, will you?"

It was hot early the following morning, and gusts of wind blew heavy with dust. In the galleries around the tomb of Shams Tabriz there were crowds of *qalandars* with blood-red eyes, women covered by dirty veils, fierce-looking ruffians smoking hashish, and prostitutes. Also fakirs with hideous faces and huge earrings, children with coniform heads, and an amazing assortment of young women begging for alms.

"So this is your culture of Sufism?" Irfan asked Sita sarcastically.

After they got out of Multan and back on the main highway, Irfan said, "Sheherzade, begin your story."

"What's the use? You know the end already."

"No, I don't. I want to find out the end."

"So that you can pass judgment?"

"So that I can make my decision."

"My, my! You non-socialists are so romantic." Then she added, "Where was I, anyway?"

"Jennifer had reached Calcutta and married Qamar."

"That's right. And barely six months later, as I was preparing some porridge for Rahul in the kitchen, our doorbell rang. When I opened the door there was Qamar. 'What brings you here?' I asked. 'You seem to have one foot in Calcutta and the other in New York.' Then he made a very dramatic statement. In his most romantic Bengali voice he said, 'Sita, I have come back because of you.'

"At first I thought he was joking, that he was probably rehearsing some dialogue. But he was serious.

"Then . . . after that. . ." Sita continued slowly, "I just fell into a new pattern of life. Jamil would often not speak to me for two or three days. He would get ready for the

office in the morning, kiss Rahul—he adored his son—
then go out and not come back home till very late at night.
At first I thought I was only seeking revenge for what Jamil
was doing to me, but the truth was. . . ." Her voice trailed
off.

"Yes? The truth was . . .?"

"That I was in fact drawing closer to Qamar—just the
way a snake's prey is pulled closer to the snake.

"One day, without bothering to tell me, Qamar went to
see Jamil in one of the bars and said to him, 'Jamil, I am
in love with your wife.'"

"Good God! No!" Irfan exclaimed.

"Jamil's first reaction was like mine, he thought Qamar
was trying out his lines from some play. But when he
realised that Qamar was serious. . . ."

"He beat the stuffing out of him," Irfan interupted.
"Then he came home and beat the stuffing out of you too."

"How did you know?" Sita asked, quite surprised.

"Because that's what I would have done if I had been in
Jamil's place."

"Amazing! But that's exactly what he did. He beat up
Qamar, then came home and beat me up. I'd never have
thought that a sweet and gentle person like Jamil would
turn into a crazy beast."

"Bravo, my lad, bravo!" Irfan said, "And then Jamil must
have said, 'Get out of my house right now!' And it was late
at night and raining."

Sita stared at him for a moment. "Yes, that's how it happened," she said in a soft voice.

"Listen, Sita," Irfan began gently, "you want everything
to be different and original . . . unique and profound. But
life's tale has been repeated millions of times. It has always been like that, and that's how it will always be. People
will fall in love just like that—then they'll be disappointed
in each other. Hearts will break; people will suffer. Sita,
you and Jamil and Qamar are not unique. The likes of you
have been seen before. You think I'm superficial, that I'm

without sentiments. But I know how you must have left
Jamil's house—which was also your house. How Jamil must
have refused to let you take Rahul with you. How you must
have gone to Qamar for help and how perhaps he, too,
refused. Perhaps such things should not have happened
to all of you, for you and Jamil and Qamar were brilliant
people. But the wheels of life turn evenly for all. As they
grind us down they don't distinguish between intellectuals and non-intellectuals. . . ."

She leaned against the car window and stared unblink-
ingly at the road ahead. Now the rich, fertile fields of
Punjab had started. A single file of peasant women in black
and red costumes was walking down a narrow track. As the
cars left Montgomery City, the sky turned blood red with
sunset. There were no other vehicles on the road. Here
and there, flocks of water-fowl circled over sheets of water.
They passed a farmer dressed in a white lungi and a huge
turban, driving his pair of bullocks homeward. There were
bells hanging from the necks of the bulls, and their clanging could be heard for some time in the utter silence of
the dusk. Sita reached forward and turned on the radio.
Radio Ceylon was playing a song by Lata Mangeshkar. The
guitar accompaniment felt like a stab in the heart.

"Turn it off," Irfan muttered angrily.

Sita switched off the radio; then she again leaned back
against the car window.

"Don't cry," Irfan said with a frown.

Sita wiped a tear from the corner of her eye, but continued to sob.

"Sita," Irfan said, "I'll do whatever I can for you. But
you know there isn't much that I can do."

"Irfan, I want my Rahul. If you have the slightest sympathy for me, please get my child back from Jamil."

"Is Rahul very attached to him?"

"Jamil loves him madly. My friends who saw them in New
York tell me that now Jamil comes directly home from work
and spends the evenings with Rahul. That he has hired an

old black woman to look after him. That now Jamil drinks
at home alone and doesn't go to bars anymore. But that
was, of course, before he got remarried. Now I hear he
has put Rahul in a boarding school. Please, Irfan . . . please
somehow get me my son."

"And what have you told Jamil's relatives?"

"What can I tell them?"

"Have you talked to a lawyer?"

"I can't. . . . But I spoke to Farkhunda Baji. She is willing to help me in every way. She has written Jamil numerous letters. But it's not an easy matter for her either; after
all, Jamil is her cousin. And now, without divorcing me,
Jamil has remarried . . . just a few days ago."

"What? Didn't you have a civil marriage?"

"No. I became a Muslim, and we had a Muslim marriage.
Jamil's father is a *mujtahid*; he had written to Jamil that if
he married a non-Muslim in the States in a civil marriage
he would disown him. Jamil told me about it. But I was so
madly in love with him that I answered, 'It doesn't matter
to me. You must meet his condition. There is no sense in
hurting the feelings of your old parents.' What difference
does it really make? Muslim, non-Muslim—I don't believe
in all that. On the marriage contract, my Muslim name
was Sayida Begum. And I insisted that I get only the strictly
legal *mehr*, which came to just a couple of dollars. I imagine he turned this Spanish girl into, too, a Muslim before
he married her.

"He wants to punish me—that's why he doesn't give me
a divorce. It was entirely my fault. I deceived him. For several months, whenever I got a chance I went over to
Qamar's apartment. Most of Qamar's friends knew.

"When Jamil pushed me out of his house, I stood on
the sidewalk in the rain for quite some time. If he had
then opened his door and said—just once—'Sita, come in
out of the rain,' I'd have thrown myself at his feet and
sworn never to be unfaithful again. But the door remained
shut. I could hear Rahul cry inside. I could see Jamil's

shadow on the blind pulled over Rahul's bedroom window. Jamil had turned the bedside lamp on and was trying to put Rahul back to sleep. I could see Jamil bending over him. He re-arranged the covers, then sat down in a chair near the bed. I kept staring at Jamil's shadow, unable even to breathe. I was hoping he call'd me back, but he sat there as if he'd turned to stone, then switched off the light.

"You guessed right, Irfan. I finally took a taxi to Qamar's place. There was a party going on. Qamar was very surprised to see me. 'What brings you here in this rain?' he asked, 'Are you all right?' I told him everything. He was silent for a while then said: 'Sita, I made a mistake. I'll never be able to give you a happy life. I'm an utterly irresponsible person. Please go back and ask Jamil to forgive you. He is a good man; he will definitely forgive you. I'll also ask his forgiveness. We let ourselves get carried away by temporary feelings. Sita dear, you can find true peace in life only with a solid person like Jamil.'

"God knows what other fancy lines he delivered. I just turned around and walked away. For a few days I stayed with my friend Grace, then I borrowed some money from Aunty and returned to Delhi. Now I've been in Delhi for one whole year. . . ."

"Did you write to Jamil about the child? Did you try to get a Muslim divorce on your own?"

"Irfan, all that is so horrible. I had willingly given myself to Jamil. Not in my wildest dreams had I thought that one day I might need the help of the law to get separated from him. I didn't want to create a big mess. If the facts had come to Daddy's attention it would have been enough to kill him. The most I did was to ask a lawyer friend to write to Jamil. He got the reply: 'That woman is morally unfit to be a mother to an innocent child.' And, you know Irfan, perhaps he was right on that score. At least in the eyes of the world . . ."

"What rubbish!" Irfan didn't let her finish the sentence.

At the railway station in Lahore, before Sita could board the train going to India, a police constable asked her some questions to complete the necessary papers. Eventually he asked, "Your religion?"

Everyone was flustered. Bilqis had already gone through and was standing near the train talking to some relatives. Only Nadir and Irfan were with Sita at the police counter. The constable opened the passport and examined it again; then he looked at the visa entries:

Name: Mrs. Sita Jamil

Reason for travel: To visit relatives.

Husband's nationality: Indian

He looked at Sita a second time. What a curious name! There was also the bindi on her forehead. Returning from Pakistan to India. It was all rather mysterious.

"Religion?" the constable asked again.

"Let me think," Irfan said with a smile. "Perhaps you should write 'freethinker'."

The constable wrote that down.

"That's just marvellous!" Nadir burst out laughing. "Bhabhi-jan a freethinker! In Tulsipur, when Jamil Bhai suddenly fell ill, she asked Bari Khala to perform all sorts of crazy rituals so that he'd get well. What a laugh!"

Irfan and Sita also began to laugh, but it sounded hollow.

(8)

The train left Lahore and reached Delhi. Bilqis got off and took a plane to Bombay that very day. Sita returned to Karol Bagh. The next day she went to see Hima. The day after that, she resumed work at the office. Her busy but empty life started its routine again, from exactly where she had left it three weeks ago when she had gone to Pakistan. *Mudrarakshasa* was to open after Bilqis' return from Bombay and all the members of the Modern Theatre were frantically busy with the final preparations.

On the opening night, Sita stood on the steps of the theatre, talking with some friends, when she noticed someone standing behind one of the pillars, intently listening to her. His face seemed familiar but she couldn't be sure. She went on talking. When they all started to go in, she noticed the man turned once or twice to look at her. At the end of the play, Sita went to Lalita's dressing room to congratulate her friends. The man was already there, surrounded by several people. He appeared to be someone quite important. Lalita introduced him as Projesh Kumar Chowdhry.

Projesh Kumar Chowdhry! The great painter. An 'expressionist' of world stature. Sita had seen his paintings in galleries as well as in books and magazines. She had read about him in American art journals. Projesh Kumar Chowdhry. And here he was before her, in the flesh!

"Hello, Sita Debi," he said, "I'm delighted. Qamar has told me so much about you. Here, let's sit down."

They settled on two stools near a pile of costumes. Projesh was speaking to her most cordially. Sita kept thinking, 'I'm talking to India's finest painter.' She felt strangely excited.

"I've heard your name since I was a child."

'What an awfully trite and foolish remark!' she thought. But she was indeed feeling quite nervous. To be overawed by important people was one of her major weaknesses. And she was well aware of it. For one brief moment all her heroes since her childhood flashed through her mind. . . .

"I don't mean to imply . . . that I'm still very young." she added, gaining some control over herself.

"Why not? You could be my daughter."

"That certainly can't be true," Sita said with a smile; then she added hesitantly, "Your daughter?"

"Yes. If I had a daughter she would've been only a few years younger than you."

Sita knew that after divorcing his Hungarian wife—who was herself a well-known sculptor—Projesh Kumar Chowdhry had not married again. Gorky used to call the entire world his university; similarly Projesh considered all the women in the world prospective slaves in his sera-glio. And he had some right to think like that, for very few women were able to resist his charm. His closest friends used to describe different 'periods' in his life——from 1938 to 1941, Projesh had been in love with Prema Bakhshi, an artist from Allahabad whose ancestors had come from Kashmir—so they called it Projesh's Kashmiri Period. Then successively there came his Czechoslovak, Gujarati, and Rajasthani Periods. The six years from '46 to '52 that the famous Hindi novelist, Raj Rani Misra, devoted to writing three mammoth novels inspired by Projesh, were called his Ganga-Jamni Period. Since then there had successively been a Marathi Period, a French Period, a Russian Period and a Punjabi Period. In between somewhere his Hungar-ian wife had come and gone. But lately no new 'period' had come to the notice of the general public.

He sat with Sita for a long while in Lalita's dressing room and talked about all sort of things—nothing complex or obscure, nothing metaphysical, just simple chitchat. How sincere and humble he was, how gentle. Sita was quite sur-prised, and when Projesh invited her to have dinner with him the following Saturday, she quickly accepted.

"Qamar and Madhuri will also be coming," Projesh added.

"How wonderful! I haven't seen him for a long time." Sita replied with enthusiasm.

That Saturday evening when she was entering the res-taurant with Projesh Kumar Chowdhry, a girl standing in the verandah looked towards them and whispered loudly to her companion, "Sugar Daddy!"

Sita's face turned crimson. 'Thank God, Projesh didn't hear it,' she said to herself.

They found a table in a corner. The dining room was brilliant with light. An orchestra played the latest tunes from America. Projesh noticed a friend at another table and went over to speak to him. Sita remained in her seat, observing the crowd. What a strange assortment of people! Actors and actresses from the newly emerging Indian theatre, Urdu poets and writers, nouveau riche Sindhis and Punjabis who only a few years ago had come to Delhi as refugees from Pakistan, bigwigs in the Central Government, film people from Bombay and Calcutta who had come to attend a seminar, political leaders of every hue. This was the crowd, the new society, on which she had done her Ph.D. research. After a few minutes, Projesh came back to his seat and began to talk to her in his sweet, soft voice. 'God! Why do all Bengalis have such enchanting voices?' Sita thought.

In a little while Qamar and Madhuri arrived. Madhuri had sindur in the parting of her hair. Projesh introduced her as, Mrs. Chowdhry.

"Congratulations, Qamar," Sita said with a smile.

"Thanks, Sita. We got married in such a hurry we couldn't inform all our friends. Also, I was told you were in Pakistan."

Qamar began to talk to her, the way two old friends talk when they meet.

Then Projesh called a Russian girl over to join them; she had come to India to do research in Urdu Literature at Aligarh. After a while two other Russians joined the party; they were engineers at the Bhilai Steel Plant. The Russians spoke either the purest Urdu or the finest Hindi. As the evening progressed the number of Projesh's guests also increased. When the party finally ended and Sita was leaving, Qamar and Madhuri insisted that she should come for dinner to their flat next Sunday. They had got married barely a month ago and had just moved into a flat in Sundar Nagar. Madhuri was a civil servant. She had her own car, so Qamar didn't have to buy one. These days they were busily decorating their home—in a most artistic manner, no doubt—and rather than go out evenings they were inviting groups of friends to come over and cook together. That was a big help to Madhuri.

That Sunday evening Sita, accompained by Projesh, rang
the bell at Qamar's building. He came running downstairs,
all smiles, and led them up to the flat on the second floor,
where Madhuri greeted them in her drawing room. Sita
and Projesh sat down on a divan under a large painting
that Projesh had given the couple as their wedding present.
Sita could see that success had changed Qamar a great
deal. He appeared more confident, and didn't pose or brag
as much as he used to. As he chatted with the guests he
would often turn and look at Madhuri with much affection. Madhuri apparently had quite an effect on him. Evi-
dently she had been busy trying to rid him of his bohemian ways.

Qamarul Islam Chowdhry was now a successful, prosperous and famous man; he was also happy and satisfied.
('How nice it is to be successful!') Now he was talking quite
casually about his British and American publishers, and
Sita saw that his words were not vain or self-glorious. ('So,
success also teaches one to be modest!') In a few days he
was to go to Moscow, then on to East Berlin where his new
play was to be staged. Just recently he had finished his
first novel, but he was in no hurry to get it published. His
collection of poems had already brought him enough
fame, he didn't care for more. ('Success makes a man content too.')

The doorbell rang and Satish Gopal and Jennifer Crane
came in. Jennifer gave a shout when she saw Sita and enclosed her in her immense arms. "Darling! What a surprise! It's been ages. How are you? I'm now Mrs. Gopal.
And you?"

Satish Gopal said "Namaste" to Sita. She had met him
once before at Bilqis'. He was a good-natured, friendly
Punjabi boy, who worked in the Ministry of Information
and Broadcasting and wrote verses in Urdu.

"So you haven't given up your project to look into the
soul of India?" Sita asked Jennifer as they settled down on
cushions around the low, Japanese style table for dinner.

"No. After I was through with Bengal, I felt I must go on to Punjab," Jennifer replied smugly, making herself comfortable on the floor.

"India has many states, Jennifer dear. You've quite a few more to go."

"Lord help me!" Jennifer raised her eyes to the ceiling in mock horror.

"Sita-ji," Satish was speaking to her. "Qamar Sahib insists that I should translate his novel into Urdu. Have you read it?"

"No, not yet."

Qamar immediately got up and brought the manuscript.

"The name is very good," Projesh remarked, glancing at the cover, *"The City of Clouds."*

When they moved back into the drawing room, Qamar sat down near Sita with the manuscript. "Some day I'll read this to you myself." he said, "Would you like that, Sita? Do you remember that stormy night in New York when you had come to me and I wasn't able to say anything to you? You remember that? I have written the account of that night in here, with my blood," he added in a whisper.

Sita looked at him with some disgust. ('You play with human beings so you can write successful novels about them!')

Jennifer was in the kitchen, helping Madhuri with the coffee; the two were laughing about something. Satish was sitting on the floor near a bookcase, examining the books; now he turned to say something to Qamar.

For a moment Sita's head reeled. These bohemians—intellectuals—playing musical chairs with marriage—so untrustworthy—and also so untrusting. Suddenly she thought of Irfan, and felt completely miserable. Who knew where he was at that moment? Lahore? Peshawar? Or 'Pindi? He was right: it was as if she and Irfan lived on two different planets.

Before her train left Lahore, Irfan had said to Sita, "You think I'm totally unsentimental, don't you? But after you're gone I'll recite a couplet over and over and cry for you."

"Really? What couplet?" Sita asked enthusiastically.

"This one," Irfan replied, with equal enthusiasm. "*She came. She left. So long ago. Still she is here in my sight. / For there she strolls, and here she comes, and there again takes flight.*"

(9)

Several months went by . . .

One night, rather late, as Bilqis was on her way to the bathroom, the telephone rang. "This must be Sita," Bilqis said to Chhoti Khala, "Only she calls at such ungodly hours." She walked into the lounge and picked up the receiver. It was indeed Sita, calling from Hima's garden house.

"Bili? I'm leaving for Colombo tomorrow morning."

"Where? For Kuala Lumpur? For heaven's sake!"

"No. Colombo." Sita's voice sounded weak.

"But why?"

"I've just learned that Jamil is there on some U.N. work."

"So?"

"I'll go and beg him for the last time to let me have Rahul."

"That's a wild goose chase, Sita dear. In any case, why should you go there? Perhaps he'll come to Delhi too. I can't imagine he would go back without coming here, when he's so close. But he didn't write us anything about this trip to Colombo. . . ."

"He's there for just one week; then he'll go to Jakarta and from there directly back to New York. I called the U.N. Information Office and got all the details."

"And you expect to catch him in Colombo?"

"Yes. I'm sure of that."

"My God, Sita, you're becoming more and more mysterious every day. How very resourceful you are! And who is going to help you in Colombo?"

"That gentleman of yours is also there these days.

There's some conference going on."

"And who is my gentleman?"

"Irfan, of course."

"How do you know he's there?"

"I . . . Because he wrote me."

"I see. So you've been corresponding with him! You're really something, Sita darling. If, God forbid, I had been thinking of marrying him, I'd have come right over to challenge you to a duel. . ."

"But because I know you're not planning to marry him, I saw no harm in answering his letters," Sita quickly explained.

"Oh . . . don't be a bore! I was only joking." Bilqis replied. "Now you've got me worried about you. Cheer up, will you?"

"So . . . yes . . . you see, Irfan Sahib is very sensible. I'll ask him—in your name—to make Jamil change his mind. In Pakistan he had promised to help me." Then she added, "In any case, I'm tired after working constantly for close to two years. I need some rest."

"There are plenty of restful places in India, Sita dear. Go to Kashmir . . . or to Kerala. There's no sense in wasting money to go so far away. And what do you mean, 'In my name'?"

"Well, Irfan is your family friend after all."

"Secondly," Bilqis continued, "Jamil Bhai is likely to become more stubborn. He doesn't like others to interfere in his life. You don't know his temper, Sita. I know, I'm his sister."

"But I'm his wife, Bilqis."

"For heaven's sake!" Bilqis exploded. "It's useless to talk sense to you, Sita. Who are you trying to fool? Why don't you come out and say that you are going there to see Irfan? You can't go possibly to Pakistan, for that's not easy . . . and might also be awkward with us."

"Bilqis!!" Sita shouted back. "Why are you talking to me like that?"

"Because you're becoming more foolish by the day. And because when people talk about your latest scandal we feel embarrassed."

"Goodnight!" Sita banged the receiver down.

"Who were you having a fight with?" Hima asked sweetly from her bedroom, where she was rocking her baby to sleep.

"I knew all of you would gang up on me one day," Sita said bitterly, and, grabbing her purse, stomped out of the gallery.

(10)

"I salute Vani and Vinayaka who created words and their meanings. I salute Valmiki and Hanuman and Bhavani and Shankara. I salute Rama and Sita. Hari-Hara, who causes this world to appear real, just as a rope appears to be a snake; Hari-Hara, whose feet are a sheltering boat in which one can cross the ocean of *samsara*, of birth and death, whose face is like an elephant's and who can burn to ashes all the evils of the Kaliyuga—may that Supreme Lord have mercy on me.

"May the lotus-like blue god who floats on the ocean of milk have mercy on me. . . My eyes shall gain eternal light from the dust wiped from the feet of Guru Ramananda. . . The nature of saints is like the flowers of the cotton plant: soft, dry and white. . . My Guru is like the holy city of Prayag embodied—from him flows the Ganges of devotion to Rama—he is Dhyana, he is Saraswati. . . The story of Hari . and Hara is like the confluence of three sacred rivers. . . Dharma is like a mighty banyan tree. . .Those who have evil in their hearts are destructive like Ketu, they are like Kumbhakarna. . .Creator and creature, wealth and poverty, king and beggar, Kashi and Magadha, Ganga and Karmanash, Marwar and Malvah, Brahmin and butcher— the Vedas have told us the difference between them. . . I write only the truth on this white paper. . . The precious wood from Malaya—no one calls it mere wood. On a full-

moon night when the raindrops of Sharada fall into an
oyster they become pearls.

"I salute the holy town of Ayodhya and I salute the sacred Saryu river. . . Sita and Rama are one, like word and
meaning, like water and wave. . . Devotion to Raghupati is
like the season of rains, and the devotees of Rama are like
flourishing paddy. . . The letters in the word 'Rama' are
like the joyous months of the rains; sincere devotion is
the forest in which Rama and Sita dwell; intelligent questions are boats and their answers expert boatmen; and
Rama's words are the safe and firm ghats where boats find
safe haven.

"Manu was the father of mankind; his grandson a devotee of Hari. Manu and his wife gave up their kingdom and
throne and took to the jungles as ascetics. The husband
and wife traversed the jungles as if Faith and Wisdom themselves were their companions. As they walked they repeated, *Om namo Vasudevaya*, till they reached the banks
of the Gomti. There they did worship for thousands of
years. Then the Lord of the World said to them, 'I am
pleased with you. Ask what you will.' Manu said, 'Lord, I
want a son who is like you.' The Lord replied, 'There can
be none like me, for I am without a second. But I will myself come down to earth in the form of your son. . .'"

"Hima! O, Hima!" Amma stuck a finger between the
pages of the *Ramayana* to mark the place, and called to
Hima. "Has Sita left? You should at least have given her
something to eat."

Hima didn't answer. She had locked her bedroom door
and was trying to put her baby to sleep. The entire Garden House was wrapped in silence. Shahzad had not yet
come back from New Delhi. Amma put on her glasses again
and began to read.

"During the reign of King Satyaketu's son, Pratapbhanu,
rivers of milk flowed through the land. He was a king, both
kind and brave. One day King Pratapbhanu went hunting
in the hills of Vindhyachala and there in pursuit of a hand-

some wild boar he arrived at a cave. A prince, disguised as
a yogi, lived in that cave. He had once opposed the King
and after being defeated had become his mortal enemy.
The King didn't recognise him. The false yogi said to the
King, 'My name is Ektanu. Since the time of creation I
have lived in just this one body, for I have gained great
powers through my ascetic acts.' The good-natured King
said to him, 'Guru, bless me so that my kingdom and I will
last forever.' That cunning man replied, 'This can happen
only if you succeed in propitiating the Brahmins, for the
Brahmins can curse and destroy the power of anyone they
wish. You must hold a banquet for one hundred thousand
Brahmins and serve them the food I shall prepare, then
they will fall under your command.'

"With the help of the false yogi, the King held his banquet, but when the Brahmins sat down to eat a voice thundered out from the heavens: 'Don't even touch this food; it
contains a Brahmin's flesh.' The wrathful Brahmins cursed
the King that he would be born a demon in his next birth.
Then the heavenly voice spoke again: 'Brahmins, you have
been hasty in your curse; the King is blameless in this matter.' But the curse of the Brahmins, once declared, could
not be revoked. So the King was born as a demon in his
next birth. He had ten heads and twenty arms, and he was
extremely brave and bold. His name was Ravana. And the
King's minister was reborn as his step-brother, Vibhishana,
who was a devotee of Vishnu and very wise.

"Then Ravana performed countless ascetic deeds.
Brahma was pleased with him and asked him to name what
he wanted as reward. Ravana said, 'I want to be invincible
against gods.' leaving out human beings and monkeys in
his pride. Brahma blessed him and granted him his wish.

"On a mountain in the middle of the ocean, Mai built a
mighty fort which was more brilliant than Amaravati, the
city of Indra. It was called Lanka. Surrounded on four sides
by deep waters, it had walls of gold studded with jewels.
Ravana made Lanka his capital and began living there with

great pomp. Now he had everything he desired: wealth, sons, comfort, armies, glory, power, intelligence—every- thing.

"Then, intoxicated with his might, Ravana declared war against all created beings. The whole world submitted to him and all goodness disappeared from the face of the earth.

"One day the Lord of the Universe said: 'Ages ago I promised Kashyapa and Aditi to grant them a boon. Now I shall be born in the Suryavanshi clan and my name shall be Rama.'

"There reigned in the city of Ayodhya the Raghuvanshi king Raja Dasharatha. A devotee of Lord Vishnu, he was a master of the Vedas and was renowned for his wisdom and piety."

A car came up the drive and stopped. Shahzad strolled in, whistling a tune. His steps resounded through the gal- lery then were muffled by the thick carpet in his bedroom.

Amma flipped several pages, then began to read again.

"When the two princes arrived outside that lovely city where countless other princes had set up their camps be- side the river, Vishwamitra said, 'Raghu, we shall stay here.'

"When the King of Mithila heard that Maharishi Vishwamitra had arrived, he himself came out to greet him. The King said, 'Maharaj, these two most handsome boys with you—of whom one is fair and the other dark—please tell me who they are. It seems as if the Absolute Being described in the Vedas as Niti has made Himself manifest in this Duality.' Vishwamitra replied, 'These brave and vir- tuous brothers are Rama and Lakshmana.'

"Then the women of the city gathered behind window screens and said to each other: 'That dark-complexioned and lotus-eyed young man who carries bow and arrows in his mighty hand is Kaushalya's son Rama; and the fair- skinned boy who walks behind him is his devoted brother and Sumitra's son Lakshmana. They have come here to watch the contest of the Breaking of the Bow.'

". . . When Sita Gauri came into the flower garden to perform *puja*, Rama heard the sound of her anklets and raised his eyes. His eyes became transfixed on Sita's face the way the moon gazes down at the *chakora* bird. Lakshmana said, 'Brother, she is Sita, Janaka's daughter, and it is with the hope of gaining her hand in marriage that all the princes are contesting to break the Bow.'

"From where she stood among flowering trees, Sita glanced at Rama and was transfixed, the way the *chakora* bird is transfixed when it sees the winter moon. She bade Rama to enter her heart through her eyes, then closed her eyes.

"When Rama returned to Ayodhya after marrying Sita . . . ."

"Amma !" Hima stood at the door. "Anand just goes on crying. Please come. . . ."

"Daughter, you never let me sit in peace to do my reading of the scriptures."

Amma got up grumbling and, book in hand, shuffled over to Hima's room. She sat down on the bed, placed Anand on her lap and propped the book against one knee; then rocking the child to sleep, she said, "All right, now you listen, too. You won't be so fussy once you hear the good name of Rama." Then she began to read some more *chaupai*s.

"Dasharatha's mind was like a forest in which pleasure whirled around like a happy bird. But now, like a Bhil huntress, Kaikeyi was to let loose the falcon of her cruel words. She said, 'Maharaj, you once promised to grant me any boon that I wished for. And Suryavanshi kings never go back on their word. Now please grant me this one boon: place my son Bharata on your throne instead of Rama, and send Rama into exile into the forest for fourteen years.'"

The child slapped at the book with his tiny hand and knocked it away. Amma picked it up and started to read where it had fallen open.

". . . Walking between Rama and Lakshmana, Sita appeared like Maya between the Absolute Being and the human soul. Crowds of rishis walked with Rama through the dark forest, and Rama didn't stop until they reached Chitrakuta on the bank of the Mandakini river."

"Amma?" Uma Jiji called from the dining room, "Amma, Bishan Singh wants to know what should be cooked for lunch tomorrow."

Anand had fallen asleep. Laying him down on his bed, Amma went to the dining room, grumbling. On her way back, she looked in on him; then she went off to her own room. After a while Hima came out of the bathroom, and began to rub cold cream on her face in preparation for bed. Just then Amma called, "Hima! Come here."

"Yes, Amma," Hima replied, coming out into the gallery.

Amma was lying on her bed, her hands covering her eyes. "Don't go to bed already," she said.

"Yes, Amma."

"My eyes hurt. Come, sit with me, and read to me the good name of Rama."

"Yes, Amma." Hima sighed, and like a dutiful daughter pulled a chair close to the bed. "Where should I start?"

"Just anywhere . . . read me the story of the exile."

"Okay."

"When Rama, whose skin had the lovely hue of a raincloud, reached the bank of the Godavari, Lakshmana said to him, 'Brother, tell me about knowledge and renunciation and about Maya. . .'"

"Skip that."

"Unhh! . . . Okay . . . 'Anasuya said . . ,' shall I read that?"

"Yes . . . read that part," Amma said, and changed sides to make herself more comfortable.

"Anasuya said, 'Listen, Princess, mother, father and brother are one's friends and benefactors, but the happiness they provide is limited. The happiness that comes from the company of one's husband is boundless. It's a base woman who doesn't honour her husband. Courage, principles, friends and wife, these four are tested when things go wrong. If the husband is old or sick or senile, or if he is blind or foul-tempered or caught in dire straits—if in such circumstances his wife doesn't show him respect, she will burn in hell. According to the Vedas and the Puranas, there are four ranks of women. The best of them is she who regards her husband as the only man alive in the entire world. In the second rank stands that woman who regards all men, other than her husband, as fathers, brothers and sons. . . . The worst woman is she who is virtuous only because she never had an opportunity to be otherwise. . . .'"

"Skip that." Amma said.

" . . . One day Ravana's sister, Surpanakha, came to the bank of the Godavari and caught a glimpse of the two princes. O Garuda, when a woman sees a handsome man she crumbles like a sandy pebble before the burning rays of the sun . . ."

"Skip that."

" . . . When Lakshmana became enraged and sliced off Surpanakha's nose. . . . Shall I read from there?"

"Hunnh."

" . . . she returned crying to her demon brothers. They got together an army of fourteen thousand demons and set out to punish Rama and Lakshmana.

"At the time, jackals were howling in the jungle. The demons and evil spirits made piles of skulls. Then male demons made drums out of the skulls and female demons began to dance to their rhythm. Surpanakha said to her brother. . . ."

"Skip that . . . start from where Sita is abducted."

" . . . Then the Satwanti Sita saw a golden deer running through the forest. 'Nath,' she said, 'Please hunt down that deer and bring me its skin.' Raghupati understood who that deer was, but in order to fulfill the wish of the

gods he picked up his bow and arrow. He said to
Lakshmana, 'Brother, there are demons prowling in the
forest. Use your intelligence and your bravery to protect
Sita.' When the golden deer saw Rama it fled swift as the
wind, but Rama pursued it and was led very far away. . . .

"When Rama's arrow struck the golden deer it let out a
loud shriek. Sita heard the sound; she trembled with fear
and said to Lakshmana, 'Brother, your brother is in
trouble. He whose mere glance caused the creation of the
Universe, is now himself caught in danger. You must rush
to his help.' And Lakshmana ran to look for Rama in distress. . . .

"Then Ravana arrived at Sita's hut in the guise of a yogi;
forcibly lifting her to his shoulder, he started off for his
own palace. Then Sita cried out, 'Raghurai . . . Raghurai
. . . Rahgurai. . . .'"

Hima was beginning to feel drowsy. She rubbed her eyes
and looked at Amma to see if she had fallen asleep, but
Amma's eyes were devotedly half-open, and one foot
moved gently to the rhythm of the poetry. She must have
heard and sung these *chaupais* thousands of times but still.
. . . Hima yawned in boredom and started reading again.

"Then Ravana placed Sita on his chariot and swiftly flew
through the air. Sita moaned and cried like a frightened
doe caught in the net of a hunter. As they flew across the
sky she saw a horde of monkeys sitting on a hill below;
uttering the name of Hari, she threw down to the monkeys the cloth that covered her hair. Then Ravana took
her to his capital, Lanka, and made her a prisoner in a
forest of ashoka trees. . . ."

Hima paused again to yawn; she looked at her mother,
hoping perhaps she would now tell her to stop.

"Now read the *chaupais* about Hanuman-ji," Amma
calmly ordered, her eyes still only half-closed.

"Okay, Amma." Hima sighed, and continued.

". . .The monkeys made a bridge to reach Lanka, and
Raghuraj came and stood on it and looked out over the

sea. Then all the creatures of the sea came to the surface
to have a *darshana* of Raghuraj, and there was such a mul-
titude on the bridge that the monkeys had to take to the
air. . . .

" . . . When they reached the shore the monkeys stuffed
themselves with all the fruit they could find. ['How sweet!'
Hima said with a chuckle. 'Unnh!' Amma frowned.] Then
they broke off rocks from the mountains and started throwing them towards Lanka. . . .

" . . . there lay Lanka in front of them . . . its cities of
gold . . . its bustling markets and streets . . . its elephants
and horses . . . its war chariots and armies of demons . . .
its jungles and arbors . . . its lakes and ponds . . . and its
bewitchingly beautiful women, daughters of humans,
snakes and *gandharvas*. When Hanuman saw the invincible
fortifications of Lanka, he fixed his mind on the image of
Narasimha; then he changed himself into the form of a
mosquito and entered Lanka. When the demoness Lankini
saw Hanuman, she challenged him, but Hanuman knocked
her down with one blow and . . . ."

(11)

"Whoom . . . whoom . . . whoom . . ." The engines slowed
and the plane made a smooth landing at Colombo's
Ratmalna Airport. Otherwise it had been a very rough flight
all the way from Madras. After disembarking, Sita immediately telephoned the headquarters of the Colombo Plan.

"No, I'm sorry there is no Mr. Kazmi here. Perhaps he is
in some other office. I can try to find out for you. Why
don't you call back in an hour?"

Sita felt her heart sink. What should she do now?

"Do you know the U.N. office here?" she asked the taxi
driver.

The taxi stopped before an impressive building. 'Jamil
must be in there somewhere, busily working at his desk . . .
suppose he comes out just now . . . what will I do then?'

She felt terribly scared and asked the driver to take her to Mount Lavinia Hotel.

It was a gorgeous day in Colombo. The dense trees with red flowers lining the roads, the groves of coconuts, the waves in the sea—they all seemed enchanted, gilded by the sun. Scores of Europeans and Americans were sunbathing on the beach below the hotel. A strange lassitude thickened the air.

Sita opened the window in her room and looked out. Not far away was the ocean, its surface roiled by choppy waves. On the beach a group of dark-skinned Sinhala ayahs were busy taking care of some European children. A Sinhala woman passed under Sita's window hawking coral strings, her hair decorated with brilliant flowers. "Beads, madam?" she called, looking upward, "Very nice beads. . . ."

Sita gently closed the window, then walked over to the dressing table. 'What's going to happen now?' she asked herself, looking in the mirror.

An hour later there was a knock on the door. A bearer dressed in a white sarong came in and presented a card on a tray: Irfan Ahmad Kazmi.

"Oh! Thank you . . . thank you."

The old Sinhala bearer smiled affectionately. Sita hurriedly fixed her hair and followed him downstairs. There, on the terrace, was Irfan, sitting under a colorful umbrella, talking with someone. He got up when he saw Sita.

"Mr. Ratansinha Jaisurya," he introduced his Sinhala companion. "Mrs. . . . er . . . Dr. Mirchandani."

"Mr. Jaisurya is an important newspaper editor in Colombo, and also an old friend of mine." Irfan added.

Sita folded her palms together with a smile. The three sat down. Not feeling quite at ease, Sita looked around. The middle-aged Mr. Jaisurya was looking at her with curiosity. At the end of his conversation with Irfan he invited both of them to join him later for dinner, then took his leave. Irfan leaned back in his chair and lit a cigarette.

"So . . . you've arrived," he said.

"Yes."

That was an extremely casual exchange for a meeting after such a long time.

"You never wrote me why you were suddenly descending upon this place," Irfan began in that half-mocking tone, "I decided you, too, were coming here to attend some conference or other. After all, Colombo is the city for international meetings."

"How could I write you everything in a letter," Sita replied. "In any case, you know the whole story."

"The fact of the matter is, I don't know anything about you."

Sita's heart sank a little, but she recovered quickly. "How did you find out that I was in this hotel?"

"Because I'm staying here too. You know you didn't even write me the date of your arrival. But I didn't have much trouble locating you."

"Have you seen Jamil?" Sita couldn't hold back any longer.

"Is Jamil here too?" he asked, pressing the stub of his cigarette in the ashtray. "So you've come to see him? You're certainly full of surprises." Suddenly he looked very disappointed.

"Why, what did you think? You thought I had come all the way just to have your *darshan*?" Sita asked with a laugh. "You certainly have high hopes."

All of a sudden the air cleared of all tension. Irfan also began to laugh.

"You should go and talk to him . . . today . . . right now. You can find out from the U.N. office where he's staying," suggested Sita.

"Who knows—he might be staying in this very hotel."

Sita turned pale. Then she began to talk rapidly, "You should talk to him . . . ask him about Rahul . . . about giving Rahul to me . . . ask him to please see me just once . . . just once."

Irfan was taken aback. To cover his surprise and anxiety he began to look in his pockets for cigarettes. "But I've never met him, Sita. How can I get so familiar with him so suddenly? I can't just walk in on him and stick my nose into such a private matter."

"But you promised. . . ."

"Yes, yes. I know I promised," Irfan didn't let her finish her sentence. "I'll go to him. But first let's think about it a bit. Here, have a cigarette. Relax."

"How can I relax?"

"That's true too." Irfan hung his head down in silence.

A group of rosy-cheeked Dutch Burgher girls walked by their table. One of the girls, wearing a blue dress, white lace gloves and a big picture hat, looked just like a painting by Gainsborough. The terrace was full of people: Sinhala and Tamil ladies in brilliant silk saris; men with glistening dark skins, dressed in expensive suits; very serious-looking Englishmen; boisterous and carefree Americans. Over there, away from the terrace, the sea was getting noisier.

"What are you doing this evening?" Irfan asked.

"Nothing."

"Come to Jaisurya's party."

"I haven't come here for social calls."

"You haven't come to do some kind of penance either."

'What sort of a man is he? How can he be so superficial? What's going to happen now?' Sita got up from her chair.

"Off some place?"

"Yes. To hell!"

"My goodness! Now you're angry. So quickly?"

'Will he also make that silly joke about the tigress and the kitten that Jamil used to tell on such occasions? Oh, my God, what's happening?'

Sita walked over to the terrace railing and watched the people on the beach. Then after a few moments, she turned around and looked at Irfan. "When are you going back?" she asked, changing the subject.

"I guess after a couple of weeks."

"Back to Lahore?"

"No. They've transferred me to Paris. I'll go first to Karachi, then a month later to Paris."

"How wonderful! Lucky you!"

"There's nothing particularly wonderful about going to Paris. And as for being lucky, that I have never been all my life."

"How long will you stay in Paris?"

"I don't know. Right now I'm going there for two years. Listen, if you're not coming to the party you'll have to excuse me. I still have to see several people at the conference. But don't worry; I shall soon get hold of your dear husband. Then I shall try to cultivate him . . . for your sake."

"It won't be hard work for you," Sita said somewhat bitterly. "I know how good you are at cultivating people."

Irfan began to laugh. "Now don't start getting angry again. Cheer up, will you? The conference starts early tomorrow morning. If I get a chance I'll phone you. Will you be coming down for breakfast?"

"I don't think so."

"O.K. I'll try to call you before I go to the conference hall. Good night."

"Good night."

Irfan strode away, down the terrace and into the hotel. Sita rested her head on the railing and gazed at the horizon where the sun had just set in the sea. A white woman in a bikini was running down the beach leaving a trail of laughter; she was being pursued by a panting white man with a paunch.

The next day, when Sita returned to the hotel in the afternoon after an aimless tour of the city, there was a note waiting for her at the reception counter. It was from Irfan: "Call me at this number. It's very important."

With a beating heart, Sita picked up the phone in her room and dialed the number. Irfan answered from his room.

"Listen, Sita. Don't get upset, but something awful happened last night. Jamil also came to Jaisurya's dinner. How-

ever, I didn't get to meet him. First he sat drinking by himself in a corner, then he joined the party but didn't exchange one word with anyone. Jaisurya told me that Jamil
was feeling so depressed because someone had told him
that his wife had run off with some Pakistani and was staying at the Mount Lavinia Hotel. Don't you think, Sita, that
Jamil is right to feel angry and hurt. After all, it's true. . ."

"What!"

"Isn't it true that you're staying at the Mount Lavinia
Hotel? Anyway, you understand why I couldn't talk to him
last night. In fact, I quietly slipped away even before dinner was over."

"What a coward!"

Irfan laughed. "I was joking. But you know it wasn't like
in some play by Agha Hashr. I couldn't just walk up to him
and say: 'Taufiq, wherefore this rage?' 'The lion is caught
in a cage!' I'm sure I'll find some better occasion to speak
to him in a couple of days. Jamil seems to be a difficult
person. Not at all like the other members of his family.
Listen, several people at the dinner asked me who that
beauty was I was having tea with on the terrace. You know
how people like to gossip. It's human nature; it can't be
changed. Now I must go back to the conference, but later
on in the evening I can come to your room and give you
the whole story. It may be dangerous to meet you downstairs, in public."

"No, you better call me after ten tonight."

"O.K."

But he didn't call. The next day she was walking down
the steps that led to the hotel garden, when he came running from the lobby.

"I'm terribly sorry, Sita," he said in a hurry, "but again I
came back very late. Listen, I'm meeting Jamil today for
lunch." They had stopped under a Gulmohar tree. "Sita,
there is a place here called St. Michel—it's an island in a
lake, with a restaurant. Come there this evening. I shall
meet you there and submit a full report."

"There won't be anyone there from India or Pakistan?" she asked rather nervously.

"I don't think so. No Indian or Pakistani would go that far out of the way. Most of them like to spend their evenings at the nightclubs in the city. You should get there by six o'clock."

"By myself?"

"For heaven's sake! You've travelled all over the world by yourself. . . ."

"Okay . . . okay." Sita quickly agreed.

Irfan turned around and strode off down the garden path.

The taxi passed through the suburbs of Colombo, and took a highway that had tall and dense groves of trees on both sides. It then entered a forest and followed a twisting and turning road to the shore of a lake. There were already a number of other cars parked under the trees. Sita got out of the taxi and went down the steps to the boat-house, where a small boat was waiting for the patrons of the restaurant. The empty boat-house with its thatched roof, was lit only by a lantern, whose red light cast an aura of mystery over everything. Sita waited. Finally a small party of Tamil men and women arrived, followed by the boatman. Everyone clambered aboard; the noisy engine was started; and the boat began to move toward the island in the middle of the lake. There was no other sound except the loud "phutt, phutt" of the engine. The groves of sandal-wood and coconut hugging the lake's shore were silent. The sky had turned a purplish red. Then the strings of lights on the island of St. Michel were above them and the boat came to a stop at the pier.

Sita followed the long wooden walkway that led to the main building of the restaurant. Colourful Japanese lanterns had been hung over the walkway. Here and there scattered couples or small groups of people stood talking. Inside, in the main hall, a handful of Sinhala Catholic boys and girls were dancing to the melancholy music being played by a small orchestra. A Dutch Burgher girl was at the microphone singing:

O, come along with me
To my little corner of the world,
And dream a little dream
In my little corner of the world.

It was all too sad and depressing.

Sita looked around. There was no sign of Irfan. She walked down some wooden steps, to the other side of the tiny island where, at a distance, a small wooden pavilion stood in the lake on some poles. A narrow bridge linked it to the island. Sita walked across the bridge and entered the pavilion. It was deserted except for a Sinhala couple who stood leaning over the railing at the other end, gazing into the gently rolling waves of the lake. The sun sank; the surface of lake first turned deep crimson, then changed into the darkness of night.

"Sita!"

She turned. It was Irfan, walking towards her from a table far away in one corner.

"You didn't see me. I was sitting over there."

They sat down close to the railing. Sita leaned over to look at the waves. "This place is so beautiful."

"Yes, it is." Irfan agreed. "But now listen to this."

"Yes?" Sita raised her eyes to look at him. Irfan was trying to appear very business-like. They could hear the singer's voice as it wafted to them from the speakers in the restaurant:

You will soon forget
that there is any other place.
And if you care to stay
in my little corner of the world,
Then we can hide away
in my little corner of the world.

"A lot has happened since yesterday," Irfan began, after lighting a cigarette. "The news has spread that you're here. And you'll agree that the fact that you're here when Jamil is here too, must cause suspicion. Also, strangely enough, people are casting me as the nasty rival. It's become quite a mess. Why didn't you think of that, Sita? Now everyone has a nice juicy gossip to enjoy after the conference sessions. Worse, given the present problems between India and Pakistan, this development is most disconcerting. Some people are totally convinced that I actually lured you away from Jamil and am keeping you under cover at the Mount Lavinia."

"How dreadful!" Sita shivered. "What will happen now?"

"The relations between India and Pakistan will get worse," Irfan said with a laugh. "A real crisis might develop, requiring our Foreign Minister to issue a statement. Questions will be raised in your parliament. There will be headlines. Just wait and see. As the poet has said: 'It's only the beginning of love now. . . .'"

"Must you make a joke of everything?" Sita interrupted him. "I want you to tell me what I must do."

"But why did you come here? If you were so anxious to meet Jamil you should've gone to New York."

"And who would have paid for the plane ticket? You?" Sita replied with some heat.

"I couldn't meet Jamil Sahib at lunch," Irfan continued. "He never came. Finally I decided to risk my neck and went over to his hotel in the afternoon with Jaisurya. Jamil was in his room, getting drunk. I sent in Jaisurya to tell Jamil that I wanted to see him . . . so that I could explain the matter and remove his doubts. When Jaisurya came out he told me that Jamil had said: 'Tell Irfan, if he loves his life he should stay away from me. Otherwise I'll give him a thrashing worse than I gave Qamrul Islam Chowdhry in New York.'"

A cold gust of wind blew through the pavilion. Sita tucked her hair under the wrap of her sari.

"Do you realise," Irfan said, slowly measuring out each word. "Do you realise you have burned your boats? It's not just Qamrul . . . Jamil has also heard about you and Projesh Chowdhry."

Sita turned pale. "Who told you that?"

Irfan didn't answer her question. "I worry about you all the time," he continued in a most serious voice. "Let me also tell you . . . and I hope it won't upset you, because though you try to be so adult about things, you never succeed . . . I'm very interested in you. And you know it. Perhaps you can't help it if people persist in taking interest in you. On the other hand, you don't break anyone's heart either . . . if you can help it."

"What you just said is so disgusting that I won't comment on it." Sita replied, struggling to stay calm. "I came to Colombo because I thought you were a friend."

"A friend! What the hell does that mean?"

In the stillness of the evening the music from the dance-hall could be heard clearly. The singer was repeating the song:

I always knew I'd find someone like you,
So welcome to my little corner of the world.

"It's getting rather late." Irfan abruptly stood up. "You better get back to Colombo. I'll come later. It's quite possible that we might be recognised here. Lots of people come to the restaurant. Good night!"

He didn't even bother to walk her to the bridge. She slowly walked across by herself and found her way to the walkway leading to where the boat was moored. As she passed the dance-hall, the Sinhala manager of the restaurant—who looked like a penguin in his dinner jacket—accosted her. "Miss, you're going back so soon? Won't you stay for dinner?" Sita hurried by him silently. Two Tamil ladies turned to look at her with curiosity. At the end of the walkway there was another Sinhala couple leaning over the railing. Their silhouette against the vast and silent night sky looked so tiny and helpless. Overhead a green and red Japanese lantern swung in the breeze. There was utter solitude all around.

Sita ran down the steps to the landing and got into the boat. There were some Russians, men and women, from the Embassy already seated in it. They all remained silent, as if they feared that any word would only destroy the magic of the place.

Next day Irfan stopped her in the lounge. "I tried to contact Jamil again today but he isn't willing to meet me. God knows what a mess you've got me into."

"I'm terribly sorry if I've got you into a mess," Sita replied, "I thought we were civilised people and could settle this entirely human issue on a civilised level."

"There you go again, spouting nonsense," Irfan retorted. "The next few days I'll be very busy with the conference. What will you do during that time? Perhaps you should go to Kandy for a week—that might end the gossip. I'll be free after next Tuesday; then we'll make some plans."

"But Jamil. . . ."

"Don't worry about him." Irfan didn't let her finish the sentence. "He's staying on for a week or more. But you should get out of here." He continued, "Find some American spinsters—the hotel is full of them—then join their tour party. You can lecture them as much as you want."

"Okay." Sita replied obediently.

"I'll check with the American Express and set up a first class tour for you right away." He walked over to the reception counter and began to dial a number.

(12)

Six-foot-three, blue eyed and tawny-haired, Dr. Leslie Vincent Marsh stopped his car in the porch of the rest-house, then turned his head to look back. He hoped to see the green Hillman which he had followed off and on all the way here from the outskirts of Colombo, and which had a most beautiful woman as its passenger. He was hoping she too would stop at this rest-house. But the gray, serpentine road cutting through the jungle remained empty.

He got out of the car and climbed the steps to the verandah. A waiter brought him a pot of coffee. After finishing his first cup, Leslie got out his typewriter and started work on his book, "The Impact of Communism on South Asia". He had promised to send the second chapter to a journal at Harvard and the deadline was too close for comfort. He still had to go to West Bengal and Kerala in India.

There were some other Western tourists relaxing on the verandah, sipping beer and reading newspapers. The garden in front was covered in bright red flowers. The sky was a brilliant blue. Leslie looked around and felt at peace. He took a deep breath and once again bent over the typewriter.

An hour later he was back on the empty, silent road, which had dense rubber-tree forests on both sides and bright yellow butterflies that fluttered over fragrant cardamom bushes. Near Kurunegala a huge rock resembling an elephant appeared on the horizon. The road began a slow ascent. The vista opened up and he could see groves of palm trees dotting the landscape. As Leslie drove through a small village market he saw the green car again. It stayed ahead of him for a while, then it stopped near a fruit stall and was left behind.

Leslie Marsh laughed at himself. He was being foolish. Why should the woman take any notice of him—wasn't he just another tourist travelling on the same road?

On the grassy paths leading off the metalled road he could see paper pinwheels spinning in the air. There were many Buddhist temples along the road. One of them had a white flag on its gate, indicating that its priest had recently died. He also caught a glimpse of an occasional Catholic church, built long ago by the Portuguese or the

Dutch. Then there were innumerable charming cottages strung along the road, with curtains fluttering in their windows.

Gradually the scene began to change, and emerald green hills spread themselves all around him. At Polonnaruwa, Leslie stopped at the rest-house on the banks of lake Parakrama Samudra. As he got out of the car he looked around expectantly, but she was not there.

In his room he washed, then came out to the glass-enclosed lounge that hung over the lake. There were huge yellow flowers stuck in the vases on the tables. Some tourists were sitting near the tall windows, sipping coffee and beer and making their usual chatter. Soft-footed and courteous Sinhala waiters were dancing attendance. As he entered the dining room a girl from the Tourist Department greeted him with folded hands.

"How long will it take me to see the ruins at Polonnaruwa?" Leslie asked.

"That depends on how interested you are," the girl replied with a smile.

"I'm an archaeologist."

"Oh! In that case you must also see Anuradhapura."

"I'm afraid I can't do that on this trip. Archaeology is only my hobby. I'm here to write a book on a totally different subject." Leslie got up to pull a chair for the girl. "Please sit and talk to me if you belong to some political party. Are you Tamil or Sinhala?"

"Tamil. But I don't belong to any political party. Now, if you'll excuse me, I have to go back to Colombo." She smiled again and walked away.

After lunch, Leslie came out on the verandah. There was a large map of Sri Lanka fixed to the wall, and another of Polonnaruwa. There was also a framed edict of Parakrama Bahu: "'Not a drop of rainwater should reach the sea without first being of use to mankind.' Parakrama Bahu."

Putting aside the manuscript on the impact of communism he took out a second manuscript and, making himself comfortable on the steps in front of the big map, started to take notes:

"Five hundred years before the birth of Christ, the Indian prince Vijay conquered Sri Lanka. The people who came with him were originally from Magadha—what is now Bihar—and were called Sinhala; that's how this island came to be called Sinhaladwipa, 'the island of lions'. Prince Vijay married the local queen. The original people of Sri Lanka were pre-Dravidian Australoids. These were the people who spread from central India, through Malaya and Java, on to Australia. Their capital city was called Lankapura. These were perhaps the people whom the Aryans of North India—out of their sense of racial superiority—called 'black demons' in their ancient epic *Ramayana*."

'Racial discrimination in Asia—"colour bar" of the East—I must do some more work on this topic,' Leslie jotted down in the margin. Then, lighting a Camel, he looked out over the surrounding lake. Finally, he managed to push away the memory of the woman in a purple sari, and returned to his notes.

"The contemporary tribal people in Sri Lanka are known as the Veddah; they are quite similar to the tribals of Orissa, and are the descendants of those early settlers of the fifth century B.C. Sinhala kings ruled over this island for 21 centuries. Anuradhapura was their capital. Ashoka's son, Prince Mahendra, was the first Buddhist missionary who came to Anuradhapura and converted the Sinhala king, Devanampiyatissa, to Buddhism. We find in the Bible the mention of a coastal city of Sri Lanka, from where peacocks and diamonds were imported for King Solomon and the Queen of Sheba.

"Sri Lanka remained under the influence of the Gupta and Maurya cultures until the eighth century, and in the ninth century came totally under the political and cultural domination of South India. To the East of the river Krishna were the kingdoms of the Cholas, the Pandyas and the

Keralas. Whenever there was a struggle for the throne in Sri Lanka the various claimants would seek help from these three kingdoms. In the eleventh century a Chola king defeated the king of Anuradhapura and annexed most of the island to his kingdom. He made Polonnaruwa his capital. But within the same century the Sinhala king, Parakrama Bahu, threw off the yoke of the South Indian king and established an independent state again.

"Anuradhapura, the old capital of Sri Lanka, flourished for 1300 years—longer than Rome, Carthage or Athens—then the jungle took over again.

"Parakram Bahu I, Sri Lanka's mightiest king, built magnificent auditoriums, stupas and temples. He created an extensive and elaborate irrigation system for the entire island which was so extraordinary that the king of faraway Kashmir requested the loan of some engineers. ('That was the first Colombo Plan,' Leslie said to himself.)

"Parakrama Bahu also created this amazing lake, this vast artificial sea." Leslie briefly lifted his eyes to gaze at the expanse of water before him, then looked at the edict posted on the wall: 'Not a drop of water should reach the sea without first being of use to mankind.'

"After him a decline set in." Leslie March continued with his notes. "And in time Polonnaruwa too disappeared under the ever spreading jungle."

Leslie looked at his watch. 'I'd better get started,' he thought, 'otherwise I won't be able to reach Sigiriya before nightfall.' Stuffing the books and papers into his briefcase, Leslie came out of the resthouse. A few feet away, on a low mound, stood the monumental statue of Parakram Bahu—it had been carved by Sinhala craftsmen nine hundred years ago. Standing in its shadow Leslie felt very humble. 'Who am I, Leslie Vincent Marsh from far away New England, to think that I can instruct the East on civilization?' he asked himself. 'That only I have the cure for all the ills of the East? That the East has no right to cure its ills on its own?'

A dark-skinned young Veddah, with ragged hair and dirty teeth, stood near the statue looking at Leslie with a greedy smile. Perhaps he was expecting some baksheesh. Leslie felt that the Veddah was the spirit of these ancient forests—a spirit that lurked in these green mountains, in this vast expanse of water and this red stone statue; a spirit which had suddenly manifested itself from out of the dark unconscious of the 'modern' world to mock him.

Leslie grabbed his camera and walked away into the forest where magnificent tall trees towered over widely scattered ancient ruins of red sandstone, and where the only sound was the rustle of the branches high above. He was seated on the moonstone of the Pavilion of Columns, adjusting the focus of his camera, when he saw that woman again. She was going down the other set of steps, towards the Fifty Room Palace of Parakrama Bahu. Leslie rushed after her. When she heard the sound of his feet, the woman turned to look.

"Hi!" Leslie said with a smile.

"Hi." She, too, smiled.

Leslie fell in step with her. "This is such a beautiful island," he said.

"Yes," the woman in the purple sari replied, "It says in our sacred book, the *Ramayana*, that the green and gold Lanka was like a garden in paradise."

"And I love this kind of architecture," said Leslie, pausing before the palace. "I feel so humble whenever I come to Asia."

"Have you seen the temples of South India?"

"Yes, I have. You're from India, aren't you?"

"I am. . . . Look over there, that's the Seven Palace Vihara. It was built by the queen Rupavati. I just looked it up in the guidebook."

"My name is Leslie Marsh; I teach at Harvard."

"Sita Mirchandani. I was a student at Columbia in 1954."

"Is it Mrs. Mirchandani?"

"Mirchandani is my maiden name."

"Do you know that I followed you here all the way from Colombo, but you never once turned back to look."

"I thought Harvard people were very serious and proper."

"That's a big joke. Did you know an Edward Marsh at Columbia, in the English department? He's my younger brother."

As they wandered through the ruins they talked about people and places in the States. He was from the same sort of background as the people she had lived with for several years, the years that had been the best in her life. Perhaps that was the reason she felt so strangely close to this brash stranger.

"I teach Political Science at Harvard, but Archaeology and Anthropology are my favorite subjects. I'm here to write a book. Are you also writing a book?"

"Oh no," Sita said hurriedly, and changed the subject. "Look, that's the lotus-shaped pool where the queens used to bathe. The guide book says that it was filled with water from the Parakrama Samudra through subterranean channels."

They took their time looking at all the monuments, all the ruined statues and palaces and temples: the Lanka Tilak Temple; the Chetavan Vihar; the Stupa of Rani Rupvati; the Keri Vihar built by Queen Subhadra, the consort of Parakrama Bahu; the numerous minor temples in the South Indian style; the immensely tall figure of Gautama made of bricks, in a temple that had lost its roof; the reclining Buddha sprawled on gray stones amidst tall grass—it showed Gautama in the state of parinirvana and at its head stood the doleful figure of Ananda, the faithful attendant, mourning the passing away of his Master. There was also a large terrace dominated by a statue of the Buddha in the 'lotus position', in front of the statue were some trees whose branches were covered with strips of white cloth tied there by visiting devotees seeking boons. Leslie and Sita watched as some Sinhala women came and prostrated themselves before the sublimely smiling Buddha. They looked at the carvings of peacocks and elephants and swans in the brackets and reliefs. Leslie was overwhelmed.

"Just look at that 'Seven Palace Prasada!'" Leslie exclaimed. "They could build a seven-storied palace in those days! I just can't believe it."

"Tulsidas has written in his *Ramayana* that the palaces of Lanka were built by Vishwakarma himself in order to please the god of wealth, Kubera," Sita said.

"What? Say that again." Leslie quickly opened his notebook.

Sita began to laugh. "And you should also note that Vishnu had built a city of magic in which Princess Vishnu Mohini lived." She sat down on the stump of a column.

Leslie closed his notebook. "May I tell you something?" he asked, "When I read the story of the *Ramayana* I wondered what Sita looked like."

"And now you have seen her?" she queried with a laugh.

'Oh, it's all so absurd,' she thought.

On their way back they saw the majestic stupa of Ranakot Vihar in the distance, its huge dome covered with plants and grass.

"How terrible!" Sita said, pointing toward the stupa. "Man is so helpless before nature."

"Yes," Leslie replied, intently watching her face, "You're absolutely right."

Arriving in front of the rest-house, Leslie said to Sita, "If you don't want me to follow you again, you should come in my car and tell your driver to follow me."

Sita spoke to the driver.

Leaving behind the ruins of Polonnaruwa, they returned to the main highway. Sita leaned her head back and closed her eyes. Last year she had been driving down a dusty road of Bahawalpur with Irfan. Now Irfan was in Colombo—as was Jamil. And here she was, going to Sigiriya with Leslie Vincent Marsh!

It turned dark very soon.

'Savitri* had said: The night is getting darker all around us.'The sun has long set. Night creatures are prowling everywhere, letting out howls of brutal laughter. Their feet make a loud noise on the leaves. There are jackals in the north-west, and their baying pounds my head like a hammer. My head . . . my head. . . .'

The rest-house at Sigiriya was wrapped in the silence of the night.

"Do you have a reservation?" Leslie asked, getting out of the car.

"Yes. . . ."

The manager of the rest-house stepped forward to greet them, "Your room is in that wing, Dr. Marsh, and. . . ."

"Fine. Thanks," and he strode off, swinging his briefcase, to the other wing.

Next morning, when Sita came out of her room, Leslie was on the verandah, busy typing.

"Good morning!" he raised his head to greet her.

"Good morning to you, professor." Sita replied and pulled a chair to sit near him.

He continued to type.

"What are you writing?"

Leslie pushed a pile of typed pages towards her.

"The Impact of Communism on South Asia." The second chapter was titled: "The Sri Lanka Freedom Party: A Fraud". Sita flipped a few pages with some annoyance, then dropped the manuscript on the table and began to look outside.

"From your remarks yesterday . . . I had thought you were a decent Democrat. . . ." she said after a few moments.

---

*In contrast to Sita, Savitri, the ideally faithful Hindu wife, after having rescued her husband, Satyavat, from the clutches of Yama, the god of death, had insisted that she and Satyavat should immediately return to his parents, and not linger in the jungle, even though Satyavat was not feeling too well.

Leslie closed his typewriter with a chuckle. "After our discussion yesterday I've decided I won't waste any more of these lovely moments discussing politics. Because once you start you don't let the other person say a thing, and that's only a waste of precious time. Anyway, beautiful girls like you shouldn't be too brainy."

Sita kept quiet, and followed him inside to the breakfast table.

After breakfast, she glanced at her watch and said, "Let's hurry and see Sigiriya."

"Why? What's the big hurry?" Leslie asked, lighting a cigarette. "I feel like staying here for a couple of days."

"But I have to be back in Colombo on Tuesday morning."

"Why? What's there to see in that colonial city built by the British?"

Sita didn't answer. She picked up his box of matches and began to form letters with the matchsticks. A very young Sinhala couple came into the room; it was obvious they were here on their honeymoon. The girl used the telephone on the counter to make a call to Colombo: Mamma? . . . yes, we're fine, very fine . . . the food? . . . yes, very fine . . . yes, I had a cup of Ovaltine last night. . . yes, Mamma, I'll send Ratna lots of picture postcards . . . now talk to George. . . .

"As you wish," Leslie finished his coffee and got up. "Let's go and see Sigiriya."

It took them a long time to climb to the top of Sigiriya's six-hundred-foot-high rockface. The wind was brisk, and a pale sun had faintly burnished the farmland spread below them. On the distant horizon they could see a range of dark blue hills.

As she surveyed the scene, Sita suddenly turned to Leslie and said, "A sense of guilt can be as hard and immobile— even as frightening—as the rock of Sigiriya."

"You know, sometimes your comments are so dense the listener could actually use some footnotes! Can you tell me where I should look for references for what you just said?"

Sita raised her eyes and gazed at him in silence.

'It's all so absurd . . . so absurd,' she thought.

They walked across a flat rock and reached the iron ladder that led up to the frescoes. Leslie stopped to look upward, shading his eyes with his hand. "What if one falls down from there?" Then he looked all around. "What was it that you just said about a sense of guilt?" he suddenly asked.

"It was nothing." Sita sat down on the low parapet.

"Do tell me . . . please," Leslie insisted.

"Last night I was reading the story of Sigiriya," Sita changed the subject. "In the fifth century Dhattusen was the king of Sri Lanka."

Leslie immediately pulled out his notebook and squatted down at her feet.

"Dhattusen had two sons," Sita continued, tucking the end of her sari in at her waist, "Kashyapa and Mogulna. And the king's daughter was married to the chief of the king's army. One day the princess told her father that her husband had struck her with a whip. Dhattusen was so angry that he had the mother of his chief burned alive. The chief, finding himself unable to attack the king directly, conspired with Kashyapa. Kashyapa rebelled against his own father, and had him buried alive.

"After Kashyapa became the king, Mogulna fled to India to save his life. But Kashyapa was pursued by his sense of guilt: he was convinced that the Goddess of Revenge would eventually punish him for his crime. And so that fear-ridden king began constructing his fort on this highest peak of Sigiriya. He built several palaces and tanks and pools and lived here, where he felt secure. But after eighteen years. . . ." Sita stood up and started climbing again.

Leslie also got up and, notebook in hand, followed her, intently listening to the story. "Careful!" he yelled, when Sita slightly stumbled on one step. "Please be careful! But do go on."

"After eighteen years, Mogulna returned from India with an army and right below this mighty rock he defeated his brother, who then committed suicide on the battlefield." Sita finished her story just as they reached an iron ladder.

On a ledge just before the top there was a narrow gallery, its walls painted with frescoes that looked like imitations of the ones at Ajanta.

"'Apsara, showering flowers.'" Leslie exclaimed. "I've seen it in reproductions so often, now I can't believe it's real."

"Have you seen the frescoes at Ajanta?"

"No. I'll try to see them this time." Leslie replied. "Just think how the artists must have risked their lives to paint these marvellous pictures."

"I don't know," Sita responded with a shrug. "After Ajanta these six or seven small paintings look rather silly to me. I must say I'm disappointed. All this climbing was for nothing." She opened her guidebook. "Let's go and look at the Wall of Graffiti."

Leslie was still engrossed in the paintings. Sita moved closer to him.

"I wonder how it would have looked if someone had painted a picture of you on some ancient rockface?" Leslie turned and looked at her intently. Then he added, wistfully, "Who knows who these girls were."

Sita pushed back a stray lock of hair from her forehead and softly said, "Vajralata, the princess of lightning . . . Meghalata, the princess of clouds . . . Heavenly dancers . . . Rambha . . . Menaka . . ."

They left the frescoes and found the Wall of Graffiti. Below them they could see the mighty statue of a lion; some tourists stepped out from between the lion's extended paws and started to climb the steps. The vast, menacing shadow of Sinhagiri lay over the fields far below.

"On this wall are preserved," Sita began to read from the guide book, "the scribblings of the visitors who came to Sigiriya several centuries ago. This wall is also called the Mirror Wall. There are six hundred and eighty sepa-

rate graffiti scratched on it by those early tourists. Some
of them are in the form of amusing verses.

"'Friend,' one of them goes, 'these pictures of golden
girls are now damaged. Their colours have faded. Is there
none alive now who loved them in their time?'

"Elsewhere, a woman has written: 'Listen, you fools, we
girls are addressing you. You who have come to Sigiriya
and do nothing but sing songs and compose poems. Have
you ever stopped to think that we are women and that we
need wine?'"

In Kandy, at the 'Chateau', Sita looked out of the window and saw the lake. It was surrounded by hills dotted
with mansions, whose red-tiled roofs could be seen above
thick, green clusters of palms. The hills also had long winding driveways that were shaded by flowering trees and were
named after the wives of various British Governors of yore:
Lady Horton, Lady Black, Lady McCallum. And there up
ahead, blocking the sky, was Bible Rock. The owner of the
'Chateau' was a Roman Catholic barrister, whose name was
partly Portuguese, partly Sinhala, and partly Tamil. The
walls of the drawing room downstairs were covered with
family photographs. The dining room upstairs had a big
portrait in oils of one of the ancestors. A plaque under
the painting had his name: Don Fernandes Da Costa Sa-
mara Sangharuna Mudaliar.

"I've seen these hybrid products in so many places, these
offsprings of the colonial East and the imperial West,"
Leslie remarked, as they sat down at the dining table. "You
can see them everywhere, from Goa to Hong Kong."

"Have you seen the dancers of Kandy?" Sita asked, un-
folding her napkin.

"Yes, I have. During the war I stopped here on my way
to Burma. In fact, we stayed in this very chateau. In those
days Kandy was the headquarters of Mountbatten's South
East Asia Command. . . ." Leslie fell silent and was lost in
thought for a few moments.

"What's the matter?" Sita asked, offering him the salad.

"Nothing," Leslie said hurriedly. "Nothing. I was badly wounded in Burma, you see, and was a POW for a couple of years. And two of my brothers were shot down over To-kyo—they were in the Air Force." Then he added, "My dear, war is a terrible thing."

"But now you want another war."

"Because, my dear, we must save your beautiful Asia from Communism."

Sita returned to her food silently.

Later, as they went downstairs after lunch, Sita said to Leslie, "Come, let's act like good tourists and visit the Temple of the Tooth."

By the time they got to the Temple, the most famous of all the sights in Kandy, the evening puja had started. Next to the temple was the wooden palace of Kandy's last king, Vikrama Rajasinha. In 1815, the British had dethroned him and taken control of Sri Lanka. The palace was now to-tally deserted. Leslie walked around volubly admiring its carved panels and decorations. Suddenly Sita remembered that in the museum in Colombo she had seen an exhibit containing the silk blouse of the queen of King Vikrama. There was a dark spot on that blouse, and the card under-neath had said: "When British soldiers were plundering the royal palace, one of them pulled off the earrings from the Queen's ears. This spot marks where her blood fell."

Sita thought: 'Rani Lakshmi Bai of Jhansi . . . Begum Hazrat Mahal of Lucknow . . . the Queen of Kandy. . . .'

Back at the 'Chateau', they didn't linger over dinner; afterwards Sita went off to her room. After three days, she was beginning to tire of talking to Leslie. Lying in her bed, she could hear the sound of his typewriter till late at night: perhaps he was working on the third chapter of "The Impact of Communism on South Asia".

Next morning they left Kandy. Outside the city, they saw many elephants being washed in the Mahavelli Ganga. Then they passed by the lovely red-stone buildings of the University, scattered over eternally green hills. Sita watched

the students. There were so many girls, soft-hued and delicate of face. Dressed in plain cotton saris, they seemed to
glide down the shaded pathways. 'Who knows what lies in
their fates?' Sita wondered, leaning back in her seat next
to Leslie. Once she, too, used to go to a university with
similar enthusiasm, tucking her books to her chest. Now
she felt she knew why the older ladies in her husband's
family responded to the greetings of young, unmarried
girls by saying: 'May Allah grant you a good fate.' She recalled how Bari Khala and Manjhli Khala and Chhoti Khala,
all three of them would respond to her greetings by saying: 'May you grow old in your marriage.' 'May you always
have sindur in the parting of your hair.'

Some distance out of Kandy, the mountains suddenly
began to get higher. There were no more clusters of palms;
now the mountainsides were covered with tall alpine trees.
Late in the afternoon they reached the hill station of
Nuwara Eliya—"the city of lights". The Grand Hotel, built
in the style of English country houses, was situated on a
hill laden with flowers. It was drizzling gently. The air was
filled with an intense fragrance of wild roses. And a western melody was softly wafting out of the hotel lobby.

"Fantastic!" Leslie exclaimed, sniffing the air he as
jumped out of the car. "Fantastic. I feel I've escaped the
hot and deadly spell of Asia once again, and am back in
my cold and safe West."

By the time Sita got out of the car and gathered her things,
Leslie had marched into the lobby and was talking with the
clerk at the counter. Sita came in and stood near him.

The clerk opened the register and looked questioningly
at Leslie, "A double room, sir?"

"Yes, please," answered Leslie.

"Your names please."

"Mr. and Mrs. Marsh."

The clerk wrote it down.

Leslie whispered to Sita, "You don't mind, darling, do
you?"

She didn't answer.

In the morning a dense fog covered the mountains. When it had finally burned away, Sita slipped on her robe; going to the window, she drew aside the curtains. Then she turned to look at Leslie.

"What's the program for today?" she asked.

"You tell me," Leslie replied, lathering his face before the dressing-table mirror, "I'm in your hands."

Sita turned away; pressing her nose to the chilly window-pane, she stared at the scene outside. There were patches of clouds floating by the peaks, and she could see several waterfalls in the distance. Leslie began to hum an old song.

At noon Leslie and Sita drove around in the surrounding mountains and came upon a small waterfall. "Will you stop here a minute?" Sita said. A short way from the falls was a small whitewashed temple. Sita got out of the car and set off towards the temple, scrambling over the scattered rocks. Grabbing his camera, Leslie followed her. The temple was at the edge of a cliff; down below rushed a mountain stream, foaming over hidden rocks. Hearing them arrive, a priest came out of the temple. He grinned with delight when he saw Leslie: how nice to see an American tourist—the god of wealth himself!

But Sita had found a passing Sinhala who, with an ivory comb stuck in his coiled hair, was telling her, "This is where Ravana brought Sita after abducting her, and kept her in isolation. When Hanuman came to rescue her he set fire to the entire mountain—that's why the ground here still looks burnt. And that's the temple of Sita Parameshwari. See that hole near the falls, madam? That's a tunnel. Through that tunnel they would bring Sita her meals from Ella. Ravana didn't live here; he lived in Ella, which is 38 miles from here."

"Good god!" Sita exclaimed, unable to stop her laughter. But Leslie carefully jotted it all down in his notebook.

"All this will be included in my chapter on popular beliefs," he confided to Sita. "I shall establish that, despite all your Communism, in all of Asia—in India, Ceylon, Pakistan, everywhere—common people are still totally devoted to their different religions. They put boundless trust in their ancient traditions. Just look at this poor Sinhala labourer. He's telling you with absolute confidence that Ravana used to live only 38 miles from here in Ella. That's the eternal power of the East. And, darling, neither your Indian Communist Party nor the terrorists in Burma, nor their fellow-travellers in Sri Lanka, can ever destroy it."

Sita was leaning over a rock to peek into the tunnel through which food was allegedly brought to Sita.

Leslie left her and went into the temple. There in semi-darkness he started to interview the priest. Then the priest put a tilak on Leslie's forehead which delighted him no end. With those red and white marks he looked quite foolish—a clown—a silly American. . . .

In that country house in Nuwara Eliya, in that room which had curtains with huge red flowers, Sita and Leslie spent four days and four nights, surrounded by the fragrance of wild roses and the music of distant waterfalls.

(13)

". . . Then Shri Hanuman went into the palace of the demon king but Sita was not there. There was another palace next to the first which had a temple of Hari. In that second palace lived Vibhishana, who was a devotee of Hari. He said to Hanuman: Here I live as circumspect and wary as is your tongue between your teeth. . . .

". . . Raghupati asked Lakshmana, 'Brother, you left the daughter of Janaka alone in the forest where demons are always prowling around?'

". . . Shri Rama wandered through the jungle asking, 'Birds, beasts, honeybees, have you seen my doe-eyed Sita? Now parrots and deer, fish, lightning and lotus flowers,

the winter moon and the quiver of Kamadeva, ducks, elephants and lions—they can all take pride in their beauty.
Listen, daughter of Janaka, the bel fruit, gold and bananas
are now happy, for you are no longer here. They are secure in the knowledge that now there is none here to rival
them in loveliness.'

". . . As they stalked through the forest, Rama said to
Lakshmana, 'Look, Lakshmana, how lovely this forest is!
Is there anyone who wouldn't be touched by its beauty! . .
When the male deer run on hearing us approach their
does tell them: Don't be afraid; you have been a deer in
every birth, but these two have come looking for a golden
deer of another kind. . . Look, my brother, see the beau-
ties of the spring season. Because I am sad on account of
Sita, Kama, the god of love, has come with his army of
birds and honeybees to help me. The vines spread over
the trees are the camps for his army. The leaves of palms
and plantain trees are his banners. The thorny bushes
laden with berries are his archers. And the piercing cry of
the kokila bird is like the roar of a war elephant. Egrets
and cranes are his camel corps; peacocks and swans are
his knights; and the wild partridges his foot soldiers. These
rocks are the chariots of Kamadeva; waterfalls are his re-
sounding drums; and fragrant breezes are his spies. O
Lakshmana, only that man is truly brave who can face the
onslaught of Kamadeva's army. And, of course, Kama's
most powerful weapon is woman. . . .'

". . . 'Now the green grass has covered the ground and
obliterated all trails, just as the arguments of heretics cast a
veil over sacred scriptures. . . . When fireflies twinkle in the
darkness of a cloud-laden night it seems as if some con-
spirators are busy secretly plotting. . . . Weary travellers have
sprawled themselves on the grass here and there just as our
senses relax after we have achieved enlightenment. . . '

". . . 'But look, Lakshmana, the rainy season is over;
autumn has arrived. Now the ground slowly turns brown,
as slowly as old age steals upon us. The earth has absorbed

all the rain water that came rushing down the gullies, just as contentment removes all traces of greed'. . . ." (Tulsidas)

(14)

The rest-house was on a rise, in the middle of a dense forest; below it, over a flat bed filled with purplish rocks, rushed the Kalini Ganga, filling the air with noise and spray. The birds returning to roost in the trees were raising their own chatter. A strong breeze rustled through the swinging fronds of the palms. Sita sat quietly at the window and gazed into the slowly darkening current of the river.

On their return from Nuwara Eliya, when Sita and Leslie had reached the rest-house, Leslie had bade her farewell and rushed off to Colombo. He had received a telegram in Nuwara Eliya that asked him to return immediately and proceed to Calcutta. After Sita saw him off, she went back to the room and closed the door. This rest-house, unlike the others, was not a glittering modern affair with fancy fixtures. Its furniture was heavy and old; its floors were covered only with coir mats; and the mirrors on its dressing tables had turned dull. There were no other tourists staying there; Sita was all alone. The driver from American Express had put the car in the garage and had gone to the servants' quarters. At dinner, the lonely waiter displayed his teeth ingratiatingly and said: "Madam, this is where they shot 'Bridge on the River Kwai'. That gorge over there, that's where the bridge was built. Alec Guiness. William Holden. All the big stars stayed in this rest house. It was so wonderful . . . madam?" But Sita had not been listening. Afterwards, she returned to the room and sat by the window looking out. Then she turned off the light and lay down on the bed. Early next morning she too had to return to Colombo.

The night continued to grow darker: the night which was set loose in the forests of sandalwood, slumbered on

the bushes of cardamom and cloves; it lay on the white
flowers spread over the steps of the temple in Kandy; and
rustled like a snake in the grass by the banks of the Kalini
Ganga. Silent as the Portuguese and Dutch churches
tucked away in forests, the night hid in the smooth rocks
at the bottom of the river. The night, proud and regal like
the mahouts of the state elephants in Kandy, was dark and
heavy-footed like the bathing elephants in the Mahaveli
Ganga. The night which was the crack of the lash, the
melody of the flute, the reel of the bagpipe, the ripple of
the sitar. . . .

In Kandy a torchlight procession is going down the road.
The procession of the Buddha's Tooth. The tooth is in a
box studded with diamonds and emeralds, and the box is
being carried by an elephant who is also covered with gold
and silver ornaments. But the Buddha who is sprawled on
the grass is laughing, showing his teeth. He has false teeth.
The Buddha has one set of teeth for eating, and a different set just for show. . . .

Priyam Mayurah Pratinrityati. The peacock dances and
comes close to its beloved. *Priyam.* God, I've forgotten all
the languages I used to know. How many do I know now?
Not one. I'm dumb. . . .

King of Words! O King of Words! I salute Vani and
Vinayaka. They created words and meanings. I am
Vishakhadatta, son of Maharaja Bhaskaradatta. Clouds are
thundering overhead. My beloved is far away. What has
happened? What is going on? The herbs of immortality
grow on snow-covered peaks. A coiled snake sits on the
head of Shiva. A coiled snake. . . .

What was that song by Chandidasa that that fool
Qamarul Islam Chowdhri sang to me? 'It's a dark night;
the clouds are heavy. How did you manage to come? He
stands among the flowers, getting drenched in the rain.
My mother-in-law is most cruel, and so are my sisters-in-
law. Chandidasa says: Dear friend . . . dear friend. . . .'

And what was that lyric by Vidyapati that the great artist
Projesh Kumar Chowdhry explained for me? 'The pupils
of Radha's heavy-lidded eyes are like the bumble-bees on
lotus flowers. The gusts of wind tickle the petals. After her
bath she puts collyrium in her eyes. Why would someone
gild a lily. . . ?'

And then she puts on a sari, dark as night itself, and
goes off to meet Krishna. . . .

Please Krishna, let me listen to your flute. Please, please
Krishna. . . .

Tulsidas has written in his *Ramacharitmanas*: A young
woman is like the burning flame of a lamp. O my soul, do
not become a moth to that flame. . . .

But no son of a bitch listens to Tulsidas now. . . .

If only I could find in Ratanpura that magic diamond
that fulfils all wishes. . . .

All the mountains in Sri Lanka are leaning. . . .

May Autumn, which is pale like the body of Vishnu, remove all your problems. . . .

I receive your command with bowed head, just as one
receives a garland of flowers. . . .

But who shall receive the garland that I'm offering? Yes,
friend, who shall . . . ?

Maharaj, may you be victorious. There was a man without a passport. He was trying to leave our camp with a
letter. He has been put under arrest. . . .

How do they give someone the third degree? The third
degree. F.B.I. C.I.D. Ph.D. K.L.M. Pan. Am. Air India International. . . .

The trees, bare of all leaves, have lined up, as if getting
ready to escort someone's coffin. . . .

Now I go to burning places and invoke the spirits of
love's magic words. May Kali of Calcutta be victorious.
There was a Hindu burning place on the way to Maripur
near Karachi. When Muslim refugees arrived from India
they set up their huts there. May Kali of Calcutta be victorious. . . .

'The beginning of the Universe is a dark secret, dark like the body of Kali. The red in the sky at sunset is the wrath of Kali; the typhoons, plagues and death are her companions. We in Bengal have seen her wrath for centuries.' Shri Projesh Kumar Chowdhri gives a statement to the press. A fraud. A painter of fake Expressionist paintings. Fraud. Fraud. Fraud. The concept of Kali is 'expressionistic'. Fraud. . . .

They drew a line on the ground to protect me, but it didn't work. . . .

Anasuya said: Listen, O princess. . . .

Virtue . . . devotion to one's husband . . . innocence . . . fidelity . . . Alas, alas. . . . Ladies and gentlemen! Comrades! Brothers and sisters! I beg to inform you that Sita is lost in the dreadful jungle of today's world. She was abducted by the Ravana of today's world. This world of ours which is divided in two camps. The world which is a prey to Anglo-American imperialism; in which innocent people are tortured but no Hanuman comes to rescue them. . . . Lata dear, the microphone is dead. . . Kailash . . . Kailash Nath Mathur, please get the power turned on quick. . . . So, ladies and gentlemen, as I was saying, in today's world where the demons of hydrogen bombs are ready to destroy human habitations, where the Sitas of Asia and Africa are daily abducted. . . . You frauds, you who read the *Ramayana*, how many Muslim Sitas did you abduct in 1947? Just count them for once. And you Muslim holy-warriors, you whose tongues never tire of cursing the tyrants of the seventh century, you tell me. . . .

Sita Mirchandani. Roll number 963 . . .?

Yes please. . . .

Yes, I am Sita. . . .

My beloved Sita. . . . My darling Sita. . . .

Sita, my love, my darling. . . .

Sweetheart. More precious than life. . . .

Tell me what you wish for most. . . .

What do I wish for? I only want all the diamonds in Ratanpura. Then you'll see how I shall put you in your place. . . .

What a petit bourgeois . . . !

Hello, hello, hello! Noises, sounds. What sounds? The humming of telephone wires. The rumble of train wheels. The sputter of the motorboat engine. The roar of the air-plane. Whrr, whrr. Phat, phat. Bang, bang. Shloop, shloop. Is that the washerman? Has he brought the clothes? . . . Bilqis *bitiya*, please check the clothes. . . . Begum sahiba, what do you want me to cook for dinner. . . .

Ah, those wonderful sounds . . . the shehnai players in Banaras . . . the band at Qaisar's wedding. . . On the island of Capri . . . the drum players at Muharram . . . hurry, it's Ja'far Bandi singing the *nauha* :

'*The nightingales love the roses, yes they do;
the roses love the morning breeze, yes they do;
but we who love Ali, Father of the Dust,
love only his grave's dust, yes we do. . . .*'

Yes, I do. . . .

Ravana is burned. Sita is burned too. All of Lanka's land is burned to ashes. . . .

Was that Rahul laughing? . . . Rahul's gay laugh. Jamil's loud laughter. The tinkle of wine glasses. . . . There was an old couple on the Brooklyn Bridge; they were whispering to each other and laughing like children. . . .

I shall die. Death will come to me. My feet will be turned towards the West so that my soul can get on board a boat and cross the ocean of Sindh. . . . The flames of the bier. . . . The candles dripping wax. Fresh flowers. The graveyard in Tulsipur. That's where we buried Jamila Baji. Who was Jamila Baji? . . . Then there was her husband; he was wail-ing and crying so loudly. Bilqis told me he remarried next month. The swine. They are all swine, the men. . . .

Jamil darling, I still sometimes have that awful dream.

That I'm taking my M.A. exam., but the questions are set
in a language I don't know. And the allowed three hours
are ticking away. Two hours left! Now one. Twenty minutes. Five minutes. One. . . .

Give me five minutes more
Only five minutes more
Only five minutes more of your charms
Give me five minutes more
In—your—arms. . . .

The rock looked exactly like an elephant. When you
climb a high rock you are likely to slip and fall. I can go
and hide on a rock twice as high as Sigiriya, but they'll
find me. . . .

May I have the pleasure. . . ?

Who me? I am Mrs. Beach Luxury Hotel. And you? Mr.
Ashoka Hotel? How nice! Please take a seat. . . .

India, that is Bharat, discovered the pillar of the mighty
King of Kings, Ashoka; discovered the Chakra of Ashoka;
discovered the Ashoka Hotel. . . .

May I have the pleasure. . . ?

Of course. This is my sister-in-law. Quite something.
Bilqis Anwar Ali. A-1 actress. Producer of great plays. Su-
per intellectual. . . . Hey you, Jamuni Begum, are you listening? Umrao Begum? Khetu Begum? . . . Where the heck
have they all disappeared to? What the hell is going on?
Hey you, Jamil's wife, look at the soles of your feet. That
will protect you from the evil eye. Hey you, Bhuri Begum,
what's making you so itchy? Why do you want to rush off
so soon. Hey you, Bundi Bua, Jamil Bhaiya is not feeling
well. . . . I think I'll go crazy from worrying. Last night I
washed Lord Ali's medallion to give us protection. . . . Just
listen to what Khetu Begum has done—she's accusing poor
Bundi of all sorts of things, as if she herself is the most
virtuous of wives. . . . You know, Urooj's wife lies like
nobody's business. Don't ever let yourself be fooled by her,
Mother. . . . What can she give to anyone? She shivers in
winter and starves in spring. . . . Jamil Bhaiya, last night

the Lord Ali himself appeared in a dream to me. Are you
listening, Jamil Bhaiya. . . ?

I'm a cow. . . .

Mr. Sandman . . . Mr. Sandman . . . Step into my heart's
Vrindavan. . . .

In my little corner of the world
Tonight my love—tonight my love. . . .

The night has come down on the Buddhist shrines. . . .
Why has the night attacked me again. . . ?
The wind has turned violent. . . .
The wind blows over Parakrama Samudra. It floats over
Kalini Ganga. It dances away towards Colombo. . . .
The wind. . . .
The moon. . . .
The moon sleeps in sandalwood branches. . . The eyes
of the people snoring in dusty cottages are filled with the
sleep of centuries. . . . Don Fernandez da Costa Samra-
sinharuna Mudaliyar . . . Ratansinha Jaisurya . . . Gunapala
Gunawerdene . . . Their eyes are filled with the sleep of
forests. . . . Portuguese covered with armor attack Dutch
castles. The spirits of English planters line the road to
Mahahinya and beg for sugar and butter from American
GIs . . . The moon swims in Mahaveli Ganga. . . . These
elephants are nothing but spirits that were held captive
for thousands of years in the jungles. . . .
The moon. . . .
The night. . . .
The night is the hair of Queen Sita. The dark-hued body
of the Lord, Rama Raghurai. The face of Mother Kali . . .
The darkness before all creation . . . We are always caught
in that primordial darkness, though we might deceive our-
selves and think that a great evolution has taken place. . . .
Dark, dark, dark. Night. . . .
I lost my sleep in New York. . . . The palm trees in the
forest have shot into air the and are touching the blood

red sky . . . the ruins of Lanka Tilaka are like a mouth full
of teeth gaping open in a hideous smile . . . the pond of
lilies is open like a sleepless eye. . . . Lilavati . . . Rupavati
. . . Sitavati. . . .

The bones collected in the stupa of Rana Vihar are busy
discussing the international situation. . . . Parakrama Bahu
I is urgently writing the fifth chapter of *Communism in South
Asia* . . . . I was devoured by the forest. . . .

God, how beautiful were the ornaments that Bari Khala
gave me at my wedding . . . the bride's jewels. . . . The
goldsmiths of Ratanpura are busy making a diamond-stud-
ded necklace. . . . All that glitters. . . . Light . . . light. . . .
The sounds of the jungle . . . the sounds of the birds, the
ocean, the roads and the highways, the sounds of the
harbour, the sounds in the stillness of the mountains. . . .

The sound. . . .

There is only one. . . .

Come here . . . come here, near me . . . come near me
. . . come. . . .

(15)

"I just got back," Sita spoke into the mouthpiece of the
telephone in her room in Mount Lavinia. "Any news?"

"Oh, hello, Sita," Irfan replied. "So you're back. How
wonderful! May I come up to your room?"

"Please do . . ."

He arrived five minutes later.

"Well, well. You look very cheerful. I'm so glad the forest air did you some good."

"Please sit down."

This was his first time in her room and he seemed rather
nervous. He paced the room once, then sat down on the
sofa in one corner. She remained seated on the edge of
her bed, busily knitting something.

"What's that?"

"A sweater for my son. I started it so that I could give it

to Jamil to take back with him for Rahul. . . . But now I don't even know how big Rahul is. It may not even fit him. I've been going by my memory alone."

Irfan remained silent for several moments, then he asked, "What else? Tell me more."

"More?" she asked with a smile.

"For the whole week I thought of you all the time. I couldn't get interested in the conference at all. God knows what I finally wrote in my report. But tell me, was your trip interesting?"

"Very interesting." She picked up a new set of needles.

"How were the doddering American widows?"

"I didn't meet any doddering American widows. Though I met an American . . . a man. But he wasn't even old."

"Bitch," Irfan muttered under his breath and fell silent.

Some moments passed, then Sita said, "You didn't ask your usual question: what happened next?"

"Tell me yourself. . . ."

"He was an archaeologist."

"Then you must've had a great time discussing Ceylonese history with him. The way you had lectured me on the history of Sindh."

"Sure." She went on knitting, unconcerned.

Irfan stared at Sita for a while. Suddenly he jumped up from the sofa and, striding up to her, slapped the needles and the knitting out of her hands. Then he grabbed her by the shoulders and pulled her off the bed.

"What else did you do besides discussing history?" he snarled.

Sita turned white.

"I asked you something. What else did you do?"

"Shut up!" Sita's face was flushed with anger. "What right have you to ask me that?"

"None," Irfan hissed between clenched teeth. "None at all. Perhaps even your husband has no right to question you—since you ran out on him two years ago."

"Shut up, Irfan!" Sita screamed. "Get the hell out of here.

Get out before I call the manager." She was trembling with rage.

For a long moment Irfan stood silently watching her, then turned around and slowly walked away. At the door, without looking back at her, he spoke once again in his normal, calm voice, "I finally managed to get an appointment with Jamil. He has agreed to talk to me tonight. I'll be meeting him for dinner at Galface Hotel. Afterwards, I'll call you. Good night."

Sometime after midnight the phone by Sita's bed rang persistently, but she didn't answer.

(16)

She wept all night. She had never wept like that before, not even that night in October 1947 when she and her family bade farewell to Karachi for Kathiawar. Not even when Jamil threw her out of their house in New York. In Karol Bagh, at night, she would often silently cry for Rahul, then in the morning she would get up early and wash her face so that her father would not see her grief. But this morning, in her lovely room in Mount Lavinia Hotel, there was no one to see her tears and feel sad or ashamed. So she stayed sprawled in her comfortable bed. The day ahead—her entire life, the world—lay empty before her: a raging sea of eternal darkness to which there was no shore. At eight the bearer knocked and came in with her breakfast. The kind-faced, old Sinhala was concerned when he saw her red eyes—he had two young daughters of his own—but he quietly placed the tray on the table and went away without saying a word.

At ten, she called the airlines office, then got dressed and went downstairs to the terrace. A hot sun was burnishing the sea and the glare was harsh to her eyes. Some white children were building sand castles on the beach. In the distance the woman who sold coral beads was walking away, her footprints still visible in the moist sand. The day felt dismal. Mount Lavinia, Colombo, the entire world felt dismal.

After leaning for several minutes on the railing around the terrace, Sita decided she would spend the next few hours driving around the city; then she would pack and leave for the airport well ahead of her flight. Just then the hall-porter came and told her she was wanted on the phone.

It was the airlines office: the delegates were all leaving at the same time and no seats were available, not for three days at least.

She opened her purse and examined her booklet of traveller's cheques. There weren't many left.

The clerk at the reception said, "Madam, have you seen the Kailaniya Temple?"

"No, I'll try to see it today." she replied somewhat hastily and came out of the hotel. A taxi-driver hurried over.

"Kailaniya Temple," she told him.

"Sorry madam." the driver shook his head.

"Why?"

"There might be a curfew. There is some chance of a Tamil-Sinhala riot in the city today."

'O my god! Even here?' She rested her hand on a tree to support herself. 'What should I do now?'

Suddenly she remembered Ratansinha Jaisurya. In this country where everyone was a stranger to her, she knew only one man beside Irfan and Leslie. Perhaps he might use his influence and get her a plane seat.

She went back into the hotel and called Jaisurya. Some emergency meeting was going on in his office but he answered the phone. He was quite surprised to hear her voice.

"Yes? . . . Yes?. . . Oh, it's Dr. Mirchandani! . . . What can I do for you?"

Sita told him the problem about plane reservations.

"I see . . . I see . . . listen, I'm very busy right now. You must have seen the morning paper."

She had not seen the morning paper.

"Perhaps you should come down to my office. When is Mr. Irfan going back?"

"I don't know . . ."

"I see. Well, come on over. I'll wait for you."

In the newspaper office everyone was terribly busy. The teleprinters and typewriters were clattering away; the editors and reporters were rushing around talking to each other in loud whispers; and the girl at the telephone board was repeatedly saying, "Good morning—*Lanka Dweep*," in a voice that was as false as it was sweet. All this only added to Sita's feeling of desolation. After a few minutes' wait she was called in by the chief editor.

When she entered Jaisurya's office he was simultaneously talking into two telephones and intermittently using the office intercom as well. Sita sat down at the edge of a chair in one corner. Jaisurya put down one of the telephones, then swung his revolving chair to look at her. His eyes seemed to bore through her clothes. Sita felt nauseated. "Dirty old man," she muttered to herself. Jaisurya put down the other phone too.

"Good morning, Dr. Mirchandani," he said with a grin, "please make yourself comfortable. Irfan called me last night and told me everything. May I call you Sita?" Just then one of the phones rang and he began to talk to someone in Sinhalese.

Sita felt her head reel. She desperately clung to the arms of her chair, and closed her eyes to calm herself. 'The earth should split open,' she thought, 'and I should disappear into it.' But this was not the world of Sita and Savitri of yore; this was Kaliyuga. Consequently, the world didn't split open, neither did Sita disappear in to some crevice. Instead, she opened her purse, took out a cigarette, and lit it.

Jaisurya finished on the telephone and turned to face her again. "Please forgive me. I should have offered you a cigarette." He looked at her intently. 'Poor thing! She appears so pale,' he thought. 'Her nerves must be very weak.' Then he said, "Don't feel bad. I know all of Irfan's secrets. Perhaps you don't know that we were together in Germany

for several years. You must have been rather young then."
He gave Sita another of those repulsive looks.

"Nothing in Irfan's private—emotional—life is hidden
from me," Jaisurya continued. "He trusts me totally. Your
secret will be safe with me. You know, journalists can be
trusted on occasion." Then he added with a smile, "Here's
some good news: there won't be a curfew today. Now, would
you like some coffee?"

"No. Thanks." Sita felt overwhelmed with self-disgust.
'Why did I come here?' she asked herself.

"I . . . er . . . the plane seat. . . ." she could barely mumble
the words.

"Sure, sure, my dear. I have to work on my editorial now,
but I'll instruct my secretary." He leaned over the intercom. "Ratna, please send Martin in. And you come in too."

His secretary and his assistant came in. But just then
the news editor also rushed in and, leaning over the desk,
began to confer with Jaisurya about something. Once again
Jaisurya forgot all about Sita and became involved in his
work.

Sita waited for a while, her eyes fixed on the ceiling,
then got up and walked into the ante-room. A young
Tamilian, with curly, raven hair and dusky skin, was standing at the window looking at the traffic below. Perhaps he,
too, was waiting to see Jaisurya. Sita moved towards the
stairs. Just then Jaisurya's secretary ran out to call her and
Sita had to go back into the office. Jaisurya spoke into the
intercom, "Ratna, tell Ramaswamy to come in."

The curtain was pushed aside and the young Tamilian
came in. He glanced at Sita with a smile then stood leaning against the wall.

While still busy with his staff, Jaisurya swivelled his chair
towards Sita and said, "Sita, meet my very naughty friend,
Ramaswamy. He is a revolutionary columnist—you might
say inflammatory. He writes for our opposition, but doesn't
mind talking once in a while to 'communalists' such as
me." Then he said to the young man, "Come, take a seat,

Rama. Meet our Indian guest, Dr. Sita Mirchandani. Being an Indian she might even share your opinions." The introductions done, Jaisurya went back to what he was discussing with his staff.

Ramaswamy folded his hands in greeting and began to talk with Sita. He was relaxed and also polite. Was she from Bombay? From Delhi? He, too, had lived in Delhi for many years as a correspondent. He knew so many journalists there. Did Sita know . . .? He also told her that half his relatives lived in Madras and that he regarded himself an overseas Indian.

Suddenly something remarkable happened. Surrounded by a bunch of Sinhala strangers, Sita felt oddly close to this young Tamilian who was roughly her own age. Just as she had felt towards that 'modern' man, Leslie Marsh, when she was with him among the centuries-old, ghost-ridden ruins of Polonnoruwa. On that occasion, Leslie was for her a part of that twentieth-century western world which was so familiar to her. He was a moment in real time, while Polonnoruwa was all of eternity. Later, when she saw Sinhala farm workers—men and women— in their sarongs and glossy hairdos, she felt closer to them than to Leslie. Now they, the farmers, were a part of her own culture, while Leslie was a foreigner—a Christian, a western man. Earlier, Sita had had a similar experience in the crowded dining hall of the Mount Lavinia Hotel when, in comparison with the fashionable men and women surrounding them, Irfan had seemed to her like one of her very own kind, for he was from the sub-continent and had a common culture with her. How strange that we simultaneously live at so many different, even contradictory, levels during a brief but complex life!

By now Ramaswamy had become involved in some heated argument with Jaisurya. The room was full of voices. Sita's headache had worsened. She suddenly stood up and rushed out of the room, down the stairs and on to the pavement. For a while she wandered aimlessly in the galleries fronting the stores then stopped at a bookstall. She asked the man how she could reach the airlines office.

"Come, I'll take you there," said a voice.

She turned around. It was Ramaswamy, a smile dancing on his lips.

"Thanks. Just tell me the address; I can get there by myself."

"After you disappeared Mr. Jaisurya was very worried. But he is so upset over this communal crisis between the Tamils and the Sinhalas that he can't even think. When you rushed out like that he was talking on the phone to his elder brother, a cabinet minister, who is in great danger of losing his position."

He walked beside her through the galleries.

"What's causing these riots?" Sita asked distractedly, glancing at her wristwatch.

"Let's sit down and have a cup of coffee somewhere," Ramaswamy said. Then he asked, "Do you have to go back to Delhi today?"

They entered a cafe where many university students and newspapermen were noisily arguing over the day's news. They sat down at a table near the door. Sita began to massage her temples with her fingers. There was so much noise, so much turmoil in the world.

"Er . . . excuse me . . . I'll be right back." Ramaswamy suddenly leaped up from his chair and went rushing after a girl in a brilliant Murshidabadi sari who was just about to leave the cafe. The two stopped at the door and exchanged some words rapidly. The girl turned and glared at Sita, then disappeared down the gallery. Ramaswamy returned to the table, wiping his moist forehead with a handkerchief.

"That was my fiancée," he said in reply to Sita's questioning look somewhat bashfully.

'How naive and intense he was!' Sita thought. He was close to her in age; she could understand his intensity and his feelings.

"'Was.' What do you mean? Is she no longer your fiancée?" Sita asked with a smile.

"That depends, as they say, on the latest political situation."

"Will you explain that to me?" Sita asked, still smiling, "If you don't mind, that is."

Ramaswamy told her everything, his eyes sadly peering into the coffee cup. The girl was a Sinhala Buddhist. He was a Tamil Hindu. The girl's parents were against their engagement. The girl was totally apolitical, but Ramaswamy had been trying to educate her. Her father was a leader in the U.N.P., and all her relatives were very rich and reactionary and thought America was God.

"Last week I had a big fight with her. I was insisting that we should go to some other city and get married in a civil ceremony. Then go to Madras for a while. But she wouldn't agree to any of it. She's such a coward." Then he added, "I don't know why I'm boring you with my long story. . . ."

"No, tell me some more about yourself." Sita ordered another cup of coffee for him.

"Did you meet any of the local people?"

"None, except for Jaisurya. Though I did hear a Dutch Burgher girl sing."

"That means, apart from Mr. Jaisurya, I'm the first true native of this country that you've encountered. The Dutch Burghers don't count; they're the Anglo-Indians of Sri Lanka. What else did you do all these days?"

"I spent almost all my time in Noruwa Eliya."

"Then you're truly a tourist. Didn't Mr. Jaisurya invite you to his dinner party?"

"He did. How did you know?"

"Perhaps you don't realise that Colombo is a small place. And that you've caused quite a stir here. In fact a colleague of mine mentioned you in her social column: the Indian lady staying at Mount Lavinia Hotel who wears extremely lovely saris. . . . She wanted very much to do an interview but you couldn't be reached."

"Good God!"

Rama looked at her with calm and serious eyes and said, "Why didn't we meet before?"   .

'Oh God, no! Not him too. . . .'

"I mean," Rama continued, "I mean if I had met you a few days earlier I could have shown you a bit of our real life. I could have taken you to some of the Tamil families and introduced you to my sisters."

"Not to your fiancée?"

"She never comes to my place. And yet I continue to hope that some day she'll leave her mansion for my three-room flat." He sounded very sad. "Sita, you don't know about the feudal class of Kandy, or the life of its European planters. This most beautiful crown colony was indeed a paradise for them . . . as it is even now. But you belong to the middle class?"

"Lower middle class, to be exact." She smiled.

"Do you know what my so-very-aristocratic Welma asked me just now? 'Is that some jet-set Indian Maharani that you're having coffee with?'"

Sita began to laugh.

"The news this morning is pretty bad," she said, taking the newspaper from Ramaswami's hands, "Another big riot in the north."

Some friends of Ramaswami's passed by the table and he looked up and smiled at them. His features were rough and his skin was dark, but one could also see he was exceptionally intelligent. And his smile was most attractive. Absent-mindedly, Sita noticed his even, white teeth.

"Tell me," she said, her head at an angle and the index finger touching her right temple, "Tell me, why there are so many riots here? You're all citizens of the same country . . . ."

"What a silly question to ask when you know everything!" He interrupted her. "You must be terribly bored. Perhaps I should get you some more coffee." He called the waiter and gave the order. "Why are there riots in your country, Sita? You're also all citizens of one country, aren't you?

Don't you see that both you and we are victims of the same kind of bourgeois, capitalist politics?"

The bitterness in his voice reminded her of Jamil. Once, in New York, Jamil was introduced to a Pakistani friend of his elder brother, who asked him if he was also from Karachi. Jamil had replied sardonically, "No. I'm still a citizen of that country which all of you only a few years ago used to call Paradise on Earth."

"They say about the Tamils that they're always looking toward the mainland," Sita remarked, "Just like the overseas Chinese who are always looking toward mainland China."

"I once wrote a series of articles for a Delhi paper on 'Sri Lanka's Indian Problem'," Ramaswami replied, "I'll send you the cuttings." Then he added, "Have dinner with me this evening."

Sita remained silent.

"Why are you in such a hurry to leave Colombo? We don't get beautiful visitors like you every day."

"Really! But so many Indian film stars come here all the time." Sita felt nervous at the increasing intensity in his voice and tried to make a joke of it.

"Do you know?" Ramaswami continued, "Do you know that when you walked into that room at the *Lanka Dweep* offices it felt as if a breeze from Kashmir had blown in."

"But I'm from Sindh." Sita protested.

"That's true. But you seem like a Kashmiri."

"Well, Sindhis aren't ugly either."

They began to laugh. At that moment, in a small cafe in Colombo, two young people—one an 'overseas Tamil' from Ceylon, the other a 'Sindhi refugee' from India—looked so happy and yet so sad. They were fully aware of the fact that ground had slipped from under the feet of their generation; that, nevertheless, they must be responsible for the world's future. Years ago, did parents have any idea what their children would have to face in the world that the politicians of their generation were creating?

"Let's take you on a tour of Colombo," Rama said, getting up from his chair.

"But the airlines office. . . ."

Ramaswami was peeved. "To hell with the airlines office," he said. "This is lunch time. All offices will be closed till three." Then he added, "Don't worry so much. I'll put you on the plane tomorrow myself."

. . . 'Perhaps you can't help it,' Irfan had said, 'if people persist in taking interest in you. On the other hand, you don't break anyone's heart either . . . if you can help it,' . . .

"Is there any place in Colombo you haven't yet seen?" That was Ramaswamy asking, as he pulled shut the taxi door.

"Kailanya Temple," Sita replied feebly.

At the top of the hill where the temple was, Sita looked all around, then said, "I don't mean the political scene, but during the last week or so I've constantly felt as if I were in South India. The same sights, the same culture. . . ." Feeling tired, she sat down on the steps. 'Why do people make so much fuss over tiny things?' she thought.

"Guide, lady? First class guide?" A Sinhala appeared out of nowhere.

Sita got up and followed the guide towards the temple. Ramaswami walked behind them, his head bowed in silence.

"Why," Sita asked the guide, "why are there so many Hindu gods and goddesses in your Buddhist temples?"

"Because these Hindu gods and goddesses protect the Buddhist dharma in Sri Lanka," the guide asserted with confidence.

Sita suddenly thought of Leslie Marsh. "Are you listening?" she turned and asked Ramaswami.

"Sri Lanka was culturally one before the Portuguese arrived," Ramaswami started, "and prior to the British hegemony there was never any conflict between the Tamils and the Sinhalas. . . ."

Suddenly he fell silent. A group of bhikshus, dressed in orange and carrying oversize palm fans, passed in front of them.

"You were saying something. . . ." Sita prodded.

"Nothing really," Ramaswami replied. "You're a sociologist, aren't you? Just now when you mentioned South India you were, of course, right. The Sinhala way of life is basically Hindu. Then there is another question: is Buddhism—or at least the Buddhism in Sri Lanka—just another version of Hindu dharma, or must we regard it as a separate religion and a separate culture? Sinhala society was based on caste distinctions, though there is no caste system in Buddhism. Then there are those Sinhala Buddhists who worship Hindu gods too."

"What is a national culture?" Ramaswami continued, "What is a purely Sinhala culture? Or a purely Indian culture? Or a purely Pakistani culture? I met some Indians and Pakistanis at the dinner given by Jaisurya. I asked them: is the Islam in Pakistan the same as is found in Egypt and Saudi Arabia? Is the culture of the Hindu masses in India the same as it was when King Ashoka ruled the land? You know, whenever I question Jaisurya about the way he interprets historical evolution, he immediately starts to lecture me on the psychology of expatriates."

"But the new middle class that appeared during the British period in this country, it must have agitated for government jobs and political privileges?" Sita asked. And there must have been some conflict between the interests of the various racial and religious groups within that middle class?"

"Naturally. And now the Buddhist Congress is demanding that an entirely new history of Sri Lanka should be written. I guess such histories are being written in every new country in Asia. But how must we interpret history?"

On one of the side-walls of the temple there were many sculpted figures of gods, including one of Vibhishana, the younger brother of Ravana. Poor Lord Vibhishana. In spite of being a god he was also a demon, and so he had two tusks sticking out of his mouth. "He was the one who betrayed," Sita confided to Ramaswami and explained a popular Urdu proverb: *ghar ka bhedi Lanka dhaye* (one who knows the family secrets can topple the whole of Lanka).

In the main hall of the temple a student from the Art College was busy copying one of the frescoes. When Ramaswami lingered to talk with the student, Sita walked ahead. In the long side-gallery, at the feet of the huge re- clining Buddha, a baby was asleep, wrapped in dirty clothes. The baby's mother lay prostrate on the cool marble floor, before the Buddha.

'Rahul . . .Rahul . . . Rahul . . .'

Carefully, so as not to wake the baby, Sita tiptoed away. In the next room there was a golden Buddha seated, as usual, on an open lotus flower, lost in peaceful medita- tion. Sita sat down on the low steps in front of the statue and briefly closed her eyes. When she opened her eyes again, Irfan was standing in front of her.

(17)

She remained silent but turned her face away, her eyes intently examining the paintings on the wall. Irfan stepped closer.

"Sita . . . please. Look at me," he said, "Listen to me. Buddha was the Prince of Peace. I'm standing before him. Please forgive me. Please . . . please . . . forgive me."

She kept her eyes fixed on the frescoes.

"Sita! . . . Are you listening to me? . . . Sita . . . Sita."

(18)

"The reason I went to the temple yesterday," Irfan said, as they stood in a balcony at the Mount Lavinia, "The reason I went was to bring some peace to my heart . . . but today I don't feel so dramatic. So let's go and paint the town red. What do you say?"

"Yes, let's," Sita replied brightly.

"We'll go to the Little Hut and see the Chinese cabaret there."

"Sure."

"We'll go to the St. Michel and ask the Dutch Burgher girl to sing our favourite songs."

"Of course."

"We'll go to the zoo and watch the elephants play the harmonica."

"Absolutely."

"But I thought you were going to the house of your journalist friend to work on some project on overseas Indians?"

"Oh, Irfan!" she laughed, "Really!"

"I don't know how you pick up these strange people. It's truly amazing." Irfan's voice had no trace of sarcasm, no bitterness. He was talking like an old friend. No longer behaving like a jealous lover: suspicious, peeved, full of resentment. How a man changes every moment!

"You'd better phone that 'Hanuman' of yours, that you can't come to his dinner."

"Which 'Hanuman'?"

"You know . . . what's his name? Ramaswami? Appaswami?"

It was a fact: she had completely forgotten about poor Ramaswami. Irfan had called her back to himself. Ramaswami's engaging youthfulness, his congenial politics, their shared culture, all these were left behind in the temple as she had walked out with Irfan. Now there was only one man in the entire world, and his name was Irfan. Irfan. The first and the last. Irfan. Only two nights ago Irfan had humiliated her and she had cried bitterly. Just yesterday she had spent a dreadful morning in Jaisurya's office and an equally dreary afternoon in a smoke-filled cafe discussing Sri Lankan politics with Ramaswami. But now that was all forgotten. There was no trace left of those events on her memory. Only the moment was present. The moment. It's in your grip. Hold on to it. Hold on to it with all your might, for days and nights are quietly but swiftly passing away. Time is soon to end.

(19)

That night, as they were returning from the Little Hut, Irfan mentioned Jamil for the first time. He told Sita that the night they had quarrelled he, Irfan, had tried to call her at midnight—because he had met with Jamil even though he had not been able to talk to him at length. But now tomorrow evening he was definitely meeting Jamil again to discuss the matter.

"These attempts of yours," Sita said, "these on and off meetings—they don't interest me any more." She shrugged her shoulders. "I really don't care. I'm going back to Delhi."

But very early next morning there was a knock on her door.

"Who's that?" She scrambled out of the bed and opened the door.

"Achchoo!" Irfan entered, sneezing and sniffling.

"Good God! How are you?"

"I'm fine. Don't worry. I didn't meet the same fate as Qamar." He sneezed again. "The fact is I've caught a cold from walking on the beach at night. The wind was too strong."

"Oh! So you were walking on the beach! With whom?"

"Well!" He sat down on the sofa and a bright smile spread over his face. "With your dear husband, of course," he said with a chuckle. "It was such fun. Your husband is now a good friend of mine." He lit a cigarette. "I must say he's something else."

"Are you going to tell me?" Sita asked, returning to her bed to recline on the covers.

"Yes, your dear husband is something else," Irfan repeated with a chuckle. "By God, he is. When I arrived at his hotel he asked me to come up to his room. As usual he was pretty drunk. Without even saying hello, he started to recite the 'Singhaladwipa' section from Ja'isi's *Padmavat*. You'd have thought Ja'isi was born again in Jamil's body. He would recite a few lines, then mention your name, then shed a few tears. Then, when he was finished with the 'Singhala Khanda', he showed me a picture of his new wife and launched into Iqbal's 'The Mosque of Cordoba': *Chain of day and night . . .*"

At the mention of Jamil's new wife, Irfan thought a shadow of anguish crossed Sita's face. He quickly asked, "Sita, what time do you eat breakfast?"

"Don't worry about breakfast. Tell me what happened."

"Well . . ." he cleared his throat, "well, a while later, Jamil switched to Tulsidas and began to sing 'chaupais' from his *Ramayana.* That guy knows so many by heart. Really Sita, what kind of a crazy person did you marry?"

Sita snapped, "Jamil is not crazy! He's a literary man. How would you know about the *Ramayana* and the *Padmavat.*"

"Oh, oh. Don't get mad," he replied cheerfully. "If you so desire I too can recite to you from Kalidasa and Tulsidas. Or would you rather hear Hafiz, or Shakespeare, or Eliot? But you see, my dear, I don't go in for such gimmicks. You women make a fool of yourselves by falling for such nonsense. Don't you know how these poets and writers, who write so blithely about love and life and so many other high-falutin' things, how they treat their own wives? But never mind. . . ." He paused, then continued, "After the *Ramayana* Jamil returned to the *Padmavat.* And all the time he kept scolding me for not drinking enough. Then he made me repeat many of the *dohas* with him over and over. God, it was strange. But he's a decent man. . ."

In his excitement, Irfan had risen from the sofa. Now he went and stood by the window. He was grinning.

"Would you like to hear some *dohas?*" he asked.

"No."

"How come? You'll have to. Just now you were complaining that I'm not a literary man."

He cleared his throat like a professional singer and began, "*Singhaladwipa katha ab gawun / awusau padaman baran sunawun**. . . Shall I continue?"

---

* "Now I tell you the story of Sinhaladwipa / And describe the beauty of Padmani."

"No."

"Why not? You can't get away now; I'll make you listen. You know, your husband nearly drove me crazy last night. Now it's my turn to do the same to you. Just listen to this . . poor Jamil wept when he recited:

Raghav jo Sita sang layi
Ravan harili kaun sudh payi
yah sansar sapan kir lekha
*bichar gaye janau na dekha**

"God, it's so moving. And listen to this:

Singhaladwipa juna nah nibhawo
yahi thanaun sankar sab saho[+]

"I think I have some experience of that."

Sita had to laugh. But Irfan paid her no attention; he leaned back against the sill of the window and went on reciting *dohas*, one after another. He looked triumphant, as if he had come back victorious from some major battle. Sita had never seen him so happy.

"And how about this one . . . just fantastic:

Muhammad jiwan jal bharan ghiriyan rahat ki rit
ghiri siwayi jyun bhari dhare janam ka bit."[#]

He sneezed loudly.

"I see my husband's madness has infected you too," Sita said, beginning to feel a bit annoyed. "Will you please tell me what happened last night."

---

* "Raghava brought Sita with him to the forest. / But who could find any trace of her when Ravana abducted her? / The world is just like a dream; / when people separate it is as if they had never met."
+ "Singhaladwipa is ancient and unconquerable. / It is a hard and narrow place to reach.
# "O Muhammad, human life is like the pot on a Persian Wheel which is emptied out no sooner than it is filled."

"Then listen, will you." Irfan paid no heed to her plea and recited two more verses:

"Hiya ki joti dip wah sojha
yah jo dip andher bha bojha
jo piya nanhin asthar dasa
jaga ujar ka kijai basa."

"What does that mean?" Sita asked.

"The poet Malik Muhammad says, 'The king saw Singhaladwipa in the light of his heart/ while this dismal world became full of darkness./ When one's beloved is not by one's side,/it matters not if the world is full or barren.'" Irfan explained.

Then he perched himself on the desk near the window and said, "Here's a really good one:

Muhammad cinaga pema ki suni mahi gagan daraye
*dhani birhan au dhani hiya jinh yah ag samaye."**

He decided not to explain this doha.

"Amazing!" Sita exclaimed. "You turn out to know so much."

Irfan bowed with a flourish. "What do you know! There's more to me than you see. You thought only your dear Jamil knew everything?"

"You're crazy," she said with a laugh.

"Sita."

"Yes?"

Irfan had his eyes fixed on his shoes; suddenly he had become very serious. Then he started playing with the pencils lying on the table.

"Sita," he said again.

"Yes? What . . . what did Jamil say?" Sita asked feebly.

---

* "Muhammad, Heaven and Earth are scared of the spark of love. Praised be the pining lover and his heart, they contain that fire."

"I explained everything to him. By the time I took him for a walk on the beach he was completely sober. I asked him to give you a divorce so that . . . so . . . . Because I want to marry you. It sounds so abominably trite, doesn't it? But you won't come to Pakistan. Or would you?"

The ticking of the alarm clock on the bedside table began to sound too loud. Then the noise of the waves breaking on the beach suddenly filled the room. After a few moments it grew quiet again.

Sita said, "What made you assume that I. . . ."

"What I assume, or don't," Irfan interrupted her, "is my business. And I think I have every right to it. You just answer my question."

"Please go away." Sita's voice was firm.

"Where? Outside? I can go—but you know I'm stubborn. You threw me out once before. But listen, I'm going to Paris next month. You . . ." his fingers were busy twirling the pencils nervously. "You . . . you should come and join me there."

Sita got up from the bed. "I don't care what Jamil does. But please leave my room now."

"All right. I'm going." But near the door he stopped and said, "Listen . . . just one more doha . . . and think over it:

Muhammad madhu jo pema ka hiyan dip tenahi rakh
*sis na deyi patang jyon tab lag jaye nah cak.**

(20)

". . . And when the god of love, Kama, set out to conquer Shambhu, all the sacred scriptures were of no avail. Self-purification, resignation, obedience to duty, knowledge, learning, disdain for this world—nothing could stand before the onslaught. Even wisdom went into hiding. . . .

---

* "Muhammad, fill your heart's lamp with the wine of love/ Like a moth, you must lose your head to gain the beloved."

Rati's husband is enraged; he strides forth, holding his bow and arrows. Who is his target? . . . The entire universe is caught in the web of love. Trees have swung low to cover vines. Rivers have fallen into the embrace of the sea. Land and sea have become one. Birds and beasts, gods and demons, men and snakes, subtle spirits and evil ones, ghosts and saints, they all have been enthralled by love. Those men of knowledge who saw the world as a shadow of the Brahmana now see it in the shape of a woman. Such was the state of things when Kamadeva approached Shambhu." (Tulsidas)

". . . The arrow of Madana was a flowery sprig of the mango tree on which Spring had set black honey-bees which looked like the letters in the name of the mind-born god himself.* The crescent shaped flowers were like nail-marks left on the forest's body by the embraces of the spring season. Spring adorned herself with the tilaka flower and put the collyrium of bumble bees in her eyes; she covered her lips—the mango flowers—from the gaze of the morning sun. The flower pollen falling from the payala bushes reddened the eyes of the deer and they went playfully leaping all over the jungle. The sweet voice of the kokila bird which never fails to melt the heart of even the haughtiest woman, was like the voice of love itself. At Madana's command branches stopped swaying, bees turned silent, birds became transfixed to branches, and deer stood still. The entire forest now appeared immobile like a painting." (Kalidas)

(21)

Sita and Irfan lived in Paris for several months. Irfan had found a lovely flat close to Boulevard Souchet, which Sita furnished and made lovelier still. Every morning Irfan would go off to his office while Sita would go and buy gro-

---

*The "mind-born" god is Kama, also known as Madana, the god of love.

ceries. Then she would prepare the food, iron the clothes, clean the house, and put Irfan's slippers by his armchair near the fireplace for his return. At night, soon after dinner, she would wrap his sleeping suit around a hot-water bottle and put it on their bed. She had turned into such a perfect, comforting and caring housewife that even Irfan was quite amazed.

Every morning Sita would impatiently wait for the postman. Perhaps today the divorce papers will arrive from New York, she would tell herself. But days passed by and the papers never arrived. On returning to Delhi from Colombo, she had not visited anyone. She had told her parents only that she had found a job in Paris and must leave. By then they had stopped asking questions or commenting on what she did. The time for such things was long gone. The day before she was to leave for Paris, Sita called Bilqis and Hima from a pay telephone in Connaught Place.

Bilqis had asked her, "How long will you be away this time?"

"I don't know," Sita had replied. "The fact is I'm not very happy here. Also, once I am in Europe it will be easier for me to go to New York. To see Rahul."

"That's right," Bilqis had agreed. "But do try to write once in a while."

"Of course."

Bilqis had not asked her the reason for her going to Paris—she knew it.

On weekends Sita and Irfan would go for walks by the Seine or wander around in the Latin Quarter. Sometimes, while sipping black coffee in a cafe, Sita would turn pensive. "What are you thinking?" Irfan would ask.

"I don't think anymore," Sita would reply, raising her eyes, "Now I only feel."

Sometimes, as they would be chatting, leaning over the parapet of some bridge, Sita would suddenly fall silent. Then Irfan would light a cigarette for her—"Here, have a cigarette"—and try to amuse her by humming some silly tune.

One day Irfan said to her, "Beyond you there's another you. When you suddenly go silent on me like that I feel totally alone again. In an instant you fly millions of miles away from me. Far, far above my reach. I want to understand you, but you leave me scared."

Sometimes Sita would herself feel frustrated by her long silences and exclaim, "Irfan, please talk to me. . . ."

And Irfan would say, "I'm scared to talk."

In autumn they went to Spain. There, in Cordova, they sat in the moonlight, on the steps of the famous mosque. A Pakistani student was also there and he played on his guitar and sang the poem by Iqbal for them : *Chain of day and night, creator of all events/ Chain of day and night, the truth of life and death.*

"Now explain these verses to me, Irfan," Sita asked.

He tried, but gave up in exasperation after a while and said, "You'd better stick to your Kalidas and Tulsidas; Iqbal is beyond you."

One day a letter arrived from the United States. Sita read it then quietly continued with her ironing.

"Sita?" Irfan called as he came into the flat.

"What?" Sita replied gruffly. She switched off the electric iron and walked over to the window.

"Ahha! So that's how it is," Irfan exclaimed, and recited a sugary Urdu couplet as he sat down in his favorite armchair near the fireplace, his arms extended in invitation.

Sita continued to look outside.

"What's the matter, Sita?" Irfan asked gently. "Please tell me."

"Nothing." Then she turned to look at him. "I got a letter today from New York . . . from Aunty. She asks, 'How many more times will I have to juggle vowels in names?'"

Irfan remained silent.

"Irfan . . . I think we made a big mistake. How long can I continue to live with you like this?"

"Why?" He laughed, but it sounded hollow. "Just a few months, and you're already tired of it. But Uma, the Daughter of the Himalayas, bore hardships for one thousand years in order to marry Shambhu. You must read *Kumara Sambhava* some day."

"To hell with your *Kumara Sambhava*," Sita retorted.

"Wonderful!" Irfan laughed again. "Didn't I tell you all your literature and poetry and philosophy were just a fraud? Isn't it true that when you see life for what it is, all else seems silly?"

Finally one day Sita gathered the courage to write to Bilqis. In her letter, she described the weather in Paris and asked about Farkhunda Baji and Chhoti Khala, but like a coward never got around to asking her if Jamil had written them anything.

Bilqis' reply came promptly, a normal, happy, impersonal letter, full of the latest news from the theatre world of Delhi: Dr. Radhakrishnan inaugurated the eighth annual session of the IPTA . . . there were many delegates from Russia . . . Gopi Nath gave a dance performance . . . everyone thought of you in Nataraj Nagri . . . the 'Nai Nautanki' group is planning to stage the 'Little Clay Cart' in the Nautanki style . . . yesterday Lalita asked about you . . . Bombay's Little Ballet Group is coming to Delhi to perform 'Meghaduta' . . . .

Sita threw down the letter in disgust and went back to her cooking in the kitchen.

Another month passed.

"Tell me, Irfan," she said one day in desperation, "Tell me what I should do."

"Try flattering Bilqis again. What else?" He responded with decided lack of interested and, putting on his coat, went off to work.

Sita sat down at the table in front of the window and started a second letter: "I couldn't talk to Jamil in Colombo. In fact, I didn't even manage to catch a glimpse of him. You were so right, it was a wild goose chase. Please, for God's sake, write him to let me go. He has punished me enough by now."

Suddenly tears began to fall from her eyes. She went on writing, one page after another, and when the letter was finished she drew a long sigh and went out to mail it.

Bilqis replied: You'll be happy to hear that Balwant Gargi's 'Sohni Mahival' has been running in Moscow for six months . . . the IPTA group from Patna came to do their play 'Pir Ali' in the Talkatora Auditorium, one of their actors turned out to be an old classmate of yours . . . Mrinalini Sarabhai is staging Noh plays in Gujarati . . . folks with the Unity Theatre are busy preparing 'Aurangzeb' . . . there's been a revival of Agha Hashr's plays . . . .

One evening, when they returned home from a movie, their concierge gave a cablegram to Sita. Irfan opened the door and walked into the flat but Sita stopped at the door to read the cable. It was from her brother: 'Daddy has passed away.'

When Irfan came into the sitting room, changed and refreshed, he found Sita doubled up on the floor in front of the fireplace.

"What's the matter, little woman?" he asked, patting her head.

"Nothing." She raised her eyes to look at him. Her eyes were totally dry. She handed the cable to Irfan.

"Oh! I'm terribly sorry." Irfan said softly.

"I'm going to Delhi."

"Fine."

"I must stay with Mummy for a while."

"Yes. Of course." Irfan said gently. "You must go."

After arriving at 'Rahmat Manzil', Karol Bagh, Sita didn't venture out of the house for several weeks. Bilqis' 'Modern Theatre' group wanted to come to express its condolences, but she asked Bilqis and Shahzad to tell them not to. By the end of the month she was pale and sickly.

One day her mother said, "Sita, what are you doing to yourself? Go out; get some fresh air."

Her mother had not asked her a thing about Paris or Irfan; she now felt that her daughter's private life was only her own business.

Then, one afternoon, Sita changed her clothes and went off to Chanakyapuri. Everyone at Bilqis' house greeted her with much affection. Farkhunda Baji talked to her for quite a while. Just then Kailash arrived with the script of their latest play.

As they were casually talking over tea, Kailash said to Sita, "Sita-ji, Projesh Babu talks of you quite often. Every time he visits Delhi he asks us about you. But now you've turned your back on us, and made Paris your home."

She smiled most courteously. "Where is Projesh Babu these days?"

"He's in Delhi. There's going to be an exhibition of his paintings."

"Where is he staying?"

"At his old place." Then he turned to Bilqis and began to talk about the play.

Sita stood up.

"You're not leaving already, are you?" Bilqis asked. "We'll play Scrabble after dinner."

"No, Bili," Sita replied, "I must get back. Mummy is alone at home."

"Stay a while," Chhoti Khala said, "Your 'Dulha Bhai' will drive you home later."

"Listen, tonight we'll make only French words. Your French must be pretty good now." That was Bilqis, who was by now busy discussing the play with Kailash.

Sita walked out into the gathering dusk.

Time flew swiftly. In the beginning Irfan wrote her every week. Then his letters became less frequent. And now for the past few months he had been utterly silent. Sita had written him countless times, but failed to get any response. In his last letter Irfan had mentioned that he was going to Germany on some official work, but that was long ago.

Now she waited for a letter from Irfan as anxiously as she did for divorce papers from Jamil. Her mother had finally received some money for the claims they had lodged as refugees for their lost property in Pakistan. Her brother was sending them half his salary from Durgapur. Because she had expected to return to Irfan, Sita had not looked for a job. Now she would spend the entire day sitting by her mother, waiting for the evening when her younger sisters would return from college and talk to her about their day. Life became darker than ever.

It was a bitterly cold winter night when, washing her hands at the tap in the courtyard, Sita suddenly told herself that she had no friend. In this wide world, in this huge, sprawling, glittering capital, in the midst of a crowd of acquaintances, she had no one to share her sorrow. Why? Why was it so? She hadn't hurt anyone. Once Projesh had said to her: Sita Debi, you're such a strange girl. You'll have a hard time finding happiness in this world—the kind of happiness you seem to desire.

"Mummy, I'm going out for a while," Sita said, after putting on her coat and stepping out into the lane. Her mother came and closed the door.

The bus to New Delhi was nearly empty. Sita sat by a window and leaned her head against the cold glass. She closed her eyes. 'I feel,' she said to herself, 'I feel as if hundreds of boats are lined up at the shore and I don't know which one is for me.'

At Projesh's hotel, she asked the clerk at the counter, "Is Mr. Chowdhry in?"

"Which Mr. Chowdhry?"

"Mr. Chowdhry from Calcutta."

"The actor?"

"No . . . the artist."

"Oh! Yes, he's in his room. That way, please."

After Sita left the counter, the clerk scratched his head somewhat puzzled. 'That's funny,' he muttered, 'I remember she came once before—at night too—must have been over a year ór so—then she had asked for the actor Mr. Chowdhry—it's all so strange!'

Projesh Kumar Chowdhry was sprawled in an armchair in his room writing something. He was astounded when he saw her standing at the door. "Sita Debi!!" He extended his arms towards her in a dramatic manner. "I knew you'd come back to me one day."

Fair and feathery Sita collapsed into the dark and burly arms of Projesh Kumar Chowdhry—just as the clear water of the Ganga merges with the dark and churning current of the Jamuna.

A few days later the artistic circles of Delhi were buzzing with the news that the 'Sindhi Period' of Projesh Kumar Chowdhry was in full swing.

Another six months passed. Sita accompanied Projesh to Srinagar for the Spring Festival. From there they went to Calcutta. In December when Projesh had to go to Japan, Sita returned to Delhi. Her mother was waiting with two letters. One had been mailed from Rome. It was very brief: "The latest news I hear about you—is it true? Irfan."

The other letter was from New York. Sita's heart beat faster: Jamil's letter . . . in his own hand. Sita's fingers fumbled as she tore open the envelope. The dusk was gathering. She moved closer to the window for more light. It too was a short letter:

"Rahul is well. I'm divorcing you. You are now free to marry anyone you want. I intend to send Rahul next year to the Jamia Millia at Delhi. I'd like him to live in his own country and become an Indian. Here he is turning into a Yankee. When he is in Delhi you may visit with him at Farkhunda Baji's house. I have no objection to that, Jamil."

Sita felt her legs give way under her. She sat down on the carpet, near the window, and leaned back against the wall for support. Her unseeing eyes stared at the picture on the wall in which the monkey god Hanuman was flying through the air carrying a mountain on his palm.

The next day she wrote an equally short letter to Irfan: "I'm waiting for my brother to arrive. He will take Mummy, Lila and Mohini back with him to Durgapur. I'll then fly back to you. Please wait for me. I love you . . . only you. And will love you for ever and ever. . . ."

'Time is flying,' she said to herself, sealing the envelope, 'Time is flying regardless. I mustn't wait any longer.'

But why should she worry about time now, she reminded herself, she'd soon be Mrs. Irfan Ahmad. She was now legally free. She would marry Irfan, who was no 'intellectual' or 'bohemian' or 'angry young man'—who was just a sensible, straightforward, solid person. Then she would go with him to Pakistan. As a Pakistani citizen she would return to Karachi—her former city—which was not hers now but would become hers once again. Then she would go back to all those places: Hyderabad, Sadh Bela, Sakkhar, Multan, that Dak Bungalow in Panch Nad where air was filled with the fragrance of the 'Queen of the Night'. . . .

Jamil—Qamar—both had wounded her soul instead of enriching it. As for Projesh, he was so engrossed in himself that he hadn't even bothered to find out if she had a soul. But Irfan . . . Yes, Irfan. . . .

Sita Mirchandani . . . Sita Jamil . . . Sita Kazmi. . . . Now all her old friends—Bilqis, Hima, Lalita—will be foreigners to her. Also her mother and sisters, and her brother, and all the other relatives scattered all over India—who no longer had any claim over the Indus. But Sita Mirchandani was going back to her Sindhu Desh. She had finally found home. She thought of Irfan and it was as if the moon had suddenly broken out of the clouds on a cold winter's night.

It took her two weeks to finish all the preparations. The day she was busily ironing her saris and putting them in her suitcase, her mother came into her room and asked, "Where now?"

"Mummy . . . I'm going to Paris to marry Irfan," she calmly replied and closed the suitcase.

At noon, coming out of the airline office in Connaught Place, Sita decided she would go and bid farewell to all her friends. It was too early in the day otherwise she would have found Lalita, Kailash and their crowd in the Coffee House.

She took an auto-rikshaw and went first to Nizamuddin West. Here, all around, were fine new homes of the Punjabi middle class. She had not been here before, and it was with some difficulty that she found Lalita's cottage. Lalita was sitting on a cot in the inner courtyard enjoying the sun; she was still in her pajamas but had wrapped a shawl over them. Her son had come back from school and was riding a tricycle around the yard. Mohan, her husband, had not yet returned from his office. In the kitchen, the cook was busy preparing lunch. Sita went and sat on the cot close to Lalita.

"The sweeper hasn't yet come today," Lalita confided to her calmly, "See, how the yard is full of dirt." (She seemed to have a cold.) "Let's move the cot over there. We'll get more of the sun."

The famous Bharata Natyam dancer seemed at peace, sitting in the security of her home.

They talked for an hour about this and that; Lalita didn't ask too many questions. When the sun began to set, Lalita said, "Let's go and sit in the front yard." Sita quietly followed her outside. Lalita brought out two cane chairs and they settled down on the tiny lawn.

After some time Sita said, "I'd better be going."

"You can't do that. Stay for lunch."

"No, I'll be late."

"But at least wait for Mohan. He should be back soon."

"Okay."

Not so far away, the high, grime-covered walls of the tomb of the saint Nizamuddin Auliya were bathed in the pale light of a winter sun, and an air of desolation lay over everything. Sita shifted restlessly in her chair. Lalita remained silent, watching the road.

The call for early afternoon prayers rose from the

mosque of Hazrat Nizamuddin. The air of desolation grew heavier.

"Lalita," Sita said, "I think I had better leave. Say hello for me to Kailash, Pradip, Kamran and the rest of the Coffee House crowd. . . . "

"Okay."

Lalita's servant went and got an auto-rikshaw for Sita. The wind was getting brisk and raising small puffs of dust on the road. Sita said goodbye to Lalita and got into the rikshaw. The Sikh driver had a long white beard which moved in the wind.

Lalita leaned over the decorative gate of her house and watched the road for a long time. The yellowing leaves of the jacaranda tree flew around them in the wind. The sun was quite pale now.

"Where should I take you, bibi-ji?" the old Sikh driver asked, after they had reached the main road.

At Bilqis' house, the washerman had just brought the weekly laundry. Chhoti Khala was on the back verandah, buying potatoes from the vegetable-seller. Farkhunda Baji's children had returned from their school and were as usual playing cricket on the back lawn with other children from the neighborhood. Bilqis was in the lounge, changing the covers of the cane chairs.

"Come in here," Bilqis said when she saw Sita, "I'll be finished soon."

. . . All my life long I was preyed upon . . .

After collecting the dirty tablecloths from the drawing room they went into Farkhunda Baji's bedroom.

"Close that door, will you," Bilqis said to Sita, "The wind is too strong today." Then she started to remove things from the dressing table. Sita helped her clean and dust. Bilqis changed the sheets on the two beds and spread new covers; she cleaned the ashtrays, dusted the pile of *The Hindustan Times* tucked away behind one of the blue curtains, and gathered all the soiled clothes.

. . . All my life long I was preyed upon . . .

In the room next door Chhoti Khala turned on the heater, wrapped herself in her shawl, and, squatting on her bed, began to chop betel nuts. Outside, children squabbled noisily. It was colder. In the diplomatic enclave of Chanakyapuri, the government flats for senior officers and the imposing structures of the various embassies stood aloof and far apart from each other. Only happy and satisfied people lived in those fine buildings. In the distance stood the Ashoka Hotel, wrapped in the gathering dusk, a tall and haughty, towering pile of red sandstone. Winter flowers filled the gardens.

. . .*All my life long I was preyed upon* . . .

Someone knocked on the lounge door. Kailash came in. Then Pradeep called. A child threw down a glass in the dining room. Butul Baji loudly said, "Hunhh!," in the middle of her prayers.

Sita left Chanakyapuri and arrived at Commissioner's Lane in Old Civil Lines. A bunch of girls standing in the verandah of the Blue House said "Namaste".

In the Garden House, Hima had retired to her bedroom with the baby. Her husband had come back from London and Hima was to go to her in-laws with him next week.

Outside the Garden House, two miniature Tibetan dogs were rolling around on the lawn. "Meet Ching and Chao," Shahzad introduced them to Sita, "They've come here with the Dalai Lama."

"Really?"

"Yes. Iqbal brought them. He was on duty, to escort the Dalai Lama from the border. You know what? He's going to be a Lieutenant Colonel."

"How wonderful!"

Amma came out.

"Oh! It's Sita. After a very long time. How have you been?"

"I'm fine, Amma."

"It's getting dark. Don't stay outside in the cold."

"Yes, Amma."

'. . . and when day and night meet, Mahadeva and Parvati

come down from Mount Kailash and fly all over the earth'—it was a cold evening much like this one when Amma had told Sita that story.

Saying goodbye to Hima and Shahzad, Sita returned to Karol Bagh when it was already quite dark. Her flight to Paris was to leave very early the next morning.

(22)

The rain was coming down in torrents that dismal afternoon of January 1961 when Sita's taxi drew up in front of that familiar building on Boulevard Souchet. Sita felt she had come home after centuries. Home, now, was where Irfan lived.

Jamil had been a romance of her immature years; it had ended after a few months. She had been attracted to Qamar because he was so casual, even careless. Projesh Chowdhry had drawn sympathy from her. Fame, honour, wealth and popularity, Projesh had all four in abundance. Women swooned over him; men were envious of him. And yet he appeared so helpless, so forlorn. For the first time Sita had felt that she, who was herself an object of pity for others, could feel pity for someone else.

That night in the Constitution House, Projesh had said to her, "Sita Debi, I have lived an extremely lonely life. The world understands my paintings, but it doesn't understand me. My friends, my critics, these throngs of admirers—none among them knows the real Projesh Kumar Chowdhry. No one knows the Projesh who used to wander through the streets of Calcutta after midnight to find his soul. Now that same Projesh sits on the throne of fame, but he isn't happy. So many beautiful girls came into my life, Sita Debi, but none could look into the depths of my soul." Sita knew Projesh was putting on a big act, but that only served to make her pity him. Projesh would often say to her, child-like, "I need you, Sita Debi," and the mother in Sita would come awake.

But Irfan . . . Irfan . . . .

Until now she had legally been Mrs. Jamil, but now that the papers had come from New York, no one would be able to deny her right to call herself Mrs. Irfan Kazmi. They would get married right away. Irfan wouldn't be just her "lover" any longer; he would be her husband . . . her god . . . her everything. The most sacred, the most beautiful of all ties would bind them together.

She ran up the stairs to the second floor and repeatedly pressed the doorbell of the flat. The door opened. An unfamiliar face looked at her.

"Yes?"

"I . . . I'm Madame Kazmi."

"Pardon! Madame Kazmi?" The stranger, a middle-aged Frenchman, moved a step closer to peer at her. "Are you sure?"

"Yes, of course . . . why . . . what do you mean?" Anger and shame made her legs shake.

"But Monsieur and Madame Kazmi left only yesterday morning for St. Croce. For their honeymoon. I'm staying in their flat while they are gone." Then he added, "Would you like to come in for a moment? Please do come in."

"Madame Kazmi. . . ?" Sita's voice sounded as if it came from the bottom of a deep well.

"She was Mlle. Dubiert before her marriage . . . Marcelle Dubiert. She used to work in his office. Mlle. Dubiert is also a former beauty queen. She's very young. . . ." The man wiped his palms with a handkerchief; then he walked over to the balcony and looked at the sky above. "It has been a bad winter. The sun hasn't come out for several days. Who knows when spring will come this year. But please do come in and sit down. The wind is terrible outside."

. . .*All my life long I've been preyed upon* . . .

. . .There's still some day left. Then it will be night. Then dawn will come. Another day. Another night. . .

. . .*The chain of day and night, creator of all events.* . .

. . .Don't ever make the mistake of keeping track of days and nights. No one has been able to measure time. . .

. . .'It checks your worth, it checks my worth, this ruthless money-changer Time'. . .

. . .This measuring of days and nights . . . . "Life is not like one of your documentary films," Bilqis had once said to Saulat, "You can't catch it all in your 'long', 'mid', and 'close.'". . .

. . .*The chain of day and night, a two-toned thread of silk* . . .
A gust of wind banged the door shut.

(1960)
(Translated by C. M. Naim)

❋ The Housing Society ❋

The Housing Society

(1)

The mist of the icy January dawn was beginning to lift from the trees. In the distance, the sun had risen from behind the sand dunes on the other side of the Gomti, and shells scattered on the river bank were glistening. Shabbarwa, the lamp-lighter, was squatting on the damp ground in front of the kitchen tent, energetically polishing silver dinner knives on a polishing board, then piling them up on one side. He was also busy singing to keep away the cold:

Moses will appear blazing like the light of Sinai;
Mohammed will show himself on Judgement Day adorned like
a bridegroom.

Then he started another *qawwali*:

See, O Saqi, if the clouds hang over the garden.

"*Bap-re-bap*, it's so cold," said Dwarka Parshad, the head peon, as he came out of the small tent for chaprasis.

"We're in for extra work tonight," Shabbarwa responded, busily polishing away.

Two indistinct forms emerged from the shadows of the mango grove. Through the mist-filled air the sunbeams had made a broad track to Shabbarwa's head. He squinted and shouted to the approaching man, "*Salaam alaikum.*" Then he said to Dwarka Parshad, "He's early with his dali, isn't he?"

Syed Mazhar Ali, with Jhinga Pasi carrying a large basket of chickens on his head, approached. He, too, carried a smaller basket of dry and fresh fruit.

Dwarka Parshad placed a towel on his shoulder, crossed the distance to the Memsahib's tent, and said from outside, "Hujur, someone has brought a present."

"Return it," replied the voice from inside.

A few minutes later, Dwarka Parshad entered the tent and said, "Memsahib, he says that. . . ."

"Fine. Just give him my salaam and return the dali."

Dwarka Parshad came out and repeated the Memsahib's words.

"All right," Syed Mazhar Ali didn't insist any further; he walked off in the direction of his village with a downcast look. He had a handspun cotton sheet wrapped over his cotton sherwani and wore a cap with earflaps. With his rough shoes, he also wore red knit socks whose heels were gone. Jhinga Pasi limped behind with the basket of chickens on his head, frequently hopping to keep up with him. Shabbarwa felt pity for him. In fact, both men seemed most pitiable. He sprinkled more powder on his polishing board and got busy with a nautanki tune from "Raja Harishchandra":

> *We dwell in palaces, O Pandit;*
> *How far away is your Kashi?*

❖

The sun got brighter and the camp started to bustle with activity. The Sahib convened the court in the mango grove. Extending far into the distance, the mud paths along the fields were lined with ekkas, bullock-carts and bicycles. Court officials, petition writers, scribes, peasants, landlords, 'witnesses' and 'clients'—all were gathered under the trees. Just then two bearers carrying a palanquin came to where the court was in session and placed their burden under a tree. The woman sitting inside started to weep softly. Her case was called; she made her statement; then she continued to cry, heaving with sobs.

Soon it was noon. An elephant emerged from the cluster of shisham trees; majestically swaying, it approached the camp. A manservant got down in front of the large tent in the centre and called out to Dwarka Parshad. Dwarka Parshad then hurried into the Memsahib's tent.

"Nawab Shams Ara Begum's elephant has come for Chhoti Bitiya."

"Send it back," the Memsahib answered as usual. She was sitting in an easy chair at the back of the tent, writing a letter to her son in Allahabad.

Chhoti Bitiya shot out like an arrow from another tent and started wailing, "Mama . . . Mama. I want to ride Jumbo. I'll feed Jumbo guavas. Mama . . . Mama." Then she flung herself on the ground.

"All right, all right, go on. Don't roll in the dirt," the Memsahib responded irritably, and returned to her letter.

Chhoti Bitiya bent over and buckled her red shoes, then raised her arms toward Dwarka Parshad so he could lift her up. Madar Bakhsh, the attendant, quickly brought her flowered silk parasol. The mahout made the elephant kneel down. Dwarka Parshad, placing Chhoti Bitiya in his lap, seated himself in the howdah and, with great dignity, stroked his long, white moustache. He was the Collector Sahib's head chaprasi, and that was no joke. Nawab Shams Ara Begum's manservant looked properly impressed. The elephant with its brocade hangings and painted howdah passed in front of the court, then set out towards the mud fort of Parbatipur.

In the court, the lament of the purdah-nashin lady in the palanquin continued. A small canvas screen had been set up on three sides behind the palanquin. Behind the screen, a fourteen- or fifteen-year-old girl, dressed in tight green chintz pajamas with a pink muslin dupatta wrapped around her head, squatted on the ground. She held the curtain of the palanquin with one hand, and with the other abstractedly drew lines on the ground. Every so often she would look up and cast fearful glances all around. Outside in the court, her name kept coming up time and time again. Peeping through a crack in the screen, she looked out. An elephant was passing by. A little, golden-haired girl was riding on it. She wore a hairy coat that looked like a bear-skin, and a white-moustached old man in uniform was shading her with a colorful parasol. It was just like in the fairy tales. The girl by the palanquin kept looking, astonished, until the elephant went out of sight. Then, bowing her head, she again busied herself, drawing pictures in the wet earth. Now she made the picture of an elephant, with four lines for its howdah; in the howdah she seated a princess wearing a crown. Then she said to herself: 'I'm the princess. I, Basanti Begum.'

"*Musammat* Surayya Sultan alias Basanti Begum, minor." Her name was being mentioned in the court again. Frightened, she tightened her grip on the curtain of the palanquin.

The elephant left the village. At the outskirts, there was a centuries-old Sufi shrine and a stepped-well. A little further was the house of the keeper of the shrine, Shah Munawwar Ali. The elephant passed along the lane beside the house. From the elephants back, Chhoti Bitiya looked into the house's dusty courtyard where a black-bearded man with long black tresses, wrapped in an orange sheet, sat on a cot gazing into the sky. Another man, sparsely bearded and gloomy, was sitting on a cane stool. Under a guava tree, a small girl dressed in tight red churidars was grinding spices on a stone. On her wrists were bangles of tarnished silver. The elephant moved on.

The sun shone fiercely and the court recessed for lunch. Lala Husain Bakhsh, clerk, wrapped up the file which contained the appellant *Musammat* Buta Begum's petition. It read:

I, *Musammat* Buta Begum, major—community: Muslim; caste: Syed; resident of village Muhammad Ganj, tahsil Harauni, district Sultanpur—am the widow of the late

Syed Zawwar Husain, cultivator in the said village.

Three years ago, Nawab Sikandar Quli Khan, alias Nawab Bhure, Ta'aluqedar of Sahroli and Durgakund, expressed the desire to marry Syeda Surayya Khatun, alias Basanti Begum, the only daughter of your humble servant, a girl who through the intercession of Holy Butul (may peace be upon her), was enriched by God Almighty, the Most Magnificent, with an abundant beauty of appearance, character and chastity. Your humble servant rejected his proposal on the grounds that the aforementioned Nawab Sahib at the age of 65, in spite of having a large number of wives, lawful and unlawful, is given to all vices and immoral practices, pleasures and frivolities. A few days later, on February 22, 1937, four hours after nightfall, the abduction of Basanti Begum, aged thirteen and a half, took place by armed men, and that young, chaste girl was imprisoned in the mud fort of Durgakund. Nawab Shams Ara Begum, Ta'aluqedar of Parbatipur, was at that time very favorably inclined towards your humble servant because in her childhood, the aforementioned learned the Qur'an from me and your humble servant lived in the fort of Parbatipur as her governess for a long time. Apart from this, the husband of your humble servant was listed among the zakirs employed at the fort. And that late-lamented person, till the end of his days, despite a weakness of eyesight, had been engaged in the imambara there as a reciter of elegies. Therefore, the respected Begum Sahiba appealed to the court on behalf of your humble servant and filed a criminal case of kidnapping against Nawab Bhure, because litigation has been going on for various reasons for generations between the estates of the aforementioned lady and those of the said Nawab Sahib.

After a few days, around midnight, masked dacoits climbed into my house and martyred with hatchets the eighteen-year-old only son of your humble servant, Syed

Karrar Husain, then disappeared. Thereafter, Miyan
Nauroz, son of Nawab Shams Ara Begum, gave a statement in the court of the Sub-Divisional Magistrate to
the effect that *Musammat* Basanti Begum was his lawful
wedded wife and that it was he who had authority over
the girl. . . .

Whereas, because of this further provocation and
fresh discord and conflict, the matter became extremely
delicate and complicated, *Musammat* Basanti Begum,
under the orders of the refuge of the people, Mr. Ram
Saran Bhargava, Sub-Divisional Magistrate, was removed
from the fort of Durgakund and placed in my custody.
But now, this death-afflicted one does not have the
strength to fight the false claim of Miyan Nauroz. Therefore, your humble servant in her extreme state of desti-
tution and grief appeals to the Collector Sahib Bahadur
of heavenly status and august dignity, the Nushirwan of
his time, that with his special orders, may he be pleased
to close all further channels of dispute and provocation in this matter. By the fact that the assistance of de-
serving people is approved by God the Munificent, this
act of yours will be a source of blessing and goodness,
and of increase in your dignity and fame.

My further submission is that in these dire times, your
humble servant can produce as a witness only Syed
Mazhar Ali, cultivator, resident of Muhammad Ganj,
who, though a tenant of Nawab Shams Ara Begum, nevertheless, because of the excellence and purity of his
nature, has. . . .

❖

The sun had now set to the level of the courtyard wall.
After Syed Mazhar Ali made a round of his fields, he returned and sat down on his stool. His elder brother, Shah
Munawwar Ali, stretched out on the cot, covering his face
with the *Medinah* newspaper. Syed Mazhar Ali's wife had

been drying red peppers all day long in the sun and the pungent peppery smell made Syed Mazhar Ali sneeze a few times. Jhinga Pasi's wife sat in the entrance picking lice from Manzurun-Nisa's head. The legs of Manzurun-Nisa's tight red twill pajamas were soiled, because all day long she had been building clay houses from the mud in front of the porch.

Shah Munawwar Ali woke up restlessly. "*Allahu Ghani,*"* he exclaimed in a loud voice. The chickens in the basket began to cluck. Just then the front door rattled and Syed Akhtar Ali entered the house.

"Bhayya is back from the tahsil," Syed Mazhar Ali's wife announced.

"Assalaam alaikum," said the newcomer, a little loudly, addressing his two brothers.

"Wa'alaikum-assalaam. May you live long," replied Syed Mazhar Ali.

Syed Akhtar Ali looked towards the basket of chickens set in one corner of the yard.

"Memsahib returned the dali," Syed Mazhar Ali explained.

"'He' borrowed a full ten rupees from Asharfi Lal to take the dali for your sake," wailed Akhtar Ali's sister-in-law, as she picked up red peppers from the burlap spread on the ground.

"So, what happened in my case?" asked Syed Akhtar Ali somewhat irritably.

"I took Thakur Sahib's recommendatory letter to the Collector Sahib. before the court convened. He said, 'I don't need recommendations. Send your petition to Lucknow. I shall speak to Johnson Sahib.'"

"Johnson Sahib will arrive this evening and early tomorrow morning he will leave to do some hunting. I had to give Lala Husain Bakhsh two rupees to get that information."

"Memsahib is English, isn't she?" Syed Mazhar Ali asked.

---

*"Allah is free from every want!"

"Her grandfather was English," replied Syed Akhtar Ali. "He was an indigo planter in Mirzapur, and married the daughter of the Nawab Sahib of Vikrampur. The Collector Sahib belongs to some family in Bihar. Memsahib got some zamindari from her father. They have houses in Allahabad and Musoorie. Also two children."

"It's all in God's greatness. That Pure Provider bestows his bounty on some people," his sister-in-law offered resignedly, as she winnowed lentils.

A silence fell over everything.

"Almighty God bestows on His lover the bounty of patience," Shah Munawwar Ali suddenly exclaimed. He then got up and went out; passing down the deserted lane, he went and sat down on the broken terrace of the dargah.

"Bhai Sahib observed many chillas for your sake, but to no avail," said Syed Mazhar Ali quietly. "Last year, for six months, he confined himself to a small hut on the bank of the Gomti. It got to be extremely cold and he developed pneumonia." Then he said to his daughter, "Manzurya, bring the hookah." She prepared the hookah and set it in front of her father. Syed Mazhar Ali, who didn't smoke in front of his older brother, took one puff and continued, "I brought Bhai Sahib back after a great many entreaties; now he is following another regimen to bring jinns under his control." He took another puff. "On your behalf, I told the Collector Sahib that my younger brother is a lawyer but he is unlucky. He practised law at the district courts but it didn't flourish, so he started in Kanpur where he almost starves. He wants to give his children higher education. We hear that a position is open in Lucknow. If your honour would be so kind as to give him a recommendation. . . . He said, 'Syed Sahib, who am I? Place your trust in Allah; sooner or later He hears everyone.'"

"In the month of terah-tezi, I'll go to Makanpur and put a chadar on the grave of Shah Madar. Only then will you get your job," Mazhar Ali's wife said as she hung the winnowing basket on the wall.

Syed Akhtar Ali looked at his sister-in-law with annoyance, then glanced in the direction of the water-stand. She rushed over, poured some cold water into a shiny bright Muradabadi katora, and offered it to her brother-in-law whom she loved like a son.

Syed Mazhar Ali stood up. He put on his muslin cap and his wooden sandals, and set out for the mosque for the late afternoon prayers. Syed Akhtar Ali picked up the copy of the *Medinah* and pulled the pipe of the hookah towards himself—he too didn't smoke in front of his elders. Far away, sitting on the terrace of the shrine, Shah Munawwar Ali let out a heart-chilling cry, "*Ya Badduh!*" The air of desperation hanging over everything could have broken even the most resolute heart.

❖

Under a neem tree by the ancient well, Nawab Bhure's nephew, Munnan Khan, who had gone and joined the dacoits, was playing Chausar with the other carefree good-for-nothings of the village. As he threw the dice he teased jobless Akhtar Ali's son, Jamshed, by singing a silly rhyme:

> *Garden birds go to the lakes to lay eggs;*
> *but Mukhtars use the holidays to lay eggs.*

Jamshed Ali squatted to one side and watched the game with no interest. When Munnan Khan repeated his little ditty for the fourth time, Jamshed swelled with anger and slapped him, overturning the playing board. Then, jumping over the conduits of the well, he strode off toward the dargah.

He hid himself behind the crumbling walls, wiped his eyelashes dry with a finger, and looked around. Under the bullrush hedge was a graveyard in which a few cottonwoods stood here and there, with their cotton flowers strewn all over. The yard was full of tall grass and thorny shrubs, aca-

cia trees, bushes of wild berries, cactus plants, pits of
sunken graves, piles of dirt, snake holes, a few whitewashed, brick graves of holy men, and many other graves
that were no better than mounds of dry mud. In the far
corner, under a shisham tree, stood the mud homes of
the keeper of the shrine and the gravedigger. The latter's
wife had lit the fire for the evening meal and its smoke
slowly rose and mingled with the early mist. Someone had
lit an oil lamp on a grave and its flame had already black-
ened the inscription niche. Wild jasmine bushes grew beside the low mud wall along the road. Two village women
driving their goats home passed by. One noticed the newly-
made grave under the bushes and remarked, "Must be the
grave of some bride—that's why the jasmine is so fragrant
tonight." In the deep silence of the evening, a cold breeze
began to rustle through the leaves.

Jamshed felt a bit scared. He shook his chappal to get
rid of some grit from under his heel; then, leaping over
the mounds of brick and dirt, set out towards the fields.
Maybe winter showers were on their way, for the sky was
filled with clouds. With his hands tucked under his arms
for warmth but still shivering, Jamshed wandered for a long
time on the narrow strips between the fields. An elephant
was coming from the direction of Parbatipur. Jamshed
stopped under a gular tree by the side of a pond to watch
the elephant. Then, as it passed by, he began to follow it
at a little distance.

Chhoti Bitiya sat in the howdah and was so absorbed in
Dwarka Parshad's story of Nala and Damayanti that her
parasol slipped from her hand and fell to the ground. The
elephant moved on.

Jamshed picked up the parasol with its silver handle and
examined it, turning it over in his hand. He called to the
mahout, but the elephant had already disappeared in a
grove of burhal trees. Jamshed turned around and walked
back home. The door to the main house was locked from
inside. He placed the parasol in a corner of the separate

baithak, then went around to the side where cattle were tied. Taking off his chappals, he wiped the dust off them and put them on the wall; then, placing one foot on a trough of fodder, he jumped into the inner courtyard.

His three gloomy-faced elders—Barey Abba, Chacha Abba and Abba—sat as usual with bowed heads on the takht in the verandah. His Chachi was in the kitchen, stirring some fried spices into the lentils, while his cousin, Manzurun Nisa, was skipping around aimlessly, chanting a nonsense rhyme:

Danda is lost, gulli is crying.
*Danda's mother is busy frying.**

Just then her mother came out in the yard, grabbed her by the arm and gave her a hard slap. "Always playing!" she yelled at her. "So big but still horsing around! Don't you see it's twilight? Go, get the water for your father's ablutions."

Manzurun Nisa started bawling and ran with outstretched arms for refuge towards her cousin, who had suddenly appeared in the courtyard. He inattentively took down his chappals from the wall and gave them to her.

"Go, put them in the room," Jamshed told the girl. Manzurun Nisa immediately stopped crying; she lovingly held the big dusty chappals in her hands as if they were her beloved dolls, and went inside.

Jamshed pulled over a cane stool and sat down near his elders. Jhinga Pasi's wife untied the cow from the shed and led it out to the water trough. Syed Mazhar Ali's wife came into the verandah and lowered the quilted curtains over its archways. Outside, lamps had been lit in the village homes. Then the call for the evening prayer sounded and darkness fell.

❖

---

*Danda and *gulli* are two sticks—one long, the other short—used in a popular game.

Shabbarwa, the lamplighter, went around to all the tents and gathered their assortment of lamps and lanterns; he then filled them with oil and set them in a row in front of the kitchen tent. Madar Bakhsh, the attendant, came and sat down facing the row and began to clean the shades and chimneys with a towel. Chhoti Bitiya came hop-skipping, squatted by his side, and started to watch this daily ritual. She took great delight in it every evening.

After he finished cleaning the glassware, Madar Bakhsh started to light the wicks, and as always, when he lit the first wick he said under his breath, "May the lamp be lighted; may my object be achieved. Blessings, blessings. Peace be upon you, O *Munkir Nakir*. The faith is my heart, the grave is my home."

"Madar Bakhsh, why is your home in a grave?" Chhoti Bitiya as always asked in astonishment.

"Shabbir! Send Bulaqan—the wretch hasn't heated the iron yet," the Memsahib's voice rang out from the far tent. Chhoti Bitiya also liked the ironing 'show' very much. She flew to her mother's tent. "Mama, why is Bulaqan a wretch?" she inquired.

"Shoo! Out!"

"No, tell me, Mama."

"Because she is," the Memsahib replied irritably. Actually she had been addressing Dwarka Parshad. "Her parents had to die soon after she was born. Then her husband took another wife. Her home was ruined. But what can that wretched woman do? One can't avoid the fruits of one's karma."

"Mama, Mama, what are the fruits of karma?"

"Come, Bitiya, the Commissioner Sahib wants you," said a chaprasi, coming inside. She shot out of the tent with the same speed.

With large mantel-lamps hissing everywhere, it was quite a spectacle in the camp that night. Tonight Chhoti Bitiya had received special permission to eat with the adults. So there she was in her high chair in the dining tent, regaling 'Uncle Johnson' with the stories of her ride on 'Jumbo' and the many pet deer and stags in the fort at Parbatipur. At the head of the table, the Memsahib, wearing a 'Parsi-styled' silver-bordered silk sari from Surat and a fur coat bought from Whiteways of Calcutta, was busy carving the roast. Her honey-brown hair was clustered over her fore-head and ears in accordance with the latest fashion, and she was wearing western style earrings that had large pearls dangling at the end of gold chains. When the Memsahib shook her head in the course of conversation, her earrings swayed, reminding some people of clock pendulums. She was of British stock, but she knew English just barely, and before her marriage she had lived in strict purdah in her parents' home. Nevertheless, the servants, fascinated by her extremely fair complexion and western features, per-sistently called her "Memsahib" instead of "Begum Sahib."

A brazier full of hot coals had been set under the table. The servants lightly stepped back and forth with dishes across the dhurrie spread over straw. The Memsahib started to tell Johnson Sahib the story of the kidnapping of Basanti Begum. "But Nawab Bhure is also a wily fellow, cunning as an old jackal. Anyone he targets has no chance. I feel so sorry for poor Buta Begum," she told him.

Johnson Sahib concurred in equally idiomatic Urdu.

The icy January wind blew hard and the walls of the tent began to shake. The light of the hissing mantle-lamp dimmed a little, but Shabbarwa swiftly pumped it back to a glow. With a flourish, Madar Bakhsh changed the dishes for the last course. When he offered Johnson Sahib the serving dish, Johnson Sahib shook his head to decline. Madar Bakhsh said to him with great dignity, "*Phinis*,"— that is, 'finish'—that is, 'this is the last course". On the occasion of formal dinners, Madar Bakhsh always spoke in English to the English guests, as his grandfather and great-grandfather had done since the East India Company times when speaking in the bungalows of the Sahib log.

Johnson Sahib complimented the hostess on her dinner service; the Memsahib informed him that the Russian service had come from Peshawar, from a store famous for its collection of pre-Revolution Russian tableware. Then Johnson Sahib began to exchange views with the Collector Sahib about the next day's hunt.

One wall of the tent shook more than usual, and two curious, amazed eyes peeked through a crack in it.

❖

Jamshed once again gathered up his courage to go inside and give the parasol to the Memsahib—but then once again he was lost in this Arabian Nights-like scene.

Now, water-filled crystal bowls with rose petals floating on top were placed on the table, but instead of drinking the water, the people dipped their fingers into it.

Jamshed looked at the little golden-haired girl who had a red ribbon tied right on the top of her head and who reminded Jamshed of his cousin, Manzurun Nisa, who wore tarnished earrings in the many holes pierced through her earlobes and cavorted around in rough and dirty hand-me-downs. When Manzurun Nisa grows up, she will be dropped in his lap and both of them will spend the rest of their lives in some dark and narrow lane in Kanpur—living in genteel indigence, just as their fathers, uncles, grandfathers and great-grandfathers had done before them. And all the while, the Memsahib, the Collector Sahib, and all their kin would continue to elegantly dip their fingers in crystal bowls of fragrant water.

Madar Bakhsh saw the tent wall ripple and took a step forward. Jamshed hurriedly jumped back.

Inside, Johnson Sahib lit a cigar. He thanked his hostess for the excellent meal, kissed the little girl on the cheek, and placing his crisp white napkin on the table, rose from his chair. Dwarka Parshad rushed to raise the entrance curtain from outside. Johnson Sahib was a tall and hefty Englishman; he bent his head as he stepped through the opening and, taking long strides, headed for his tent. His courteous host, the Collector Sahib, strode beside him. Dwarka Parshad, dressed in his red broadcloth chapkan, again took his place on the stool outside the dining tent. Then he heard a noise. "Who's there?" he demanded threateningly.

Jamshed, scared out of his wits, fled, but he tripped on a tent rope and the chaprasis caught hold of him. "Thief, thief!" they shouted, and grabbed the parasol from his hand.

"Thief . . . rogue!" snarled Dwarka Parshad as he slapped Jamshed's face.

"I'm not a thief," Jamshed shouted back angrily, and again tears came into his eyes. "I came to bring Bitiya's umbrella. I found it lying by the pond."

"You lying crook, you think you can fool me!" Dwarka Parshad roared and slapped him some more.

"Madar Bakhsh," the Memsahib's voice rang from inside, but Madar Bakhsh, too, had rushed to the scene.

Chhoti Bitiya peeped from the doorway, "Mama, Mama, Dwarka Parshad has caught a thief!" she happily exclaimed.

"What's all the ruckus?" the Memsahib inquired, coming to the entrance.

Jamshed immediately wiped his eyes dry and boldly struggled forward. "I'm not a thief. I'm not a liar. I'm Syed Jamshed Ali, nephew of Shah Munawwar Ali of the dargah sharif. My uncle, Syed Mazhar Ali came to pay his respects . . . ," then he quickly changed his words, ". . . came to meet you but you sent him away from outside."

"Shah Munawwar Ali?" the Memsahib repeated with some interest, "Shah Munawwar Ali. I've heard about him. Doesn't he bring jinns under his control?"

"No, Barey Abba doesn't have any jinns under his control," Jamshed replied, bitterly. "His continued poverty has affected his mind." Jamshed's teeth began to chatter from the severe cold, and he sniffled.

"Why are you standing out there? Come inside. Madar Bakhsh, set out a plate."

"No, thank you. I ate at home before coming."

The Memsahib noticed the look on his face. He reminded her of her son, Salman, who had the same sense of pride and self-respect. Jamshed stepped inside the tent but remained at the door.

"Bitiya, thank Jamshed bhayya. He came in this cold weather to give you your parasol."

Holding her parasol, Chhoti Bitiya said in a small voice, "Thank you."

"Now say 'Goodnight'."

"Goodnight," she obediently repeated, then went off with Bulaqan.

The Memsahib again turned to Jamshed. "You are connected with Shams Ara Begum, aren't you?" she inquired.

"No. My uncle cultivates some land she owns. We're in no way related to rajas or nawabs."

The Memsahib was taken aback. The bitterness in his voice sounded so familiar to her. When her darling son came home from the University, he would gab about God knows what with his friends—'the feudal class' . . . 'British exploitation' . . . 'agrarian revolution' . . . incomprehensible words and terms.

"Do you study somewhere?"

"I'm in 'Second Year' at Kanpur."

"Very good!"

"Now, if you'll allow me. . . ."

"Have some coffee."

Coffee. He had never had coffee before.

"No, thank you," he answered firmly. "My home is at the other end of the village; it will be very late by the time I get there." Then he said, "Adab Arz," and stepping out of the tent, disappeared in the darkness.

When he reached home, Jamshed stepped lightly into the narrow hall. On one side, on cots laid out side by side, the three brothers were fast asleep. Chachi Amma and Manzurun Nisa slept on the other side on a takht with their heads covered with dirty, Farrukhabadi print quilts. He quietly dropped onto his own cot and pulled a thin quilt over himself, but he still felt cold, so he pulled down a coverlet that was hanging on the clothesline above him, and spread it over the quilt. Huddled up on one side, he finally fell asleep.

❖

At *tahajjud* time, Shah Munawwar Ali got up, and groping in the dark, found his way to the head of Jamshed's cot. He muttered a prayer under his breath and blew upon the boy's forehead. He then took an amulet from under his pillow, tied it on the boy's arm, and went back and stretched out on his cot again. Jamshed had come awake, but he remained silent and still, only wishing he could have a nice cry. After a while, Chachi Amma woke up and lit a lantern. Manzurun Nisa instantly got up also. Both mother and daughter threw their thin quilts over their heads, went to the kitchen, and began to prepare the food for Jamshed's journey. He dozed off again. The cock crowed from the courtyard wall while it was still dark. Jamshed got up quickly. He didn't have a watch. He hurried into the totally dark room at the back and brought out his tin box of clothes; then he rolled up his beddings in a dhurrie, and going to the door of the hall softly called, "Manzurya, where are my chappals?"

Manzurun Nisa came running. She lit the little oil lamp that was hanging from a nail in the wall and took his chappals down from the shelf, then she brought him his coat and muffler. She also fetched some warm water so that he could wash his face. Then Chachi Amma came with the stuffed tiffin-carrier and put it near him on the takht; she then returned to the kitchen to prepare tea.

"Bhayya, I myself made the puris for you," said Manzurun Nisa.

"Fine." Jamshed, tying his shoe-laces, looked at her with some affection, and his heart melted. 'Poor, poor unfortunate girl,' he said to himself.

Gobindwa arrived and called from outside. Jamshed's father and uncle woke up. Chachi Amma tied an *imam zamin* to Jamshed's arm. He climbed onto Gobindwa's ekka and set out for the railway station.

Mist was beginning to ripple over the chickpea fields and the moon's light had paled. The solitary lanterns of the Collector Sahib's camp were twinkling in the distance. The sound of the train's whistle could be heard from across the river. Mango groves, the dargah, the pond, Hanumanji's temple, Jhinga pasi's hut, Barey Abba, Chacha Abba, Chachi Amma, Manzurun Nisa—all the receding silhouettes disappeared into something greater and more nebulous. That night while returning from the camp, he had resolved that when he went back to Kanpur, he would work very hard. He would make the top of the class. He would compete in the services tests. And one day his name would read: S. J. Ali, I.C.S. Then when he would visit Muhammad Ganj, the peasants will say, 'The Gent Sahib has come on his rounds.' Gent Sahib. Collector Sahib. Commissioner Sahib. . . .

The ekka bumped wildly on the dirt road. He quickly grabbed its canopy and with his other hand, took out a packet of Passing Show cigarettes and matches from the pocket of his coat. When he struck the match, Gobindwa turned around and looked at him.

"What are you doing?" he asked plaintively.

"Please, Gobind Chacha, don't tell anyone at home," Jamshed entreated. One look at the frown on Gobindwa's face and all his dreams of the I.C.S. instantly vanished into thin air.

"Well, I won't, but don't you go picking up these city ways." Gobindwa whipped the mangy horse again. "Why can't you move, sasur? You need a cigarette too?"

Jamshed took a long puff and exhaled through his nostrils. Just then Gobardhan Chacha came into sight. He carried a plough on his shoulders and was driving a pair of bullocks towards his field. In a panic, Jamshed hid the cigarette in his fist. If Gobar Chacha had noticed the cigarette, he would have pulled Jamshed down from the ekka, hit him with a shoe fifty times, then lost count.

How sickeningly conservative life in the village was, he thought angrily. Villages of Hindustan! Ha!

Little did he know that this morning would be nearly the last time he would set out from his village; that he would never visit Muhammad Ganj the way he did now, or sit in Gobindwa's ekka; that he would never again have any reason to fear Gobar Chacha's wrath.

(2)

Jamshed arrived at his home in Kanpur. Several years earlier, Syed Akhtar Ali had sold his share of the land in Muhammad Ganj and bought this house in the city where he had started his law practice. Posters for "Bhabhi" and "Pukar", the hit movies of the year, and notices for public meetings organised by the Congress were pasted on the wall across the lane. Jamshed climbed the few steps and, raising the chiq hanging over the door, entered the narrow baithak. In the centre, on the bare brick floor were a table and, for clients, three or four chairs. Thick, dusty law books were arranged on the shelves of a cupboard in one corner. On one wall there was a picture of Syed Akhtar Ali, in which he wore a B.A., L.L.B. gown as he stared into the camera. The remaining walls contained a picture of Sir Syed Ahmad Khan, a picture of the Taj Mahal, and three framed calligraphic prints: "*Muhammad * Ali * Fatima * Hasan * Husain*"; "There is no God but Allah and Muhammad is His Prophet"; and "We place our trust in you, O Omniscient". There was also a calendar with a picture of the tomb of the Prophet in Medinah. In another corner on a shelf were some bound volumes of *Nizam al-Mashaikh, Din-o-Duniya* and *Medinah* and a copy of the ever-popular Sufi memoir, *Tazkira-e Ghausiya*. A large, framed print of the shrine of Sultan-ul-Hind Khwaja Gharib-Nawaz in Ajmer was placed on the cornice piece. Jamshed raised a dirty cotton curtain and entered the women's quarters. There was only one long, narrow room, whose four doors opened onto a verandah. The room contained his cot and the cots for his brothers, Asghar and Anwar, and his sister, Aliya. They were all younger than he. There was a small table at the head of his own cot, heaped with his books which had been carefully protected in covers cut out from newspapers and illustrated magazines. The embroidered tablecloth was grimy and showed a big ink stain. His bicycle stood in one corner. His consumptive mother lay out in the verandah; Aliya was in the kitchen.

He set his luggage on a cot and stepped into the verandah; sitting down on a takht, he began to untie his shoelaces.

"Bhayya, did you bring the money?"

Jamshed started at Aliya's voice. "What money?" he asked.

"Abba said that he'd get some money from Chacha Abba. He has been gone for so long. Then you, too, went there for the vacation. Now we owe money to all our neighbors."

"No, I haven't brought any money. But maybe Abba will soon find work. Otherwise, I myself will quit college and get a job. Hey, why are you crying, you silly?" he said, stroking her head.

Amma, whom years of confinement to a cot had made extremely irritable, started her usual shouting and coughing. Jamshed sat silently on the edge of the takht.

A huge 1935-model sedan pulled up to the portico of the old-style bungalow in Civil Lines, Allahabad. A sensitive-looking, light-complexioned young man got out excitedly and rushed into his room. He quickly pulled out the drawers of his desk and rummaging through the papers, found a wallet. He then took out a red-coloured, folded card from his pocket, glanced at his name written inside, and carefully placed it in the wallet.

A servant brought the mail. When Salman saw his mother's handwriting on the envelope, he smiled lovingly. "As soon as our tour ends," he read, "we'll come straight to Allahabad. Now you must prepare for the I.C.S. examination. I'm sure Niyazi Begum has not looked after you properly in my absence. Now you are, by the grace of God, ..." Salman finished the letter and put it back in its envelope. A sad smile flickered on his lips. He walked to the large by window and lit a cigarette. 'What words,' he thought, 'What words can I use to tell Baba and Mama that I'm about to wreck all their bright dreams?'

Seated on the broken terrace of the dargah, Syed Mazhar Ali began writing a postcard in his old-fashioned scrawl:

Young man of auspicious appearance, comfort of my life, dear Jamshed Miyan, may you live long. Let it be known that for several reasons, your father is still in Muhammad Ganj. The 'camp' has moved on. Your father has sent several petitions to the office of the 'Sikattar' Sahib in the city of Lucknow. God will certainly do what He thinks is right. Further news is that the hearing of Buta Begum's case has been postponed. The Collector Sahib very kindly has taken her under the wing of his benevolence and during the course of the case, Buta Begum and her daughter will live in the city of Allahabad under the patronage of the Collector Sahib. Nawab Shams Ara Begum has spread hostile and improper gossip amongst everyone in this regard. Further, your father says that you are to sell your bicycle.

Six months later, Jamshed received another postcard:

Dear, light of my eyes, may God protect you. It was of some comfort to learn that you have begun tutoring. An oppor-

tunity for your father's employment still hasn't materia-
lised. Now, all day long, he sits in the dargah. My greatest
worry is that, God forbid, his mind may have become un-
hinged, because last night he told me he was hearing voices
that told him good news. Revered Bhai Sahib is also extremely worried about him. Keep praying to God. He is
the resolver of all difficulties.

Two years later, another postcard came:

. . . Light of my eyes, Manzurun Nisa, may God protect
her, has reached the age when she should be sent to her
husband's house. Therefore, please come and take her
away in due manner during the month of Eid. Your Abba
is now permanently living in a hut by the bank of the river.

Wearing a garara of red satin costing two rupees a yard
and a kurta and dupatta of red muslin—the latter pulled
low over her face—Manzurun Nisa, the bride, wrapped in
a burqa got down from the tonga in front of the house in
Kanpur. She had around her neck a tauq of silver and a
hamel made of 'Queen Victoria' silver rupees; in her ears
she wore silver balis and patte; and a long mubaf of imita-
tion gold threads trailed from her braided hair. Fake gold
lace was stitched onto her outfit. On her wrists she was
wearing thin red glass bangles from Firozabad and silver
bracelets. Her fingers had only a few silver bands on them,
but her palms were glittering with bright red henna. Silver jaushans were tied to her arms. On her feet were silver
chhares and chhagals that jingled as she walked; she was
wearing red silk socks and English-style gurgabi shoes. But
the large three-pearled nose-ring was really her very own,
the rest were all originally a part of her mother's dowry.
Syed Mazhar Ali had been able to borrow from Lala Asharfi
Lal only enough to buy seven sets of clothes, a silk achkan
for the groom, four copper kitchen pots and a Muradabadi
paandaan. As for the other seven copper pots, they had

been carefully put together by his wife since the day Manzurun Nisa was born; they had been brought out of the back room and carefully re-tinned.

The wedding feast was held under the neem tree: mutton and potato curry, nan, and saffron-colored sweet rice. The food was served in earthen dishes to all guests except the groom, the Maulvi Sahib and a few special people— they were served in flowery, enamelled plates. At a distance under a banyan tree, a meal which was served on banana leaves was prepared for Hindu friends under the supervision of Pandit Lachhmi Narain. There was the music of shahnai, and the task of amusing the guests was given to Chapati bhand. Syed Mazhar Ali was deep in debt because of the wedding but Manzurun Nisa was his only child, and he lived to see her face. He just wished he could forget about the compound interest that Asharfi Lal charged so that he could realise his every wish for his daughter's wedding, but the ghost of his poverty haunted him at every step. He could only suppress, and suppress again, his feelings. When the time for the bride's departure neared, he left and went to sit silently on the terrace of the dargah. When they cajoled him back to his daughter's red palanquin under the neem tree, he bade her farewell by saying to Jamshed in a tearful voice, "Bhayya, this poor, meek girl will always be your slave. Please never do anything to break her heart."

Manzurun Nisa, wrapped in a red cotton cloth decorated with large mica flowers, crouched in the palanquin and listened to her father's words with head bowed. Then the bearers lifted the palanquin and proceeded toward the station. Jhinga Pasi and his sons followed behind, carrying the dowry trunks on their heads. Leading the procession was Jamshed, wearing a bridegroom's bright clothes and garlands and holding a red handkerchief, seated once again in Gobindwa's ekka.

Manzurun Nisa stepped down from the tonga and entered her new home. City-bred Aliya gave her a critical look;

then, making a sour face, she called to her mother: "Amma, Dulhan Bhabhi has arrived." Manzurun Nisa was taken into the tiny room by the side of the verandah and seated on her bridal bed. There the women of the neighbourhood came to see her. Each woman would lift the veil from the face of Manzurun Nisa—she would quickly squeeze her eyes shut—look at her face, then drop a rupee or two on the red handkerchief spread before her.

For a whole week Manzurun Nisa spent her daylight hours sitting on the bed, with bowed head, motionless. Then she opened her eyes and looked around. The small house seemed like a palace to her. It had electric lights. Tables and chairs. China. Paper flowers in blue glass vases set in niches in the wall. And her ever so smart sister-in-law Aliya was learning English at the school!

Jamshed was now in his M.A. (Final), and did tutoring until late at night in order to pay the household expenses. He had also rented out the baithak and stopped smoking. Already in his early twenties he had become bitter and pessimistic, an old man, both in mind and at heart.

Manzurun Nisa took upon herself all the housework. She prepared all the meals. She looked after her mother-in-law with devotion and took silently all of her chiding and remarks. She was good to her brothers-in-law, and held her sister-in-law Aliya in the greatest awe. Jamshed never spoke to her pleasantly, but even this didn't bother her. It was her duty to serve her husband, and she worshipped him.

But after she returned to Muhammad Ganj to wait for the birth of her first child, Jamshed lost all interest in her. He even stopped replying to Syed Mazhar Ali's at first anxious, then increasingly pleading, letters.

Three years had passed since the war started. Jamshed became a Havaldar Clerk in the Office of Military Stores. Within the year he was promoted, so he rented out his city house and moved the household into his spacious and airy official quarters. Now he was making four hundred rupees a month; there was also the continuous flow of goods from the canteen. His only regret was that he couldn't apply for emergency commission because of his weak eyes. During this period, after puffing away a whole tin of cigarettes in a single night, he mailed Manzurun Nisa a letter of divorce.

❖

When Manzurun Nisa's baby girl was born, Syed Akhtar Ali was forcibly brought back from his hut to whisper the words of the azan in his grand-daughter's ear. Shah Munawwar Ali blew his breath over the child after reciting numerous prayers. The neighbourhood women came and made special sweets to celebrate the event. Outside, under the neem tree, Syed Mazhar Ali sat with his friends on a cot, enjoying the hooka and the mimicry of Chapati bhand, while the village's only 'professional dancer' sensuously shimmied and sang. When she came close to nudging Syed Mazhar Ali with her hip, he took two rupees from the knot of his scarf and placed them in her hand. Inside, before the women, Jhinga Pasi's wife, her face veiled with her odhni, was dancing with her hands aggressively placed on her hips. Haidari domni and her sisters had also come to sing maternity songs. A few days later, special food offerings were made to honour the Prophet's daughter, Fatima, because Manzurun Nisa had only barely escaped death in childbirth.

At the *aqiqa* ceremony, Syed Mazhar Ali named the child Farhatun Nisa Begum. Shah Munawwar Ali loaded her with amulets and talismans. A dholak was placed in the courtyard around which women gathered to sing, while Manzurun Nisa, wearing a purple outfit of glossy satin, sat on the charpai with the baby in her lap and, as usual, told her girlfriends endless stories of the marvels of Kanpur: "'Trains' go jingling down the streets in Kanpur. There are such huge factories; if you sleep in the courtyard, you wake up all smoky in the morning. Once I even went with 'him' to the cinema."

Just then, Sambhu Dada who was also the village post-man, came with a registered letter.

❖

Syed Mazhar Ali's wife sat silently pulling the string of the cradle. All the women of the village gathered in the court-yard. The newborn baby, wearing a black string around her wrist and a black mark on her forehead to ward off the evil eye, was squealing. Outside, under the neem tree, Tauqir Miyan, Gobar Chacha, Lala Majlis Rai, Shaikh Ramzan, Maulvi Muhammad Hasan, Pandit Lakshmi Narain, Gosain Kaka, and Gobindwa sat with their heads bowed. Shah Munawwar Ali was quietly sitting inside the dargah. He gave out only one cry, "Praise be to Him, He has bestowed a great bounty!" As for Syed Akhtar Ali, he remained absorbed in meditation on the bank of the Gomti; no one gave him the news.

Several years passed. The child was raised by her grand-mother. Manzurun Nisa would do the chores, then usu-ally sit silently staring into the sky. Every morning, she would get up, do her ablutions, then sit under the khirni tree reciting *munajat* poems:

> *You are the Master. You are the Almighty.*
> *Why did you delay so when my turn came?*

Sometimes she would sit with the *Milad-e-Akbar* open before her and silently move her lips:

> *When the Gardener of the World started*
>   *tending the flowers,*
> *He chose one flower from all that were there.*

In the quiet of long summer afternoons, in the chilly darkness of winter nights, in the wet afternoons of the rainy season, her voice would echo in the small house:

You are Holy, O God, and Most High in Your Glory.
You are the Just Lawgiver, and Most High in Your Glory.
You mete out as you wish, O Most High in Your Glory.

Often while she was rolling rotis, braiding Farhatun Nisa's hair, or winnowing rice, she would hum the couplet she had heard from Maulvi Muhammad Hasan's wife:

Two flowers bloomed together, but each with a
*   different fate.*
One was placed in a wedding garland, the other
*   upon a grave.*

Her heart would be pierced with pain and she would think, 'Who knows what flower will now be woven in "his" wedding garland?' Every day she expected the news that Jamshed had married some 'B.A. Pass' girl in the city. But the day would go by without any news. Then she would hope that perhaps Jamshed would return to her. At twenty years of age, Manzurun Nisa looked broken and twice as old.

A long time had passed since Salman Mirza moved to Bombay. Sometimes he would return to Allahabad, but after a few days vanish again. For some years past, Buta Begum and her daughter, Basanti Begum, had been living in a room in a wing of "Qasr-e-Salman". Her case had gone all the way to the Chief Court where she had won, and thus humbled both Nawab Bhure and Nawab Shams Ara Begum. Now she only prayed for Basanti Begum to be married to some upstanding, gainfully employed young man of decent background. At "Qasr-e-Salman", Buta Begum's position was like that of a housekeeper. She also read the majlis every Thursday; and when Chhoti Bitiya came home for vacations from the convent school in Mussoorie, she took care of her clothes. And every waking moment, she called for God's blessings upon the Collector Sahib. The Collector Sahib had now retired. He just sat in his room, half reclining in an easy chair, and read books about Sufism. Basanti Begum was going to a school, and at home she would sit in a spare room painting pictures in water colours.

The day Basanti Begum won one hundred rupees as first prize at her school's annual exhibition, Buta Begum fell to her prayer rug in prostration and cried for a long time. For the first time in a very long while she had held one hundred rupees in her hand. Whatever she had—her bits of jewellery, her three bighas of land, her ancestral home in Muhammad Ganj—had been devoured by the court case. Now, the Memsahib paid her twenty rupees monthly and also took care of her paan expenses and Basanti Begum's school fees, books and clothes. Twice a day, meals were set on the takht on the back verandah for Buta Begum and her daughter and Salman's old nurse, Niyazi Bua.

Often, after she had finished the night prayers, Buta Begum would remain prostrate, bitterly crying at the memory of her son who had been killed in the bloom of his youth, and her tears would leave a large spot on the prayer rug. During the month of Muharram, she would pass her hands over the banners dedicated to the martyrs of Karbala and then crack her knuckles against her temples as a token of devotion. She would sweep up the dust of the *zarihs* and *ta'ziyas* with her fingers and touch it to her eyes. She would stand before the replica of the cradle of the infant martyr, Janab Ali Asghar, or before the horse that represented the martyred Imam's charger, Zuljinah, and supplicate: "O my Master, O Resolver of All Difficulties, O Chief of All Martyrs, O Unjustly Oppressed Imam. Please unlock Basanti's fate. Let her be settled somewhere with honour and respect." And so when Basanti Begum put the hundred rupee note in her mother's hand, Buta Begum felt a shiver go through her. This huge amount was a reward for the talent and hard work of her poor, unlucky daughter. "God, bless her with good fortune," was all she could manage.

Anand Mohan Ghosh was the younger brother of the school's headmistress; after seeing Basanti Begum's paintings in the exhibition, he wrote to L. M. Sen: "I'm sure you wouldn't believe it if I told you that I have discovered a near-genius."

The next time L. M. Sen, Principal of the Lucknow Art School, came to Allahabad, Miss Reba Ghosh had him meet her most talented student.

The following year, after her matriculation, Basanti Begum entered the Lucknow Art School on a government scholarship. But when she was still in her third year, her mother became seriously ill and she had to return to Allahabad. There, she started college. She also abandoned her name of Basanti Begum, because it was a constant reminder of her painful childhood. After passing her F.A. examination, she became an art teacher in her old school. She told Buta Begum, "I've been tossed around since I was thirteen. We've lived in this mansion for seven years and I'm ashamed to be living on charity. I've found a job which pays 125 rupees a month, and will also give lessons in the evenings. I'm going to get a house in the city. Come on, Mother, pack your things."

"Bitiya, how will you live alone?" asked Buta Begum, shocked.

"Mother!" She was fed up and gave her reply once and for all, "I'm not that same Basanti Begum whom Nawab Bhure's minions could abduct. Secondly, I am not alone. The toiling masses of the country are with me." She repeated the words of Anand Mohan Ghosh, who had passionately told her, "'Soorya', the toiling masses of the country are with you."

Buta Begum couldn't make any sense of what this new, astonishing Basanti was saying. She went and told the Memsahib.

"I know," the Memsahib quietly answered. "My own son

has rejected the comforts of home and taken to a life of wandering. This is how children are nowadays. It's futile to try to make them understand anything. They only do as they please. But, you'll still come on Thursdays, won't you? I'll send the car for you."

Buta Begum burst into tears.

❖

When Salman next came to Allahabad, Anand Mohan Ghosh mentioned Surayya Husain, who could become a people's artist in the truest sense because she herself was from a peasant family. That evening he took Salman to a dingy house in Purana Katra and knocked on the door. Buta Begum peeked from inside.

"Is Miss Husain in?" Anand Mohan Ghosh asked.

"Who?"

"Miss Husain."

Buta Begum still did not understand. "Basanti," she called. She came to the door.

"Oh, Basanti Begum!" Salman exclaimed, happy and surprised. "How mysterious you have become. Here I was, so nervous about meeting the great Miss Husain."

Surayya laughed light-heartedly. "Please come in. Do come in."

Buta Begum covered her head with her dupatta and quickly disappeared into her room. Surayya took the men into a small room that was also her studio. Salman looked all around. "This is really something. Fantastic!" At "Qasr-e-Salman", he had seen Surayya only as Basanti, the *Atuji*'s daughter: a girl who would seldom appear before him and was usually closeted in some room or other. Now she was Surayya Husain, the talented artist, and he was standing in her studio. He looked at her closely and wondered where she had been hiding herself all this time.

Salman had been sent back to Allahabad by the Party for an extended period. He began to take Surayya with him to public meetings, social occasions, and political and literary gatherings and she became a part of his circle of friends. For those young men, Surayya belonged to a class that was their guiding light. She herself had been a victim of the dreadful ways of the feudal system. They would listen to her stories of her six months in captivity in the mud fort of Durgakund. She would describe that fateful night when a gang of masked men butchered her poor brother. She would reminisce about her blind, poverty-stricken father who could recite Muharram elegies and mourning songs in such a pain-filled voice that the hearts of his audience would be filled with terror. To Salman's comrades, she was a heroine, and to Salman himself, his ideal. During the same period, she also passed her B.A. examination as a private candidate.

At that time Chhoti Bitiya was studying in Crossthwaite College. Buta Begum went to "Qasr-e-Salman" every Thursday and recited the majlis, but Surayya rarely went with her. Buta Begum's heart fluttered thinking about the friendship between Salman and her daughter. 'What will the Collector Sahib and the Memsahib think of this ingratitude?' Just thinking about it made her tremble. She did not dare say anything to Surayya but she felt very uneasy when she went to "Qasr-e-Salman". The Memsahib never made any reference to the matter.

In April 1947, Chhoti Bitiya took her Intermediate Examination and then as usual went to Mussoorie with her parents for the summer holidays. Salman remained in Allahabad. In June the scheme for the Partition of India was announced.

After the war, the department in which Jamshed was em-

ployed had been disbanded. By then, because he had
passed the age limit, he could not compete for either the
Indian or the Provincial Civil Services. Immediately after
the Partition in August, Jamshed left for Karachi to try his
luck there.

❖

It had been raining the whole day. Pulling the collar of his
raincoat over his neck, Salman Mirza hurried to Surayya's
house. Evening had set in, and frogs of the rains were
croaking in the lane. A radio was on in the house next
door; the announcer was reading the names of those who
had fled from Delhi and Punjab for the benefit of their
relatives in Pakistan and India. An air of desolation and
foreboding lay over everything.

At the sound of Salman's footsteps, Surayya peeped
through the barred window and let him in. She pulled a
chair close to the window for him. "It's suddenly become
very stuffy," she said. Her voice sounded hollow.

Salman sat down, glanced at his watch, and lit a cigarette. "There isn't much time," he said in a steady voice,
"but I know that you won't fail in any crisis. You'll always
help us—won't you, Surayya?" Suddenly a child-like tone
emerged in his voice, a tone much like Chhoti Bitiya's.

"Don't lecture me," she responded, fed up. "I've been
hearing your never-ending speeches for years: crisis, ideals, principles, values. . . ."

Salman was shocked. "My girl, you too are disappoint-
ing me?" he asked with great pain. "Don't disappoint me,
please."

"Disappoint you? You're still not cured of your wishful
thinking about mankind?"

The radio echoed in the lane: "Shri Nawab Chand
Khanna's family is arriving in Amritsar on the Dakota from
Peshawar . . . Janab Fazal Din Advocate's family has safely
reached Lahore from Hoshiarpur . . . A Dakota is being

sent to Jhelum for Chaudhuri Tika Ram and his family . . I repeat. . . ."

Surayya closed the window.

"Surayya," Salman said with the same pain, "Painting those abstracts all the time, you've completely cut yourself off from reality."

"That's another of your presumptions, Salman Mirza. I don't wish to discuss art with you, it's not your field."

A sudden gust of wind blew open the window shutters.

"I sit here every evening listening to the news. I haven't heard anything about your family." There was a faint trace of malice in her voice.

The radio continued: "I repeat. Janab Qamaruddin Mirza, Begum Mirza and Miss Mirza"—Salman stopped breathing and turned pale—"left Mussoorie with an army convoy on Sunday, for Lahore. Dr. Hari Ram Malhotra, Sirdar Khushhal Singh and Lala Gulab Chand. . . ."

For some moments, complete silence reigned in the room. Salman sat still. Surayya gave him a worried look, and felt ashamed of her churlishness. She hurried out to make some tea.

"A letter came from Mama a few days ago," Salman said softly while stirring sugar into his tea. "She wrote it the day after their Mussoorie house was burned down. She was most worried about Chhoti Bitiya . . . hundreds of young girls have already been abducted."

"Don't worry," said Surayya, placing a hand on his shoulder. "They will get there safely."

Suddenly the lights went out.

"Please light me a cigarette."

Surayya, groping on the floor, found the cigarettes and matches and gave them to Salman. He lit a cigarette. Surayya remained silent. After a while, Salman haltingly began, "Baba was born into a Sufi household, accustomed to austerity. He grew up in the shade of a dargah in a famine-stricken village of Bihar. Though he was nominated to the P.C.S. and entered a powerful middle class, mentally he remained otherworldly. But I'm worried about Mama and Chhoti Bitiya. They'll have to face some severe shocks."

"Your Mussoorie house was burned down?" Surayya asked.

"Yes," came Salman's voice through the darkness, "the fanaticism that the system gave birth to, burned down its mansions. But Surayya, that has only made the existing contradictions more vivid. The mansions of the past have burned down, but the mansions of the new bourgeoisie will soon rise on their debris in both countries. Yesterday's feudal lords will give way to today's capitalists. Our real struggle begins now." He struck a match to look at his watch and stood up. "Surayya, I'm being sent across the border . . . will you come with me?"

She didn't reply.

"It will be a hard life," he continued, "and God knows, you deserve a little comfort and stability. But with me, at least your heart will be content and your mind at peace. My deep love. . . ."

"You may have to move from place to place after you get there. Where would I stay?"

"You're a soldier, Surayya. Our war continues, only the front will change."

She remained silent.

He leaned against the wall. "Surayya?" he asked for the last time.

She still didn't respond.

Someone lit a lantern in the house across the lane and its dim light crept through the window into the room. Salman looked at Surayya and closed his eyes for a moment—as if he wished to capture a last picture of her in his mind. He stood up. "O.K., Surayya, I'm going now. I have to start tomorrow morning," he said in an overly normal voice. "'Life waits with open jaws. . .' and all that," he added with a short laugh. "Goodbye." He put out his hand, "Come on, shake hands like a man."

She remained seated, silent.

Then suddenly she too got up and clasped him in her arms.

"Salman. Salman," she said, pressing her face into his shoulder. "I've been a coward, Salman, a pessimist—but just for a moment. I'm with you. I'm always with you. You can trust me. I'll never disappoint you."

Salman gently freed his arms and took her into his embrace. Caressing her curly hair, he softly asked, "Promise?"

"Promise," Surayya repeated in a tear-filled voice.

"Shake on it," Salman said.

"But not like a man," Surayya answered, laughing and crying at the same time. A flood of motherly affection that every girl feels for her lover surged in her heart.

"Friends?" Salman asked again.

"Yes, friends, you crazy fellow. Did I scare you? You know how moody I can be."

"Don't put on airs, you Picasso's aunt, you. . . . Now tell me, when will you be able to come over?"

"Just as soon as the school accepts my resignation. When you get there, Salman, send me a note to let me know how you are."

At the door, he paused for a couple of moments to look at the lonely, courageous girl standing in the half-lit room, then quickly stepped out into the lane.

He stopped short at the turn and took a last look at that small house. For so many years he had made it a symbol of his struggle, the centre of his desires. So many evenings he had spent there, arguing Marxism with his friends. He would bring Surayya books by his favorite authors: Tolstoy, Gorky, Romain Rolland, Jawaharlal Nehru, Christopher Caudwell, Howard Fast most of which Surayya didn't read beyond the first few pages. He would read aloud to her, particularly about the Spanish Civil War, while she quietly stood at her easel, painting. Sometimes he would chide her irritably: "Surayya! You ignoramous! Listen to what Lenin says about art." Or, "Don't be a fool, Surayya. Read Balzac." Or, "Surayya, you should attend the university this term."

"The world is my university," she would roll her eyes and dramatically intone Gorky's statement. Then they would both laugh. One night he read her Julius Fucik's diary and when he had finished, he began to cry.

Total mental companionship, complete emotional harmony—how beautiful and perfect their friendship was. Surayya Husain and Salman Mirza. What respect their names carried among their friends. Salman found his dreams realized in this soft, delicate, intelligent, attractive, brave 'peasant' girl. Woman of the future. Heroine of the coming society who could prove herself perfect as a sweetheart or sister, wife or mother, in every feminine role. Not even unconsciously could she regret being deprived of some family prestige or having some mansion burned down, because she belonged to a class that had nothing to lose but its chains.

She didn't have even one silk sari, was a stranger to jewellery, and was completely disgusted by cosmetics. Descriptions of fashionable dinner parties incensed her. She considered Chhoti Bitiya an extremely pitiable creature, and would often benignly think of her, 'Poor girl! She'll spend her entire life driving from one party to another, from the swimming pool to the skating rink!'

Salman would say to his sister, "Bitiya, let's go to Surayya's. Maybe you'll pick up something sensible."

"Never," Chhoti Bitiya would answer. "For one, today is the Fancy Dress Day at my college, and for another, Surayya Baji speaks to me in such lofty tones that I could cry. Truly."

"You don't want to understand Surayya." Then he would add, laughing, "But I don't blame you. You're a girl who truly represents her class."

That year, Surayya's paintings were sent to Delhi for the All India Exhibition. Then, an exclusive show of her work was held in Allahabad under the auspices of the Students Federation. L. M. Sen himself came from Lucknow to inaugurate it. Well-known writers and intellectuals came to see her at her rundown home whose furniture consisted of a few stools and a couple of chairs.

Only Salman knew how proud he was of Surayya. But today he was leaving her all alone—for who knows how long—and going to a faraway place.

The window of Surayya's room closed. Salman lit another cigarette; then, taking quick steps, he walked away into the dark night.

(3)

After he arrived in the new country, Salman lived 'underground' for a year. He couldn't find out where his family was. Perhaps they had been killed while crossing the Beas river. Then one night he got the news that his parents and sister were in Larkana, and as soon as conditions permitted, he left to join them there. As he passed through the noisy, dusty bazaar of Larkana, he could see all the Sindhi *amils*' homes which were now occupied by refugees from U.P. Finally, he arrived at the address that was given in the message.

It had been the house of some petty Hindu shopkeeper. Statues of Hanuman, Lakshmi and Ganesh-ji were fixed above the door. Colourful designs were painted on the steps. He peered inside with a trembling heart. Mother was busy preparing food at a stove in the courtyard, Father lay on a cot reading.

Salman entered quietly.

"Bhayya!" Father said, putting *"Diwan-e Hafiz"* away to one side and sitting up against a pillow. "I can't get up to welcome you because my legs are paralysèd."

Later, as she was setting food in front of him, Mother said, "Bhayya, if it is possible, get a house in Karachi, then send for us. It's difficult here to get him treated. All kinds of ailments have taken hold of him."

"The pension papers of the Provincial Service people are still stuck in red tape and our 'Qasr-e Salman' has been declared 'evacuee property'," Father announced calmly. "The Allahabad Bank has informed us that it has frozen all accounts until both countries have come to some agreement regarding moveable property." Then he added,

> *"No pain or pleasure will remain;*
> *In the end, only God's name."*

Chhoti Bitiya came home from teaching school. She looked at Salman with confusion. He had become very thin and his fair skin had turned dark. Chhoti Bitiya's colour had also wilted in the desert sun. Brother and sister embraced, and cried like children.

The next day, Chhoti Bitiya, too, said to Salman, "Bhayya, if it's possible, take us to Karachi. This is the second wasted year of my education."

"I've heard of a place there called Ilahi Bakhsh Colony," said Mother, "The quarters are cheap to rent. Take the money you'll need and make arrangements."

"You have money?" Salman inquired.

"There is still some jewellery left that we brought with us from Mussoorie," Mother answered. "But Chhoti Bitiya is not a graduate yet, so her salary is very low."

"Chhoti Bitiya should get a B.A.," Father added, "and also a teaching degree."

"Bhayya, as soon as you get there look for a house," Mother reiterated.

"All right."

"Have some tea."

"Fine."

"Look after yourself in Karachi."

"O.K."

Salman had been living a perilous, haphazard life for a long time. The Memsahib had apparently become accustomed to it, but she remained uneasy in her heart: what silly game had her darling son been playing? It made her heart bleed. Her hopes for him had been dashed to the ground. Over there, at 'home', her peers used to criticise her. The women of the family would say, "Oh, Anjuman

Ara's only son, look how he's turned out! Every day the police come inquiring about him. He's already been jailed three times. Who, I ask, would give him their daughter?"

And Salman? He wanted to marry Surayya, Buta Begum's daughter! The poor mother was such a simple, god-fearing soul, but the daughter had grown to be so peculiar. "Bhayya needs a girl who will look after his comfort and meals, and not some intellectual, socialist, 'artist-shmartist'," the Memsahib had once exclaimed.

"Well! Surayya Baji isn't even such a big intellectual," Chhoti Bitiya had responded, quite peeved.

"You talk about poor Surayya just like a jealous sister-in-law," Salman had burst out laughing, "but if you don't, who will?"

"Has Surayya Baji come?" Chhoti Bitiya suddenly asked.

"I don't know," Salman answered. Then he got up, confused. "It will be good if I catch the afternoon train. I've to go for an interview for a newspaper job the day after tomorrow." He lovingly caressed his sister's head. "Don't be too upset, Bitiya. Things aren't so bad." Then he said goodbye to his parents and left.

Outside, a dust-storm was raging. Burning yellow sand grated in every eye. A jungle of tall wind-catchers stood on the roofs of the colourfully tiled homes of the Hindu evacuees and warm air whirled and whistled through their funnels. The muhajirs from Rajasthan, Delhi and U.P. were rambling around the lanes. Every day a pitiful caravan of them crossed the border at Khokhrapar and settled down here. What hardships they had faced coming from India, and what hardships they were now going to face here! Salman set out down the road to the railway station. Sindhi women wearing long, red robes passed by on mules. Indian film songs were blaring from the tea houses. He passed a filthy restaurant with the sign, 'Cafe de Paris'; several muhajirs from Rampur sat on steel chairs in front of it, conversing loudly.

"Hey, Chunnan Khan, so you got a house allotted all to

yourself? Didn't give your friends even the slightest wind of it! And now you're trying to fool us. Listen, you might be smart, but I'm super-smart. Just wait till I report this to Jhamman Miyan."

"Go ahead. Who gives a damn? I am Riyazat Husain Khan. I'm not inferior to anyone. Talk about yourself!"

"Don't let it go to your head. I tell you. . . ."

Salman worked on. The bazaar was ringing with sound. So many languages, so many different accents. So many hawkers' cries. Everyone was struggling to make a go of it again in the new land. Salman kept his eyes fixed ahead of him and proceeded swiftly.

At the station, too, there was a mass of muhajirs. Salman looked at them thinking, 'Who knows who these people are or where they are from?' People from eastern U.P. and Bihar whose faces bore an un-eraseable sadness. Dandies from Rampur and Bareilly wearing round, velvet caps and velvet waistcoats. Brass-workers from Muradabad. Lock-smiths from Aligarh. Bangle-makers from Firozabad. Dyers from Farrukhabad. Embroiderers and poets from Lucknow. Artisans from Delhi. Weavers from Azamgarh and Banaras. Carpet-weavers from Mirzapur. And their burqa-clad wives and many children.

There was still some time before the train left. Salman sat on the platform and watched the confusion raging around him. Then he pulled out his *"Sindhi Reader, Part III"*. (He didn't have money to buy a magazine.)

❖

There were holes in the ground and patches of mud on both sides of the two-room house in Pir Ilahi Bakhsh Colony, and garbage was piled high against its back wall. The rooms looked grimy and pieces of cardboard and newspaper were pasted in the doors instead of glass panes. The neighbours were muhajirs, most of them employed by the government. Their lives were quite devoid of comfort, but there was a strange enthusiasm and nationalist spirit hovering over everything.

Chhoti Bitiya had entered college to get her B.A. Salman was most concerned about her. She was always brooding about their new, déclassé life; it had almost ruined her health.

One day when she returned from college, she said, "Mama, please get me a black burqa."

"What?" asked Salman, surprised. He lay on a cot reading the paper.

"People on the bus stare at me and I get embarrassed. Their eyes pierce right through me. Sometimes when I'm standing at the bus stop, I wish the earth would split open and suck me in. At least, in a burqa no one would know who I am." Her voice choked with tears.

Salman sat up.

"Then those buses—just looking at them scares you to death," she added, wiping her eyes dry.

"But Bitiya, those who ride the buses are human beings just like you," said Salman, "There's no difference at all between you and other people."

"Bitiya," Father called from his cot. "It's all in your mind. No one looks at you thinking that you are Chhoti Bitiya. You don't matter to the people that much. They have enough worries of their own."

"But Father, I feel so humiliated in front of our old friends, Raziya Baji and others. They see me waiting at the bus stop every day and speed away in their cars. Then today. . . ."

"What about today?" Salman asked.

"Today, after waiting for the bus a full hour, I started walking towards the Sadar when Aliya Syed—you know, the table-tennis champion—drew up in her car and said, 'It's so hot. Get in, I'll give you a lift.' It's lucky she doesn't know me." Then she ran off sobbing, to wash her face in the bathroom.

❖

When he arrived in Karachi, Jamshed hustled and within a few days started an import-export business in partnership with a friend. They took over an abandoned office on Macleod Road. It was easy for him to establish his business, for this was the time when Hindu businessmen were fleeing. When a two-storied house at Amil Colony No. 2 fell vacant after the riots of January 1948, Jamshed had it allotted to himself. Through hard work and devotion, he expanded his business so that within one and a half years he had firmly established himself in this bustling, new trading world of Karachi.

The next year, he went back to Kanpur and told his mother, "After Asghar and Anwar have sat their exams, come to Karachi with them. Or else, you and Aliya come with me now; the others can come later. I have arranged for you to stay at a very nice sanatorium."

"Won't you go to Muhammad Ganj to see Farhat Bitiya?"

"I don't have the time. I'm a busy man. You can either come with me now, or come later."

The following week he returned to Karachi with his mother and sister. Aliya had got her B.A. in Kanpur; and began her M.A. in Karachi. She had won several table-tennis tournaments while at Kanpur; here in Karachi she quickly became the university champion.

Jamshed had never quite forgotten his childhood dream of being called an I.C.S. officer. He was rolling in money, but he knew that it was something else to be a high government officer. He decided that he would have his brothers take the exams for the Civil Service of Pakistan. What could be better for a businessman than to have his brothers as high-ranking officials?

Jamshed had never seen his daughter, Farhatun Nisa, who was growing up in a mud hut in a poverty-stricken, backward village in some far-off world. For some time he had been tormented by the thought of her. One day, he hesitantly wrote a letter to his uncle; then he got a visa, and set out for India.

Jamshed returned to Muhammad Ganj after an absence of eleven years. (The last time he had come was in 1941 for his marriage to Manzurun Nisa.) He couldn't believe his eyes when he got off at the station and saw that Gobindwa with his ekka was waiting for him, just as if he had come home from school for the Dussehra holidays.

"Bhayya, you have come!" Gobindwa said, approaching him.

"Gobind . . . Chacha?" (He hesitantly added 'Chacha'.) "What brings you here?"

"The Younger Shah-ji told me that you'd be coming by the train today."

Jamshed had difficulty climbing into the ekka and, feeling a bit embarrassed, looked at the crease in his expensive trousers.

Almost the entire village had gathered at Syed Mazhar Ali's house. Shambhu Dada, Shaykh Ramzan, Maulvi Muhammad Husain, Tauqir Miyan, Pandit Lachhmi Narain, Gobardhan Chacha, Rahmat Bhayya, Gosain Kaka —god knows who else. Small children were now young adults, those who had been youths were now entering middle age, and old folks looked as if they would fall into their graves any moment. Gobardhan Chacha hugged him and started to wail. Jhinga Pasi, ecstatic with happiness, was grinning broadly and gaping at Jamshed like a fool. Everyone had heard the news: "Jamshed Bhayya has come from Pakistan." "He has become very wealthy." "His gold watch is this big." "He looks just like a Gent Sahib."

Jamshed searched for several familiar faces that were not present. Chapati bhand had died. 'Buck-toothed' Salamo, who used to sell cigarettes and paan at the corner, had also passed on. Nawab Munnan was alive—and still an active dacoit—but was in jail at the time.

Ever since she had heard that Jamshed was coming, Manzurun Nisa had been scurrying around like a scalded cat. She swept the rooms and scrupulously scrubbed every utensil in the house to a shine. With Jhinga Pasi's wife, she freshly plastered the mud floors of the hall and the porch. She picked and cleaned rice for the pulao and firni, and got up at midnight to prepare breakfast for the morning. Her parents saw her rushing around doing a dozen different things and lowered their eyes in pain. For three days she had sat in the courtyard until nightfall, sewing a new dress for Farhatun Nisa.

When it was time for Jamshed's train, Manzurun Nisa bathed her daughter and dressed her in the new outfit with gold lace. She oiled and braided the child's hair. Then she set out the breakfast things on the takht, tucked away her stray hairs under her soiled dupatta, using the same to wipe her perspiring brow, and went up to the roof. There she crouched behind the parapet and fixed her eyes on the road through a drain hole. She watched, wide-eyed and trembling, as Jamshed got down from the ekka. He bent down to greet Mazhar Ali, embraced the villagers, and stepped inside to tightly hug his little daughter.

Shah Munawwar Ali came out from his cell at the dargah and stroked Jamshed's head, but didn't say a word. Then he returned to his cell. Several men ran to get Syed Akhtar Ali, but his hut by the river was empty. He had vanished.

Jamshed stayed there a week and spent the whole time telling Syed Mazhar Ali and his friends such astounding stories about Karachi that their mouths fell open. He had to strive hard to explain to the old men what was meant by 'export/import' and 'black market' and 'pagri', and what were 'license', 'permit', and 'allotment'.

"I get it," Shambhu Dada said, nodding. "You might say that 'pagri' is the same as the dali we used to give to the sahibs. Just a different name for the same thing."

"I know all about these things," Pundit Lachhmi Narain said, stroking his whiskers. Of all the people in the village, he alone knew these mysteries because his 'English-knowing' nephew had been a 'contractor' in Delhi for several years and had now started some 'import/export' business, too, in Bombay. Once he had come to Muhammad Gunj and told his uncle the most incredible tales about Bombay and Delhi.

"This village has produced only two really great men," Tauqir Miyan proudly declared to the Pundit, "One is your Phigu, the other is this Jamshedwa."

"Karachi is an Islamic capital city," Maulvi Muhammad Husain began, "There must be innumerable mosques there now, one more magnificent than the next."

"Yes," Jamshed briefly replied.

"The *firangis* must have a lot of trouble in your country," the Maulvi Sahib went on.

"Why?" Jamshed was baffled.

"Because now the *umm al-khaba'ith** must be prohibited. It is an Islamic country, by God's grace."

Jamshed thought to himself, 'If these poor folks only knew what their dear nephew nightly gulps down at the Karachi Gymkhana Club. . . .' "No, so far it hasn't been prohibited," he responded a little indifferently.

"Here they have imposed a restriction," the Maulvi Sahib said.

"But what are restrictions?" Pundit Lachhmi Narain, the knower of mysteries, said. "Phigu tells me that people consume much more liquor now, but on the sly."

'What are restrictions' Jamshed thought philosophically, 'these moral, religious, and political restrictions?' He recalled an Urdu verse: '*Saqi, the time has passed when drinkers quaffed secretly // Now the whole world will be the tavern, and everyone a drinker.*' Then his wandering mind returned to the shade of the neem tree at the shrine.

"Bhayya, just tell me this. What's the national dress of Pakistan?" Tauqir Miyan asked. "Here, the officials are ordered to wear the national dress when they go abroad." (He was a regular reader of the *Medinah* and the *Qaumi Awaz*.)

"The women in Pakistan must be in purdah, aren't they?

---

* "The mother of all abominations"—alcohol.

It's an Islamic country," the Maulvi said. "Here they have become very free."

Sheikh Ramzan, Tauqir Miyan and the other old Muslim men listened to tidbits about Pakistan with the utmost devotion.

"What has Farhatun Nisa been studying?" Jamshed asked his uncle, changing the subject.

"I myself teach her Urdu and the Holy Qur'an. Shambhu Bhayya teaches her the 'A, B, C, D'. Gosain Bhayya is teaching her Hindi," Syed Mazhar Ali proudly told him.

It seemed to Jamshed that the village's people considered his daughter to be their personal responsibility. He was about to announce his intention of sending Farhatun Nisa to a school in Switzerland after she had spent some time in Karachi, but felt too embarrassed. He would be making fun of these poor innocent people. He became painfully aware of his own unworthiness before them. He lowered his head and started to draw lines in the dirt with a twig.

Now that she had been divorced by Jamshed, Manzurun Nisa was in purdah from him, but as long as he was there, she kept peeking at him through the cracks of the doors. Once her mother caught her at it and exploded, "You wretched, ill-born girl! Now Bhayya is a na-mahram to you. To be seen by him would be a sin—a great sin."

"He may be a na-mahram, but he's still my uncle's son," Manzurun Nisa muttered under her breath, boiling with rage.

"Shameless hussy!" Mazhar Ali's wife grumbled, as she stomped off to the kitchen to finish cooking the pulao for the guest. Manzurun Nisa slipped to the floor and, resting her head against the door, sobbed softly.

Jamshed took Farhatun Nisa with him to Karachi. The day after he arrived, he hired an Anglo-Indian governess for her; he also had her admitted to a prestigious private school. Aliya took charge of her niece's upbringing. Farhat was now called 'Feri', both at school and at home. Within a few years she became a smart, sharp teenager who wore narrow-legged shalwars, tight, sleeveless shirts, and a scarf-like piece of cloth across her shoulders instead of a proper dupatta over her head. She was now an expert at rock and roll, and never felt the need to remember her grandfather's courtyard.

Aliya sometimes wrote to Syed Mazhar Ali to inform him of the latest: "Today, Bhayya bought a new car. By the grace of God, it cost forty thousand rupees." "Yesterday, Bhayya left for Europe on a business trip. This is his fourth trip to Europe." "Next month I'm going to New York. It's a very large city in America." "Feri Bitiya has gone to Murree with other school girls. Murree is a hill station in West Pakistan."

❖

"I'm sitting writing these lines at the restful and green Circuit House at Sylhet. The Surma is flowing at the foot of the slope in front of the house. Behind, there is a huge lake surrounded by trees. By the side of the house, an unending procession of pedestrians, cycle rickshaws and infrequent cars is passing over the handsome red bridge that spans the river. I'll sit here on my bed near the window all day writing a letter to you, then I'll hide it at the bottom of my suitcase. How many such long letters have I written to you over the past few years, only to lock them away or destroy them? When I feel suffocated trying to get my thoughts across in those vague and circumspect one or two lines which we have been exchanging under assumed names, I sit down and write long, copious missives to you. Whenever that strong urge overwhelms me to write without deleting anything—to give details and gossip, I get out my pen and paper. Then I sit, thinking: if only these wads of letters could reach you! But I'm certain that the day will come when I'll put this whole pile in your hands—then we shall converse in retrospect.

"Now the old, affectionate, sparsely bearded, buck-toothed bearer of the Circuit House has come with my tea. He often tells me charming stories about his village and about the Sufi saints of Sylhet.

"At night, the lights of the bazaar glimmer in the distance and create an unreal, fairyland scene. Next to the Circuit House is the grave of some British officer from the time of the Mutiny. All day, a cow grazes on the lush grass around it. How endlessly peaceful it is here! Yesterday, I wandered all day long in the tea gardens and sketched.

"Today marks the end of the sixth year since I have been in East Pakistan, but it seems like only yesterday that it was the end of 1949 and I got word that you might be here. Trusting the vague news, I resigned from my teaching job and came to Dacca, only to find out that the news was false. Once again I started the life of struggle and toil which makes you so proud of me—and which has now worn me out. Your words echo in my ears: 'God knows, Surayya, you deserve some comfort and security.' Many a time, crossing the Padma, I have had the uncontrollable urge to end it all by throwing myself into the water. But then, I hear your words in my heart, 'You, too, disappoint me? Don't disappoint me, brave girl. Warrior girl.'

"Sometimes I think this is nonsense. You've gone mad. You're wasting time. I've gone mad. I, too, am wasting time. But then, a hope for the future stops me and I try to convince myself that some day I'll certainly have my happiness. Hope! What a wonderful thing! As the poet has said: *But for this endless illusion, man would die.*

"Now it is vacation time at the school where I teach. I have come to Sylhet with a friend. Her husband is here on a tour of duty and they have been gone to Maulvi Bazaar since yesterday. Today, all day, I'll talk to you.

"How beautiful East Bengal is! How loving its people! Will the day come when we'll be together and I'll paint pictures of these forests and rivers in your presence?

"You may have read it in the paper—some wit has announced that I have begun my 'Bengali Period'. What nonsense! I'd only like to begin the most important, most beautiful period of my life, and you know what it will be called. I've had two exhibitions in Dacca. Without you, this rigmarole wearies me.

"It's also my thirty-first birthday today. That is, thirty-one years ago, I entered bawling into this 'vale of tears'. In the world where I opened my eyes there were only smoking lanterns and clanging cowbells instead of silver candelabra and gay shouts of 'Happy Birthday'. Birthdays were never celebrated in that world of mine. I didn't know of chocolate cakes; we had only the dung cakes that we used for fuel. You were born in a magic world. There, on your birthdays, fancy dress parties were held at the "Qasr-e-Salman". Anyway, right now, for the first time ever, I'm celebrating my birthday. And I've decided to celebrate it by writing you a thirty-one page letter. Then I shall add a further thirty-eight pages, which is the number of your years. Accordingly, our collective age is sixty-nine; we are two old people of sixty-nine years of age. Just now I closed my eyes and imagined that we had spent these sixty-nine years together. Passions, longings, dreams of youth. The emotional balance of maturity. The empathy, companionship and quietude of old age. '*Calm of mind, all passion spent!*'

"When I got here last week and went to mail a brief note to Qamar Jahan Begum, I didn't know the way to the post office. I just walked down the road and entered a low government building which I mistook for the post office. I walked straight into a room where a Bengali lawyer in a worn-out black gown stood in front of the magistrate conducting a cross-examination. I had walked into the district court! At that moment it suddenly dawned on me how you and I, both of us, have so many associations with the courts.

"Your last letter reached me six months ago. In it you only wrote, 'Father died the night before last. If you had been with me, I'd have covered my eyes with your hands

and had a good cry. Father never complained that if his
son had been a government officer he wouldn't have had
to suffer such hardships.'

"Since then, you have been completely silent. Earlier
you wrote to me regularly. I'm going crazy with worry.

"Now the twilight's hues have spread themselves on the
Surma and candles have begun to twinkle in the bazaar,
and. . . ."

Jamshed was in his drawing room, mixing cocktails for a
few guests, when the servant came.

"Sir, there is an old gentleman outside. He says he's your
father."

"My father?" Jamshed rushed outside.

Wrapped in an orange *kafni*, Syed Akhtar Ali sat in an
auto-rickshaw. A small metal box, a meagre bedroll and
his lota were at his feet. He raised his eyes, looked at
Jamshed and smiled.

"It was revealed to me that I should come to Pakistan,"
he announced serenely.

"This is to let you know the big news: I'll be arriving in
Karachi very shortly. I'm writing these lines from a launch
headed for Narayan Ganj. I have saved enough to get to
Karachi, and until I find a job, I'll. . . ."

❖

One day after coming home from teaching school, Chhoti
Bitiya read the "Jobs" column of the morning paper as
usual, as she sipped her tea. There was an opening for a
receptionist in a large firm.

The next morning, she took leave from her school and

went to the shiny new building at the address on West Wharf.

On the third floor, an Anglo-Indian girl asked her, "Yes, please?"

Chhoti Bitiya, very confused, took the newspaper clipping out of her bag. "Who interviews the candidates?" she asked.

"The managing director himself. Do you have an appointment?"

"No."

"Please give me your application."

"I . . . I haven't prepared one."

The girl noticed Chhoti Bitiya's confusion and distress and felt pity for her. "Wait here, I'll speak to the boss."

She returned a few minutes later and took Chhoti Bitiya through a cool, softly lit, glimmering gallery and into a large air-conditioned room. A green carpet covered the floor and across a huge desk, below a long window fitted with pale-green blinds, sat the managing director in a revolving chair, signing papers. He was a rather handsome man, not too dark, and appeared to be in his forties. His eyes looked thoughtful. After signing those papers, he briefly spoke into the dictaphone and then got busy writing again. The Anglo-Indian girl had left and Chhoti Bitiya stood alone in front of the table, but the managing director remained engrossed in his papers. (This was his special way of impressing upon visitors how valuable his every moment was.) Finally, he closed the file and looked up.

"Salaam Alaikum," Chhoti Bitiya said.

"Alaikum Assalaam. Tell me, what can I do for you?"

"You have a job opening here."

"Yes, yes. Please be seated."

He sized up the candidate with expert eyes. The girl had tremendous sex appeal. She was petite and fair-complexioned, with honey-coloured eyes and golden brown hair. 'Just a like a Japanese doll,' he thought. She had braided her hair into a single, thick braid which looked unique and very attractive in contrast to the current fashion of short hair.

"May I ask your name?" he inquired, having made an instantaneous decision.

"Salma Mirza."

He wrote it down on a piece of paper.

"Qualifications?"

"B.A., B.T."

"Have you worked before?"

"No . . . yes . . . what I mean is, I have never worked in an office. I'm a school teacher."

The managing director smiled to himself at the girl's diction. After a pause he said, "Very well. The only job we have open at this office is that of receiving our foreign clients. In addition, whenever I take foreign businessmen or high officials to the Metropole or to the Gymkhana, you'll also come along to give me a hand in entertaining them."

"But. . . ." Chhoti Bitiya tried to interject.

The managing director ignored the interruption and continued, "You must surely be familiar with western ways and also know how to dance? Please excuse the question. A few days back I hired a Pakistani girl for the position but she felt too uncomfortable conversing at parties and wasn't well-versed in table manners. What I mean is, these days public relations are extremely important for big business. I could easily hire a foreigner, but you know how European and American men are, fascinated by eastern women."

"Yes, but. . . ."

The managing director was quick to detect that the candidate was hesitant to accept the position, but he also knew that he wouldn't easily find another extraordinarily attractive girl like her. He knew how to sell an idea, too. So he chit-chatted about something else, but got back to the subject a few minutes later. ". . . for example," he said, "prominent western airlines have their stewardesses wear saris and kimonos, just so that the passengers. . . ."

"Yes, but. . . ."

"And in New York, at the U.N., I have myself seen how tourists throng behind female guides from eastern countries. It's nothing to worry about. So, now it's settled. I feel you'll prove to be perfect for the job. Your appointment starts on the first, the salary will be seven hundred and fifty rupees per month."

He watched the candidate's reaction from the corner of his eye and rang a bell. A dark-complexioned, Goan clerk appeared like a genie from behind a heavy curtain.

"Mr. Patrick, this is Miss Mirza. I'm appointing her as my social secretary. Please start a file on her."

"Yes, sir."

Within fifteen minutes she had been hired—and at an unbelievable salary. This seemed very strange to Chhoti Bitiya.

"But I thought you had advertised for a receptionist," she demurred once again.

"Yes. But when I saw you, I changed my mind," said the managing director, giving his chair a turn. He had noticed the girl's growing anxiety. 'She's a very simple girl, even a little silly,' he thought, 'but very needy, and doubtless, quite inexperienced.'

"And another thing," he said a bit loudly, "where do you live?"

Chhoti Bitiya gave her address.

"Oh!"

Chhoti Bitiya rose from the chair, adjusting the pallav of her sari.

"You don't accept the appointment?" the managing director asked.

She closed her eyes momentarily.

After Father passed away and Bhayya went to jail, she had taught for a while at a wretched private school for less than two hundred rupees a month. Every Sunday she wanted to take her brother fresh fruit, his favourite cigarettes, and the latest books and magazines, but it was impossible on her salary. Then Salman was sent to some other jail far away and she managed to get a job as second mistress in a girls' school in Bahawalpur district. She entrusted the house in the Colony to a relative who had migrated to Karachi from Bihar and went to Bahawalpur with her mother.

She spent five searing years in an obscure little town in that burning desert. Then Mother started to have heart problems and because it was impossible to treat her there, they returned to Karachi. The past year, they had lived in one room of their Colony house—the rest of it was now firmly occupied by that Bihari relative—and Chhoti Bitiya was again teaching at that private school. She had worn herself out at the local Rehabilitation Office, chasing the file concerning the property they had lost in India, but to no avail. The drudgery of daily life and the unending rounds of clinics and hospitals had further sapped her strength.

Now and then, a letter would come from Bhayya bringing her some loving, encouraging words, and Chhoti Bitiya would again lift her head and get busy with life's struggles. How rapidly the time was passing! How long it was since Father had died and Bhayya had left the house! It was now 1961. In the past fifteen years, there had not been a single day or night when she was free from worries and cares, when she didn't have to toil to eke out a living. Seven hundred and fifty rupees per month! Incredible! Girls the world over were working in offices, there was nothing demeaning about being a secretary. How many times Bhayya had explained to her, "Bitiya, there is absolutely no difference between you and other people." And during the past fifteen years, she had proved to Bhayya that in fact there was none. Bhayya was so proud of her—"My brave sister, my warrior sister," he wrote.

She made up her mind. "Yes, I do."

"Good! At 8:30 on the first, our minibus will pick you up."

Suddenly, Chhoti Bitiya again felt perturbed. "But . . . but, I don't know shorthand or typing."

"Never mind. We have a half dozen girls to do the typing. Now remember, 8:30 on the first. Goodbye, Miss Mirza."

When she got home, Chhoti Bitiya was out of breath with excitement. "Mama . . . Mama . . . I've found a job which pays Rs.750 . . . all of seven hundred and fifty rupees! . . . and a car for getting there and back. . . ."

"Fine," Mother responded briefly. She had recovered from her grief over the Collector Sahib's death, but after Salman had gone away she had almost taken a vow of silence.

While squatting on the verandah and splashing her face with water from a mug, and afterwards while having her meal, Chhoti Bitiya kept thinking: the managing director seems to be a decent enough person. But immediately, the special nature of the relationship between a secretary and her boss and the jokes and stories connected with the relationship flashed through her mind. What will people think of me? That I am a cheap secretary? What will people say? 'Bitiya, it's all your imagination. People really don't care about you that much. They have enough worries of their own,' she remembered Father's words.

She quickly tried to picture seven-hundred-and-fifty rupees. So much—every month. Fantastic! She hadn't seen that much money for a long time. She began to make out her first month's budget. First of all, a heap of things for Bhayya. To begin with, a nice shaving set. How worn out his old set must be by now. Next, new pajamas and shirts. Several boxes of chocolates and tins of cigarettes. Last time, Bhayya wrote for a book which he wanted very much. When I went to Thomas & Thomas to buy it, I saw that it cost twenty-five rupees. But now, what's so hard about buying a twenty-five rupee book? Next, saris for myself. This month I'll buy only a few plain saris, and a pair of black sandals that should go with all of them. But the managing director said that I'll have to go to his parties. What should I do? Parties need really nice saris . . . and some make-up things, too. Well, no. I'll never wear make-up. Bhayya hates girls who put on make-up.

Furthermore, if the man tries anything funny with me, I'll resign on the spot.

She felt somewhat comforted with these decisions, picked up the dirty dishes and headed for the kitchen.

Syed Akhtar Ali's room was on the second floor of Jamshed's house where he spent his days lying silently in bed. His wife had recovered and returned from the sanatorium, but she rarely saw him. For the first time in his life, Syed Akhtar Ali had found peace and comfort. Now he had plenty of good food to eat and endless time to sleep; he also had a servant who waited on him alone. This life of absolute contentment gradually improved his mental health too, and when he began to think normally he grew tired of his continuous idleness. Jamshed, who everyday came across all kinds of normal and 'abnormal' people, had become quite an expert in human psychology. "Abba," he said one day, "why don't you give the Company Law books a look from time to time? My firm could use your legal knowledge." And so, Syed Akhtar Ali eagerly lost himself in law. After almost eighteen years, he was again able to put his legal training to use. He started going occasionally to Jamshed's office and gradually got fully involved in his son's business.

When Surayya arrived in Karachi, she stayed in Nazimabad with a girlfriend who had been a teacher with her in Dacca some years earlier. Hesitantly, she began to make inquiries about Salman, but whoever she asked gave her suspicious looks. Eventually she learned that Salman had been sent away from Karachi to some unidentified place—for an undetermined length of time. Now she began to search for Chhoti Bitiya. Salman had been careful never to make any mention of her in his letters to Surayya. How was she to locate her? Karachi was a vast city and Chhoti Bitiya was a person of no consequence. Finally, one day Surayya learned that Chhoti Bitiya also was not in Karachi any longer, that she was teaching at a school in some distant, little-known place and no one knew the address. In the meantime, Surayya, being a reasonably well-known artist, got appointed as a lecturer at a girls' college.

Some of her colleagues had bought small plots of land in Nazimabad and the P.E.C. Housing Society and were having their homes built. They convinced Surayya that she would go bankrupt if she kept paying rent in Karachi, and that she should take a loan and have her own house constructed. Surayya bought a plot of 400 sq. yds. in the 'Society' on instalment, took a loan for construction, and six months and twenty thousand rupees later her cottage was ready. Buta Begum had the kitchen built to her own liking. Because both mother and daughter had come from East Pakistan by sea, Buta Begum had packed each and every kitchen utensil in a large gunny sack and brought them along with her. But, Surayya didn't have any money left to buy furniture. She had her paintings, but they were not much in demand yet. Also, there simply were not that many art patrons in Karachi. She borrowed some money from her friend in Nazimabad and bought a couple of second-hand chairs and tables and two beds, and borrowed a few miscellaneous pieces.

Many years ago, in Muhammad Gunj, when Buta Begum went anywhere she would travel in a covered doli. Even in "Qasr-e Salman" she maintained her purdah and never quite unveiled herself before the Collector Sahib. In their house in Purana Katra, however, she did away with her veil in front of a few of Surayya's friends—they would all call

her Amma and prod her into telling stories about her life
in Parbatipur. Once she got to Dacca, Buta Begum began
to wear an occasional sari, though she still didn't give up
the burqa. But Karachi was something else. Here she
couldn't maintain her purdah for long. The cottage was
built under her supervision and so she had to confront
the contractor and all the masons and labourers. After that,
she had to run around to get the furniture. She put away
her burqa and started going all over the city in buses and
cycle-rickshas to get various chores done. She got to know
other U.P. women in the neighbourhood. She was now
called Begum Husain and could regularly be seen going
to Bori Bazaar in a cycle-ricksha, decorously covering her
head with the end of her sari, holding a brown plastic purse
and a grocery bag made of pink plastic mesh.

Surayya worked all day long and tried to forget Salman.
In the silence of the night, she would feel more tormented
thinking and worrying about him. But there was no escape. Everything in her life was associated with memories
of Salman—books, magazines, politics, and especially
painting. She was hard pressed for money. Most of her
salary went in paying off the two loans. Buta Begum's old
asthma problem had returned and required regular treatment. Surayya had no new clothes to wear and was still
using her old saris from Dacca. Even while painting, she
kept thinking of the money she needed but didn't have.

One day, she was standing in front of her easel finishing a painting when a shiny Chevrolet pulled up outside
the house. A very smart looking girl wearing stovepipe
pants came in with two American ladies.

"I'm Aliya Syed," the girl said, "I got your address from
the college. My friends here would like to buy some Pakistani paintings."

The newcomers looked around; seeing that there was
absolutely nothing in the room to sit on, they squatted on
the floor and started looking at the paintings. (The two
second-hand chairs were in the back verandah, covered

with the laundry done by Buta Begum. The lone stool was in use in the kitchen.) Surayya felt terribly embarrassed.

The Americans immediately bought two Sylhet landscapes at three hundred rupees each. Surayya thanked Aliya Syed and Aliya gave Surayya her phone number. She said she had long been wanting to meet such a fine artist and invited Surayya to her house.

That same day, Surayya went to the market and bought a sofa set, a small bookshelf and a table lamp. When she got home and arranged the new things, she thought that the room would really brighten up if she had a nice carpet and some curtains. But, fifty of the rupees she had spent on furniture had come out of her household budget and her debts were increasing every month.

When a few days later she learned that ad agencies pay excellent salaries to artists, she thought of Aliya Syed—who seemed very influential—and phoned her from college.

Aliya's brother, Jamshed Ali Syed, answered the phone and when he learned that it was the noted artist, Surayya Husain, speaking, he said "What a remarkable coincidence! Aliya was mentioning you just yesterday. Some American friends of mine too are interested in paintings. Would you like to meet for lunch some day?"

That Sunday, Surayya went in an auto-ricksha to the Karachi Gymkhana. Jamshed was waiting for her in the grand room facing the tennis courts. In a little while, Aliya also came in from playing tennis.

In the course of conversation, Aliya openly asked, "Surayya, you're a 'Red', aren't you?"

"'Red'?" Surayya was startled and a little disconcerted. "No, why?"

"Oh, it's nothing. I just heard. . . ." said Aliya, in an offhand manner.

Jamshed laughed. "She might have been in her college years." But when he noticed Surayya's continued uneasiness, he added more seriously, "Miss Husain, you can get a job in any advertising agency. Don't worry about it. But your views . . . if they're such, then please. . . . What I mean is, don't express them openly. It's mostly American tourists who buy our paintings and they pay a good price. Your paintings can easily be sold to Americans if . . . I mean, if they don't know. . . ."

Surayya laughed, but it sounded hollow. Aliya had to go somewhere, so she left them to their lunch.

In the next few months, Surayya sold several paintings through Aliya and Jamshed. She bought some beautiful handloom curtains printed with ancient Mohenjo Daro designs for her sitting room. She also bought a colourful, artistic sort of jute rug and put in an application for a telephone. The following month, Jamshed himself bought one of her large paintings for his office for seven hundred rupees and an American tourist bought another for a full thousand. This time, Surayya bought a small refrigerator. Then, she had a dining room set and a dressing table made for a modest amount at the Central Jail. Soon the telephone was installed. Now her cottage was in full bloom, and even if some very important person were to come, she wouldn't be embarrassed.

But her expenses were also growing: the telephone bill, Buta Begum's doctor's bills, bills from various shops. She needed more saris. She couldn't wear the same sari two days running; her students were each more fashionable than the other. Her circle of friends was expanding too— every evening she had to go somewhere. She needed saris to suit local fashion. In Dacca, six or seven saris had been plenty for the whole year. Apart from this, she was now 'someone' and couldn't just go out in ordinary clothes. Her standard of living was constantly rising and getting more expensive. Then fortunately, she got a job—at nine hundred rupees per month!—at an ad agency which handled all the publicity for Jamshed's business. Now most of her financial problems were solved. She had been working there for about a year when she received a very generous scholarship. She moved Buta Begum in with her friend in Nazimabad, rented her cottage out for four hundred rupees per month, and went to Paris for two years. On her way back in March, 1961, she bought herself a Volkswagen 'Beetle' in Germany.

❖

When her boss threw a big party at the Beach Luxury, Chhoti Bitiya had been working with him for a month. He told his social secretary over the intercom that she should be ready at seven and that he himself would come to collect her.

When Chhoti Bitiya received her salary the first month she went straight to Elphinstone Street and bought an 'Indian' sari at twice its actual price. At the office, Miss DeSouza had insisted that it was absolutely essential to wear make-up at least in the evening—otherwise one's face looked insipid and lifeless. So Chhoti Bitiya bought a light-coloured lipstick too.

It got dark as she sat by the window applying her make-up. She always kept the shutters closed because the window opened onto the side lane. But today, she opened one shutter in order to hang the mirror from the dusty screen, and sat on the edge of her bed. As she was rubbing foundation cream on her face, her limbs suddenly went cold. It hit her that this was the first time she was going out to do the job that she had been hired for: she had to 'entertain' the boss' foreign friends. She would be the 'hostess' of the party and, inevitably, would also be considered the boss's 'mistress.' 'Allah. Allah Miyan, why don't I die!' She rested limply against the wall. 'Ya Allah, why doesn't my life just end!'

A long, red Chrysler stopped outside her door. Its dusky horn sounded. She quickly put on her lipstick, closed the window, picked up her bag, and went into the other room.

"Mama, I'm leaving for the party. I should be back by ten or eleven."

"Fine."

Jamshed had brought his car up to the verandah. As he rested his arms on the steering wheel, he looked at the sad homes of the Ilahi Bakhsh colony which looked even more dismal in the twilight. 'What dreary lives most people in the world lead,' he thought. Then, Miss Mirza came out. He leaned across and opened the car door; she sat down next to him.

The Chrysler passed majestically through the muddy, pot-holed lanes and came out on to the main road. Jamshed turned to look at his attractive social secretary, smiled, and politely inquired, "So, how are you this evening, Miss Mirza?"

"Fine, thank you."

The car was now edging its way through the crowds at the main intersection. Noisy, smoke-spewing buses were trailing after each other and lining up in the dusty yard nearby. Hordes of people were returning from their offices. The shops of the sweet-sellers and tea-vendors were glittering with bright neon lights. In row after row of small houses, bamboo screens hung on the verandahs and small nameplates were nailed on the doors. What stories lay behind those names! Huge signs were painted on the walls, advertising homeopathic doctors, 'Genuine German Treatment with Water, Electricity and Steam', and private colleges.

Jamshed took a deep breath, then looked at the girl beside him. He liked to take personal interest in the welfare of his staff and always tried to treat them with sympathy.

"How do you like the office work, Miss Mirza?"

"It's all right," she answered.

Then the car passed by the Central Jail's high wall. Suddenly Jamshed noticed that his secretary had turned pale and was clamping her eyes shut to force back her tears.

"What's wrong, Miss Mirza?" he anxiously asked.

"Nothing."

"Do tell me. What happened?"

"Nothing at all," and Chhoti Bitiya turned her face away.
Jamshed fell quiet. 'She's a very nice girl, but so nervous,' he thought. 'Well, she'll be all right soon.'

"If you're this quiet at the party, then my business will
have had it," he said after a while, trying to be light-hearted.

She forced herself to laugh politely. Jamshed lit a cigarette.

"Don't you smoke?"

"No, thanks."

The girl's vulnerable dignity awed him. He didn't have
the courage to ask any further personal questions; instead,
he began to chat about other things.

Later, when the party had ended, Jamshed went up to
her and warmly and enthusiastically took her small, fair
hand in his.

"Miss Mirza, you even know French! What a hidden genius you are! And you took care of your social duties so
beautifully. People kept telling me that if all secretaries in
Pakistan were as charming and perfect as you are, they
would readily transfer their businesses here."

"Please take me home now."

"Certainly. But, Miss Mirza . . . you're generally so quiet
and earlier in the evening you looked so depressed. I'm
delighted that you enjoyed the party. Today I saw you laugh
for the first time. But why did you hesitate so long before
tasting the sherry? An educated girl and so conservative?
Be happy. Enjoy life to the fullest. As they say, we only live
once. And laugh, do please laugh. . . . Damn it! I've had
enough of this formality. You're my secretary. I'll just call
you Salma. You should throw off the mental cloak of a
school mistress. Remember, if you adopt an old maid's
attitude, you'll remain an old maid all your life—and that
would be a great tragedy. The pleasures of youth have a
higher claim on you. . . ."

Jamshed's eyes were a little red.

❖

That night when Jamshed Ali Syed got home, he was floating on waves of mild intoxication and was thinking that
although he didn't have the least information about the
girl's lineage, she was really lovely and spoke English like
any Memsahib. Perhaps her mother had been from England. She will make an excellent wife: quiet, hard-working, well-mannered. But she lives in the 'Colony'! Status
will be a big problem. How can I take my baraat to the
'Colony'?

But, after he had changed his clothes and was ready to
go to bed, his wooziness wore off and he thought: Hell!
What nonsense am I thinking? What marriage? Whose
marriage? I shall groom this girl. She'll prove to be an
excellent 'contact' person. Even the wiliest crook will fall
for her innocent face and spill out business secrets. Business worth millions will be settled in minutes. . . .

He lay on the bed, switched off the table lamp, and lit a
cigarette. 'What a lucky dog I am,' he gloated to himself.

In the next room, Syed Akhtar Ali was exchanging views
on lost-property claims with some visitors.

"How large a claim have you filed for, Vakil Sahib?"

"Only for three hundred thousand rupees," came the
voice of Syed Akhtar Ali.

"But you must have owned some agricultural land too?"

"Yes, I did. But my brother is still in India," Akhtar Ali
answered. "He is stuck there. I have written him so many
times to come here, but he doesn't listen to me. For the
time being, I've filed only the claim for my residence in
Kanpur. Even if it's approved, I'll get only forty per cent of
the amount claimed. But I'll thank God and be content
with it. What else can I do? Here, plundering is the order of
the day. No one listens to you in the Rehabilitation Department. If you ask me, there is no justice left in this country."

"Rightly said, Vakil Sahib."

Jamshed felt thirsty. He turned on the light, got up, and
took out bottles of whiskey and soda from the cabinet. He
filled a glass and went to sit on a chair.

He could still hear his father's voice. Syed Akhtar Ali was saying, "Just look, Jamshed Miyan had two thousand square yards of land put aside in his name in the 'Society'. He began constructing the house, but then cement and steel disappeared from the open market. He has already spent three hundred and fifty thousand rupees, but the construction isn't finished."

Jamshed gulped down the remaining drink, then went back to bed and closed his eyes. Suddenly, a dreadful realisation filtered through the dimness of his mind. It was he who had made a liar and a cheat of his father. It was he who had made a forger and a hypocrite of a simple old man who had been otherworldly and resigned to divine will—his god-fearing father who was once a member of the small, innocent circle of Syed Mazhar Ali, Gosain Kaka and Maulvi Muhammad Husain. 'What a dog . . . what a dirty dog I am!'

He punched his pillow hard, covered his face with the blanket, and went to sleep.

❖

Mansur Ahmad had met Surayya in Paris. He was an intelligent, successful and hard-working journalist. After spending several years in the United States learning PR techniques, he had recently returned to Karachi and was associated with an English daily.

Today, he was sitting in the Press Club doing a write-up on Surayya's upcoming exhibition. Surayya had presented one of her large paintings to the Press Club, and Mansur had asked her to come and hang it to her satisfaction. After that they were to have lunch together. It was a Sunday afternoon and only a handful of journalists were present in the hall, engrossed in a chess game in one corner.

Mansur was winding paper into the typewriter to begin his article, when he suddenly remembered that he was supposed to prepare an important note on India and submit the copy to his editor as soon as possible. He strode over to the long table that was covered with magazines and newspapers, and started to scan the latest English and Urdu periodicals from India. He picked up a relatively obscure Urdu paper from U.P. in order to review the north Indian scene. Most of the news were about upcoming·Urs celebrations at various shrines and the affairs of diverse Islamic madrasas and auqaf in the state. There was a small headline in the column of district news:

Shah Munawwar Ali Passes Away: Makhdumzada Shah Munawwar Ali, may God bless him and make his grave resplendent, sajjada-nashin of the shrine of Muhammad Gunj in the district of Sultanpur (Oudh), was among those venerable and perfect saints of this pure and heaven-like land of Hindustan. . . . ('Pure land?' Mansur Ahmad thought to himself, 'Only Pakistan is Pure Land.')

He read on wearily. There was another uninteresting piece of news in that same column:

Janab Nauroz Husain Khan of Parbatipur (District Sultanpur), member of the Swatantra Party in the State Assembly, yesterday. . . .

Mansur skipped ahead to news about criticisms of ministers, demands to end black marketing, bribes, caste conflicts, regionalism, communalism, and so on. One headline caught his eye: "Comrade Anand Mohan Ghosh, M.P.'s question in the Parliament." 'This could be important.' He began to read.

"Hello, what's up?" Surayya asked, approaching from behind.

'Hello, Surayya," said Mansur, closing the newspaper and turning toward her.

"Excuse me for being late," Surayya smiled. With her was Abid Ansari, the chief reporter of Mansur's rival paper. The two were very good friends, but when it came to getting a scoop, each always wanted to outdo the other. "I took Abid to show him my mural and it took a whole hour."

"The one you're doing at the airport?" Mansur inquired.

"No, this is in the lounge of Jamshed House."

"Jamshed House? Oh, you mean the new house of Jamshed Ali Syed."

"A lot of artists had their eyes on the job; he pays so generously," Abid Ansari added.

"Shall I get a photographer? We can print a picture of it too with the article," said Mansur Ahmad.

"Not just yet. I've still to do the elephant's trunk," Surayya answered. "You can see it at the house-warming."

"So, you've used an East Pakistani motif for that one too." Mansur leaned over the table and made a note of it. Then he said, "Surayya, you'll have to concede you couldn't have received better advance publicity than you're getting from me. I'm writing one article in my own name; then there will be four more, under other names, by next week. And the brochure of the exhibition looks just lovely."

"Thanks, Mansur. You're sweet."

"Go ahead, the two of you, and order food. I'll join you soon as I finish this urgent note."

"Don't be long," called Surayya, heading for the dining room.

Mansur Ahmad quickly finished his note about India; then put a fresh sheet of paper in the typewriter and rapidly began to type:

Miss Surayya Husain needs no introduction to the art circles of Karachi. Miss Husain, whose father was a prominent landholder in Uttar Pradesh (India), was educated in a convent school in Mussoorie and after that at Santiniketan and. . .

(4)

Countless cars were parked all over a still unpaved road of
the P.E.C. Housing Society and dignitaries alighting from
them were gingerly making their way through them to the
spacious compound. The prominent Karachi businessman,
Jamshed Ali Syed, had invited almost all the V.I.P.s of
Karachi to his house-warming. Through the picture window in the lounge, the expansive green lawn looked like a
technicolor scene on a cinemascope screen. Bright lights
in the trees. Colourful Japanese lanterns. Flowerbeds bursting with blooms. Sofas scattered all over the lawn. Boxes
of expensive cigarettes on little tables. Rows of long tables
loaded with food and drink. Wine cooling in buckets of
ice. White-uniformed bearers. Cabinet ministers, secretaries and other senior officers, ambassadors. Press and Com-
mercial Attaches. Big name industrialists. Packs of journalists busily taking notes. Photographers strolling around
flashing bulbs. Pakistani ladies dressed in alluring 'Indian'
saris, foreign women in evening gowns and cocktail dresses.
A band played on the terrace and several couples were
dancing. There was the louder noise of rock and roll on
the second floor of the house where Feri and her young
friends were having fun. Below, on the lawn, Aliya Syed,
wearing a priceless white brocade sari from Banaras and a
single strand of real pearls, was busy with her duties as the
hostess. In one corner Syed Akhtar Ali sat on a sofa, looking smart in a suit and smoking a cigar. Further away stood
both of Jamshed's younger brothers, laughing raucously,
in a cluster of young girls just back from the U.S.

Inside, in the lounge, a number of guests were intently
discussing the mural on the wall. Surayya, who was wearing a French chiffon sari with large red flowers on it, stood
nearby talking to her admirers. Her hair was done in the
latest 'beehive' style and the air around her was fragrant
with Chanel No. 5. The daring cut of her blouse left her
entire back exposed.

"Miss Husain, I can confidently say that you have now totally freed yourself from the influence of Jamini Roy," a well-known critic of Pakistani art was saying. "Your forms and colours are now beginning to reflect a national character and style."

"The future of Pakistani art entirely rests in the hands of our new generation of artists," commented a second critic. "Your Paris pictures clearly indicate that you are working towards your own cultural heritage."

"For example, Monsieur Vigier, observe the trunk of the elephant," an intellectual addressed a fat Frenchman. "The elephant"—he cleared his throat—"the elephant is a symbol of the culture of East Pakistan. As are the rivers, the boatmen and. . . ."

"The fish, the boats and the jute strands," interjected another intellectual.

The plump and rather stupid looking Frenchman edged his glasses towards the tip of his nose and peered at the painting. "This kind of elephant is found in India, too," he declared, amazed.

"Miss Husain," the first intellectual turned to Surayya, "Please explain the symbolism in your masterpiece to Monsieur Vigier. Your search for the roots of Pakistan's cultural traditions and your expression of the various aspects of the collective artistic unconscious of the Muslims and. . . ."

A bearer walked up with a tray loaded with glasses and bottles. The group, fresh drinks in their hands, continued to discuss the fresco.

Crooked, disarrayed mango trees stood on the glistening, green surface of the wall. A dark blue river flowed in the background and an elephant with a yellow jhul and a square howdah was moving across in the foreground. A small girl was seated in the howdah. The entire mural had been done in the style of Bengali folk art.

"Surayya," someone called from outside, "Jamshed has been looking for you everywhere."

She excused herself to the guests and came out on the lawn.

As she strolled down the formal walk, she saw a petite, golden-haired girl wearing a hot pink sari with twinkling stars, approaching her. The girl's hair was piled high on her head in the shape of a crown or a fan, adding a few inches to her height. And her make-up was perfect, with lightly shadowed eyelids and deep rosy lips.

They came face to face and froze. Several seconds passed. They kept staring at each other.

"Chhoti Bitiya!" Surayya finally found the words.

Salma, dumbstruck, lowered her eyes and looked fixedly at the grass.

"Chhoti Bitiya. . ."

Salma remained silent.

"Chhoti Bitiya . . . you . . . I. . . ."

"Oh, hello Surayya," a guest suddenly appeared next to her. "Long time no see. I got tired of trying to reach you by phone. By the way, where do you live?"

"In the 'Society'," Surayya answered in a voice that she couldn't hear herself. Then she repeated, "Here, in the Housing Society."

"Fine, tomorrow evening, I'll come over with Aliya," and he disappeared into the crowd.

Jamshed, approaching Surayya from behind, placed one hand on her shoulder while he held a cocktail glass in the other.

"Darling," he cooed drunkenly, "'*I wearied myself searching for you//In every forest, through every lane.*' Where were you? And why do the two of you stand here so silent? Haven't you been introduced to each other? Surayya, this is Salma Mirza, my most efficient social, personal and confidential secretary." He put his glass down on a table—"Come on, darling, let's dance"—and grabbing Surayya by the shoulder, he whisked her onto the terrace. As they disappeared in the swirl of the dancers, the band struck up a fast tune.

Salma somehow made it to a nearby sofa. Her heart had

sunk to the bottom of some deep, dark ocean. 'Surayya Baji,' she thought to herself, 'Bhayya went off to serve years in the jail with your name on his lips. By the time his confinement ends, his hair will be white and he will have grown old. But no, my Bhayya will never age—he will never be defeated or lose hope. But you, Surayya Baji . . . you accepted defeat so easily . . . you, who gave Bhayya light . . . heart . . . courage. . . .' She closed her eyes tightly so as not to see anything of the party.

"Hello!" exclaimed someone coming from behind and placing a heavy hand on her shoulder. She was startled. The sixty-five year old cotton king, Mr. Zhaveri, stepped up in front of her, grinning through his false teeth. These days, it was Salma's duty to keep him entertained. "Hey, why are you sitting here like a loony? Don'tcha wanna dance wid me?"

"No, thank you. I can't dance right now," Salma answered in a trembling voice. "Please excuse me this time."

"Honey, wha'ssa matta? Not feelin' well?" Mr. Zhaveri asked, the same way some people ask their wives.

Salma shuddered.

"Ohkay. C'mon, yer friends are waitin' for you at the 'boofay'."

Salma rose to her feet. 'How can I blame you, Surayya Baji? I myself have accepted defeat.' And she went off with Mr. Zhaveri to the tables where the buffet had been laid.

At the end of the dance, Surayya stepped down from the terrace and returned to the lawn. She saw Salma sitting on a sofa with Mr. Zhaveri, who had his eyes fixed on her. The leer on his face reminded Surayya of the eyes of Nawab Sikandar Quli Khan of Durgakund alias Nawab Bhure.

Suddenly, there was a huge explosion and the technicolor, cinemascopic scene before her eyes shattered. Black smoke and red sparks danced everywhere in the air. Far away, a volcano began to erupt. Hot lava spread everywhere. Through the explosions of the volcano and the rumbling

of the earth, through the band's music and the noise of
rock and roll, through the tinkling of laughter and the
clinking of glasses—a sad, sweet voice echoed in Surayya's
ears: 'The palaces of the past have burned down, but in
both countries the palaces of the new bourgeoisie will rise
on their debris. Today's capitalists will replace the feudal
lords of yesterday. . . .'

Surayya shuddered in fright and closed her eyes. This
was not the ultra-modern Jamshed House designed by an
Italian architect, glittering with cut-glass chandeliers from
Belgium. No, this was the half-lit mud castle of Durgakund
estate in Sultanpur where she, Basanti Begum herself, was
imprisoned. Then the mud castle of Durgakund changed
into Jamshed House where Chhoti Bitiya was confined.
Opening her eyes, Surayya tried to identify the people
strolling across the lawn under the Japanese lanterns—
Mr. Zhaveri . . Mr. Ghasletwalla . . Mr. Burton. She closed
her eyes—Nawab Bhure . . Miyan Nauroz . . Munnan Khan.
She opened her eyes again. Nawab Bhure, Miyan Nauroz,
Munnan Khan once again changed into Mr. Zhaveri, Mr.
Ghasletwalla, and Mr. Burton. She raised her eyes. Jamshed
was standing in front of her.

"Darling." One could hear the whiskey in his voice.
"Come, drink to this Jam-e Jamshed* which is called
Jamshed House. This is my 'World-revealing Goblet'," he
pointed all around with his hand, "This is Jamshed's Cup,"
then he picked up his glass and gave another to Surayya.
"Cheers!"

"Cheers."

He put his arm around her waist and they meandered
over to the drawing room, where a few foreign and local
businessmen were perched on stools at the bar. Mr.
Patrick—immaculate in black pants, white coat, and black
bow-tie—was carrying out his bar duties. Jamshed joined
them and had Surayya sit next to him.

*Jam-e-Jamshed, "Jamshed's Goblet," a fabulous cup in which the
legendary Persian king, Jamshed, could see the whole universe.

Pouring more whiskey into everyone's glasses, Jamshed started talking about business matters.

"Jamshed Bhai," interjected Seth Isa Bhai Musa Bhai Ghasletwala who had just come to the bar, "tell me whether or not you received that cable from your London office."

"It hasn't come yet, Seth Sahib," Jamshed answered carelessly and returned to the foreigner he was talking to, "Yes, George, what was I saying? Oh, yes, I had asked for applications from London and I have appointed a Mr. S. D. Johnson to my Manchester office. He said in his application that he had been a Collector and all that in the Indian Civil Service and was well acquainted with the subcontinent. I'm sure he will do well at Manchester. I always hire only such natives for my overseas branches who are not strangers to the affairs of the subcontinent."

"Gimme my answer, Jamshed Bhai," Seth Ghasletwala slurred, downing another glass of whiskey, and pounding his fist on the shining counter top. "Didja settle my deal?"

Now, Mr. Zhaveri too came in and joined the group. Surayya, tiring of the business talk, got down from her stool and went over to a divan in the opposite corner.

Suddenly a fight started at the bar. Seth Isa Bhai Musa Bhai Ghasletwala smashed his glass on the floor and grabbed Jamshed by the collar. "Saala . . . you've cheated me of five lakhs . . . I'll sue you."

"Shut up, you old fool," and Jamshed pushed him away.

"You shut up . . . you dirty black-marketeer," thundered Seth Ghasletwala, and pushed back.

"Oh, for god's sake!" George said in a tired voice, waving a finger at them.

"Saala . . . you cut a deal with the Khan Brothers, then lied to me . . . you cheated me out of five lakhs . . . you're trying to destroy my business . . . you do any hanky-panky with me . . . I'll sue you if you double-cross me . . ., scoundrel, cheat . . . " and Seth Ghasletwala punched Jamshed hard on the nose.

The other men at the bar considered it all great fun.

On hearing their shouts, Salma hurried into the room while Mr. Patrick quickly bolted all the doors from inside.

Surayya put her dry martini on the table and looked across dopily at Salma, "Come, have a drink, Salma dear."

Mr. Patrick promptly poured some sherry for Salma, who joined Surayya on the divan.

Glasses were smashed and the honoured guests raised a few ecstatic cries as they pushed and shoved in drunken horseplay, but Seth Ghasletwala was hell-bent. He kept punching away at Jamshed until he fell to the floor and cut his face and hands on shards of glass. Surayya and Salma calmly watched the scene from the divan.

Outside on the terrace, most of the guests were busy doing the latest Latin dance to the loud and measured beat of the drums. Then the drums changed to some wilder, African rhythm and the couples started to whirl around the floor, wildly clapping to the beat.

Inside the drawing room, Seth Isa Bhai Musa Bhai Ghasletwala continued his litany, "Saala . . . liar . . . scoundrel," until Mr. Patrick picked up a full jug of water and poured it on his head. Now he was sprawled on the floor and went on muttering, "Full five lakhs . . . full five lakhs." Mr. Patrick prepared fresh drinks. Suddenly Seth Ghasletwala got up and, swift as a wily cat, pounced on Jamshed again. "Thief!" he shouted at the top of his lungs.

"Surayya Baji. Hey, Surayya Baji. Mr. Ghasletwala has caught a thief," Salma woozily confided to Surayya.

Jamshed freed himself from Seth Ghasletwala's grasp but fell to the floor again. For a moment there was complete silence, then Mr. Zhaveri stepped forward and dragged Seth Ghasletwala out of the room. Jamshed propped himself up on his elbows and wiped the blood from his hand and face with a handkerchief. Then, he started crawling on all fours like a dog toward the girls. He was sobbing loudly. When he got near them he stood up, leaned over Salma, and said, "I'm not a thief . . . Salma, tell him I'm not a thief . . . tell him 'Jamshedwa' is not a thief."

"You're merely very drunk, Mr. Syed," said Salma, turning her face away in disgust.

Suddenly Jamshed started an old theatre song, "The fire was kindled, the Sunderbans burned down . . ."

Surayya took a deep breath and got up. With Salma's help she led Jamshed to the big sofa and laid him on it. By then the honoured guests had left the room. Mr. Patrick too finished wiping the soaked counter of the bar with a towel, and went out.

Jamshed, lying on the sofa, changed to another, older theatre song:

> *I'm a spark of mischief.*
> *I can make them dance. I can set them on fire.*
> *I never miss a throw.*
> *I'm lucky, I'm lucky, I'm lucky. . . ..*

"Hurray . . . hip, hip, hurray . . . hip, hip . . . hip. . . ."

"Shut up, Jamshed," Surayya scolded him sternly; she went to sit on the sofa under the picture window.

"Yes, sir . . . All right, sir," Jamshed got up, saluted, and then stretched out.

Mr. Patrick came in with a bundle of mail. "Sir, a cable has arrived and there are two urgent letters from Chittagong in the evening mail. Please take a look."

"Get out!"

"Sir, the Khan Brothers' agreement . . . Mr. Johnson's cable," Mr. Patrick persisted. "Most urgent, sir."

Jamshed stood up on the sofa and reverted to the original song,

> *Shirin showed wonders to everyone.*
> *When she reddened her palms with henna.*
> *Her lover's heart was set on fire*
> *And the Sunderbans burned down.*

Salma, who was perched on the table, resting her head on her knees, stared at the floor. Jamshed jumped down from the sofa and staggered over to her, singing,

> *Her hair was sprinkled with the red powder*
> *of Holi, but the tulip said No, it's a fire*
> *set in the musk of Tartary.*
> *And the Sunderbans burned down.*

He lovingly caressed Salma's hair, but she angrily turned her head the other way. Jamshed leapt on to the table, dropped to his knees in front of her, and kept roaring,

> *Love, only in you, did I see this happen*
> *that when you were angry your face turned crimson.*
> *The nightingales thought that the garden was on fire.*
> *And the Sunderbans burned down.*

"Do shut up, please." Salma was now livid with anger. But Jamshed flung his hand in the air in a flourish, and continued,

> *What can I say about her innocent ways!*
> *My love sees the twilight's red and says,*
> *'How strange! The old heaven is on fire.'*
> *And the Sunderbans. . . .*

"Surayya Baji," Salma called, getting off the table. Surayya, who was half stretched out on the sofa dozing, opened an eye.

"My sweet . . . tell me, how is she your 'Surayya Baji'?" Jamshed inquired, waving a finger in Salma's face. "How? From which side? Etcetera, etcetera. . . ."

"Sir," Mr. Patrick made another effort, "please, look at the mail."

"All right, all right, you black man, jackass, my slave's slave, my servant's ass-kisser, show me the cable from Mister S. D. Johnson Sahib Bahadur, I.C.S. retired . . . and look, if you've wasted my time, I'll give you such a thrashing that you'll wish you'd never been born." He started tearing open the business envelopes. Mr. Patrick quickly offered him a pen. Jamshed barely glanced over the letters, signed a form, then threw them all on the floor. Mr. Patrick rushed to pick them up, then hurried out after handing Jamshed an envelope that had Indian stamps. Still swaying on his feet, Jamshed tore it open and cast a glance at its brief contents. His forehead wrinkled and his eyes opened wide. He re-read the letter very carefully:

In the name of the Most Holy

Near Dargah Sharif,
Muhammad Ganj Village,
Tahsil Harauni,
District Sultanpur (U.P.)
14 June 1961

My 'son' of auspicious nature, light of my eyes, Jamshed Miyan, may God preserve you. Let it be known that on Friday night, the 12th of June at 10 p.m., the light of my eyes, Manzur-un-Nisa, may God's peace be upon her, departed for the world of non-existence due to her suffering from high fever. 'From God do we come and to Him we return.' The blessed one was buried in the graveyard of the Khanqah Sharif by the sacred side of Bhai Sahib (may his grave be illumined), whose place of rest is paradise. The blessed one pardoned you at the time of her death. May your God also pardon you. That's all for now. My blessings be on you.

Your uncle, Syed Mazhar Ali.

Jamshed crumpled the paper in his fist over and over, then he straightened it out and read it again. Then he slumped to the carpet in silence.

Surayya and Salma had dozed off on the divan in the corner, their heads resting on their arms awkwardly thrown across some cushions. Outside, the dancing had stopped and guests were thinning out.

The silence of the graveyard came rustling into the room. All the shutters of the desolate khanqah blew open in the wind and began to rattle. 'Almighty God, what a great bounty you do bestow on your lover . . . the bounty of patience'. Bare Abba shook his shoulder-length hair, gathered his orange robe, and peeped out of his cell. He clomped down the staircase in his wooden sandals and re-entered his grave. The wind began to whirl through the cottonwoods. It was a bitterly cold wind, but suddenly changed to burning gusts. Whoosh, whoosh. Zhoon, zhoon. A heavy rain started pouring down. The un-protected dirt grave got soaked. Then the clouds broke and the moon came out. The sun was setting in the red sky but a moon was also out. 'It must be the grave of a new bride, that's why this jasmine gives off such a strong fragrance,' said a girl as she drove her goats home. Jamshed gave a loud sob.

"Haven't you sobered up?" Surayya, opening an eye, mockingly asked, then went back to sleep.

Abid Ansari, leaping over the steps, ran panting into the lounge and called, "Mansur! Mansur!"

Mansur, a drink in one hand and telephone receiver in the other, was hunched over the phone. Abid ran up to him, looked all around and hissed, "Mansur. Something dreadful has happened."

Mansur raised his head, looked at Abid, and covering the mouthpiece, quietly responded, "I already know." He put his ear to the receiver for another minute, then slowly slumped to the floor.

The lounge was empty. Abid reached for the telephone.

"It's useless," Mansur stretched out an arm and stopped him.

"The police insist that he committed suicide, but the jail officials say that the police used the 'third degree'. . . ." Abid cautiously looked around and stopped. The drawing room window softly opened.

Voices from the lounge had awakened Surayya. She opened the connecting window and peeped in. "Hello, Mansur . . . Abid . . . you so and so. What are you guys cooking up?" Then she closed the window again, fell onto the cushions and went back to sleep.

The two men sat in the lounge under Surayya's mural in total silence. After some fifteen or twenty minutes, Mansur quietly quoted Faiz:

When we decided to sell our lives, we sold them without
   asking a price.
*Oh, people of Egypt, note our ceremonious ways.**

Abid glanced at his watch and got up. "I'm going to the press."

"Sit down," Mansur pulled him down onto the floor, "There's a 24-hour blackout on this news." He reached for the bottle of whiskey on the nearby table and splashed some into his glass. After downing it instantly, he poured some more.

Abid, too, filled his glass. He was perspiring badly. "I'm going," he repeated, "This is my biggest scoop."

Mansur peered into his drink and softly muttered, "Eh . . . my scoop . . . *'Which is greater than you or me.'"**

"*'This night . . . this night . . . is a tree of that pain,'"** Abid, sobbing loudly, offered the previous line and resting against the mural, hiccuped.

The two fell silent again. Abid drained the whiskey in his glass.

An allusion to the story of Joseph. The next three verse quotations, marked with a, are also from Faiz, but from other poems.

"'*We who were killed on pitch-dark tracks. . .*'"* he hiccuped again, "Well done, Faiz Ahmad Faiz, the great man. . . ."

"Well done. Cheers! . . . To your good health!" Mansur added, getting up from the floor. Then he sat down again. The prevailing silence was broken only by the sound of the cuckoo clock in the drawing room. A half hour passed.

"Who. . . ?" Mansur wanted to ask, but after looking around, he stopped.

"Yes, 'Who?'" Abid asked, between hiccups.

"Who was it. . . ?" Mansur tried again.

"'*Who was he . . . who cast his corpse . . . on the path . . . of youthful days?*'"# Abid sang out.

"'*We had just then passed . . . by the battlefield. . . .*'" Mansur picked up the verse.

Some giggling foreign girls, wearing rustling gowns that they had hiked up to their calves, passed through the gallery and went up toward Aliya's rooms.

"'*He twisted the tyrant's wrists and set out,*'" Abid said.

"'*It was a desolate night . . . yet he set forth,*'" Mansur added. Then he continued, "*But whose corpse was it that its legs were still chained?*'"

"The officials at the jail say that nails had been hammered into his palms. Hic!" Abid confided.

A bearer came in with a silver tray laden with brimming glasses. The two men lifted their heads and looked at him. He walked over to them, took the empty glasses from their hands, gave them each a fresh drink and went out.

"'Almighty God bestows on His lover a great bounty . . . the bounty of patience. . . '" came Jamshed's voice from the drawing room where he stood on the sofa, waving his hands in the air.

"'*It was a reflection of that grievous dusk / It was like a warn-*

---

* From Faiz.
# This and subsequent quotes in this section are from a poem by Ali Javad Zaidi.

ing shot / It was something to trample upon / Why should it be saved in a grave?" Mansur rambled on, "Tell me, Mister Abid Ansari," he emptied his glass, "Tell me, *'why should it be saved in a grave?'* . . . *'No, no'* . . . *'Keep marching on. Trample it down.'*" He waved a finger in the air, "*'Trample it down'* . . . hic . . . *'This corpse is like an autumn bud / This figure of Death has scared us enough / It is soaked in blood from head to toe / The congealed blood smells of me. . . .'*"

Mansur said "*me*" with such vehemence that Abid jumped, and bellowed even more forcefully, "It's my scoop. I tell you, it's the biggest scoop of my career." Then he clambered through the picture window onto the flower beds below, and staggered across the lawn. Knocking onto chairs where one or two guests were still nodding, he made it to the gate, to Surayya's blue Volkswagen, and sped off to his newspaper office.

Mansur watched his progress and shook his head. "Abid Miyan, I had telephoned the news to my office even before you got here." The he too climbed through the window, trampling the flower beds, and walking crookedly like a crab disappeared into the darkness.

Surayya awoke. She rubbed her eyes to banish sleep, and shook Salma's shoulder. "Wake up, Salma, or do you intend to sleep here all night?"

"Please let me sleep, Surayya Baji. I'm so tired," Salma whined, shifting from one side to the other.

Jamshed got off the sofa and staggered over. Sticking his face into Salma's, he asked, "Tell me, darling, how is Surayya your Baji, eh? How? From which side?"

Salma hastily sat up and pushed Jamshed away with all her strength. "Keep away, you dirty dog!" she hissed, contemptuously.

"What did you call me, my fair one? I'm a dirty dog? And you? What are you, you dirty bloody bitch?"

258 ❀ A SEASON OF BETRAYALS

Surayya shot up from the sofa, enraged, and slapped him across the face. "Jamshed Ali Syed, you may be very drunk, but if you insult Chhoti Bitiya in front of me I'll knock your teeth out. I'll kill you!"

"Ha, ha, ha . . . ho, ho, ho. Now there are two, instead of one. Chhoti Bitiya. She's your Chhoti Bitiya . . . and you are her Amma Jan? Her mother, eh? . . . What a riot! I'm gaining some great insights tonight. All the fourteen . . . no, twice that many . . . realms of the universe have been opened to me." Then he sang out a line from a song, *"Tonight . . . tonight, my love . . . don't touch the strings of the saddened heart!"* and flopped down on the carpet near their sofa.

Salma was trembling all over. She clung to Surayya as though begging for shelter.

Surayya had suddenly sobered up. She spoke in a calm and measured tone, "Jamshed, Salma has worked in your office for four months and you still have no idea who she is? Whose daughter she is?"

"I've no reason to know her ladyship's lineage," Jamshed said, aggressively, "I'm not concerned with her history. My man of all tricks, Mr. Patrick, deals with her personal file. All I care to know is that she's my employee . . . my clients' sweetheart . . . a real killer. . . ." Again he started to sing, an old rustic song,

No one ever blossomed like her . . .
Ten goons walk in front of her,
and ten behind.
No one ever blossomed like her. . . .

Surayya exploded. She hit Jamshed across his face several times, while he tried to shield himself with his arms. Salma, trembling with fright, pulled her away, but she freed herself and closed in on Jamshed again. "Yes, Jamshed Ali Syed, it's certainly your night for insights and revelations."

The look on Surayya's face unnerved Jamshed. "Darling, please don't hit me again," he pleaded with folded hands, "Please, please don't scold me."

Surayya turned like a caged lioness. "Jamshed, today I met your father for the first time at the buffet table. I immediately recognised him. In Muhammad Ganj, he often came to our house to visit with my father."

She laughed when she saw the effect of her words on his face. "I'm not the daughter of any ta'aluqedar. I was not educated at some convent in Mussoorie. I never even saw the gates of Santiniketan. I'm the daughter of the late Syed Zawwar Husain, marsiya-reciter and cultivator in the village of Muhammad Ganj, district Sultanpur. And you aren't the son of some 'famous advocate' of Kanpur. You're the nephew of Syed Mazhar Ali, cultivator in Muhammad Ganj, district Sultanpur, and you were not educated at Colonel Brown's School in Dehra Dun. You and I . . . we're both the creations of our PR man. Long live Mansur Ahmad Khan! . . . Now, Jamshed, my throat's dried out," and she sat down.

Jamshed silently went and got two brimming glasses from the bar.

"Come," Surayya clinked her glass against Jamshed's, "Come, let's drink to the long life of our precious Mansur Ahmad Khan."

Jamshed watched her, slightly scared, 'So she was Basanti Begum . . . Buta Begum's daughter,' he thought.

Surayya went on, "Your uncle, Syed Mazhar Ali, risked his life when he gave evidence against his master, Nawab Shams Ara Begum, and got me released from the clutches of Miyan Nauroz. He was my guardian angel. He was also your guardian angel, but you didn't recognize him. You didn't value his worth.

"Then Chhoti Bitiya's father, Mirza Qamaruddin Ahmad, took me under his wing. He too believed in doing good deeds without expecting a reward. My third . . ," she suddenly stopped; then she pulled herself together and continued, "My greatest guardian angel of them all is Mansur Ahmad Khan . . . and my final refuge are those Swiss banks where you keep your wealth. Come, let's drink to your Swiss accounts." She clinked glasses again. She had never drunk

so much as she did that evening, not even when she had
been in Paris.

Jamshed looked at Salma, who was rubbing her eyes with
her fists like a child and, clutching the edge of Surayya's sari,
crouched behind her in fear. 'In a mist-shrouded mango
grove, inside a cosy well-lit tent, a little girl accepted her lost
parasol and mumbled, Thank you.'

A terrifying silence filled the room. The two desolate, helpless girls looked to Jamshed like the figure of Sita in that
temple in Muhammad Ganj. Slowly he kneeled before them
and whispered, "My Manzuriya forgave me before she died.
Surayya, Salma . . . you should forgive me too."

"*Che sera, sera. . .*" the melody wafted from upstairs and
echoed in the stillness of the night. In Feri's quarters the
party was still going on, and someone had put the Doris
Day record on the radiogram.

Jamshed leaped up from the floor and rushing to the
foot of the stairs, yelled, "Hey, *Farhatiya*, knock it off!" His
voiced boomed throughout the house. Feri nervously
peeped out from upstairs, frightened by her father's vol-
ume and tone. Daddy had never called her by that old,
rustic name before.

Jamshed returned to his place on the floor next to the
two girls. The cuckoo clock sang out two a.m.

Surayya clamped her eyes shut and whispered to herself, "Salman . . . you should forgive me too. Wherever you
are . . . however you are . . . do please forgive me. Don't let
me die like this. . . ."

Jamshed was sitting holding his head in his hands as if
he was a gravedigger, resting after burying many dead.
"*The fire was lit and the Sunderbans burned down. . . ,*" he
muttered hoarsely. Then he gulped down the contents of
his glass and wiped his eyes with his palms. In a low, pain-
filled voice, he began to sing,

Separation consumes my bones,
My sweetheart, come to me soon,
for now even my shroud's on fire.

Then he said to Surayya, "Basanti Begum, do you re-member Chapati bhand of our village who used to sing that poem?"

Surayya moved closer to him and joined in,

My sweetheart, come to me soon,
for now even my shroud's on fire.

Then they both fell silent.

Salma kept staring at the carpet.

Surayya started a different refrain, "'*Beloved, my eyes never rest . . . never rest . . . my eyes never rest . . . never rest. . . .'*"

"Surayya Baji," Salma nervously placed her hand on Surayya's shoulder, "Surayya Baji. Please lie down. Drink some water."

"I'm absolutely all right, Chhoti Bitiya," Surayya an-swered and wiped her face with the end of her sari, but tears gushed out of her eyes. She turned to Jamshed. "Jamshed," she said softly, "I too remember one of Chapati's songs. Shall I sing it?" Then she spoke the words in a heart-rending voice,

You didn't come by day,
but couldn't you have come by night?
You didn't have henna on your feet to stop you,
nor was it raining.
There was no reason but indifference.
In truth, you had no desire to see me.
You had no desire to see me. . . .

Then she fell silent, her hands clasped in her lap. The three of them sat with bent heads, surrounded by shards of glass, scattered bottles, puddles of spilled drinks, and knocked-over tables—as if the world had come to an end and they were the last earthlings alive.

❖

The door burst open and Seth Isa Bhai Musa Bhai Ghasletwala came in. He waddled over to Jamshed and waved a sheet of paper under his nose, "The long distance call from Chittagong came, Jamshed Bhai. Here, sign the paper. I must go home."

Jamshed raised his head and looked at him. He rubbed his eyes and slowly recognised Seth Ghasletwala. Then he stood up and looked at himself properly. He was the prominent business magnate, Jamshed Ali Syed. This was his house-warming for a house that had cost him four hundred and fifty thousand rupees. All its rooms were air-conditioned and equipped with intercoms. He was counted among the city's best-dressed men, and most upper-class unmarried girls would be only too eager to be called 'Begum Jamshed Ali Syed'. That morning he had struck a million-rupee deal and must now send a cable back to Mr. Johnson. He must also make a long-distance call to Chittagong. Then tomorrow afternoon, he should leave for Europe for negotiations with a German firm concerning another contract. He took a deep breath, lit a cigarette, and went off with Seth Ghasletwala to his office.

❖

It was now half past three in the morning. Mr. Patrick briskly strode into the room and spoke to Salma, "Miss Mirza, Boss wants you."

Salma got up. She took a mirror from her bag, cleaned her face, and set off towards the office with firm steps.

"Miss Mirza."

"Yes, sir."

"I have to bother you even on Sunday morning, but Mr. Wilcox and his group are coming on the BOAC flight at nine. Then by 9:30, the two Japanese should also arrive. Please meet them at the airport. Also, book them rooms at the Metropole and see that they have lunch." Jamshed kept his eyes on the papers before him. "I won't be able to join them . . . I have much work to finish before my flight in the afternoon."

"Yes, sir," said Salma, standing upright, speaking in a normal and firm voice. "Goodnight, sir."

"Goodnight. Mr. Patrick, tell Qadir Bakhsh to drive Miss Sahib home."

Salma left.

Then Mr. Patrick again went to the drawing room. "Miss Husain, Mr. Syed wants you."

Surayya got up, took a mirror from her bag, cleaned her face and resolutely walked to the office.

"Surayya," said Jamshed, without raising his eyes, "your ticket came in the evening. You may start packing when you get home. Get to the airport by 2:30. I just got a cable from Paris. Your exhibition is set to open on the 18th. In the interim, we can stay in Geneva. I'll see you tomorrow. Goodnight."

"Goodnight."

Surayya left, but returned after a few minutes. "My car's gone. Perhaps Mansur or Abid took it."

"Mr. Patrick, tell Fateh Gul to take Aliya Bibi's car and drive Miss Sahib home."

"Yes, sir."

❖

On Sunday, after finishing with the overseas guests, Salma bought a lot of things from the Metropole shops: expensive chocolates, toffees, boxes of biscuits, dry fruit, a full carton of Three Castles cigarettes, bottles of aftershave and shampoo, a nice shaving soap, toothpaste, and a great many paperbacks and magazines. Thus loaded, she came home and showed her mother each and every item. After dinner, she made a big parcel, placed it at the head of her bed, and fell asleep with her hand resting on it.

She had a parcel sent to Salman every fortnight through a certain man who would come to her house to get it. But the last time he told her that he wouldn't be able to come himself, so Salma said that she would herself bring the package to him on Monday.

Next morning, she took the parcel with her to the office and was looking for the man's telephone number in the directory, when Mr. Patrick came into her room and handed her an envelope. "A note from the Boss," he said and left. Then Miss DeSouza came and left a batch of papers on her table. Salma walked over to the window and opened the envelope.

Chhoti Bitiya,

With utmost sincerity, I seek your forgiveness for my impertinence to you last night when I was extremely drunk if not totally out of my mind. I know that I don't deserve to be excused. Despite my disgusting behaviour, you took my orders with the same dignity and obedience as before, and today carried out your duties as hostess, as usual.

When I gave you the instructions I had already made a most important decision concerning you. It was that I could no longer trouble you with your job which is an insult to you and is totally incompatible with your family's dignity and status. I don't know what to write or in what words to assure you of the respect I have for you in my heart, nor do I have the courage to tell you what I must. I have sought without success for words that may communicate my intentions without further hurting you.

Chhoti Bitiya, last night I pulled a lot of forgotten skeletons out of the closet, and after dusting them off locked them away again. I did a post-mortem on my own corpse and then placed it back in the morgue of life. Today, I'm that same Jamshed Ali Syed whom you have known for the past four months. You well know that I'm a heartless, loathsome, base opportunist. I'm one of those people for whom words such as 'principles', 'nobility', 'traditional values', have lost all meaning. But the other night when I learned that you're the daughter of the late Mirza Sahib, the earth shook beneath my feet. Simultaneously, my mind registered a second shock threatening my business instinct and my selfish commonsense—you are not only Mirza Sahib's daughter, you are also your brother's sister.

Chhoti Bitiya, by now you must know that I'm a self-made man, and my greatest concern is my own self-interest. You also know which country I do most of my business with. When they find out that my confidential secretary is the sister of such a person, you can guess what a devastating effect that could have on my business.

I'll secretly help you, Chhoti Bitiya, in every possible way. I'll get you a suitable job in some other office. My first duty is to serve you and your respected mother. Now Bitiya, I'd like to offer you some advice as your 'elder'. You already know that the world is a disgusting place. I, too, am a member of it. Your brother wouldn't compromise with the world, so he is suffering the consequences. I hope, and believe, that he will soon find out that his fanciful analyses and idealism are completely wrong. Forced by need and circumstance, you made some sort of a compromise with the world through me, just as Surayya also made her compromise through me to make a place for herself under the sun. I'm sure she struggled a great deal before she made the final decision, but now she knows—and you've also seen—that today's world is a great, big black market. Here intellects and minds and hearts and souls are bought and sold. I've seen big-name artists and intellectuals, believers and non-believers, all being sold for a price. I myself often trade in them.

I write you all this, Chhoti Bitiya, so that you should become mature mentally, and so that no illusions or wishful thinking of any sort should further linger in your heart. Otherwise, you're in store for shocks till your dying day. I want you to stop being frightened by life; I want you to face life's vileness, hypocrisy and deceit with those same weapons. Most of us in the world are like beasts, and we must all follow the law of the jungle. I knew from the first day how scared you were in your job—I want you to get over this fear of life as soon as possible.

I'm writing to you from the airport. Surayya and I are going to spend a month in Europe and we both hope that when we return, we'll find you happy and in good health.

Finally, I have another 'elder brotherly' suggestion to make: you should get married now. To that end, your present place of residence cannot have any good effect on your future. As soon as I get back from Geneva, I'll try to find you a reasonable flat in my own neighbourhood, so that you too can move into the Housing Society.

Please extend my humble greetings to your respected mother. All my good wishes are for you. Be assured that I shall always remain your true and sincere friend. May God be with you.

Yours faithfully,
Jamshed

The letter fell from Salma's hand. Nearby, on a chair, lay the morning paper. Its front page carried Mansur Ahmad Khan's 'scoop' in bold headlines.

(Translated by Suzanne Schwartz Gilbert
Revised by C. M. Naim)

A Note on Names

In addition to proper names, other words indicating real or assumed relationships—and expressing respect or affection—are used in Urdu both for reference and address. These may occur by themselves, or together with an actual name—either before or after it. Some of them also have diminutive forms, which add either a further quotient of affection, or sometimes, paradoxically, an attitude of contempt. Included in the translations, they are explained below. (Other Urdu words are mostly understandable within the context, but some are also explained in the glossary.)

Abba: Father (Added to other 'male' terms, it makes them more respectful.)

Amma: Mother (Added to other 'female' terms, it makes them more respectful.)

Baba: Father. Father's older brother or cousin.

Baji: Older sister or female cousin.

Barey Abba: Father's older brother.

Barey Bhayya: Older brother.

Bari Khala: Senior aunt (mother's sister).

Bhabhi: Brother's wife.

Bhayya: Dear brother. Little brother. Diminutive of 'Bhai', brother.

Bibi: Lady. Little lady. (Added only to feminine names.)

Bitiya: Dear daughter. Little daughter. Diminutive of 'Beti', daughter.

Chacha: Uncle. Father's younger brother or cousin.

Chacha Abba: Senior uncle.

Chachi Amma: Senior aunt (father's brother's wife).

Choti Bitiya: Little daughter.

Choti Khala: Younger aunt (mother's sister).

Dada: Paternal grandfather.

Devar: Husband's younger brother or cousin.

Dulhan: Bride. Often used to address a daughter-in-law.

Dulhan Bhabhi: "Brother's bride".

-jan: Added for affection to other terms.

-ji: Added for respect to names.

Kaka: Uncle (father's brother).

Khala: Aunt (mother's sister or cousin).

Mamun: Uncle (mother's brother or cousin).

Manjhli Khala: Middle aunt (mother's second sister).

Miyan: Added to male names, it expresses either respect (for an older person) or affection (for someone younger).

Nand: Husband's sister or cousin.

Saala: Wife's brother. (May be used as an abuse.)

Sasur: Father-in-law. (May be used as an abuse.)

Glossary

Adab Arz: " I pay my respects." A greeting more expressive of the synthesis of a synthetic Indo-Muslim elite culture than any particular religious identity.

Achkan: Another name for sherwani. (See below.)

Auqaf: Plural of Vaqf. Family or public trusts set up under the Islamic law.

Amil: A high caste of Sindhi Hindus, whose members formed the professional and mercantile classes.

Aqiqa: The formal name-giving ceremony among Muslims, traditionally requiring a shaving of the head and the sacrifice of a goat or sheep.

Assalaam alaikum: see Salaam alaikum

Azan: The Muslim call to prayers.

Baithak: An old-fashioned sitting room.

Barat: The wedding party that goes with the groom to bride's house.

Bhand: A caste or community of entertainers, usually Muslim and frequently identified with Kashmir, that specialised in mimicry, acting and satire.

Burqa: The covering garment used by Muslim women as a head-to-toe veil.

Chaprasi: Usually translated as "peon" in South Asian English. The all-purpose male servant at any civil office or in the entourage of any civil officer. Frequently garbed—even now—in some tawdry Mughal-style costume.

Chaupai: A four line stanza in Hindi poetry.

Chilla: A forty-day confinement—with prayers and fasting—undertaken for the sake of obtaining a boon.

Dali: The gift in kind that a subordinate or inferior presents to a superior.

Dargah: A Sufi's tomb or tomb-complex. Often followed by 'Sharif' (noble) to show reverence.

Darshan: A visual encounter of ritual or spiritual significance.

Dholak: A two-faced drum; the traditional instrument used by mirasins and bhands.

Doha: A couplet in a certain fixed metre.

Doli: A small palanquin employing only two carriers.

Domni: The female member of a traditional caste of entertainers.

Dupatta: A thin scarf or length of cloth to cover a woman's head and shoulders.

Ekka: A high, two-wheeled, horse-drawn carriage that has almost disappeared. It was considered more rustic than a tonga. (See below.)

Firangi: Englishman. European.

Hari: A Sindhi peasant.

I.C.S. Indian Civil Service.

Imambara: The building or room dedicated to the martyr Imam where *ta'zias* and other items related to Muharram are kept, and where majalis are held. (See below.)

Imam Zamin: A coin or prayer dedicated to the Imam and tied to the arm of a person, particularly for protection during a journey.

Kafni: A long length of cotton cloth, usually white or yellow, that some Muslim fakirs wear, partly tied around the waist and partly used to cover the upper parts of the body. Literally, shroud.

Katora: A wide-mouthed metal bowl for drinking water, now replaced by tumblers and glasses.

Khanqah: A sufi hospice or retreat. Often followed by 'Sharif' (noble) as a token of reverence.

Khuda: God as opposed to Allah.

La Haul va La... A shorter version of the longer expression meaning "There is no power nor might except with God," which Muslims use to deprecate a situation or remark, or to show their rejection of something immoral or evil.

Lota: A small, spouted pot for keeping water.

Madrasa: A traditional Islamic school.

Majalis: Plural of Majlis, which in its specific meaning refers to a gathering for the purpose of commemorating the martyrdom of Imam Husain. A particular practice of the Shi'as of South Asia, it may consist of a sermon or a reading of elegaic poems. (See Marsiya.)

Marsiya: An elegy; more particularly, an elegy about the martyrdom of Imam Husain and his companions.

Mehr: The amount of money fixed at the time of marriage which the groom ordinarily must pay to the bride before the marriage may be consummated.

Mirasin: Women of a Muslim caste or group that provided musical entertainment to their traditional patrons.

Muhajir: A term now used in Pakistan to refer to the North Indian Muslims who migrated to Pakistan and who are perceived as Urdu-wallas.

Muharram: The first month of the Muslim calendar. (*See* Ta'zia)

Mujtahid: A Shi'a religious scholar and jurist.

Mukhtar: An attorney-in-fact, not a fully qualified lawyer.

Munkir Nakir: The two angels who, the Muslims believe, visit every dead person person in the grave and ask about his/her faith

Munshi: Originally, a writer of formal letters and documents at royal courts; now a public scribe, petition-writer or accountant.

Na-mahram: Any man that a Muslim woman may be eligible to marry and hence may not be seen by.

Namaste: "I pay my respects to you." A greeting mostly used by Hindus.

Nauha: A dirge.

Nautanki: A form of musical folk-drama in North India, identified more with rustic audiences.

Pagri: Literally, turban; but in the urban culture of South Asia, the cash bribe a tenant may have to pay to a landlord in order to rent or buy a flat.

Pallav: The end of a dupatta or a sari, often used by women to cover the head as a show of respect.

Paandaan: A metal box with compartments to hold various ingredients for the favourite chew of South Asia, the paan or betel leaf.

Pasi: Name of a low Hindu caste in U.P. whose members were often employed by zamindars and others as watchmen and enforcers.

Purdah: The elaborate system of veiling and seclusion as observed by Muslim women in South Asia.

Purdah-nashin: Literally, those who sit in purdah; the women who fully observe the traditional practice of veiling and stay out of the sight of men.

Qalandars: Wandering Muslim fakirs or dervishes easily distinguishable by their colourful garb and habits.

Sajjada-nashin: The hereditary care-taker or spiritual heir of a sufi.

Salaam alaikum: A colloquial form of "*Assalaam alaikum*", (peace be upon you) the greeting more closely identified with Islam, the response to which is "Alaikum assalaam".

Sanyas: Renunciation of mundane life.

Sanyasin: A woman who has renounced the world.

Shalwar: Baggy cotton pajamas.

Sherwani: A long coat worn by men. (See also Achkan.)

Sindur: Vermilion, a red powder used to decorate the parting in the hair of a married Hindu woman; a symbol of the woman's auspicious married state.

Ta'aluqedar: A titled land-holder in U.P., with more rank and wealth than a zamindar.

Tahajjud: A very late, night prayer; not obligatory, but performed by pious Muslims.

Tahsil: A sub-division of a district; also refers to the headquarters of such a division.

Takht: A rectangular low-legged platform of wood, used as an all-purpose piece of furniture.

Ta'zia: A large or small replica of the tomb of Imam Husain, the grandson of the Prophet, whose martyrdom at Karbala is commemorated during the month of Muharram. These are usually taken out in procession on the tenth day of Muharram and buried in the ground.

Terah-tezi: The name given by Muslim women in India to the month of Safar of the Muslim lunar calendar.

Tonga: A two-wheeled, horse-drawn carriatge, lower and more comfortable than an ekka. Also considered more urban. Now, in its turn, replaced by rickshaws and taxis.

Urdu-walla: A speaker of Urdu who also closely identifies himself with its North Indian culture.

Urs: The annual event held at a sufi shrine to commemorate the saint's death.

Vakil: Lawyer.

Wind-catchers (badgir): A distinctive feature of traditional domestic architecture in Sindh. An air shaft, which runs from an inverted L-shaped chimney on the roof to the ground floor, to ensure circulation of cool air throughout the house.

Zakir: One who narrates the travails of the Shi'a Imams in a formal, prose discourse.

Zamindar: A relatively small or large, hereditary owner of rural properties with authority over his tenants and peasants. Originally the middle-men collectors of agricultural revenue.

Zarih: A larger, more distinctive looking *ta'zia*. (*See above.*)